Theresa et al.

A Novel

Jean Hackel

An excerpt of "Kubla Khan" by Samuel Taylor Coleridge appears on page 15. Published in *The Oxford Book of English Verse: 1250-1900*, 1919.

Edited by Kerry Aberman

ISBN 13: 978-1-64343-722-4
Library of Congress Catalog Number: 2022911873

Printed in the United States of America
First Printing: 2022
26   25   24   23   22   5   4   3   2   1

Book design and typesetting by Tina Brackins.

Pond Reads Press
939 Seventh Street West
Saint Paul, MN 55102
(952) 829-8818
www.BeaversPondPress.com

For Paul

I felt a cleavage in my mind
As if my brain had split;
I tried to match it, seam by seam,
But could not make them fit.

Emily Dickinson

1

Theresa did not want to have an abortion. She wanted a healthy child—boy or girl—born of the love she and Charlie shared. A child who would become an independent adult someday. A child with a high IQ, a friendly smile, and a body that functioned well.

She knew now that child had never existed. As of that morning, the child of her imagination—real as she'd seemed—had ceased to be. And all Theresa could do was mourn without Charlie.

Sitting on a redwood picnic table under a steel pavilion, the sound of rain magnified around her, she absorbed what she'd found out at the clinic. May 9, 2018, was a day she'd never forget—the day the new life she and Charlie had created revealed itself to be *not typical*. Wasn't that their phrase?

Theresa knew *not typical* had to be bad—so bad they wouldn't even put a name to it.

She stared at her still-flat belly. Her father always said if she yoked herself to a plow and set herself in a given direction, no force on earth could alter her path. But she hated the thought of abortion.

———•◦•———

The previous night—the night before she knew—had been cloudy with high winds. About three in the morning, after the wind died down, the sky cleared. She fell into a deep sleep and didn't wake until nearly seven, when lightning flashed close to the window, followed by a deafening thunderclap.

She got up and looked outside. The oak tree in the backyard had lost a big branch. It hung from the trunk by a sliver and swayed back and forth above the crabgrass that passed for lawn. She could smell burnt wood through the window screen.

The sky commenced to pour water on the land. It came down relentlessly, like the shower down the hall where, minutes later, Theresa scrubbed her skin and washed her hair with her usual ferocity. Combing it out, she noticed an ugly brown stripe at her roots. *No coloring now,* she'd thought. *It isn't good for the baby.*

She shook her hair dry, got dressed, and walked into the kitchen at 7:25, just as her soggy, scowling father was coming in from outside.

"Get rid of that limb," Tom said to Theresa's brother Greg, who'd almost finished his oatmeal and was about to start on a plate of bacon and eggs. Tom washed his hands at the kitchen sink.

"What limb?" Greg asked.

"The goddamn limb in the yard. Didn't you see it?"

"I don't appreciate your language," Maureen Haig complained to her husband. "We can take a little storm damage without cursing about it." She handed a platter of food to Tom, who sat down, picked up a fork, and pulled bacon and scrambled eggs onto his plate.

"You want me to chop it for firewood?" Greg asked.

"What the hell else you going to do? Where's the bread?"

Maureen cut three thick slices of her homemade whole-wheat bread and tucked them into the napkin-lined basket on the table.

Theresa collected her prenatal pills from a cupboard near the refrigerator, set them in front of her plate, poured herself a glass of orange juice, and took one of her mother's Morning Glory muffins.

"Where's Annie?" she asked.

"Annie!" Maureen trudged upstairs, stopping outside a bedroom door at the front of the house. "You ready?" she hollered.

"In a minute," yelled a voice inside.

"Hurry up," Maureen hollered back before returning to the kitchen. "Theresa, are you going downtown today?"

"I have a clinic appointment at eleven."

"Would you pick up some groceries?" Maureen stared at Theresa's plate. "Oatmeal would be better for you than a muffin, and you should drink milk, not orange juice."

"Give me a list," Theresa replied, adding, "The label on the orange juice says it's spiked with calcium."

Greg got up from his chair, scraping its feet across the oak plank floor Maureen kept "polished 'til it gleamed."

"I'll do the tree branch when I get home," he said.

Tom raised his gaze from his bacon sandwich. "I'll need you in the fields when you get home. Do the tree at lunch."

"OK," Greg said, grabbing the keys to the family pickup on his way out.

Tom turned his attention to Maureen. "My back is killing me," he told her.

Annie appeared in time to grab a muffin and rush out of the house, just as Greg was turning the keys in the ignition. Maureen watched them speed down the driveway.

"Why does Annie never take time for a proper breakfast?" she complained. She turned toward Theresa. "You look tired, sweetie."

"I couldn't sleep last night," Theresa said. "Those winds went on for hours."

"We needed the rain, not the wind," Tom remarked. "Any more bacon?" He gave his remaining piece to Zip, the family's lab-terrier mutt.

"That was the last," said Maureen. "It's on the grocery list."

Theresa yawned. "I'm going back to bed for a while," she said, wandering out of the kitchen.

Tom looked at Maureen. "What're we running here, a damn boarding house?"

"I don't know what's bothering you, but you keep cursing like that, you'll never see bacon again," Maureen informed him.

Tom raised his hand, palm forward, and smiled at her. "You know you're the only woman on earth can talk to me that way."

"I better be."

"We could have used a nice two-day rain," Tom grumbled. "Instead, we get a downpour that's flooded the low spots. It'll kill what's pushing up . . . That and those blasted tariffs. And what I owe the goddamn bank."

"What did I just say?"

"You said: 'Tom, darlin', I trust in the heavens and you.'"

He kissed the back of her neck before departing, Zip at his heels.

"Mostly the heavens," she yelled after him.

The Haigs' middle daughter needed a lot more rest these days. Theresa slept until ten and arrived at her obstetrician's office shortly before eleven. The waiting room was crowded with pregnant women in a community where annual babies were still the norm.

"Nature taking its course," Maureen always said. "Let Mother Nature have her way. She's God's emissary."

Julie, the red-and-pink-haired receptionist, seemed to be distracted. She didn't even look up when Theresa entered. Theresa sat down and picked up a magazine. Before looking through it, she checked her phone again. No message from Charlie.

Her appointment had been scheduled for eleven, but she knew it would probably be closer to twelve by the time she got to see Dr. Ryan. He had a habit of overbooking.

She pulled out her phone once more, checking again for Charlie. No message had arrived in the intervening minute. He was in Afghanistan, ten and one-half hours away. It was nine thirty in the evening over there. *He might be asleep,* she thought, *especially if he's active tomorrow.* But he hadn't called or sent a text yesterday either, and that was unusual.

He'd insisted he didn't want to know the baby's gender, so she decided she wouldn't tell him; she did want to know, though. They both hoped for a girl. Charlie said he wanted a girl. She recalled her parents wanting boys. They sure got them.

Mary was the oldest Haig child, but then there were Matthew, Paul, David, Mark, John, Andrew, and Luke. They were followed by herself, Gregory, and Annie.

Maureen had named all her sons after either apostles or doctors of the church, except for David and Paul. Of course, Paul wasn't an original apostle, but he was considered an important add-on, an honorary thirteenth apostle. David brought to mind the ancient King of Israel.

As for the girls, Maureen assumed every Catholic family had to have a Mary. Theresa, she'd named for the founder of the Carmelites, St. Teresa of Ávila. Theresa, for no reason Maureen could figure out, inserted the *h* when she entered high school.

Annie was named for Saint Anne, the Virgin Mary's mother and the grandmother of Jesus. If the Lord had sent Maureen one more child, she would have named him Patrick after the patron saint of Ireland. But the Lord had not been so generous. Maureen often laughed about it.

"The Haigs have to make do with only eleven," she told people.

Now, Mary was gone, a ghost for all practical purposes. Annie was on the cusp of adolescence. At twenty-five, Theresa was the only full-grown daughter still at home, and that was only temporary. Greg was the only boy left.

The family wasn't keen on Charlie, Theresa's husband. Maureen thought he was a member of a cult. He was not. Theresa couldn't correct her parents' misimpression after Charlie had joked at their wedding that he and his "kin" were pantheists. She'd never forget the look on her mother's face.

Maureen Haig had no use for liberal thinking or anything else that smacked of *moral relativism*, a phrase she'd learned in Faith Renewal class. She mourned the Latin Mass—though it was gone prior to her own childhood; and on at least one occasion she'd had words with her pastor, Father Schmidt, about society's general decline in decency—a downhill slide she attributed to Vatican II.

"There's no reverence for tradition anymore," Maureen frequently told her family. "Moral relativism, that's all there is."

"Theresa?" A nursing assistant hesitated just a moment before repeating, "Theresa."

Surprised to hear her name so soon, Theresa stood and followed the woman down the hallway. The fresh-faced assistant (whose name tag said *Jane*) had her step onto the scale in the inner hallway. She noted her weight (120.6 pounds) and measured her height (5'8") before leading her into one of the examination rooms. She took Theresa's blood pressure (115/65) and motioned toward a paper gown on the examination table.

"Put that on," Jane said crisply without eye contact. Theresa decided she didn't like her.

"I'm not here for an exam," Theresa said.

"In case he wants an exam," Jane replied, partially closing a curtain as she left the room.

Theresa changed into the paper gown. Like every woman she knew, she hated these scratchy, disposable coverups. They invariably tore every time she put one on. She sat at the edge of the table and waited, glancing occasionally at her phone. Nothing from Charlie.

Seven minutes and several checks for Charlie later, Dr. Ryan walked in with two women behind him. Neither wore clinic uniforms.

"Hi," the first woman said. "I'm Lucy Meyer, nurse-midwife. I'm here to make sure you have everything you need to help you through your pregnancy."

"Really?" Theresa asked, looking at the women. The older one had red hair. The other was young and mousy, her wide forehead tapering to a pointed chin. Theresa hadn't signed up for a nurse-midwife.

"I'm Sarah Peters," the other one said. "Consider me backup."

"What do I need backup for?" Theresa asked them.

"Every pregnancy is unique," Lucy replied. "You're young and healthy, and will surely be fine, but we're here to reassure you in the months ahead."

Dr. Ryan sat down in his swivel chair, his wide midriff pulling his white lab coat taut. Heavy black glasses dominated his features. He had an odd look on his face.

Theresa had seen Dr. Ryan for every checkup since she was fourteen and began having periods. He was avuncular but distant—the closest thing she could get to medical care by machine—and that was a good thing. Plus, he answered questions without evasion and allowed her to see him without her mother in the room. Several of her high school friends had mothers with an unnatural interest in observing their daughters' progenitive powers up close. Theresa found that level of parental voyeurism revolting. Maureen, at least, could be held at bay by embarrassment. Even when Theresa was fairly young, her mother didn't want to be in the room.

"What are my test results?" Theresa asked, more loudly than she had intended. Dr. Ryan's silence was unnerving. He took off his glasses and set them on his desk.

"I have them here," he said. "Your report is one of the reasons I don't encourage testing early in pregnancy. Chorionic villus sampling is an invasive procedure. It carries a risk of miscarriage, plus there is a significant chance of a false alarm. Had you asked me, I would have recommended against the test."

"I haven't had a miscarriage," Theresa pointed out.

"No, but you did take that risk. And I see you went to a clinic in St. Paul. May I ask why you didn't consult me first?"

"It's not listed in your pregnancy services. Also, I thought they'd have more expertise in a perinatal clinic. I did ask them to send you a copy of the results," Theresa replied, unwilling to feel guilty about it.

Dr. Ryan glowered; there was no other word for it. Theresa began to wish she were not wearing a piece of paper.

"You had it done last week?"

"Yes."

"You were about eleven weeks pregnant by your own estimate?"

"Yes."

"Did you experience any fever, chills, or leaking of fluid?"

"No."

"Did they tell you there's a chance of getting a false positive—that is to say, something that turns out to be untrue?"

"Yes, they told me . . . I'd like to see my results."

"Theresa, we're here to reassure you," said Lucy. "Dr. Ryan wants you to have all the facts."

Dr. Ryan raised his palm, interrupting her.

"The good news," he said, "is that your pregnancy is progressing normally. Everything is in place for you to look forward to the birth of a child who may or may not be typical, but he or she will be a source of great joy for you and your husband."

"I want a copy of my test results," Theresa repeated, frightened by the phrase *may not be typical.*

"Tests don't mean much before twenty weeks," Dr. Ryan went on. "I wouldn't put a lot of weight on anything done earlier. But of course, you can get a copy at the front desk after you sign the standard release. The main point is not to worry."

"What are you telling me? When you say my child may not be typical, what does that mean?"

"Every child is unique," Lucy interjected. "I've assisted at the birth of over two hundred babies in my career, and I can tell you—no matter the gender, or birth weight, or any challenges in the child's life, parents fall in love on the spot just as soon as they see their child. After all, everyone's baby is always atypical because he or she is theirs and no one else's. You'll fall in love too."

Theresa disliked the lilt in the woman's voice. Lucy *whoever-she-was* sounded like someone trying to convince herself. Theresa glued her eyes on Dr. Ryan as he looked down at the paper in his folder. She was too far away to snatch it, but for a brief moment she contemplated getting off the exam table, grabbing the whole damn folder, and—and then what? She couldn't leave the clinic in a paper gown. It would still take her several minutes to put on her clothes, and what would happen to the report in the meantime?

"Would you please leave?" she said, looking at the nurse-midwives. She wanted to have this out with Dr. Ryan one-on-one.

Lucy responded tersely, "Sarah and I would like to talk to you separately, my dear."

Dr. Ryan closed the folder. "Try not to feel anxious, Theresa," he said, standing up. "We're here for both you and your baby. It's possible these tests will end up telling us nothing of importance."

"Could you be more specific?" Theresa asked him.

"I think we're getting ahead of ourselves." Dr. Ryan replied. "All your indicators look good. Your heart rate and the baby's, your blood pressure, your blood glucose levels . . . they're all fine. Please try not to worry. I'd like to see you again next week. And in the meanwhile, stay calm, Theresa."

Then he left the room.

Shaken and astonished, Theresa held still for a moment.

Her mind embraced calm, true enough, but it was not Dr. Ryan's calm. It was a strange, dizzying calm, the air inside her sinking into a storm's eye. She felt a wall of resistance forming around her, swirling, her need to escape paramount.

"Out," she practically yelled at the nurse-midwives. "Lucy, Sarah, whatever-your-names-are, get out."

They stayed put.

"I'm getting dressed," Theresa insisted.

Still, neither of them moved, though they stole a glance at one another.

"Perhaps we could talk in the lunchroom after you change, dear," Lucy suggested. "I brought along some chocolate chip cookies and herbal tea. Isn't that one of the great things about being pregnant? You get to eat for two."

Still, they didn't leave.

"OK," Theresa snapped. "I'll get dressed in front of you if you won't get out. But you can expect a letter to the clinic's administrators telling them you refused to give me privacy while I was changing clothes."

Abruptly the two looked at each other, got up, and moved toward the door.

"Of course," said Lucy as she opened it, "we're just here to help, dear."

Theresa ignored them. Once dressed, she went to the front desk and asked for a copy of her test results. Julie gave her a form. Theresa didn't like the look on Julie's face. She signed the form.

"How long will it take?" she asked.

"It might be a while," Julie said, still not making eye contact. "We're short on staff today. Could you come back tomorrow?"

At that point, Theresa realized she might wait for hours and still not receive the information she was entitled to. She looked around. The reception area wasn't crowded. She began to suspect they'd decided not to give her anything solid to go on. If they wouldn't tell her specifically what the test revealed, that was a huge red flag.

Outside, it still wasn't over. Lucy reached Theresa's car just as Theresa turned the ignition key. She must have exited a side door as Theresa came through the front. Luckily, her windows were closed, and the car doors were locked.

Lucy knocked on the glass. She was a tall woman with surprisingly little hands, bare of a wedding ring. Her short nails were polished red. For some reason, that detail stuck in Theresa's mind.

"Please don't leave like this," Lucy begged, stooping to put her face at Theresa's level. "There are so many things for us to talk about."

Theresa backed up the car, turned sharply, and left the parking lot. She sped past the strip mall next to the clinic, veering onto University Drive. At first she found herself going in circles. Then she neared Riverside Park and the gardens at the edge of the Mississippi.

How would she tell Charlie? What could she tell Charlie? The words *not typical* kept reverberating. Not letting her know what was wrong with the baby meant *not typical* was so bad, they didn't dare put it into words.

What could it be? A mutation, some kind of defect in the way the cells divided? Had a genetic code been transposed somehow, or did an infection cause some microscopic damage that turned her normal pregnancy into something abnormal, maybe something grotesque?

Theresa wondered how she could not have known. She would have expected forebodings—a gut feeling, an alarm system in her subconscious. She also would have expected her body to do something about it. Isn't that what miscarriages were for? The body's rejection of a pregnancy gone awry.

A miscarriage hadn't happened. She had imagined her baby many times, and every time her tiny daughter had been perfect. Until that morning, she hadn't the slightest inkling anything might be wrong. If an old friend hadn't encouraged her to undergo a prenatal test, and to drive all the way to a specialist in St. Paul to get it, her present predicament would have gone undiagnosed until it was too late.

Theresa pulled out her cell phone and called her friend, but it went to voice mail. "Hi, it's Theresa," she said in as normal a voice as possible. "I need to come back to St. Paul. You were right about getting tested in the Cities. They won't even give me the results here. So, I'm going to call the perinatal clinic and make another appointment. Is it OK if I stay with you?"

She pulled her car into a parking spot and crossed the sidewalk toward the picnic tables beneath the pavilion.

A parterre of white and yellow tulips danced in the breeze. Small children played on a swing set too far away to hear them. A hawk circled the heights above the river. A woman on a path let herself be pulled by a large brown dog. Theresa sneezed, scrounging in her pocket for a tissue.

The pain was visceral. She searched for a point of comparison. The worst agony she'd ever endured had been appendicitis when she was eight. Her mother had gone to a funeral that day, then to some other appointment. Her dad was unreachable. Mary and Matthew weren't living on the farm anymore. Her older brothers were at school, and Greg hadn't been born yet. Theresa was home alone, sick with an aching stomach that got worse as the day progressed. She knew she should call 911, but she worried she'd be blamed for an unnecessary medical bill if it turned out to be nothing serious.

Finally, her mother returned and took her to the ER. The doctor had been angry that they'd waited until Theresa's appendix had actually burst. "If your daughter hadn't been in a hospital, she'd have died," he'd told her mother, who'd later said she'd never felt so humiliated in her life.

How did that compare to this? Theresa took a while to measure and decided it was about equal, though her earlier pain had been local to her side, and this one mushroomed to encompass every cell in her body.

She put her head to her knees and let out sobs. She could not stop crying as cars zoomed along the highway. She coughed and kept crying. She had no idea how long she cried. Her body could do nothing else.

In sympathy, the sky opened, and more rain came down. Her father called rain "liquid gold." There was nothing golden about it that day. Theresa shivered as the air temperature plummeted. She stared ahead and thought about what to do. She considered the awful alternatives endlessly, as the rain continued, until finally she decided that she might have to have an abortion.

———•◦•———

Theresa moved like an automaton back to her car and took the road to her parents' house, ignoring the grocery list on the passenger seat. She parked in her usual spot near the pole barn and did not see anyone as she came through the front entry, climbed the stairway, and followed the hallway to her bedroom, shutting the door and engaging the deadbolt behind her.

Her dad had installed a lock at her insistence. She didn't want her mother snooping in her room. She didn't like living at her parents' house at all, but money was tight. They needed to save for after Charlie's most recent deployment. If she'd known Charlie's family better, and if there'd been an obstetrical clinic closer to his home, she would have lived with them. But that was water over the dam. At the moment, Theresa needed to get to the perinatal clinic in St. Paul to find out exactly what was going on.

She felt tired, though—so incredibly tired that she decided to lie down for just a little while. She fell asleep almost instantly. When she woke, the clock on the bureau said 3:17.

Was it really that late? She realized she'd better leave if she expected to make it to St. Paul before dark. As she pulled her suitcase out from under her bed, she heard a knock. It was Annie, home from school.

"Where are you going?" Annie asked after Theresa let her in.

"The Cities," Theresa replied, pulling an outfit from her closet.

They heard a car drive up. Theresa looked out the window and saw two women emerge with umbrellas. She vaguely recognized them. Another car drove up, and another woman got out. A third car followed with three women inside. Then a blue van. Theresa turned to Annie.

"Will you do something for me?"

"What?"

Theresa pulled a black pouch out of her top bureau drawer, stuffed her cell phone and wallet inside, and gave it to her sister.

"Take this to the mailbox and stay out of sight. I might have to bulldoze my way out of the house, and I don't want any of Mother's friends grabbing it."

Annie looked at the pouch. "You think her friends would steal your purse?"

"They may want to stop me from leaving."

"Why?"

"Annie, please don't argue. Just do this for me, OK?"

"OK," Annie said and hurried down the back stairway.

For once, Theresa didn't lock her bedroom. She might have to rush back upstairs to escape a mob, she thought—an idea she realized was ridiculous, even as she carried her suitcase down the stairs toward the front door. At the bottom, her mother stood in her way. Right beside her was this Lucy person.

"Where are you going?" Maureen asked.

"To St. Paul," Theresa replied.

"Why?" her mother asked.

"That suitcase looks heavy," Lucy observed.

"It's not heavy at all," said Theresa.

The front door opened, and someone else entered—Suzanne, she seemed to recall—a white-haired, broad-shouldered woman about her mother's age. Through the archway she counted bodies in the living room: eight women with vaguely familiar faces, all of them staring at her.

She understood then that the roughly one hundred feet between herself and her parked car might as well have been ten miles. Her father was nowhere in sight. Neither was her brother Greg.

"We need to talk to you, dear," said Lucy.

"I'm leaving," Theresa told her.

"We have to talk first," Lucy insisted.

Theresa looked at her mother, who stared back. At that moment, Theresa knew that she could expect no help from the one person who should look out for her, who should love her absolutely. The truth was, without Charlie, she was alone. She felt weak. Skipping lunch had been a bad idea, especially since she hadn't eaten much at breakfast.

"Fifteen minutes," she offered.

"Can't you give your unborn child more than that?" asked Lucy. She put her hand on Theresa's shoulder.

"Take your hands off me," Theresa snapped, jerking her shoulder free.

"*Please, dear,*" Lucy remonstrated, placing the same hand on Theresa's back and pushing her toward the sofa. Theresa momentarily considered collapsing as dead weight, faking loss of consciousness. She decided against it. The situation was ludicrous enough already.

Several women brought in chairs from the kitchen. Two perched on the window ledge, which Theresa noticed had been cleared of knickknacks, doilies, and plants. Lucy occupied one side of the sofa. An unknown person sat on the other. Theresa was stuck in the middle.

"We'd like to get to know you, dear." Lucy reached for Theresa's hand. Theresa pulled it away and folded it inside her other hand in the center of her lap.

"Sarah and I just met you this morning, so we're starting from zero," Lucy continued. "These friends of your mother's are—"

"I'm not interested in who they are," Theresa snapped.

"Remember me? Suzanne O'Brien," announced the white-haired woman, ignoring Theresa's response.

Beside Suzanne stood a onetime high school acquaintance, a very-pregnant Agnes Olson, now Agnes something else. She met Agnes' gaze, and it wasn't friendly.

"Louise Swanson," said a blond woman sitting near the coffee table. "You babysat for us, remember?"

"Roberta Wells," said a woman with the angular face of a model. She looked out of place in Stears County. Her nails were long and professionally manicured. She wore a tan blazer over a crisp, black-cotton shirt and black slacks. More *Vogue* than *Shoppers News*. Theresa was sure she'd never seen her before, yet she sat beside her on the sofa—too close—flanking her left side as if to keep Theresa from moving an inch.

"Kathleen Peterson," said a woman she thought might be a distant cousin. Kathleen Peterson was pregnant too, about six months, Theresa guessed.

"Helen Swanson," said an older woman standing in front of a window that looked out on Maureen's vegetable plot. "Louise is married to my son, George. We live next to the orchard in St. Augusta," she added.

"Rosemary Schmitz," said another woman standing in front of the picture window.

"Liz Mueller," said someone Theresa had seen in the clinic. She suspected that Liz Mueller had something to do with Roberta Wells. They kept looking at each other.

Theresa exhaled in exasperation.

"Have you imagined what your baby looks like?" Lucy asked.

"No," Theresa lied.

"About this time, it's taking human shape," Lucy continued. "Bones and cartilage are forming, and it's got these little dimples on its legs where knees and ankles will be. We understand you want a girl?"

"I don't want this baby at all."

With that, Theresa attempted to stand up. As if expecting her to do so, Lucy gripped her arm and held it back while Roberta's flat hand and mother-of-pearl fingernails pushed against Theresa's shoulder.

She felt light-headed. The smell of cookies on a platter in the middle of the coffee table aroused an absurd desire to eat.

"Have some milk," Maureen suggested, handing her a half-filled glass. "Milk goes well with cookies, and it's great for the baby."

Theresa took the glass mechanically. She was beginning to feel not just hunger but panic.

"Your baby is the most important person in this room," said Roberta. "Your child is an innocent life. He needs to be the focus of your world right now."

Theresa set the glass of milk on the coffee table and refused to give in to fear. What could these women do, really? There would be hell to pay once she got away from them.

"Did you know you're expecting a boy?" Lucy asked.

"Your son, yours and Charlie's son," Suzanne chimed in. "That's your husband's name, your mother tells me. Charlie. So, your son will be Charles Junior? Unless you have another name picked out."

Theresa wondered how long they could keep her like this. It must be going on four o'clock. Her dad was still planting, probably. Greg would be out with him. They might not come in for another two hours.

"Let's talk about where your son is at this point in his development," Roberta Wells continued. "Your chart says eleven to twelve weeks, so—"

"How do you know what my chart says?" Theresa interrupted angrily. "You have no right to view my chart."

"We all know," Roberta replied. "Everyone in this room knows."

"I needed to tell people so we could help you," Lucy explained. "No one should go through this alone. We're here to accompany you on your journey, Theresa. Your mother is here. Your friends from church. We're sure your husband will be as supportive as we are. From all we hear, he's a good man, the kind of man who defends his country and his family."

"You know nothing about him!" Theresa yelled, "If Charlie were here, he'd—" She stopped. This was pointless. Their minds were closed.

"It's a little early for an ultrasound, but in your case, I think we could arrange one. I'm sure Dr. Ryan would agree, if it made the difference between your imagining your baby abstractly and actually seeing his little body moving in your womb. Would you like that, Theresa?" Lucy probed.

Theresa didn't answer. They wanted her to convince them she would definitely allow this pregnancy to continue. But that would be a lie, and she refused to say it.

"My cousin in Sauk Rapids had a baby with Down syndrome," Helen Swanson said. "He's almost thirty now and doing very well. He has a job. He lives in one of these group arrangements where there's oversight but still enough freedom to go to movies, classes, museums . . . My cousin and her family adore him. He's their anchor, she says."

Roberta interrupted again, "The important point is that his parents recognized his right to be born. They understood things don't always turn out the way we anticipate. But we don't get to dictate what happens. It's God's job to give us opportunities to grow close to him, and it's our job to make the most of those opportunities. You may have slid off the path God meant for you, Theresa, but it's not too late to recognize that Providence intervenes for a reason. Your son is a blessing. He has a right to his life."

Theresa had never wanted to strangle anyone before, but Roberta Wells, with her persistent white claws clutching her shoulder, her arm, the back of her neck—Roberta Wells came close to releasing a monster Theresa never dreamed existed.

"We'll answer all your questions," Lucy offered. "There's so much information available. You wouldn't believe how much medical science has learned about Down syndrome, and how much progress has been made."

"So, *not typical* means Down syndrome," Theresa said sharply. "Well, I'll tell you right now, I'm not having this baby, and your opinions, your convictions, whatever you want to call them—they mean nothing to me."

No one had anything to add after that. Lucy turned toward Theresa's mother and said, "I need to be alone with her. Would you ask everyone to leave the room, Maureen? Roberta, stay nearby."

Lucy's minions left the room, blocking the exits. After they'd scattered, Theresa felt no freer, though at least they were no longer in her face. She and Lucy remained on the sofa.

"I'd like to share something with you," Lucy said quietly.

"I'm not interested," Theresa snapped.

"It's a war story," Lucy continued. "It happened to my uncle Ted in Korea. He was only seventeen. He'd lied about his age to get into the army. He and his unit were put ashore on the coast. There wasn't much of a beach where they landed. It was full of rocks, some the size of a car. They had to climb their way up a hill through those rocks, and it took all morning. Along the way, my uncle Ted saw a bundle. Turned out someone had wedged a baby between two rocks. It was wrapped in white cloth, still alive and crying, but it wasn't going to last long. The baby's skin was turning blue because it was freezing. It was February or March. My uncle Ted stopped and picked up the bundle. The infant still had her umbilical cord attached. He might have thought, *There's nothing I can do here, this isn't practical.* But he didn't. His buddies helped him take the baby with them. They unloaded my uncle's gear from his backpack, took everything out but his sleeping bag, and put the baby inside. Then they split up his rations and ammunition and the rest of his stuff among their own loads, and they all climbed that hill. When they got to the top, they kept going. Around noon they came to a road with refugees streaming south, including some nuns. My uncle went up to the nuns and gave them the infant. He didn't understand their language, and they didn't understand his, but they all knew the right thing was to save that baby, so they didn't need to speak."

Theresa said nothing; her eyes glazed over, not even looking at Lucy.

"He never talked about the war, and he never told anyone that story until one of my neighbors adopted a baby from South Korea in the '70s. The orphanage there sent a picture, and when Uncle Ted saw it, he blurted out the story to me and my sister. We were just kids, but I never forgot it."

Theresa did not respond and continued to avoid Lucy's stare.

"That infant, whose parents probably couldn't afford her during the war—that infant would have died *for sure*, Theresa. But thanks to my uncle, she got to stay alive. She got to live her life."

Lucy's words registered vaguely.

"Theresa, you can do that. You don't have to raise your little boy if you feel you don't have it in you. But you can bring him up the hill. That's all God asks. Bring him up the hill so he can live his life. Give him that chance."

Since Lucy's spiel seemed to be over, Theresa turned and faced her.

"I'm leaving this house," she said. *"Now."*

She started to rise. That's when she felt something sharp in her upper arm.

———•◦•———

Annie considered Theresa to be the most sophisticated, gorgeous, brainy woman in the entire history of the world. Her perfect husband made their story the stuff of legend.

Just last month, she'd come across a poem that could have been about them. It was written by an English poet, Samuel Taylor Coleridge, who, she'd read, had composed it in an "altered state" (whatever that meant).

She'd found this "dream fragment" in a copy of *The Oxford Book of English Verse.* Someone had sold it to the used bookstore downtown. Its spine was wrecked, but the contents were intact. Annie bought it for only one dollar. She took it home and added it gently to her stash so it wouldn't disintegrate further. It started in a sort of chant.

> *In Xanadu did Kubla Khan*
> *A stately pleasure-dome decree:*
> *Where Alph, the sacred river, ran*
> *Through caverns measureless to man*
> *Down to a sunless sea.*

Annie imagined that Theresa *dwelt* (she didn't just *live;* Theresa *dwelt*) in a stately pleasure dome. She had no idea where or what Xanadu was, but she thought it might be a mystical city on a mountain peak high in the Himalayas. In Annie's mind, the sacred river ran through caverns of love.

She half-slept at the base of the old oak tree that shaded the Haig mailbox. Annie was the family's mail fetcher, which meant, if she wanted to, she could send away for anything and no one would be the wiser when it came. The mailbox was about one hundred and fifty yards from the house, and the driveway meandered toward it along a line of white oaks and sugar maples. Her dad loved sugar maples. Every time an oak got diseased, he'd cut it down for wood and plant a sugar maple instead. That had been his habit since well before she was born. Most of the maples were fifty feet tall now. They were the kind that turned electric pink in the fall. She had inherited her father's fondness for them.

Annie didn't have a watch, but she guessed it was long past time for Theresa to drive by the mailbox on her way to the Cities. She wondered if their mother had convinced her to sit and talk with the St. Philomena ladies. She heard the noise of a car and half-turned. Theresa might not be able to see her in all the vegetation. She was about to get up and wave her arms when she realized it wasn't Theresa's car. It was one of the church ladies' cars, followed not very far back by another car, and finally a blue van.

Just her mother's friends finished with their meeting, Annie guessed. She liked the fact that her mother held these gatherings at their house because Maureen baked up a storm beforehand. There were always plenty of delicious leftovers.

More minutes went by, and still there was no Theresa.

It occurred to Annie that something was strange. This waiting had gone on too long. And then there was the exceedingly goofy request to hold onto Theresa's black pouch so no one could grab it. What was that about? And why did Theresa tell her to "stay out of sight?" That was goofier still.

None of the church ladies would think of stealing someone's purse. Annie opened the zipper. She found Theresa's wallet, cell phone, a pad of tissues, a pen, a lipstick, and a bottle of eyedrops. She decided to walk back to the house, but first, the pouch needed to be stashed somewhere safe. She considered various possibilities and decided the base of the mailbox was the place. Down about two feet into the culvert, her dad had set rocks that Annie could move only by straining every muscle. She pulled one out, tucked the pouch beneath it, and rolled the rock back into place.

A lifelong taste for mystery novels had taught Annie to question everything. If Theresa was inside the house, no foul, no miss. But if she was not there, Annie wanted to know where she was, and why she had asked her to take the pouch and meet her secretly.

One car remained near the house. It had an all-letter license plate, easy to remember. Annie entered through the kitchen door, took off her tennis shoes, and put them in the laundry room. She glimpsed her mother and another woman around the corner, but there was no sign of Theresa.

"It couldn't be helped," insisted the woman. "She didn't drink the milk."

"You didn't give her a chance to drink the milk," her mother said angrily.

"Trust me, Maureen. I know what I'm doing. I wouldn't inject anything harmful."

Her mother didn't respond to the injection remark. Annie wished she could see their faces better.

"Her stress levels must have been through the roof," the unknown person continued, "and that's not good for the baby. For heaven's sake, you could see it just looking at her."

"I don't—" Maureen started to say, but the person interrupted again.

"When the body puts out cortisol, the mother's heart beats faster, and so does the baby's. I used my professional judgement, Maureen. Someday she'll thank us for saving her from herself."

Annie cleared her throat. Neither woman seemed to have heard, so she cleared it again. They both turned.

"What are you doing home?" her mother asked, rather indignantly. "You said you'd be rehearsing your play."

"Rehearsal got canceled," Annie told her.

"Well, go upstairs and take a shower. You've got mud all over your legs. And put clean clothes on. Two outfits in one day! Do you think I run a laundry?"

Annie wondered whether it would be wise to ask about Theresa now when her mother was arguing with this definitely suspicious lady who had just talked about injecting something. Probably not, she decided. She resolved to bring it up later, and first to her dad.

"Sorry," she said. She climbed the back stairs until the corner put her out of sight. Then she stopped and sat down.

"I have to go," the other woman said. "I'll call you when we're settled."

"Who will watch her?" Maureen asked.

"Don't worry. We'll be careful."

"What if she needs a doctor?"

"I'm a certified nurse-midwife, Maureen. I'll see her every day, and I'll call you if anything happens."

"I can't tell Tom," her mother said, almost in tears. "I never expected—" She coughed and couldn't seem to find her voice again.

"You shouldn't tell your husband. We'll handle this ourselves as women supporting each other."

Annie stretched her neck, but she couldn't make out much except that the suspicious lady was patting her mother's arm.

"And remember! It's to help her in her time of disordered thinking. A life hangs in the balance. Keep that foremost in your mind, Maureen."

Her mother nodded. The lady kissed her on the cheek and left through the kitchen door.

No use talking to her mother now, Annie decided. Maureen looked ready to cry. She went upstairs, where she found nothing—no sign of Theresa, nor Theresa's suitcase. Theresa's bedroom door was open. That was unusual.

Annie knew that she'd better write down what she'd heard while it was fresh in her mind. She took a notebook from the collection in the desk drawer in her own bedroom and copied into it everything she could recall. It was a little black notebook, two inches by three inches, with gold edging and a black pen attached to the back cover. She chose it because it would fit into her pocket in between taking notes—perfectly surreptitious.

She walked back to Theresa's room. The bed was made, as always. Grandma's hand-sewn blue-and-white quilt was folded in three across the foot of the bed. The king-size for-show pillows in starched white cases leaned against the wooden headboard her dad had carved from one of the fallen oak trees. The pillows Theresa actually put her head on were in front, and the sheets were turned over just so. The front pillows and sheets were slightly wrinkled, indicating Theresa had taken a nap. Annie didn't find that surprising. Theresa would have used clean sheets every day if not expressly forbidden, but sometimes she took naps, so the bed didn't always look perfect. It looked close to perfect, though; certainly not the way it would look if a struggle had taken place.

She found nothing illuminating under the pillows, beneath the bed, in the bureau, or in the closet. Theresa's laptop sat on a side table, but Annie didn't have the password. She tried *Charlie,* but that didn't work. She looked around for documents, or maybe Charlie's dog tag numbers, but she couldn't find any clue that might suggest a password. She opened her notebook but realized she didn't have anything new to write down.

Annie went to her parents' bedroom next. This part of the investigation would require a whole higher level of stealth, she thought. She decided not to even try it while her mother was home. Annie tiptoed away from the door and down to the kitchen. It was empty. There were coffee mugs and dishes left on the counter. A Post-it note had been attached to the coffeepot. It said "Church meeting. Lamb stew in fridge."

Another meeting right after this afternoon's meeting, and at suppertime? She wrote in her notebook, "Second church meeting suspicious. Most significant info so far—unknown person injected someone, according to conversation between Mother and unknown person. Was Theresa injected? They talked about a baby. Is Theresa pregnant? Someone watching over someone—are they watching over Theresa?"

Annie went back upstairs. Her parents' bedroom door did not have a lock as some of her friends' parents' bedrooms did. She went in, looked around, opened drawers quietly, and even surveyed the closet. Her parents' bed was made but did not smell of starch the way Theresa's had. Annie saw nothing she considered unusual.

She left her parents' room and closed the door behind her. Zip stared up at her in the hallway. Her dad's dog wandered the farm at will. He shoved his black nose into her thigh. Annie wondered if he'd been in the house when whatever happened to Theresa had occurred. *Maybe he witnessed something*, she thought. But he'd have no way of telling her. More probable was that her mother had let him in when she'd left, and now he was curious.

With Zip in tow, Annie walked further down the hallway to examine the paperwork her dad kept on the desk in his office. His desk sat in the middle of the room. It was a massive oak heirloom that her grandpa's father had made almost a hundred years ago.

She didn't think her dad would know anything about Theresa, so she wasn't surprised when all she found were farm materials, invoices, and other boring detritus.

Before leaving, Annie decided to use her dad's computer to send an email to Mary. She knew his passwords because he kept them on a slip of paper next to the computer.

"Strange goings on," she typed. "Help! Urgent. —Annie"

Annie went back downstairs and sat at the kitchen table. Her mother was nowhere in sight, but she knew there had to be a clue somewhere. She didn't think a person could just disappear with no explanation. It didn't make sense.

The injection remark still bothered her. She pictured crime shows where the bad guys put a needle in someone and the victim crashes to the floor. Then the bad guys pick him up like a sack of flour and take him to a room with no windows, tie him to a chair, and torture him until he spills his secrets.

Her mother's apron hung on a hook in the corner near the coffeepot. Annie examined its pockets. The first one was empty, but the second had a note on scrap paper. *Lucy Meyer*, followed by a phone number. She wondered whether she should call the number. It was long distance, so there might be a record on the phone bill. Also, she didn't know what she'd say. She didn't want to make wild accusations.

But the phone number was definitely an anomaly. She copied it and Lucy Meyer's name into her notebook.

It was almost seven o'clock when her dad and Greg came home. Tom was not in a good mood. Annie warmed the lamb stew on the stove and told them that Maureen had gone somewhere, "with some woman or group of women. Mostly church people, and at least one total stranger." She also told them she didn't know where Theresa was.

Neither her father nor her brother made any comment.

Annie heated bowls in the microwave and set the table with plates, rolls, and butter while her father and brother cleaned up at the kitchen sink.

"Theresa went missing today," she said again as her father and Greg sat down and started to eat.

Her dad looked at her, his eyes tired. "Theresa is an adult," he said. "She doesn't owe you or me an explanation for her comings and goings."

He ate the stew fast, probably because he hadn't stopped for lunch.

"She packed a suitcase," Annie explained, "and next thing I know she disappeared after all these ladies came over. I was supposed to give her something before she left for the Cities. And someone talked about an injection. What if that was for Theresa?"

"Mind your own business," said her father.

"Can I be excused?" Greg had wolfed down his stew even faster than his father. "Homework," he added.

"When'll you be done with homework?" Tom asked grumpily.

"Two more weeks," Greg said, "and sweet freedom!"

"Not around here there's no freedom," Tom answered. "We got two fields not draining. There's no freedom for me, so there's none for you neither."

"Yeah. Any dessert?" Greg asked Annie.

"Ice cream in the freezer," she responded. "Peanut butter cookies in the cookie jar. They've got those chocolate kisses."

Greg went to the counter and took a handful of cookies from the jar with the rooster on top.

"They're fresh, from a church meeting right before Theresa disappeared," Annie added.

No one responded. Greg left the kitchen. Annie decided to confront her dad. "Your daughter's missing, and you don't seem to care," she accused.

"Theresa's not here," said Tom. "Doesn't mean she's missing. Why do you make a drama out of everything?"

"I'm not making a drama. I'm pointing out—"

"Last week, you and your mother argued nonstop about some stupid thing."

"She wanted me to quit the play because she said the book was banned, and I wouldn't do it—"

"Give me some *peace*," her father interrupted. "I've got bigger problems to worry about than you going into a panic every time you don't get your way."

Annie shut up and gave him some peace. She didn't think he believed her about the injection, or any of the rest of it. She'd have to wait for Mary to get back to her or for some new information to surface. In the meantime, to stop her mind from worrying, she decided to work on her lines upstairs. Her part was minor, but she wanted everything her character did and said to come out perfectly.

By the time her mother came home, her dad was already in bed. Annie went downstairs when she heard the car engine. She hoped someone might be dropping Theresa off.

Her mother walked through the front door, took off her headscarf, and set her purse on the hallway table. She looked as if a relative had died.

"What's wrong?" Annie asked. "Where's Theresa?"

"Nothing's wrong. Go back to bed."

"Where's Theresa?" Annie repeated.

"Theresa's fine," her mother said. Then she went upstairs.

Annie followed her up. She could hear her parents' voices as they talked behind their bedroom door, but she couldn't make out what they were saying.

——•◦•——

The next day, as usual, Annie's father left the house at dawn. Annie got out of bed early and watched him go. Her mother was in the kitchen. Annie could hear the sounds of baking sheets being pulled from the cupboards.

Standing next to the kitchen table, she wolfed down a bowl of cereal and a glass of orange juice. Instead of waiting for Greg, Annie walked to school alone. The long trek helped calm her down. Clearly her mother was in no mood for questions.

It was a normal day at school. Annie decided not to tell her friends about Theresa's disappearance. They were otherwise consumed by a rumor about the math teacher, Mr. Thomas, who was said to be in hot water with the principal for reasons yet unknown.

All week she returned home late after rehearsals for *The Bridge to Terabithia*, a play the school's drama teacher had reframed for older students. It was originally written for ten-year-olds, but it dealt with mature themes and even had some profanity. Annie would have given anything to play the lead, a girl who dies tragically because a rope snaps. Ropes aren't supposed to snap. Her father had taught her how to double a rope and tie the strongest possible knots so it wouldn't ever break. The heroine in *The Bridge to Terabithia* didn't know practical things like that.

Days passed, and Theresa still did not come home. Annie made a schedule of events in her notebook. She had last seen Theresa on the ninth of May in Theresa's bedroom. May 9 was a Wednesday. It was now May 19, a Saturday. In all that elapsed time, Annie had found only one significant detail besides the phone number for Lucy Meyer, and that was Theresa's car. She'd discovered it at about six thirty on May 10, after she got home from rehearsal. The car was behind the thresher in the pole barn. To get it there, someone had to make a very tight maneuver around the bulky machine. It was clearly a hiding place, since Theresa never normally parked toward the back. She parked near the front of the barn.

She couldn't find anything unusual inside the car. There were no foreign smells, no cigarette butts or stains that might be blood, no needle that might have been used for an injection. The glove compartment was clean. The keys were in the ignition. There was no suitcase. Annie even opened the trunk. Nothing.

In the following days, Annie sent her sister Mary two more emails but still got no reply.

On Saturday, May 19, she didn't have rehearsal until two o'clock, so she was home when a cherry-red pickup drove toward the house and parked in front of the living-room porch. She recognized the man who got out. It was Charlie's father. She was 99 percent sure. He had been best man at Charlie and Theresa's wedding. Annie hadn't talked to him at the wedding, but her mother had, and she didn't like him.

Annie knew he was here to ask about Theresa. She also knew her mother would give him the runaround. That was confirmed when her mother came outside and spoke to him on the porch instead of inviting him in like she would do for anyone else.

Her dad and Greg were in the fields. No one else was around. Annie could tell by her mother's body language that she'd be sending Charlie's dad away soon. So she ran as fast as she could downstairs, out the kitchen door, and along the driveway until she reached the mailbox. Her sides ached from the quickness of it. She didn't have to wait long for his truck to come back up the drive.

His pickup had a blue-and-red confederate-flag license plate on the front. She couldn't believe she didn't notice it when he drove in. It gave her reason to consider letting him drive by.

But then she thought, license plate or not, he might know something she didn't. It would be foolish to miss out on new information, especially since Theresa's absence was becoming scarier with each passing day. Annie stood up by the mailbox and waved her arms until she came into his view. Then she jumped out. The pickup slammed to a stop. The man inside rolled down his window.

"You Theresa's sister?" he asked, his drawl giving her pause as she tried to decide if it sounded creepy or just odd.

"And you're from a slave state," she told him.

"Now, that's just not true, young lady. Slavery's an abomination long gone from the free state of Alabama, which is where I'm from . . ."

"Only since you lost a war is it a free state," Annie retorted.

"That was a *long* time ago," he insisted.

"Not long enough for you to take that ugly license plate off your truck."

"It's a Southern Heritage plate," he said. "Got nothin' to do with slavery."

"That pile of manure won't wash up here," Annie said indignantly, remembering *Uncle Tom's Cabin,* a historically important book she'd read about the South.

The man strummed his fingers on the steering wheel and didn't say anything more. Annie's breathing was the only other sound she could hear. Even the wind had gone silent.

She began to worry he might drive off without either of them finding out anything they didn't already know, so she made a split-second decision to be less emotional and more strategic. She might despise his stupid license plate, but Annie didn't want Theresa's father-in-law to take off just yet, especially since he could probably find things out easier than a kid could.

Charlie's dad got out of his truck. He was thin and middle-aged. His face was impassive. That was the only way she could describe him.

"I'm lookin' for your sister," the man said, coming right up to where she stood. "Your mama doesn't seem to know where she is."

"I don't know where she is either. She went missing the afternoon of May ninth, and she hasn't been home since."

"Did anyone see her leave?" Charlie's father suddenly looked scared. At last, she thought, someone was taking her seriously.

"I saw her right before she disappeared. She gave me a pouch to keep for her. We were going to meet here at this mailbox so I could give it back," she said, climbing into the low spot by the foot of the mailbox post and stooping to pull out the rock at the base.

He knelt beside her. "Let me do that," he said. He pulled the rock away with less effort, revealing the pouch. Then he picked it up, opened its zipper, and looked closely at the contents— especially the wallet and cell phone.

"Things she needs," he said. "I don't suppose you know the password to this cell."

"No, sorry," Annie said. "I tried to figure out the password to her computer upstairs in her bedroom, but none of my guesses were right."

"Maybe Charlie knows," Woodrow said. "I'll ask him. Meantime, you hold onto this pouch. I'll mention it to your sheriff. He might want an expert to look at the cell phone."

"OK," Annie said. "Be sure to tell him Theresa's driver's license is in the wallet, and that she put the wallet in the pouch herself and asked me to keep it out of sight. Theresa was planning on driving to the Cities, but she didn't. I know because I found her car in the pole barn the day after she disappeared."

She pulled out her notebook. "Also, here's this note I found in my mother's apron. It's got a name and phone number on it. I was afraid I'd get caught snooping if I called it, and anyway, I didn't know what to say when somebody answered."

Annie told him that Theresa had packed a suitcase and had probably used the front stairway because it was wider and would have been closer to her car. Annie described how she usually used the back stairs that wound around into the kitchen. Theresa must have run into the large group of ladies who had just arrived for a meeting with their mother. She thought some of those ladies might have been blocking Theresa's way.

"I waited at the mailbox a long time, and when I got back to the house, Theresa was gone."

She also told him about the unknown woman talking to her mother in the kitchen, and the mention of an injection and a baby. She described the remaining car's license plate, the one that had been all letters. "It probably belonged to the woman in the kitchen who was the last to leave. I remember it exactly. SAV ALL."

"That's a good catch," he said, "thinkin' to memorize the plate."

"She's my sister. She asked me to meet her here, but she didn't show. She gave me this pouch and she didn't explain why. Now she's missing. I'm *really* worried."

Charlie's father didn't say anything to that. She figured he was thinking over all she'd told him.

"I'm in a unique position to notice strange behaviors, because no one here pays attention to me," Annie added.

"You're certainly good at it," he agreed. "Can you tell me if anyone called the police?"

"Not that I know of," she said. "By the way, what's your name? You *are* Charlie's dad, right?"

"Yes, ma'am. I'm Woodrow Cole."

She wrinkled her nose. "I'm not *ma'am*. I'm thirteen. I'll be fourteen in a few months. My name's Annie Haig."

He smiled. "Annie Haig," he said her name distinctly, "you were supposed to meet Theresa right here on the afternoon of May ninth, but she didn't arrive."

"That's right, and no one's seen her since."

"And no one called the police?" He pronounced *po-lice* as if it were two words.

"No. Nobody but me thinks she's missing. I tried to tell my dad and brother, but I'm the only one worried about her."

"No, you're not. Charlie's worried sick. He hasn't been able to get hold of her since about when you say she disappeared, and your mama acted skittish as all get-out just now. She made it plain she's offerin' no help. So, I'm tryin' to figure out where to look next."

"Don't go see the police with that thing on your truck," Annie advised, pointing to his license plate. "By the way, I've been trying to reach Mary for advice."

"Mary?"

"My oldest sister. She wasn't at Theresa's wedding. She divorced the family years ago. That's her word for it. But she comes home for Thanksgiving sometimes. Anyway, I've been sending Mary emails, but she doesn't answer."

"OK, would you give me that name and phone number you found in your mama's apron, and Mary's phone and email and where she lives?"

"Mary's somewhere in St. Paul. She's a teacher. I don't know where she lives exactly, but she works at a school called Metropolitan."

Annie wrote Mary's and Lucy's information on an empty page in her black book. Then she tore it out and handed the sheet to Woodrow.

"You can look at my notebook, but then I want it back," she said, adding, "No one in my family is even talking about Theresa being gone. All my dad can talk about is getting the planting done, and my mother is acting really weird, like she doesn't even notice Theresa's missing. And now I find out Theresa's pregnant . . . Nobody told me. It's true, isn't it?"

"Yeah," he said, "it's true."

"It's like I don't count. I have to listen in on other people's conversations just to find out what's going on. Somebody should have told me Theresa's pregnant. Maybe then I could have helped her more so she wouldn't have disappeared."

"You're helping her now."

"But not enough to bring her back. Not so far, at least."

"That's why we're gonna work on this together."

"OK," Annie agreed instantly. "If I find out anything new, I'll let you know right away. Write down your phone number."

"You've got a deal, sweetheart," he said. His eyes were big, and he

25

sounded sincere. She liked his straight-to-the-point attitude. She suddenly remembered his grin at the wedding the moment his son kissed the bride. He wasn't grinning now. He pulled out a pencil.

"I need to get the timeline as clear as possible. Last time you saw Theresa was when on May ninth?"

"Middle of the afternoon, about three thirty," Annie said.

"Was this Lucy Meyer the woman with your mama when you overheard them?"

"I don't know. She didn't say her name. Mother doesn't introduce me to people."

Woodrow wrote his phone number in her book. "Day or night," he said.

"OK, we're partners, then."

"We are," he said. "And you, little darlin', are a treasure. I'm most beholden to you."

Annie beamed. Hardly anyone ever complimented her. She'd give it up in a second, though, if Theresa would come sauntering across the lawn.

Woodrow got back into his truck and drove away. For the first time since the afternoon Theresa disappeared, Annie felt she was making progress. At the very least, her evidence had convinced one person to pay attention. Now the question was why nobody else did.

Annie took a deep breath and held it before expelling as much air as she could. For a bleak moment, she tried to imagine how her parents would act if she disappeared. Did they even care about their kids? They didn't seem to care that Mary hardly ever called or came home to visit.

All her dad could talk about was the farm. She knew he worried a lot about financial things. But didn't he worry about Theresa too? And all her mother seemed to care about was God. Her mother wasn't worried about Theresa. "Theresa's fine," she'd said. What did that mean? Theresa was pregnant and nobody could say where she was. How was that *fine*?

Maybe Mary could figure it out, she hoped. If she'd ever answer her emails.

———•◦•———

A few miles from the farm, Woodrow pulled off the road and checked his phone for the location of the St. Dominic Police Department. It was in the same building as the Stears County Sheriff's office. He decided to visit in person, ruminating about the Haigs along the way.

Something was really off with his daughter-in-law's mama, Woodrow concluded. He thanked his lucky stars for the kid behind the bushes. She'd been in the wedding procession when Charlie married Theresa the previous fall.

Their nuptials had seemed, to put it mildly, subdued. Charlie's new Minnesota relations were standoffish. The Coles hadn't been formally introduced to anyone. There wasn't an ounce of gusto in the hymns. The light in the church was dim. And from a safety point of view, Woodrow thought the towering plaster-of-Paris statues at the altar might come crashing down if anyone sneezed.

Charlie hadn't cared much about the minutiae of his wedding, though. He told Woodrow afterward he'd have married Theresa in a bog with ducks for guests.

Now, reviewing everything, Woodrow tried to remember what exactly Theresa's mama had said on the porch. She'd had her arms crossed and wore a don't-mess-with-me look on her face. Few words had come out of her. She'd stood her ground, not invited him in, and acted as if she hardly remembered who he was. She hadn't even expressed surprise at his unexpected appearance. She'd mostly just stared down at the steps, avoiding eye contact.

Woodrow took her unusual deportment as a cue to stay put on the ground below, but he'd used considerable charm—a soft voice, the sincere expression on his face, his cap in hand—as ancillary armaments. Usually such things worked with persons of the female persuasion. With Theresa's mama, they'd fallen flat.

His simple request, "Could I speak with Theresa?" had prompted a crisp reply.

"Theresa's not here," and not one word more.

Maureen, Woodrow remembered—her name was Maureen.

"Well, as you'll recall, I'm her father-in-law, and I'm here because my son is mighty worried 'bout her. Seems he hasn't been able to connect with her for over a week. He asked me to come up here and talk to her, if that's possible, ma'am."

"She's not here," Theresa's mama repeated.

"And where might she be?" Woodrow inquired politely.

"She needs time to think. She's with friends."

"And which friends might those be?"

"I told you, she needs time alone," Maureen had retorted. "She doesn't want to be bothered."

"Alone? You said she was with friends."

"I don't know why you came all the way up here!" Maureen exclaimed, giving Woodrow momentary hope for some reason he couldn't explain.

"Well, that's the point, isn't it? My son's overseas, and he's worried sick, and that's dangerous 'cause he needs to focus on his job. He can't be worryin' 'bout whether his wife is OK, so he asked me to come up here. She's not answerin' her phone. It was days past the last time he talked to her when he called on me to check. And it was a couple days more before I could head up. I've driven straight through, stoppin' only to get some sleep, and now you can't tell me where she is or what's going on. You can see how that'd be a mite nerve-rackin', can't you, ma'am?"

"I told you, I don't know where she is. I know she's fine. She'll call your son when she's ready."

"What the hell—"

"There's no need to curse at me." With that, Maureen went into the house and closed the door. Woodrow thought he heard it lock.

He'd stood at the base of the porch, mad as could be, unsure what to do next. He'd decided to leave for the moment, thinking he'd come back when the husband was home. Then, at the mailbox, this girl had come out of the bushes saying she didn't know where her sister was. The details in her notebook had scared him shitless. He'd wondered whether he should even believe her at first, but his gut told him she wasn't like her mother. She wasn't playing games.

He took Highway 15 to 23 east into St. Dominic, north at the Tenth Avenue exit, right at Second Street and right again at Courthouse Square. The "square" comprised an assortment of red brick buildings, including one with large *Law Enforcement Center* signage across the front. Nothing stately, Woodrow noted. Nothing that didn't look as if it sprang from the prairie the day before yesterday. In other words, he considered it a far cry from the grandeur of a Southern courthouse.

Woodrow backed into a parking space in the center lot and walked inside. A young woman sat in front of a computer screen. Her name tag said *Jennifer B.* "How are you today, Miss Jennifer?" he asked, looking straight at her.

"I'm just fine." She answered with a smile that showed off perfect, white teeth, likely the product of pricey orthodontics. "What can I do for you?" she asked.

"I'd like to inquire 'bout someone who may be missin'," he returned.

"You don't know if this person is missing?" she asked.

"I just came into town," he continued, "and I can't locate her. She's my son's wife, and he's overseas, and he's worried as all heck about her 'cause she's not answerin' phone calls or Skypin' him. He asked me to come here and find out what's what."

Miss B. made notes in her computer. Then she picked up a phone, pushed a button, and spoke, "Antoine, there's someone here looking for a possibly missing person."

A deputy entered the lobby from the street. He was a heavyset man in a white shirt, black epaulets and tie, an American flag above his left pocket, and a sheriff's badge on his right. He glowered at Woodrow.

"You got that Confederate plate outside?" he asked.

"No, sir. That's a Southern Heritage plate, and I'm truly sorry if it's rubbin' you wrong. There's no intention to offend."

The deputy stiffened but said no more. He looked Woodrow up and down before leaving the lobby.

"Someone will be right out to help you," Jennifer B. said, her smile gone.

"Thank you, kindly." Woodrow sat on one of the lobby's plastic chairs.

These people were not going to make anything easy, he realized, especially with him smelling of a day and a half on the road and his vehicle sporting a license plate that seemed to send Northerners up their silos.

Another deputy entered from an office area and motioned Woodrow to follow him. They went into a cubicle where Woodrow took a chair in front of the desk. The nameplate read: *Lieut. Antoine Harrison.*

"You're here about a possibly missing person?" he asked.

Woodrow appreciated men like Harrison, guys with a military demeanor who looked like they'd been through the mud at some point. Antoine Harrison was well-proportioned, about thirty-five, his thick black hair slightly receding. It was the energy behind his eyes that attracted Woodrow. Harrison radiated intent, the kind a commander wanted in an officer, the kind Woodrow needed right now.

"Yes, sir, I'm here on behalf of my son. It's about my daughter-in-law. She and my son were married last fall in St. Dominic. My son, Charlie, is in Afghanistan. He enlisted with the US Army Recruiting Battalion out of Montgomery, Alabama. We're from the town of Lafayette, a couple hours north of there. Charlie's wife's name before their marriage was Theresa Haig. Now, while he's overseas, she's livin' at her parents' farm. Tom Haig's her father's name. Her mama's Maureen . . ."

"What makes your son think she's missing?"

"No text messages or emails, no phone calls from her in ten days. Just nothin'. She's not Skypin' either. They Skype every chance they get. He doesn't get callbacks when he leaves messages. He's damn near goin' out of his mind. I don't need to tell you, sir, that it's dangerous for a soldier to have to worry about his family back home. Also, my son says his wife is pregnant."

"Have you talked to her parents?" The deputy typed notes into his computer.

"I tried talkin' to her mama. She didn't invite me in, and she seemed nervous out on her front porch. I don't know what to make of it. She wouldn't tell me much, and you know the Irish, normally they talk you to death."

"The mother's Irish?"

"Ah," said Woodrow, "I'd say she's Irish extraction. She's got reddish-blond hair. Dark eyes, though. No brogue, so her family musta been in this country awhile. It was mostly the look of her . . . and her tone of voice."

"Let me make a few calls," the lieutenant interrupted. He left the cubicle.

Woodrow waited about ten minutes before the guy came back and sat behind his desk.

"I spoke to Theresa's mother. She didn't sound nervous. Her daughter has gone on a spiritual retreat with some friends, and she doesn't want to be disturbed. I got the impression she and your son had some kind of marital spat, and Theresa would like to be left alone for the time being. Her mother is sure she'll contact your son when she's back."

He handed Woodrow a form.

"You can fill this out, if you like, and I'll keep it on file. But for now, I don't think the sheriff's office will be putting anyone on it." He smiled slightly, as if apologizing.

Woodrow didn't return the smile.

"If your son's wife doesn't contact him by next week," the lieutenant continued, "let me know and I'll go out there myself and talk to the parents. Here's my card." He pulled a business card out of his breast pocket and handed it to Woodrow. "Call me if there's no word by mid-week."

Woodrow stood up. "I don't rightly believe her," he said.

"Well, the sheriff's office has no reason not to at this point, but like I said, I'm willing to go out there."

"Is there any way I can find out who these friends are? The ones who went on this retreat?" He put an emphasis on *retreat*, but his skepticism didn't seem to make an impression.

"I'll ask the parents," the lieutenant said. "By the way, if my wife stopped calling me or taking my calls overseas, I'd talk to my unit's chaplain . . . see if he couldn't get the army to look into it. It's not good for morale, guys worrying about their wives."

"I doubt Charlie talks much with his chaplain," Woodrow said.

"Tell him to start," the lieutenant advised, "and fill out this form with your information. Leave it at the front desk. And, this is important—" he added with a stern look, "try not to panic. Situations like this happen all the time. Young people get into fights, but they generally work things out."

Woodrow filled out the form. Then he remembered the pouch. "Another thing," he told the lieutenant. "Theresa has a younger sister. She gave that sister a pouch that had her wallet and cell phone in it. The wallet has her driver's license. Theresa wouldn't have gone anywhere without those things, not willingly. I think you should check that out. The younger sister's named Annie."

Lieutenant Harrison made a note about the pouch, and Woodrow left his office, still agitated. He was not about to call Charlie and say, "We have to wait a week before they'll look into it. And, oh, by the way, talk to your chaplain."

The only thing left to do was to go after the other sister Annie mentioned. Mary at Metropolitan School. He returned to his vehicle and pulled the notebook pages from the glove compartment. Annie had given him Mary's email address and phone number. He tried calling the number. It was disconnected. This was not his lucky day.

He'd have to drive to St. Paul. If he found Mary, maybe she could tell him the names and whereabouts of Theresa's friends. He'd been near St. Paul on his way to St. Dominic. He headed back to Highway 52/I-94, south toward Maple Grove. He planned to pull into a truck stop to wash up, change clothes, and eat something. He knew soon he'd have to get some sleep.

Woodrow noticed his radio wasn't tuned to local stations. He hadn't turned it on the whole trip, that's how scared he'd been for Charlie. He drove until he saw a Walmart visible from the freeway, got off at the exit, and parked near a line of RVs at the far end of the lot, where a man and woman were peering behind an open panel on an old Winnebago. It had a Tennessee decal on its rear end right above a Tennessee plate.

"You folks havin' trouble?" Woodrow asked.

The man turned around. He was bald with a pot belly. His clothes looked too nice to wear while working on equipment. He had grease smudges and a grimace on his face.

"Boy, are we," he said.

"Well, you're in luck. 'Cause there's damn near nothin' I can't fix. Let me take a look."

"That's mighty nice of you," the woman replied, smiling broadly.

"No trouble at all, ma'am," Woodrow said, smiling back. "I had one miserable pup of a day today, so it's time for somethin' to go right."

An hour later, with a new part installed in the RV, they let him use their shower and served him a homemade meal on a table outside under the canopy. He described his mission.

"I wish you luck," said the man, a retired breeder whose son had taken over his horse farm back home. This was their first trip to Canada. They planned to start in Winnipeg and drive west.

"I'll tell you one thing," the lady said, "you'd best get that plate off your truck. These Yankees don't take kindly to anything of that sort. You'd think they lost the war."

"That's what people been tellin' me," Woodrow said, smiling at her.

"Well, my recommendation is you get on their good side," she continued. "You deposit that plate somewhere else, and don't put it back 'til you're halfway home."

"Yeah, I know I should do that. I guess I'm just too ornery to take the hint."

That night, the couple offered to let him sleep on their sofa inside the RV, but Woodrow preferred the back of his truck, so they parted ways.

—•—•—•—

There was no Mary Haig currently teaching at Metropolitan State University. Google found no other school in the area with the word *Metropolitan* in its name. No publicly available database revealed that any Mary Haig had ever worked at a place called Metropolitan.

However, a Claire Haig did currently teach at MSU, as Woodrow had noticed in the faculty directory online. A woman in the admissions office confirmed it for him. She allowed Woodrow through the glass door despite the fact that the administration section of the building was officially closed. It said so on a placard next to the door that he hadn't bothered to read. His pitiful expression had induced her to let him enter anyway.

"Whatever you want, it better be quick."

The woman was in her mid-fifties; her name tag said *Linda*. She wore polyester slacks and a short-sleeved cotton shirt. Her left hand lacked a wedding ring so Woodrow assumed she had never married or was long divorced. He also concluded—based on her rough haircut and cracked plastic belt—that her job didn't pay much. Her eyes were warm, though. Instinct told him a nice person hid beneath that gruff facade.

He slid into a charm offensive. What a middle-aged woman would do for an attentive man, even a stranger, could be downright remarkable.

"I think it unseemly that a lady such as yourself should be cooped up on a beautiful day like this," he said, looking straight into her wide-set blue eyes. "And I sincerely apologize for takin' up your time."

She was in her office on a Sunday to help the teaching staff meet their twenty-four-hour deadline to upload semester grades into the university database. It takes codes and spreadsheets, she told him almost breathlessly. In particular, she was trying to help the newbie professors. Woodrow kept looking into her eyes.

"End of semester comes so fast," she said. "It crashes down on us right after finals. There's this mad dash to get grades in. Final grades can mean the difference between a student's scholarship continuing or being cut off. It can be a mess if we do it wrong."

"You have an important job," Woodrow said. "So many people depend on you."

"That's right," she admitted. "One semester a professor gave a student an incomplete to hide the fact she'd missed the deadline. The student complained so much the professor nearly lost her job. She wasn't tenured, so that can happen. And then there's the school's reputation to consider. If grades don't get out in time, or if they're not accurate, it costs us in enrollment. Keeping enrollment up is crucial."

Woodrow nodded. She asked him for identification. He showed her his driver's license, leaning in to explain the rhyme and reason for his search. She grew warmer, even smiling as she made a copy of his license and had him sign into the visitor's log. She told him how to get to the cafeteria in the student center while she attempted to contact Claire Haig.

Woodrow left her office, followed the stairway to the cafeteria, and waited. It was eleven thirty. A few people meandered in, bought sandwiches, and took them outside. Woodrow ate a ham and cheese on sourdough along with fries and a Coke at a table that gave him a clear view of the door. He put in a call to the Minnesota National Guard and left a voice mail at the chaplain's office, following up on the lieutenant's advice.

It was a little after twelve thirty when he noticed a woman flying down the same stairway he'd taken. She reminded him of Theresa. Haig women devoured space—that was for sure. But this one didn't have Theresa's sparkle. Her eyes looked sad. He stood up as she approached his table.

"Woodrow Cole?" she asked, glancing at a paper in her hand.

"Yes, ma'am," he said. "I'm Charlie's father."

"Charlie being?"

"My son, who's married to Theresa Haig. I'm looking for her sister Mary. Are you Claire Haig?"

"Yes. There is no Mary." He assessed her, taken aback by the way she'd annihilated a person well-known to Annie.

"What does that mean?" he asked. "You were Mary, but you changed your name to Claire?"

"Precisely. What do you want, Mr. Cole?"

Her rushed response suggested she'd be harder to charm than Linda in the admissions office.

"Well, my son and your sister Theresa—they got married last October, and now Theresa's missin' and was maybe taken by force, strange as that may seem. I thought you might know where she is or who her friends are."

She stared at him. "I have no idea," Claire Haig finally said.

Woodrow tried to keep his breathing relaxed and regular despite how much he had riding on this woman's cooperation.

"Could we go somewhere and talk?" he suggested.

She didn't reply.

"Charlie's in Afghanistan, and he can't be searchin' for Theresa himself. He's worried sick, so I really need to find out where she's at. For his sake. And also for your sister's, of course." He knew he was talking too fast.

Claire still didn't react.

"They were married here in Minnesota," Woodrow added as if that meant anything. Claire had not been at the wedding. He would have remembered her. He felt like a fish flailing in the air after getting yanked out of his natural habitat.

"She was livin' with your parents after Charlie deployed," Woodrow continued at a slower pace. "Charlie says she's expectin' a baby. Everything seemed fine until about ten or eleven days ago when she up and disappeared. I tried at your family homestead, but I can't get a thing out of your mama. I think she knows where Theresa is."

Claire stood like a stone wall on a battlefield.

"Could we please go somewhere and talk it over at least?" he reiterated, lowering his voice. He'd get down on his knees, if that's what it took.

"Here is fine," she said, taking a seat at the table. He sat across from her.

"I talked to your sister Annie," he said. "She's been tryin' to contact you. She sent you emails. Did you get them?"

"No." Claire shook her head.

"Have you checked your email lately?" Woodrow asked.

"Constantly, especially during finals. Unless—" she paused.

"Unless?"

"Annie probably doesn't have my Gmail address. She could be using a Yahoo account I haven't checked in a while."

"In other words, your family can't reach you by email. Can they phone you? Text you?" These Haigs were incredible.

She shook her head.

"So," he concluded, "you're unreachable to the people closest to you?"

His frustration sounded like an accusation. Hell, it was an accusation, he realized. He cared more about her missing sister than she did.

He found it unfortunate that she was good-looking. On average, he found attractive women harder to talk to. He noticed she wasn't in the first bloom of youth, though. He put her in her mid-thirties, at least.

"My family's not close," she replied matter-of-factly.

"Why is that?"

"Mr. Cole, I'm not giving you time I could spend grading exams to explain my personal relationships. Suffice it to say that people in my family tend to go their own way."

So, he concluded, she wasn't close to either of her sisters. He figured he might as well cut to the chase.

"Do you care that Theresa's missin'?" he asked point-blank.

"How do you *know* she's missing?" Claire asked him.

"Find your sister's emails," he suggested.

She pulled out a phone and scowled. "I can't remember my Yahoo address." He watched as she typed in possibilities until she found it.

Woodrow remained silent while she read. Her face was expressionless. Damn, she was getting on his nerves. Then she punched in a number and put her cell on the table between them. The volume was set on high. He could hear it ringing.

"Yeah," said a young man's voice.

"Greg?"

"Who's this?"

"Your sister formerly known as Mary," she said. "I call myself Claire now."

"Yeah, Mary!" he replied. "What's up?"

"I'd like to talk to Theresa. Is she there?"

"Nah. She's gone."

"But she was living with you at the farm?"

"For about a month. But then she went somewhere."

"Do you know where?"

"Mom knows, I think."

"Did you talk to Theresa before she left?"

"Not exactly."

"She didn't tell you where she was going?"

"Nobody tells me anything, except Dad when something needs doing."

"Greg, is Annie home?"

"She's in her play today. Mom and Dad are there too. They're only putting it on this one weekend, so Annie talked Dad into going."

"Greg, I'm going to give you my cell number. Would you pass it on to Annie?"

"OK."

"Tell her to call me as soon as she can." She gave him her number.

"Yeah, got it."

"Thanks, Greg."

"OK. Bye."

He hung up. Claire's head was bent over the phone, but when she looked up, Woodrow could see that, put together, Annie's emails and this call were the game-changers he'd been hoping for.

"They took her," Claire said.

"What do you mean?" he asked.

"Mother and her tribe of do-gooders kidnapped my sister." She said it as if the matter were self-evident.

"You don't think she went off with friends on some kind of retreat?" Woodrow asked.

"Not if Annie is telling the truth."

"And you think she is?"

"Yes. The clincher is—why would Theresa go through that cloak-and-dagger business with her purse if she weren't afraid something was going to happen between her bedroom and the mailbox? You said she's pregnant?"

"She told Charlie she was."

"Did she tell Charlie anything was wrong with the baby?"

"Not that he said. He would have said."

"So, our first stop has to be her doctor's office."

Woodrow liked the way she said *our first stop*. "You don't think you should talk to your mama first?"

"My mother and I have an oil-and-water relationship. According to Annie, you didn't get on with her either. So, what's the point of letting her know we're working together?"

Woodrow liked *working together* even more than *our first stop*.

"My truck's outside," he said. "When can you leave St. Paul?"

"Not for another day," she replied. "I've got papers to read and final grades to post." Woodrow's hopes crashed again.

"Tell you what," she added, "I'm done here for the moment. I'll go to my place and work on papers and meet you somewhere tomorrow. I might be able to leave for St. Dominic in the afternoon."

"I'll drive you home," he suggested, standing up. "Or do you have a car?"

"I take the bus here," she said, putting her cell in her pocket.

"Then let me drive you. It'll save you time to work on grades."

"You'll have to find a motel tonight," she remarked as they left the cafeteria.

"No problem," he replied. "I'll sleep in my truck." Claire didn't say anything to that.

When they got outside, they walked around the building. She stopped in her tracks when she saw his vehicle. He had parked parallel to the sidewalk, and they came on his truck front first. She stood before his pride and joy, a 1940 red Ford pickup that he had restored over many years, washed twice before sunrise in an open-air carwash, and dried in circles with a microfiber towel. He'd cleaned the windows and chrome until they sparkled like mirrors, and vacuumed the inside so that anyone, however fussy, would feel privileged to enter a conveyance in such immaculate condition. He'd gassed it up. It was ready to go.

"If you think I'm getting into that thing, you're in the wrong state," Claire said.

Woodrow sighed. "You mean the plate."

"Of course I mean the plate."

No use arguing, he decided. He needed her too much. Woodrow located his toolbox, pulled out two long screwdrivers, a wrench, and a rolled-up mat. He spread the mat under the front of the car, slid in, and twisted and turned the fasteners until he could pull the plate free.

There was damn near nothing he wouldn't do for his son, he thought to himself. Woodrow turned the key in the truck's ignition, and the engine purred to life.

"I got a pack of cigarettes in the glove compartment. Any objection if I light one?" he asked.

"Long as I don't have to breathe in what you breathe out," Claire said.

"Jesus," he muttered.

"Just drive," she said. "I'll tell you where to turn."

Her apartment comprised the upper half of a blue-and-white duplex on the west side of the city, a grand old Victorian with an expansive front porch, and above it, a balcony. Woodrow guessed it was built in the nineteenth century, or maybe around the first World War. It needed a new paint job, he noted, and soon, new shingles.

"Looks like a gentrifying neighborhood," Woodrow observed as he pulled to the curb.

"The rent keeps going up," Claire said.

"Yeah," Woodrow acknowledged. "That's a given."

Claire opened the passenger door with one arm and held paperwork in the other. "I'll call you when I'm ready to leave," she told him as she pushed the door shut.

"Hold on," he protested, jumping out. "Don't be in such a damn hurry. You had lunch today?"

"I can't waste time going out for lunch," she told him.

"No need. I'll whip somethin' up. I make a mean omelet."

"You think I'm going to invite a total stranger into my house?"

"Yeah, I do. We're on a mission and time's wastin'."

"I don't have food on hand," she said.

"Well then, this is your lucky day. I'm gonna do the shoppin'. Just point me in the right direction."

Claire said nothing at first. "Well," she finally said, "I'm not getting dangerous vibes off you."

She gave him directions to a grocery on Snelling Avenue and went into the house by herself. Woodrow rang her doorbell an hour later with an overflowing bag in his arms. He found a frying pan in her kitchen, a bottle of olive oil, a slightly cracked mixing bowl, a mishmash of plates, cups and saucers, the coffeepot, and a wire whisk. By the time he slipped an omelet onto her plate, Claire was too distracted by the smells to keep on reading.

"I called Charlie," Woodrow informed her.

"And?" she asked.

"He already talked to his chaplain. The army's goin' to contact someone in the Minnesota Guard. I left a voice mail for the chaplain here."

"I'd like someone like that with us when we talk to my mother," Claire said.

"You think he'd untangle her tongue?" Woodrow hoped Claire knew something he hadn't figured out.

"She might feel intimidated enough to let something slip."

"She didn't seem easy to intimidate. But I'll call the chaplain's office again tomorrow morning before we set out."

Claire didn't reply, and he got the feeling she was thinking something she'd likely not share. He tried another approach. "Help me understand . . . You think your sister's disappearance has to do with her bein' pregnant?"

Claire nodded. Her mood was improving with each bite, as Woodrow expected. "Yes, I think it has to do with Theresa's pregnancy," Claire said. "I also think it has to do with my mother's church."

"That's what Annie said. Church ladies. The same church where Charlie and Theresa got married?"

"It's the only church my family knows, and—"

"What's this church got to do with Theresa bein' pregnant?" Woodrow interrupted.

"I'm guessing something is wrong with the baby, and the women at my family's church think she won't have it."

"So, they abduct her?"

"They probably consider kidnapping a lesser evil."

Woodrow shook his head. "I know a lot of crazy Baptists, but I'm not acquainted with anyone who goes around kidnappin' people."

"You need to realize who they are," Claire told him. "These women are obsessed. They look for causes—something that makes them feel important. Something they think can't be questioned, like a baby's right to be born. That's my guess."

Woodrow began to wonder if Claire were a bit tetched herself. He studied her closely, as a soldier sizing up a potential ally or foe.

"Didn't the South do that?" Claire asked, raising her voice. "Come up with a *cause* to cover the ugly truth?"

Woodrow met her gaze. "You sound like a zealot," he said.

"Evangelicals in your neck of the woods make the same arguments about abortion," she insisted. "I mean, wouldn't they do *anything* to stop one."

"Truth be told, I don't have much truck with evangelicals, and they don't have much truck with me. Though my brothers' wives are born-again, one in particular."

"This feels like the same craziness," Claire continued. "The Salem witch trials, the Great Awakening, revival tents. We live in a superstitious country, Mr. Cole."

Woodrow was not in the mood for lectures and must have telegraphed his impatience, because Claire went back to grading papers while he cleaned up in the kitchen. When he asked to use her shower, she nodded and even locked herself in her bedroom to give him privacy. Woodrow fetched a change of clothes from his pickup.

Her bathroom reeked of lemon. Lemon soap, lemon shampoo, little beveled glass bottles of pale-yellow oils, white subway tile on the walls that she probably cleaned with lemon detergent. Woodrow pegged her as a one-track woman. Anything she took a shine to, she overdid.

He adjusted the shower head for maximum pressure, lathered up, and let hot water sluice the sweat off. Finished in less than two minutes, per Marine protocol, he grabbed a white towel from a shelf next to the shower and rubbed his skin dry. He put on a clean T-shirt, socks, and underwear, then pulled his old pants back on before taking a closer look around the place.

She had two walls in a second bedroom lined with books—mostly literature, art history, and philosophy. But she lived in a void when it came to war and conflict, topics Woodrow felt essential to understanding the world.

Next to the longest wall was a sofa. It would make a nicer bed than his pickup, he decided, so he stretched out and slept the rest of the afternoon. By the time she woke him, she was done grading papers. It was still light outside.

"We can leave as early as you want," she said, shaking his shoulder, "but I've decided you need a long-sleeved shirt to cover those tattoos."

Woodrow's olive drab T-shirt exposed *semper fi* in black cursive on his left bicep and a blue eagle descending with talons outspread on the other, its feathers drawn so fine you could practically stroke them.

"You can still buy one tonight," Claire continued. "White and long sleeved. My mother can't tolerate tattoos, and she's a sucker for white."

Ordinarily, Woodrow would not take orders from a woman he just met and had no personal interest in. In this case, he made an exception. The

Target six miles away had his size. He washed the shirt in her kitchen sink, let it dry overnight, and ironed it at five the next morning. They needed to get on the road. He was guessing, since she hadn't mentioned a motel again, that she had been OK with him on her sofa.

———•◦•———

They had breakfast in a suburban cafe on their way out of the metro, a pot of coffee on the table for Woodrow—who took it black—and juice for Claire, who had never found a restaurant that could serve a decent cup of coffee. They kept it on the burner after it was brewed, she said, and the oils turned rancid. She gave Woodrow a lecture on the subject.

She was getting on his nerves. No cigarettes within a hundred yards of her. No bluegrass or country on the radio. She preferred FM, news, or classical music—preferences he ignored. He kept the radio off, and they drove for the most part in silence.

Except for family, Woodrow didn't let other people behind the wheel of his pickup. Ten years prior, he'd bought it at auction "as is" for fifteen hundred cash, meaning it had no warranty, and there was no bringing it back for a refund. He had inspected it as much as a buyer could in the half hour before bidding. It might have been in a flood, of course, which would mean a new engine. The odometer registered 192,905, but he couldn't be sure someone hadn't rolled it back from 292,905 or more. The body made it worthwhile. Solid red, no dents he couldn't pound out, and immaculate chrome. There were four other people interested, but they dropped out short of fifteen hundred.

Woodrow was glad he'd taken the chance. At this point, most of the guts had been replaced, some from salvage, some new. The engine purred, the chassis shone, and he didn't worry about it breaking down, not after he'd installed a brand-new turbo 350 automatic transmission.

He could tell Claire regarded his truck as simply another wheeled instrument capable of moving her from point A to point B. It was no surprise that she didn't ask about or compliment him on the aesthetic or functional beauty of his prize possession.

"I called Charlie," he told her as they continued northwest on Highway 694. "It was two thirty in the afternoon there. Charlie said a Captain Mortensen from the Minnesota National Guard called him. The captain's going to meet us at your mama's house at nine o'clock."

"We shouldn't confront my mother until we know more," Claire objected. "We need to visit Theresa's clinic first."

"We aren't confronting her. She agreed to meet us," Woodrow countered.

"If we don't go straight to your mama's house, we'll miss our chance to connect with this guy."

"I still think you've got the cart in front of the horse," Claire said. *None too originally*, he thought.

"Maybe," Woodrow conceded. "But Charlie needs information, and your mama has it. You ask me, this whole fucking mission is taking too long."

"Stop!" Claire screamed, loud enough to rattle them both.

Alarmed, Woodrow slowed to a crawl on a narrow shoulder marked *Emergency Only*. He wondered if she were having some kind of panic attack.

Highway signs announced *No Parking* every couple hundred feet. If the state police came by, he'd get a summons or worse. He could get towed. He looked closely at Claire's expression as she sat staring straight ahead, half expecting her to upchuck breakfast. She loosened her seat belt when he stopped, got out, and walked away. He followed her into a stand of tall grass.

"What the hell's wrong with you?" He put his hand on her shoulder.

She shook it off. Her face didn't look like she was sick. Just mad.

"First of all, don't use the f-word to me. Ever. Under any circumstances. You can take your male contempt and swallow it, but don't you ever speak like that in front of me again."

"I wasn't expressin' contempt," he said defensively. "I'm frustrated, Claire. Every day we don't find Theresa is another day my son is under pressure that might get him killed."

"Second," she said, "you don't set the agenda. We do that together. I spent close to a year married to a man who thought he ran the world and me in it. I'm not going to let anyone get away with treating me like that again, not for one minute."

Now it was starting to make sense. He reminded her of her ex. He wondered if every guy reminded her of her ex.

"OK, I get it, calm down," Woodrow said, trying to calm himself as well.

He waited for both of them to breathe normally. Then, in a softer voice, practically a whisper, he said, "You're not goin' to bail on your sister, are ya?"

His training told him to focus and improvise. Tune out the traffic behind him, the city pace unfamiliar to a man who grew up in small town Alabama.

"Yes, I'll bail if we don't get some things agreed on," Claire returned, her shoulders square, her gut pulled in, exactly the stance he'd taken. "We have civil conversations from now on. Agreed?"

"Absolutely," he said. "Can we also agree that your sister is our first priority?"

"Yes," Claire said. "But keep in mind, you don't know my sister. I've been thinking about how tough she is. She's tougher than I'll ever be, and she's surely tougher than any of those nutty women who took her. They can't keep her forever. You think they're vicious enough to hurt her? I don't think so."

"They're sure as hell hurtin' my son's peace of mind. How do you know they're not hurtin' your sister?"

Claire put her hand to her throat, as if she were choking.

"You OK?" he asked, not daring to touch her.

"Yes," she got out. "My esophagus squeezes shut sometimes. All I can do is wait for it to relax." Woodrow waited with her. Claire had to get back into the pickup on her own. He needed her, so temporarily, her rules had to be *the* rules. He looked at his watch. They had a slight margin for error. It was already 6:40.

Cars whizzed behind them—SUVs in overdrive, semis moving back and forth between lanes, everybody on everybody else's tail. They stood in the grass another minute, then Claire walked back to the truck.

Woodrow moved quickly around to the driver's door, climbed in, turned the ignition over, and gradually merged his vehicle from the shoulder back into traffic. He didn't speak the rest of the way for fear of a new scene, and she returned the favor. By the time the signs for a town called Monticello came into view, the traffic had thinned, and they were sailing along at seventy-five miles per hour.

Closer to their destination, Claire sent him onto a side road that eventually led to the farm. It was not the route he'd taken before, and it shaved a couple minutes off the trip. His watch said 8:48. They parked at a field's edge until they saw the chaplain's government-issue car coming down the road from the opposite direction. The vehicle turned into the Haigs' long driveway. They followed, parked the pickup alongside his car, and got out.

The chaplain, Captain Roy Mortensen, wore his dress blues with full military insignia, including captain's bars. Woodrow liked that. He thought it might impress Theresa's mama. Captain Mortensen remained inside his vehicle for several minutes, making notes while they waited. When he emerged, Woodrow and Claire introduced themselves and shook his hand. Woodrow mentioned that he'd spoken to Charlie that morning, but his son still hadn't heard from Theresa.

There was no need to underscore the urgency, the chaplain assured him. He was well aware. He would take the lead in the conversation with Theresa's mother, who had agreed to see the three of them together. Mrs. Haig had seemed gracious on the phone, he said. Woodrow recalled she'd been gracious talking to the Stears County Sheriff's deputy too, but gracious didn't bring Theresa back.

The front door opened, and Maureen came onto her front porch, blinking in the bright spring sun. The dew was not quite gone from the grass, and the day shimmered. Maureen put her hand to her forehead, shading her eyes as she watched them approach. She wore a yellow cotton dress with a lacy white apron, and her hands showed dabs of flour she had failed to brush off. No doubt a cake had been baked, the coffeepot set. Woodrow watched Claire and her mama stare at each other, their eyes sparking like crossed wires.

———•·•·•———

They perched on chairs in the dining room, everyone ill at ease. Maureen had laid the table with her rosebud china, silverware, and white linen napkins. She set a lemon blueberry cake in the center with a crystal-handled knife and server beside it. The place mats were bright yellow with white stripes, and a silver creamer and sugar set sat on a porcelain plate with tiny silver spoons.

She poured coffee into four cups with delicate handles too small for a man's fingers to slip through. Woodrow and the chaplain raised their cups with the saucers held firm underneath, and then proceeded to hoist the steaming dark liquid to their mouths using thumbs and index fingers as pincers on the handles. Neither Woodrow nor the captain took a second sip.

When Maureen finally sat down, she focused entirely on the officer.

"Thank you for inviting us into your home," Captain Mortensen began. "I think you know how urgently your daughter's disappearance needs to be explained to her husband. I spoke to your son-in-law's chaplain this morning, and he told me he'd talked to his superiors, and they are very concerned. They want me to convey that concern to you and your husband."

"My husband's busy in the fields," Maureen remarked.

The captain cleared his throat and looked Maureen full in the face.

"Charlie's dad here has been in touch with Charlie just about daily," he told her. "As you know, Charlie's in and out of his basecamp. There are no safe places in Afghanistan, Mrs. Haig, even in the cities. I've been there. I know we need our units to remain cohesive. Every soldier has to have his mind on his job. Not only his own life but those of his fellow soldiers depend on his ability to concentrate on the role he plays on his team. So, it's a danger to everyone around him if his mind is engaged elsewhere." He paused to let Maureen respond. She didn't, so he continued.

"Charlie's chaplain tells me that Charlie feels distracted by worry for his wife. We've got to change that. If necessary, we'll bring Charlie home until she's found, but I hope, and his superiors hope, that we can locate her soon so it doesn't come to the point of a long journey back for him."

Maureen didn't say anything to that either. "Mrs. Haig, what do you know about her whereabouts?" Captain Mortensen asked.

"Really, I don't know where she is," Maureen replied tonelessly. She seemed composed, hands in her lap, and looked straight at the captain.

"Are you worried about your daughter's whereabouts?"

"Well, perhaps I should be, but Theresa has always been her own person. She has a large group of friends." Maureen waved her hand listlessly in the air, to what aim Woodrow could not fathom. "That's why she returned here instead of remaining with her husband's family in Alabama," Maureen went on. "I think she felt more freedom here, more closeness with her friends."

No one contradicted her. "I'm sure Theresa will call Charlie eventually," Maureen concluded.

"Charlie says they were both excited about Theresa's pregnancy," Mortensen said, "which is all the more reason for him to worry when he couldn't reach her. Did you know she was pregnant, Mrs. Haig?"

"Yes," said Maureen. "She's in her first trimester."

"Mrs. Haig, I'm going to ask you again: do you have any knowledge of her whereabouts?"

"No, I'm sorry to say." Maureen didn't sound offended, something Woodrow thought suspicious in itself. Mortensen had practically accused her of concealing where Theresa was.

"My, my!" Maureen exclaimed suddenly. "No one's touched my cake. It's just out of the oven. You must have a slice."

Woodrow shook his head, as did Claire. Captain Mortensen ignored the suggestion.

"Excuse me for putting things bluntly, Mrs. Haig, but you don't seem overly concerned by Theresa's disappearance," he said.

"I haven't been," Maureen replied evenly. "We think whatever happened between her and Charlie is their personal business, and we should keep out of it."

"By *we*, you mean you and your husband?"

"Yes, my husband Tom."

"May I ask why he couldn't be here for this meeting?"

"He's somewhere out on the farm with our son Greg. They have to get the planting done before the heat starts in."

"Does your husband know I'm here?" Captain Mortensen asked.

"I told him at breakfast. He wondered what I could tell you, since we don't know anything."

"Did Theresa leave things behind? A diary or some kind of note?"

"I don't go into her room."

"Would you mind if I take a look?"

"Of course. I'll show you up."

"And if I could get a list of the names of her friends?" Mortensen added.

"I don't know them personally," Maureen replied.

From the look on Mortensen's face, Woodrow could imagine what he'd say to a recruit as intractable as Maureen. But Maureen was not answerable to him.

"Do you have a priest or minister you've talked to about Theresa?" Mortensen inquired.

"Our Father Schmidt has a lot on his plate these days. I wouldn't bother him with family matters like this."

"Have you talked to anyone else about Theresa's disappearance?"

"No," said Maureen. "Should I? I don't think it's a disappearance in the sense of someone missing."

"What do you think it is?"

"I just think she's not here at the moment," said Maureen.

They were getting nowhere, and that was precisely what Maureen intended. Woodrow was sure of it. A moment later, the captain pushed his chair back and stood up.

"Thank you for your time and hospitality, Mrs. Haig. I'd like to speak to your husband before I make a report back to my counterpart in Sergeant Cole's unit. Would you ask him to call me?" He handed a card to Maureen, who took it and smiled.

"Of course," she said pleasantly.

"Could we go upstairs now?" Captain Mortensen asked. Maureen nodded, and they left the room, leaving Woodrow and Claire alone at the table.

"Wow," was all Claire could get out.

"I'd like a little more than *wow*," Woodrow said.

Claire shrugged. Within minutes, Mortensen returned. Maureen escorted him to the front door, and Woodrow followed, nodding as he passed his son's mother-in-law in the hallway.

Claire walked a few steps behind, but she halted in front of her mother. "How long do you think you can keep this up?" she asked. Maureen didn't respond. "If Charlie comes back, you'll have to answer to him," Claire said.

"Don't talk to me like that," Maureen retorted. "I'm still your mother, even if you pretend you came from the stork." Words failed Maureen at that point. She collapsed on a chair, quietly crying.

"Theresa doesn't belong to you," Claire said. Maureen continued to cry, louder now. Claire knew she couldn't talk to her mother when she wept. She opened the screen door, letting it close gently behind her, and joined Woodrow beside his pickup. Captain Mortensen's car was making its way down the drive.

"He wants to talk to your dad," Woodrow said, "and so do I. Let's see if we can find him."

"We'd be better off coming back this evening," Claire demurred. "Right now, I think we should check out Theresa's clinic." Her voice had an edge.

Woodrow nodded. "The clinic it is. Do you know where it's located?"

"Of course," Claire said.

———•◦•———

She directed him toward the west side of downtown, where a medical office sat tucked behind a strip mall. It had its own parking lot, and at the far end, with sight lines clear to the entrance, they found an open space for the pickup. There were maybe twenty other vehicles between them and the door.

"I should go in alone," Claire said. "More discreet."

"OK," Woodrow agreed reluctantly. He leaned back in his seat. "But we share everything?"

"Yes," Claire replied, adding, "was there anything else from Mortensen?"

"He didn't say, but I think he's leaning toward getting Charlie compassionate leave to sort this out. I told him about that pouch Annie has, the one with Theresa's wallet and cell phone. He's going to ask your dad if he can look at the phone. Not sure what he could do with it, unless your dad knows the password."

Claire opened the pickup door. "If I'm not back in ten minutes, assume they've got me locked in a closet and call the sheriff."

"Reckon I'll do that," said Woodrow.

Claire returned well before ten minutes elapsed.

"What happened?" Woodrow asked.

"They wouldn't let me see her records," she said. "Patient privacy, HIPAA regulations, all that. So no facts. But I did get a possible lead. What time is it?"

"Almost noon. What's your lead?"

"Someone I knew in high school was behind the counter. Patricia Conroy."

"What'd she say?"

"We didn't talk yet."

Woodrow exhaled loudly. "This is getting us nowhere!"

"She probably knows something since she works there," Claire insisted. "Let's wait and see if she comes out for lunch."

They remained in the pickup. Woodrow hardly moved. Claire couldn't hold still. Several patients arrived, but no one left.

Claire broke the silence. "I don't think my mother knows where Theresa is," she ventured.

"What makes you say that?"

"She could lie without getting flustered because she was telling the literal truth. Theresa has always had plenty of friends. She does come and go as she pleases. And I'll bet my mother *doesn't* know where Theresa is, not precisely. But does she know people who know? I'd say yes. Wish I'd thought of that earlier."

"How do we get it out of her now that you've thought of it?"

"We need to find this Lucy Meyer. From what Annie says she overheard in my mother's kitchen, I'll bet she's the brains behind this whole thing."

People went in and came out of the clinic as they watched. Claire said nothing until a woman in a white blouse and navy-blue skirt emerged. The woman walked down the street in the opposite direction.

"Follow her," said Claire. "That's Patricia Conroy. Drive slowly, 'til we see where she's going."

They followed at a distance for a half dozen blocks, until the woman ambled toward the back of a tiny house that looked like it was built in the 1940s. She climbed two steps, opened the screen door, and put a key in the lock. Woodrow drove right up the driveway. Patricia Conroy turned at the sound of his engine behind her.

She looked mousy, not someone people would ordinarily notice. Woodrow and Claire got out of the pickup. Patricia Conroy seemed frightened for a moment, but her expression changed when she recognized Claire.

"Mary? You were in the clinic just now."

"Yes, hi, you remember me?" Claire asked.

The woman nodded. "Mary Haig."

"I changed my name to Claire."

"Really?

"Uh-huh. Patricia, this is Woodrow Cole. His son is married to my sister Theresa. You remember her?"

"No. Is she older or younger than you?"

"Younger, and as it turns out, she's missing. She's also pregnant, and we think she was at your clinic to see Dr. Ryan."

Patricia's face lit up. "Oh, yes. The one with the bad result. I didn't connect her with you."

"Can we come inside, Patricia? We need to talk to you about her situation," Claire asked, her voice cracking.

Patricia Conroy looked uneasy. A silence ensued and lasted too long. Woodrow decided to change the subject.

"That your vehicle over there?" he asked, pointing toward something covered by a blue tarp.

"My Volvo. It broke down in March. There's a bunch of stuff it needs, but they tell me it's mostly a broken transmission and bad brakes."

"Expensive repairs," Woodrow said.

"I'm saving up. I can't *not* have a car in winter, but for now I'm walking. I'll get it fixed by October for sure."

"You mean by October if it's just what they found the first time your mechanic looked it over," Woodrow suggested. "There might be problems he missed."

"I hope not," Patricia moaned.

Woodrow approached her with the most winning smile he could muster. She mattered right now beyond any other woman in his life.

"'Course, it doesn't have to cost an arm and a leg. We could do a trade on the labor."

"Woodrow's a mechanic," Claire pointed out. "A good mechanic, he tells me."

"Yeah, and I'll be in the neighborhood awhile. I could work on your car and guarantee I'd get it runnin' like new, and I'll do the labor for nothin'. If—*big if*, you'll answer our questions. All our questions."

Patricia froze. He could see ambivalence in her eyes.

"I can't lose my job," she said in a whisper.

"You're not goin' to lose your job, 'cause we're not goin' to talk to anybody," Woodrow promised. "And I mean *anybody*. What you tell us does *not* come back to you, I give you my word on that." Patricia remained rooted to the concrete stoop. "With my whole heart and soul," Woodrow added. He spoke to her the way he hunted, quietly and with extreme caution.

They moved inside her house then, as if Woodrow were taking her inside his house, and the three of them sat at her kitchen table. She had lived with her grandparents since high school, she said, but her grandpa died two years ago and her grandma passed away six months ago, and now she was alone. Patricia had nursed both of them and handled everything for their funerals, which swallowed up the rest of their assets, except for the house. She followed their wishes to the letter, she said.

When Patricia Conroy stopped talking, Woodrow let some time pass.

"First off," he started when the silence grew strained, "would you kindly tell us 'bout those test results?"

Patricia met Woodrow's gaze. "What about parts?" she wondered aloud. "How much will *they* cost?"

"I don't know," said Woodrow, "but whatever the cost, I'll minimize it. There's lots of good parts in salvage yards. You have to know what to look for. I've been searchin' salvage yards since I was a kid fixin' tractors. It's amazin' what you can get for very little money. I'll fix your car for just the cost of parts. That should save you half or more . . . Now *please*, tell us what you know."

Patricia looked at Claire, who nodded. "You can trust him," said Claire.

"She came in about two weeks ago," Patricia began. "The whole clinic knew about the tests. She had them done in St. Paul, and they sent them to us. Turns out her baby likely has Down syndrome, and that doesn't happen very often in someone so young. The risk goes up as a woman gets older. Anyway, she had the tests done in St. Paul, which Dr. Ryan wasn't happy about. He doesn't believe in prenatal tests, except for ultrasound. We do a lot of those. But these Dr. Ryan sent to a local lab for a second look, and when the report came back, he was upset. I heard him say he couldn't just call Theresa until there was a plan in place to help her understand. So, he contacted a group in Minneapolis, and they sent this woman, Lucy Meyer, and she came with another woman to help when Theresa came in for her appointment. But it didn't go well."

"What happened?" Claire and Woodrow asked almost simultaneously.

"Theresa left the clinic. She just went out the front door, and Lucy Meyer ran after her, but Theresa wouldn't talk to her. So, Dr. Ryan called your mother. He talked to her with Lucy Meyer on the line."

"Do you know Lucy Meyer personally?"

"Not very well. She's been in the clinic a couple of times since. I think she and Dr. Ryan both want to help Theresa make the right decision."

"By right you mean for her to continue the pregnancy," Claire suggested.

"Of course," said Patricia. "Everyone just wants what's best for her and the baby. But she got so emotional. It's too bad she didn't bring her mother in with her. Dr. Ryan regrets not calling your mother right away when he got the results."

"What about HIPAA regulations? Would Dr. Ryan have been within his rights to share patient information with someone like Lucy Meyer?" Claire asked.

A horrified look appeared on Patricia's face.

"I'm sharing patient information right now. I shouldn't be doing this," she blurted in panic.

"But we're not goin' to tell anybody 'bout this conversation, remember?" Woodrow reassured her, taking Patricia Conroy's hand in his. "We're goin' to keep this private, totally, absolutely, private. We'll protect you."

He glanced at Claire and stood up.

"Patricia, thank you. And don't forget, I'm goin' to come back soon as I can to work on that car. I give you my word," Woodrow said.

She looked at him with a blank face. They were about to leave when she started talking again.

"I probably shouldn't tell you this either, but Lucy Meyer is staying at the

Best Western on Raymond Street, you know, where Raymond meets Main. I know 'cause Dr. Ryan is paying for it." She looked at Claire. "And she drives a rental car from Enterprise. It has a sticker on the back window. It's not the same car she drove here from Minneapolis. I think the other woman took that one back to the Cities."

"You mean the car with the vanity plate, SAVE ALL? My sister Annie saw it when she was at my parents' place."

Patricia nodded.

"What model is the rental?" Woodrow asked.

"It's gray. I think it has four doors," Patricia replied, adding, "I hope you find Theresa." She stood up and walked outside with them.

"It's going to be OK," Woodrow assured her. "You've helped Theresa more than you know, Patricia. And none of this'll ever come back to bother you. I promise."

He hugged her before they left. Patricia looked startled to have been hugged. Startled, but not displeased.

"We took advantage of her," Claire observed as they backed out of the driveway. "She really might get fired."

"I'd do a lot worse to find out what Charlie needs to know," Woodrow said.

"Will you fix her car?"

"'Course I'll fix her car," Woodrow said, "but like I told her, soon as I can. First, we've got to find your sister. That remark about HIPAA didn't help, by the way."

"I know," said Claire. "I just got so mad."

"We can't afford to get mad," Woodrow said harshly. "Where is Main and Raymond?"

"Turn right two blocks down."

—•◦•—

They ended up in the Best Western parking lot near, but not too close, to a four-door gray Ford Focus with an Enterprise sticker affixed to its back window. Woodrow got out to examine it and saw nothing on the seats, front or back. New vehicle, less than twenty thousand on the odometer. Locked. Dirt on the front seat floor mat. He got back in his pickup and checked his phone. No messages. It was close to one o'clock. They would wait.

An hour and a half later, three women came out of a side door of the Best Western and made their way to separate cars. One got into the Focus. She was the tallest at about six feet. She had reddish hair and wore a brown pantsuit and sensible shoes. Woodrow pegged her at between forty and fifty years old. He followed her car, keeping a half block's distance as it headed toward the edge of town, then drove north toward Sartell, according to a road sign they passed.

"Who do you know in Sartell?" he asked Claire.

"Whom do I know."

"Just answer my question!" Woodrow snapped.

"Let me think," she snapped back. "My mother has a niece up there—Mary Lou. She lives on a farm with her husband, Dennis. I haven't seen them in years."

The Ford Focus left the highway and disappeared into a large, wooded front yard. Woodrow had increased the distance between them, but he could still see the dust cloud where the Focus turned in. He drove past.

"What'd you do that for?" Claire demanded. "It's their farm. I'm sure of it. If Theresa's inside—"

"If Theresa's inside, what do you propose we do?" Woodrow asked her peevishly. "I've got a weapon in my toolbox. You think I should assemble it, and we go chargin' in like assault troops? That your recommendation?"

Claire leaned forward, unbuckling her seat belt as Woodrow pulled alongside a newly planted cornfield that edged the highway. They were roughly an eighth of a mile from the mailbox at the entrance to the driveway, but there were so many trees, they couldn't see the Ford. Woodrow retrieved a set of binoculars from his tool chest, got out of the truck, and crouched down. Claire joined him.

"I don't like your attitude," she said in a whisper. "We're in this together. So cut the mean streak and tell me what you're thinking."

"Don't worry, they can't hear us," he said. "But they'll see us if we're not careful. As for the attitude, sorry 'bout that. I'm worried as hell, and it's gettin' to me." Claire didn't reply. "Question now," Woodrow continued, "is should we try to get into that house to find out if Theresa's there, or should we wait for help? I could call that sheriff's deputy an' see if he can get a warrant."

"I doubt we have enough evidence for a warrant," Claire said.

"Maybe not. It's worth a try, though." Woodrow pulled Antoine Harrison's card out of his wallet and punched in his cell phone number. He got an answering machine.

"What's their last name?" he asked Claire. "Mary Lou and Dennis, what's their last name?"

Claire exhaled in frustration. "Mary Lou's mother was one of my mother's older sisters. But Mary Lou would have taken her husband's name for sure." She sighed. "I can't remember their last name."

"Maybe he can get it from the cell phone GPS," Woodrow said. He left the deputy a message asking him to call back as soon as possible. Then he wondered aloud whether they should remain where they were, leave the area, or move in for a closer look. Moving in was risky, but it might be even riskier to leave. There was no guarantee Theresa would still be there when a sheriff arrived, if the sheriff would come. They decided to move in for a closer look.

"You stay here," he ordered Claire.

"No way," she said.

"OK, but keep low. Take that vest off."

Claire tossed her yellow vest through the open window and onto the passenger seat of the pickup. Her shirt was light brown, her pants a few shades darker. Woodrow took off his white shirt and pulled on a green-and-brown camouflage tee retrieved from his toolbox. Crouched down, they followed the rock-strewn culvert that edged the cornfield until it reached the end of the driveway.

Lucy Meyer's rented Ford was parked near the door in back. The blinds were down in what they guessed was the kitchen, and the drapes were closed in the front-facing rooms.

"Windows closed, shades drawn on a pleasant day. That alone's suspicious," Woodrow said in a low voice.

"I'd say the odds Theresa's inside are mounting by the minute," Claire whispered back.

"The way I see it, we got three options. One of us goes to the front door and knocks and gets let in or not—either way it's a distraction—while the other enters through a basement window. *Or* both of us go to the door and see if we can talk our way in, barge in if we have to. *Or* we take pictures, go back to the pickup, and keep watchin' the house from there. At the same time, we text Harrison the photos."

"I thought you said you had some kind of gun," Claire recalled.

"Not bringin' firepower into a situation like this," Woodrow told her, peeved again.

"OK, but I'm not sure any of your other options will work."

"We need to pick one," Woodrow said.

"I vote for option one," Claire said. "Which of us breaks into the basement?"

Woodrow laughed. "Ever break in somewhere?"

"I'm not the outlaw type," Claire said. "I suppose you are." He didn't answer.

"What you goin' to say at the door?" he asked.

"The truth. I'm lookin' for my sister. I'll tell them I have a message from our mother."

He shrugged. "Just stay low-key. Don't start an argument. If they give you grief, make your way back to the pickup. We don't want anyone gettin' hurt."

With that, Woodrow sprinted, still crouching, through the yard to the front of the house, so close they could have reached out a window to touch him.

Claire waited until he was out of sight, then walked to the kitchen door instead of the front, thinking the kitchen might be unlocked. She climbed the back porch's rickety wooden steps, opened the screen door, and turned the inner door's knob. The door wouldn't budge, so, reluctantly, she knocked. It took a minute before it opened—a minute that felt like five.

"Who are you and what do you want?" a woman asked belligerently. She wore a pink-and-white polka-dot dress that had been washed so many times, Claire could barely see the dots.

"Hi," Claire said cheerily. "I'm your cousin, Mary Haig. Theresa Haig's sister. My mother has a message she wants me to deliver."

Behind Mary Lou, another woman appeared—tall, red-haired, wearing a brown pantsuit—Lucy Meyer, for sure. The two stared in unblinking recognition, each knowing an antagonist when she saw one.

Mary Lou looked at Lucy, who said simply, "Let her in."

There was no doubt who was in charge. Mary Lou pushed the screen door wider, and Claire slid inside. Four undressed bulbs glared in a hanging fixture over the kitchen table. A long florescent buzzed above the sink. There was no sign of Theresa. Claire wondered whether she should call out. Theresa might be upstairs or in a back bedroom.

"Yes, she's here," said Lucy Meyer, gesturing toward a chair, one of five around the table.

Claire had no intention of sitting down. "I need to see her," she said.

Lucy sat down, gesturing again toward an empty chair. "Please," she said.

Claire ignored the order.

"Theresa doesn't intend to come home just yet, nor will she discuss her reasons with you. Inform your mother that if she has a message, she should call me."

"I need to hear that from Theresa herself," Claire insisted.

"Let me explain," Lucy's diction was clipped and precise. She gestured toward the chair again. "*Sit down*. You too, Mary Lou."

"It's like this," said Mary Lou, sitting, "the Lord has a plan for each and every one of us. He has a plan for Theresa."

"And you, of course, have access to this plan?" Claire asked sarcastically.

"That's right," Lucy replied. *"For I know the plans I have for you, declares the Lord, plans to prosper you and not to harm you, plans to give you hope and a future."*

"The Lord has plans for Theresa," underscored Mary Lou, "and *His* will be done."

Mary Lou had hardly pronounced those words when they heard shouting from below, then noise that sounded like a fight. Before Lucy or Mary Lou could get up, Claire rushed to where she guessed the stairway to the basement began and clambered down the steps. She reached the bottom and found an unfinished cinder-block room where a boiler stood alongside a water tank. An older man looked down at Woodrow motionless on the floor, Woodrow's face pressed into the concrete, his head bleeding and the muzzle of a hunting rifle pushed against the skin on the back of his neck.

"I could kill you," the older man shouted. "I could shoot you dead and it would be castle domain. A man's home is his castle. A man is king within his walls. No one would convict me for giving you what you deserve, you mangy dog."

He turned the weapon upside down and hit Woodrow's back with the stock. Claire didn't dare rush him and grab the rifle. He could push her back and then what would he do? Shoot Woodrow?

"He's with me," she yelled. "He's not a burglar. Leave him alone."

The older man turned to look at the source of the interruption. "Who the hell are you?" he demanded.

She could hear someone behind her.

"Please, Dennis," Lucy pleaded, "no violence. Put the gun down."

Dennis pulled the rifle away from Woodrow, who still wasn't moving. He shifted its muzzle toward the ceiling.

"Ain't a *gun*," he pointed out, shaking his head. "What you callin' it a gun for? Beats me how people can be so ignorant."

Lucy Meyer moved past Dennis, knelt beside Woodrow, and checked his pulse.

"It's steady," she said matter-of-factly to Claire. "You need to get him out of here *now*."

Claire reached into her back pocket for her cell phone, but Dennis grabbed it. He took Woodrow's too.

"Where's your vehicle?" he snarled.

"Down the road. You realize there are people who know where we are."

"Get it," Lucy ordered. "Park in front of the house, and Dennis will help you put him inside. Otherwise, you're responsible for what happens to him."

Claire thought for only a few seconds before reaching into Woodrow's pocket for his keys. She ran all the way to the pickup, adjusted the seat, got the engine going, turned the vehicle around, and drove to the driveway, backing in toward the front door. Her hands trembled as she approached the group huddled over Woodrow's unmoving body.

Dennis carried him by his armpits, Mary Lou by his feet. Lucy held the door open. Woodrow's head was bleeding through the bandage that someone, probably Lucy, had tied around it. Claire glared at all three of them. Mary Lou and Dennis eased Woodrow into the passenger seat.

As she drove away, Claire looked up at a gable window on the second floor. The curtains were drawn, and no sound emerged. It would help if she could testify that she had heard or seen Theresa. But she couldn't.

———•◦•———

A half hour later Woodrow sat on an exam table in the ER at St. Dominic Hospital. Claire was relieved that he'd regained consciousness. The doctor wanted to admit him for observation.

"No," Woodrow said. "Not gonna happen."

"You need a CT scan," the doctor replied.

"I'm fine," Woodrow maintained.

"I've seen people who thought they were fine until they collapsed in the parking lot. We have to find out if there's bleeding inside your brain, or a clot. We won't know anything until we get images," the doctor insisted.

"I'm fine," Woodrow repeated.

"Mr. Cole, I'll get you scheduled." She left the area, pulling the flowered curtain behind her.

Woodrow slid off the exam table, wobbling a bit, and walked toward Claire, then past her all the way to the ER desk. An employee looked up. Woodrow gave her an ashen smile.

"May I help you?" she asked. Her name tag said *Lori*.

"Lori, sweetheart, would you loan a guy your cell phone? Mine got lost, and I gotta make a call." He looked straight into her wide-set brown eyes.

"Don't call me sweetheart. I'm not your sweetheart," she said, then handed him a cell phone. "Five minutes. In front of me. No calls outside the country."

Woodrow nodded. He looked faint. Claire took the receptionist's cell phone and the card Woodrow pulled from his pocket. She punched in the number for Deputy Harrison, who answered on the first ring. Woodrow took the phone and filled the deputy in.

Antoine Harrison said he was on his way. Woodrow gave the cell phone to Claire who handed it back to the woman at the desk.

Ten minutes later an orderly showed up with a wheelchair, but Woodrow wouldn't get in. Eventually the orderly left. Not long after, Antoine Harrison found them in the waiting area and listened as Woodrow and Claire described their ill-fated attempt to save Theresa.

"Can you get a warrant now?" was Woodrow's main question.

Harrison wrote what they said in his notebook, interspersing questions, not much impressed that Woodrow had removed a basement window to slither inside.

"You might've got yourself killed," Harrison told him. "Everybody's armed to the teeth around here, especially farmers. They feel as much right to shoot a man who breaks into their house as they do a fox that gets to their hens."

"I s'pose you're right," Woodrow admitted. "But we knew they had Theresa inside."

"How did you know?" Harrison asked.

"Lucy Meyer admitted she was there," Claire said.

"Who's Lucy Meyer?" Harrison asked.

"One of the kidnappers," Claire replied.

Harrison ordered them not to go back to the farmhouse. "Theresa's disappearance needs to become an official investigation," he said, "and you need to stay out of it." He left abruptly, and as the sliding doors closed behind him, Woodrow took off his bloody T-shirt and put on the white shirt Claire had retrieved from the pickup.

"Let's talk to your father," Woodrow said, "soon as I start seein' straight. You drive."

"You have to get those tests first," Claire reminded him.

"My mama's insurance's got a massive deductible. Not gonna burden the corporation."

"You think she'd want you risking your life?"

"This is my call, Claire. Stop interfering."

"OK, but it could also be your funeral. Literally. Guess I'll have to find Theresa alone."

"No, you won't."

———•◦•———

Claire pulled up to the kitchen side of the Haig farmhouse a little after six. She cut the engine and put her hand on Woodrow's shoulder. He woke with a shudder, shifted his body from its half-curled position, and sat up straight. Claire waited a moment, wondering if she should drive him back to the hospital.

Through the window, she could see her mother in front of the stove, and her brother Greg at the kitchen table. Annie walked in from the hallway just as Tom emerged from the laundry room.

Woodrow unfastened his seat belt, indicating his intention to keep to the plan. Claire rushed around the pickup to make sure he didn't collapse as soon as his feet hit the ground.

"You really want to do this *tonight*?" she asked again as he leaned his weight on her shoulder.

"No time like the present."

They hobbled toward the house and entered though the screen door. A startled Maureen turned around, skillet in one hand, tongs in the other. The pan held sausages, probably the spicy kind her father ordered whenever he slaughtered a pig. Maureen turned off the burner and set the sizzling pan back on the stove.

"What's this?" Tom asked in a booming voice. He strode toward Claire but stopped when he took in Woodrow leaning on his daughter.

Her dad looked at her quizzically.

"Sorry to intrude, Mrs. Haig," Woodrow got out, pulling his arm free to deposit himself in a kitchen chair. "Hope you don't mind comp'ny."

"You remember Woodrow Cole," Claire said to her father. "We were at the house this morning. Along with a Minnesota Guard chaplain inquiring about Theresa."

Tom looked at Maureen.

"Since then, we've run into trouble," Claire went on, "as you can see from Woodrow's head."

"Get more chairs in here," Tom snapped at Greg and Annie, who rushed out of the kitchen. Tom sat down in his usual spot and faced Woodrow. "What's going on, Mr. Cole?" he demanded to know, looking back and forth at Maureen, Claire, and Charlie's dad.

Woodrow talked in fits and starts, breathing heavily in between. "We got close to . . . Theresa this afternoon," he said. "They had her in a farmhouse in Sartell . . . Claire and I got inside . . . but they stopped us . . . before we could . . ."

"What's the hell's Theresa doing in Sartell?" Tom cut in. "And who's *they*?"

Maureen did not correct his language.

"Your daughter has been abducted, Mr. Haig . . . My son can't reach her . . . I think your wife knows why."

Tom looked at Maureen. "I'm waiting for an answer," he said impatiently. "Who's *they*?"

"Mother's niece, Mary Lou, and her husband, Dennis. Dennis did this to Woodrow," Claire said, gesturing toward the bandage. "They're part of a criminal conspiracy to kidnap Theresa."

"I have nothing to say," Maureen announced. "And I don't know where

Theresa is. That's the truth."

Everyone fell silent. Annie and Greg returned, each with a chair.

"OK! I want the whole damn story," Tom bellowed suddenly. "I want to know exactly what's been going on around here, and I want it from your mother first."

"I tried to tell you," Annie cut in, earning a scowl from her father. "You wouldn't listen to me," she accused. "So I told Charlie's dad. He listened. Now he's got his head bashed in because those church ladies took Theresa!"

"Church ladies?" Tom repeated.

"Church ladies Mother is friends with," Annie went on, looking straight at Maureen. As if she hadn't heard, Maureen calmly used the tongs to lift sausages one by one from the frying pan onto a white platter lined with paper towels.

"Will somebody tell me what's going on!" Tom demanded.

Maureen put the platter of sausages on the table, alongside a ramekin of sauerkraut, a bowl of spring beans drizzled with olive oil, a basket of home-made whole-wheat bread, a dish of home-churned butter, and a porcelain tray holding a variety of pickles and condiments. The meat and beans were steaming, but nobody reached for them. Maureen picked up the platter of sausages and handed it to Tom, tongs poised at the edge.

"I don't want any goddamn food 'til I know what's goin' on with Theresa," Tom roared.

Maureen set the platter on the table, sat down herself, and began to cry. Head hovering over her lap, her body heaved. No one could see her face.

Tom sighed and looked at Woodrow and Claire. With Annie's help, they laid it out for him, starting with when Theresa came back to the house after her doctor's appointment.

"Mary Lou and Dennis live on a farm on Route 10 in Sartell. You're familiar with it?" Woodrow asked Tom in a voice that sounded more like his usual self, Claire thought.

The food cooled in front of them. Greg let his hand hover over the sausages, at one point reaching to grab the tongs. Annie hit him with her elbow.

Woodrow finished his story. All the while, Maureen sat with her head down in the chair across from her husband.

"OK," Tom said when Woodrow stopped talking. "Now, straighten up, Mother, and give me your version."

Maureen lifted her head, looked for a moment as if she were about to speak, but instead stood up and rushed out of the room. They heard her climb the stairs, and then a door slammed.

"She's in the bathroom," Annie said matter-of-factly to Woodrow. "That's where she goes."

Tom leaned forward, his chest against the edge of the table. He wasn't looking at anyone in particular when he said, eyes glazed, "I'll talk to her. Now the rest of you get out of this kitchen." He got up and left.

"Where are we supposed to go?" Greg asked plaintively. "We didn't even get to eat!"

"I think he means Woodrow and me," Claire said quietly.

"I doubt she'll open the door to him," Annie said.

Greg helped himself to sauerkraut and buttered a slice of whole-wheat bread before adding mustard. Annie left the kitchen to see if her father had managed to get into the upstairs bathroom.

"We should leave," Claire told Woodrow.

Woodrow agreed, reluctantly. She helped him get up. He seemed even less steady than when they'd come in. Slowly, they made their way to the pickup.

"You think your daddy'll get it out of her?" Woodrow asked as she drove.

"I'm hopeful," Claire replied. "But right now, you have a choice to make. Sleep somewhere or head back to the ER?"

"Bed," he answered.

"That's not the one you should pick."

"I told you. My kin's got a business. One sick person can wipe out a year's profit. You think I'm goin' to saddle them with bills, when there's nothin' for it but rest?"

Claire found a motel, specifying two separate beds. "Ordinarily, there's no way I'd spend the night with you," she informed Woodrow curtly as they settled inside. "Or with anybody for that matter. But in this case, I'm making an exception so I can call 911 when I can't find your pulse."

"Let's get some sleep," he said.

Claire checked Woodrow's wrist when she woke the next morning at seven thirty. She took a shower, got breakfast across the street, then checked Woodrow's pulse again at nine o'clock. He was still sleeping. She dashed off a note and departed.

She believed Annie's version of what had happened. It fit with her own hypothesis that her mother had orchestrated the whole thing to prevent an abortion. She drove Woodrow's pickup to the St. Philomena campus. A sign on the porch of the rectory identified Father Mark Schmidt as pastor. She rang the doorbell. An elderly woman appeared, probably the housekeeper, Claire guessed. The woman let her in, but she said Father was at church. She couldn't say when he'd be back. Did Claire have pressing business?

Yes, quite pressing, Claire told her. The woman nodded and led Claire to a sofa in a spartan living room and offered her coffee or tea.

"Tea, if you'll join me," Claire said sweetly. She'd noticed how nicely Woodrow behaved toward people and how people reacted in kind. That hadn't been her style, but if it worked, so be it.

The woman smiled warmly and ten minutes later came back with lemon tea and a plate of ginger cookies.

"I'm Mrs. Wegand," she said. "I was here before Father Schmidt arrived. That was more than a decade ago. It's unusual, having a pastor that long. We think the bishop forgot him."

"How well do you know him?" Claire asked.

"Very well, I should say. When you launder a man's underwear, there's not much that stays a secret!" Mrs. Wegand chuckled.

"Do you think he's likely to concern himself with problems in the parish?" Claire asked.

"Oh, my, yes. He's not one of those standoffish types. Though he's not gregarious, and some people criticize him for his voice."

"His voice?" Claire wondered if she meant a speech impediment.

"He has a—let's call it an *unfortunate* singing voice. Our choir director, Helen Swanson, tried to train him, but he doesn't have an ounce of talent. So, she lets him sing off-key."

"Oh," Claire said, bemused.

"Beggars can't be choosers, you know. The best singers go to the rich parishes. Like everything else in life," said Mrs. Wegand.

Claire nodded.

"Now if you ask some in the parish, they'll say a man can't be a good priest if he can't sing, and he doesn't even look the part. And that's about the summing up for Father Schmidt. But, and here's where I differ from certain individuals, Father is as good as can be where there's real problems. He'll go out any time, day or night, to give the sacramental blessing for the sick. It doesn't even matter if the dying person is a parishioner, and I know there are some who feel if you're not paying your dues, you don't deserve the final blessing. But that's not Father Schmidt. He gets mad as all get-out if the ladies in the church office don't pass on requests from those who are in arrears or even someone who left the church altogether. And, let me tell you something else . . ."

Mrs. Wegand patted Claire's hand.

"Last year he paid the rent for a woman who was about to be evicted. And she wasn't even Catholic, never had been! That, to me, is what you call a man of God. Not these fancy bishops with their coverups. You heard about the coverups?"

Claire nodded yes. Mrs. Wegand smiled.

"Well, I should be getting back to the kitchen. You just stay here. Father should be back soon."

But he didn't come back soon. Claire almost gave up. Finally, a little after eleven, Father Schmidt walked through the front door. Claire stood up.

"I'm Claire Haig," she told him in a rush, "and my sister—her name is Theresa—has been abducted. I think my mother, Maureen, and some people in this parish are behind her kidnapping."

The priest took a while digesting what she'd said.

"How long has she been missing?" he asked. His face didn't tell Claire anything.

"Since May ninth."

"Come into my office." He motioned toward a door that led to a tiny study. It held a walnut desk with a sheet of glass on top, a black swivel chair behind the desk, and in front, two folding chairs for visitors. Claire sat on one.

"Tell me what you *know*," the priest said.

"I know my sister Theresa is being held at a farmhouse in Sartell. I know her husband is in Afghanistan and can't reach her. I know my mother saw her, along with a group of women from this parish, in my family's home on the day she was taken. I know she is pregnant and went to a clinic to get some test results. I know she packed a suitcase and was planning to meet my other sister outside, but my other sister waited a long while, and Theresa didn't appear. So my other sister went back to the house, but Theresa wasn't there anymore. I know a number of vehicles left the house about that time. I think this is about preventing an abortion," Claire blurted, knowing full well she'd lost whatever calm she'd possessed on entering the rectory.

The priest was listening, but so far, he'd had nothing to say.

"I'm all but certain my sister was kidnapped by"—Claire knew she shouldn't antagonize this man, but the words came out of their own volition—"by pro-life extremists."

Father Schmidt looked at her impassively.

"My question to you is what do *you* know about it?"

He shook his head. "This sounds like a matter for the police."

"We talked to a sheriff's deputy who's looking into it. Father, let me ask you, do you know a woman named Lucy Meyer?"

"No, I don't," he replied.

"I think she's behind the kidnapping."

Father Schmidt sighed. "My child, this sounds pretty far-fetched. I think you should go back to the authorities."

"Would you talk to your parishioners, ask if anyone knows anything about Theresa's disappearance?"

"That would sound like an accusation without evidence. I have no way to evaluate your story. I don't think the parish can get involved."

He stood up. She was being dismissed, Claire realized. She wasn't likely to get any new information from Father Schmidt.

Meanwhile Woodrow might have awakened in her absence. He might be walking around outside the motel at that very moment, dizzy and disoriented and wondering where she went in his pickup. And all the while she had wasted precious time on this conversation with what amounted to an administrator who didn't have a clue what went on in his parish, or worse, knew full well and lied by omission. Without another word, Claire left, manners be damned.

——•◆•——

Woodrow's eyes were still closed when she got back to the motel. She wasn't sure whether to feel relieved. He might be bleeding inside his skull. Claire was tempted to call 911. She put her hand on his forehead. It wasn't hot. That was a good sign. And it woke him.

He looked at her and blinked several times.

"Don't move," she admonished. "Think about it before you get up. Then, if you want, I'll help you."

He nodded. With one hand at the nape of his neck and the other at his shoulder, Claire tried to steady him.

"Bathroom," he said. Claire guided him to his feet and toward the bathroom door. He shut it behind him, but it didn't sound as if he'd locked it. She heard water running.

When he finally came out, he seemed unsteady on his feet, still wearing badly wrinkled clothes. The bandage he had tried to push off his head had fallen over one ear.

"No toothbrush," he complained with something like his old smile.

"I'll get your stuff from the truck," she said. "Lie down and stay that way until I get back."

An hour later, they were both feeling better. Woodrow had showered and changed clothes and looked halfway presentable. They headed to a diner nearby. It was well after noon, but Woodrow ordered breakfast. He asked for grits too, but they didn't make them. The waitress said she wasn't even sure what grits were.

Claire told Woodrow word for word about her encounter with the priest.

"No surprise," Woodrow remarked. "He's not about to incriminate his own outfit."

"I expected more," Claire said.

"Why don't we take another crack at the sheriff's office? See if they got a warrant. We should also report our cell phones stolen."

Claire continued to help a still-unsteady Woodrow maneuver his way in and out of the pickup. She drove. When they got to the sheriff's office, they had to wait almost an hour to see Deputy Harrison, who took them to his cubicle with a stern expression on his face. Woodrow asked Harrison about their next move and what resources the sheriff's office was prepared to deploy.

"It's out of my hands," Harrison said. "The search in Sartell didn't go well. That's not for attribution, you understand. But in this job, you develop instincts. Mine told me both residents of the house were lying. But without proof, that's just conjecture. Nothing a prosecutor hates more. The warrant didn't produce a single piece of evidence, admissible or otherwise, and I'm sorry to say we didn't find your sister."

He nodded toward Claire.

"And we didn't locate extra phones in the house," Harrison continued. "The property is registered to a Dennis and Mary Lou Peterson. Inside, the basement was clean, no blood on the floor, the window was in place. It had fresh putty, but that doesn't prove anything. The owner's rifle was locked in a cabinet. No sign it had been used to beat someone's head in. Owner's got a permit for it, everything in order. And the couple denied you were even there. So, all told, we looked pretty foolish. When I got back, I shared my suspicions, and that's when my superiors decided to assign the case to an investigative unit."

"Aren't you an investigator?" asked Woodrow.

"Not at the level required for felony kidnapping, or so I'm told."

"Do you agree a kidnapping occurred?" Claire pressed him.

"Doesn't matter what I agree on," he said, sounding annoyed. "I'm not part of the investigative team. I briefed the two detectives who are looking into it, and that's it. Though I can likely track your phones."

"I feel like we're sinkin' in quicksand," Woodrow said.

The deputy shrugged.

"Who's on the case now?" asked Claire.

"You'll have to make a written request for that information. They'll give you a form at the front desk." Harrison stood up.

"Who's going to talk to my parents?" asked Claire.

"The investigators, I'd imagine," Harrison replied, exhaling in what seemed like exasperation. "OK, guess I can give you their names. Hold off a day or so before you bug them. They're not going to tell you much anyway.

It's an active investigation."

He wrote the names on the top sheet of a notepad. *Jeffrey Webster, Daniel Smits.* "They've been around awhile," he said, handing Claire the paper. "By the way, that Minnesota Guard chaplain's been trying to reach you, Woodrow. He called this morning. Got his number someplace."

Harrison found it on his desk and handed it to Woodrow.

"Thank you for what you did. You tried," said Woodrow.

Harrison nodded, and they left, Woodrow's attention glued to the piece of paper.

———◆◆◆———

Claire and Woodrow stood in full sunshine outside a T-Mobile shop near the law enforcement building, Woodrow looking about as low as Claire had seen him. She found it amazing how protective she felt about someone she'd known only a few days and whose manners and attitude left a lot to be desired.

"They may have destroyed our phones," Woodrow said after he purchased a new cell. Claire held off, hoping her old one would turn up.

The captain answered immediately. Woodrow identified himself and held the phone between them so they both could hear.

"I have news," Captain Mortensen said.

"What?" Woodrow almost yelled.

"Can we meet somewhere?" asked the chaplain.

"Tell me now," Woodrow said.

"I can't over the phone. Where are you?"

"Sheriff's office in St. Dominic."

"I'll see you soon as I can get there. Let's say around six o'clock."

That made no sense. The Joint Force Headquarters was in St. Paul, seventy-five miles away. The only reason to make the drive from there to St. Dominic so late in the day was if the news were as bad as it could get.

"OK," Woodrow said, ending the call.

"Let's find somewhere to sit down," Claire suggested.

They walked across the street to the same diner they'd patronized earlier. She had an egg salad sandwich on honey wheat bread. Woodrow wouldn't order anything. He wouldn't even have coffee. Claire watched him closely. His eyes still seemed a bit glazed. They sat in a front booth with a clear view of the sheriff department's front door.

"No use assuming the worst," Claire remarked at one point. Woodrow didn't respond.

When they finally saw Mortensen's car pull into a parking slot, Woodrow jumped out of the booth, wobbly as he was, and met the captain before the officer could pocket his keys. Mortensen was in full dress uniform. Claire put enough money on the table to cover the bill and rushed to catch up.

"What do you have to tell us?" Woodrow asked.

"There's a conference room inside the courthouse," Mortensen replied. "Let's find a place in there. Do you want your son's sister-in-law present?"

"Yeah, that's fine," Woodrow said.

No one spoke another word until a security guard unlocked the conference room and the three of them were seated at a long shiny table.

Woodrow felt a sense of dread he had not experienced in decades. This meeting had something to do with Charlie's presence in Afghanistan. He could see it on Mortensen's face, and in quick succession, he relived flashes of his own hot days and cold nights in the first Iraq war. The omnipresent dust, exploding wells, and mutilated bodies left out to rot in the fields. The attacks his unit fought off to rescue a city full of civilians, who, it turned out, mostly didn't survive their wounds. To the rest of the world, Woodrow's war was a short, cheap victory. But cheap victories are only cheap at a distance. Up close, it had been total insanity. How a soldier ended up came down to luck and training. He needed both. Woodrow wondered if Charlie had run out of luck.

Captain Mortensen cleared his throat. "I don't have good news," he said, focusing on Woodrow. "But first I need to tell you that your son is alive. He was injured in an incident north of Kabul yesterday evening, Afghanistan time."

"Where is he now?" Woodrow interjected.

"On a plane to Germany," Mortensen said.

"So, it's bad."

"Bad enough to be evacuated, but I don't know the extent of his injuries. Fortunately, there was no IED at the scene. So, no blast wave damage." Mortensen paused and drew a deep breath.

"Was Charlie with his unit?" Woodrow asked.

"No. He had a high priority pass for the next plane out of Bagram. He was on his way there." Captain Mortensen was sweating in the air-conditioned room.

He wiped his brow with a white handkerchief and carefully put it back in his pocket just as Woodrow's fist hit the table. Woodrow apologized.

"I understand your frustration," Mortensen told him. "I'm going to put you in touch with people who can give you better information. I can tell you now that a lot of soldiers emerge with far better outcomes than it looks like in early days. Our doctors in Germany are the best battlefield medical team to be found anywhere."

"Thank you," Woodrow cut in. "Is the army flying family to Germany?"

"That's done on a case-by-case basis, so I can't tell you right now. I can tell you he'll be back on American soil as soon as he's stable enough to make the trip. The sooner they send him back, the better the prognosis. That's what I'm told."

Woodrow stood up. Claire remained seated.

"You've acquired quite a bruise on your temple," Mortensen remarked, standing up himself. "How'd that come about?"

"Just a scrape," Woodrow replied.

"I'm free for the next three months," Claire announced suddenly to both of them. "I've decided to spend whatever time it takes to find my sister, all summer long if need be. Knowing Theresa's safe should help Charlie recover."

"That's good to hear," Woodrow said.

"Yes," Mortensen agreed, pulling a single folded sheet of paper from his inner breast pocket. He handed it to Woodrow. "Here's a list of information officers who can give you more detail about Charlie's condition. Is there anyone else in your family I should contact?"

"I'll tell them," Woodrow said. He took the folded sheet and offered Mortensen his hand. They shook. Mortensen shook Claire's hand too.

"I hope you find your sister," he said. "That'd do Charlie a world of good."

"I'll do my best," Claire said.

The captain led the way out of the conference room. The three of them emerged into sunshine that seemed warmer than when they went in.

"What are you planning now?" Claire asked Woodrow as they approached his pickup.

"Headin' home," he said.

"When?"

"First thing tomorrow. I'll call my mama, soon as I get a grip. I want her to hear it from me. Won't be long 'fore the army contacts her, that's for sure. Wish I knew more to tell her."

"Will you fly home? I can loan you money."

"Nope. I'll take the truck."

"With your head bashed in? That's a ridiculous idea!"

"This operation has been full of ridiculous ideas," Woodrow snapped.

"Well, I can tell you this much," Claire said vehemently, "you can't drive alone to Alabama."

Woodrow kept walking. Claire increased her stride, arriving at the pickup just in time to jump into the driver's seat before he did.

Woodrow called home as Claire headed toward St. Paul. "Mama there?"

he asked when someone picked up. A pause. A full minute later, he spoke again. "What'd they tell you? When was that?"

With the noise of traffic, Claire couldn't hear a thing on the other end.

"Sorry I didn't call sooner," Woodrow said. "I just found out. Yeah, he's in Germany or maybe on his way home . . ."

Claire thought the conversation sounded calm under the circumstances. Calm and tense.

"They didn't say," Woodrow continued. "I don't think they know. Did they tell you when they'll call back? . . . He was coming home on compassionate leave . . . No, she's still missin' . . . I don't think so. Her mama tried to say that, but I'm not buyin' it. You know she's pregnant . . . We think it has something to do with it . . . *We* is me and her sister and a couple of other people, including the sheriff's office. I think she was kidnapped . . . It's complicated. Right now, I need to concentrate on Charlie . . . I know, Mama. Any way to contact Josie? . . . Maybe so, but she has a right to know . . . OK. I just thought you might be in touch . . . I'm comin' back. Leavin' tomorrow morning. I should be home late Sunday, or early Monday. I'll call you from the road. Write this down—"

He gave her his new cell phone number, adding, "You hold on now, ya hear? See ya soon." He ended the call, and to Claire's astonishment, kissed the screen as if his mother were in there wanting to be comforted and this was the closest he could get. Something about his kissing the screen stayed in Claire's mind for miles.

She put her hand on Woodrow's back. He was damp with sweat. She felt a muscle spasm under his shirt and then, half-turned, she saw him crumble. His head dropped between his knees. He didn't move or make a sound after that. She put her right hand on his head and tried to keep her attention on the road as she kept on driving. It might have been a half hour before he sat up again. They didn't exchange a word until she maneuvered the pickup into the alley behind her duplex, and then, only spoke in monosyllables.

They went upstairs, took showers, and slept—she in her bedroom, Woodrow on the couch. She vaguely heard the sounds of his walking around about three o'clock, getting ready to leave, she guessed. A bit early. It wouldn't be light for a while.

When she woke again, she sat up in bed, wondering if he were still in the bathroom. That's when she heard him drive away. It wasn't even dawn.

Claire prepared a boiled egg and toast, drank an espresso, checked the voice mail on her landline, and answered emails from several students unhappy with their grades. She busied herself with administrative paperwork the rest of the morning to keep herself from "going off half-cocked," as her dad liked to say.

She needed to put thought before action. Charging into a farmhouse, enlisting the help of a sheriff's deputy, and sitting around in a church rectory had all achieved nothing. Henceforth, there had to be more method to her strategy.

Whoever took Theresa was part of an organization. Claire was sure of that much, and she knew that organizations functioned in predictable ways. Before she did anything further, she had to find out more about Lucy Meyer— who she was and how and where she was likely to operate in her SAV ALL crusade.

Claire spent the next three days researching anti-abortion groups in the Twin Cities, searching for a connection to Lucy that might take her back to St. Dominic. She visited a "Life and Human Dignity" office run by the archdiocese. She talked to pro-life advocates, pretending to be of their opinion. She read their literature and news articles about them. But she couldn't find a roadmap to Theresa, and, of course, no one ever admitted, "Oh, yes, we kidnap pregnant women," or even "I know Lucy Meyer."

Finally, on Sunday morning, May 27, she packed her car with clothes and toiletries and headed north, hoping against hope that Theresa would be at her parents' house when she arrived, released from whatever captivity her mother had orchestrated.

The Haig farmhouse was empty, left unlocked as usual. Since it was a Sunday, Claire figured they'd be in church for Mass, and they'd probably stop off in the church reception room afterwards for coffee and sweets.

She went up to Theresa's bedroom. The door was open. Theresa's computer sat on the edge of the bed. Claire wondered whether the police had been on the premises—maybe those two detectives the deputy mentioned. Surely, if they'd searched her room, they'd have taken Theresa's computer with them. But there it was.

Claire looked around the rest of the house, hoping her mother had been careless enough to leave a list of her friends' names and addresses lying about. She went into Annie's room too. The walls were covered with movie posters, and the shelves packed tight with books, some of them wildly inappropriate for a thirteen-year-old. No one noticed, apparently.

She heard cars and looked out a front-facing window at the end of the upstairs hallway. Her younger siblings were getting out of their vehicles; Matt and his wife, Mary, in a van with their kids; Paul in his Jeep; David and Mark in a black SUV; John in a second SUV with his wife, Amy, and their infant; Andrew and Luke, both unmarried, rode behind the procession on big Harleys. Claire was sure they'd all been summoned for a family meeting about Theresa.

Her parents' white Cadillac was last into the yard. Her father got out wearing a suit. Tom Haig did not often wear suits. He didn't even go to church with any regularity. Greg and Annie got out of the back seat. Claire hurried downstairs.

In the kitchen, Maureen looked surprised to see her oldest daughter, but she didn't make a point of it, turning her attention to the general hubbub instead. Claire's brothers lived in a different galaxy, happy to have fled the farm but pleased to visit occasionally. Matt was a chemical engineer at 3M. Paul and David worked in construction. Mark was a high school math teacher in Brainerd, about sixty miles to the north of St. Dominic. His wife, Jennifer, taught American history in the same school. Jennifer's family were academics with no faith, according to Maureen. She and Jennifer had little use for each other, so it wasn't surprising that Jennifer was nowhere to be seen.

John was the gentle soul of the family, always the peacemaker. He probably made a wonderful father, Claire thought, as she watched her brother take his six-month-old son out of his car seat. His wife, Amy, came from the western suburbs of Minneapolis. Her parents were wealthy, and John worked for them, doing what, Claire had no idea.

They all gathered around the kitchen table, made longer by the addition of three massive leaves Tom had fashioned years ago from some stricken oak tree. Maureen brought out her largest tablecloth, much used, its blue-and-white expanse marred by food stains that would not wash out without bleach. Maureen shunned bleach, unless it was absolutely necessary.

She unfolded the cloth on the table, smoothing occasional wrinkles as best she could. Matt's wife Mary laid out coffee cups and spoons. Tom took charge of the coffee maker. He hated weak coffee. He called the coffee at church receptions "brown water."

Claire greeted everyone, hugged and kissed her brothers, and even got to hold baby Liam for a while as she watched his big brown eyes bore into hers. She examined him in return. He laughed, reaching out little fingers to grab her mouth. She wondered what was going on in the mind of a six-month-old. He didn't even know yet that his fingers and hands belonged to him. Liam's mood vacillated, though, and he reached toward his father in a sudden bout of anxiety. Reluctantly, Claire handed him back.

Being childless hadn't bothered her until recently. The thought of bringing an infant into the world was something Claire had abandoned when she'd divorced Rob. Prior to the last few months, it hadn't occurred to her that she might someday change her mind, that a gnawing need would eat its way into the quiet of her womb, demanding its primordial right to reproduce just as her fertility drained away.

They sat at the table. Maureen said grace. Claire was about to describe the kidnapping, in case some in the family weren't aware, when suddenly her father stood up.

"I'm sorry Andy and Luke couldn't make it, but maybe the rest of you will pass on what I have to say." He sounded on the verge of an oration.

Baby Liam looked at him in amazement.

Claire breathed deeply, stifling a cough. Was he going to expose Maureen's involvement in Theresa's disappearance in the same way he approached everything else? When something mattered to him, her dad didn't let sentiment interfere. He focused bluntly on the problem.

"Our farm is going to remain in this family," Tom said. "You all know that's been my dream since I took over from your grandfather in 1979."

He glanced at Claire, who felt a tremendous urge to object. With great difficulty, she stifled the impulse.

"That was the year Mary was born. The year my brothers walked away. It broke my father's heart. They didn't want to be farmers, they said. Well, I'll tell you right now, none of them did as well as this family has. Farming is a good living if you manage it right, and if you're willing to put your heart and muscle into it every day of the year. Up 'til now, as you boys went off one by one for the big city or whatever . . . " He practically sneered the words. "I kept hoping there would be at least one farmer in the bunch. And now I've found him. Greg will be eighteen soon, and he's going to start out at the extension program here in the county, and if he does well, I'll foot the bill for him to get a degree in agriculture at the U in the Cities."

No one said a word. Baby Liam began to fuss. Amy took him to another room, presumably to breastfeed in private, but also, Claire guessed, to get away from the tension in the kitchen.

"Now, just maybe, one of you other boys has had a change of heart. If so," Tom continued, holding up his right hand in a fist, "now is the time to say it. Greg would be glad to team up with any of you if you have a genuine interest in running this farm. There's plenty of room to build another house, hell, another half dozen houses. And I'm still fit enough to help."

No one spoke. Claire saw the annoyance on her father's face, and she knew what he was thinking. He had run into this wall of resistance for years, with Matt especially, and it rankled him. It felt like ingratitude.

Of course, since she was a daughter, not a son, it had never occurred to him to sell her on the farm, not that any of his girls had ever expressed a desire to take up farming.

What about Theresa? Claire wanted to shout. Instead, she waited.

"OK," Tom grumbled. "I can talk to you boys privately one-on-one. I can talk to two or three of you. But you come to me *now*, or you hold your peace after. Just don't complain at my funeral that you were left out."

He let his message settle, and then he sat down.

"Let's eat," Maureen said, getting up. "I have a baked ham, two loaves of whole-wheat bread, potato salad with hard-boiled eggs, a cucumber salad, sweet pickles, dills, a red Jell-o with bananas, chocolate pudding I made from scratch, and a Bavarian cream pie. Let's get it on the table."

Claire caught her mother's eye. Maureen looked back with not the slightest hint of fear, totally focused on getting everyone fed. That was too much.

"What about Theresa?" Claire practically yelled at a volume necessary to penetrate the din of conversation.

Maureen pulled bowls and platters from the refrigerator and handed them to Matt's wife, Mary, who placed them, along with serving spoons, over every available space on the tablecloth.

"What about Theresa?" David repeated in a more moderate tone.

"Did you know she's missing?" Claire asked.

"She's missing?" John echoed.

"She's been missing for over two weeks. Eighteen days, to be precise. When I saw everyone gathered here, I thought she was the reason."

Her siblings looked at her, clearly flummoxed. *None of them know,* she realized. Her father, sitting at the head of the table, said quietly, "After we eat, Mary, then we'll talk about Theresa."

"My name is Claire."

"Just quit that nonsense," he ordered.

For the second time since they sat down, Claire caught the exasperation on Annie's face as the family ate and conversed with gusto. No one mentioned Theresa again. After the meal ended and the women started cleaning up, the men went outside. Claire would have followed, but Maureen thrust a soapy platter into her hands, and in a ritual ingrained from childhood, she rinsed and dried it, continuing 'til the last dish was done and back in the cupboard.

Annie motioned to Claire as the kitchen emptied. They walked to the barn together. Annie stopped in front of the thresher.

"Here's where her car was," Annie said.

"Who moved it?" asked Claire.

"No idea. I asked Dad, and he said 'Mind your own business.' *And* Father Schmidt came to see Mother yesterday. I heard them arguing. He said if she knew where Theresa was, it was her obligation to tell. He said otherwise the church might be blamed."

"What did she say?"

"That she didn't know. I don't believe her. Whatever's going on, I think Dad's in on it too. It's a conspiracy," Annie whispered.

Claire found that hard to believe. If her father were part of a plot to kidnap Theresa, the few certitudes that remained of her childhood ceased to apply.

"Hey," John called out. He was the middle child, with five siblings older, five younger. Once a reedy boy, John seemed to have developed more muscle in his arms since the last time Claire had seen him. Baby Liam fidgeted against his chest, a pacifier in his mouth. John motioned from the open barn door, probably to keep Liam away from the dust inside.

"What's this about Theresa?" he asked. Claire and Annie told him everything they knew. He shook his head.

"You really think they'd break the law?" He sounded skeptical.

"I don't think they'd consider it breaking the law. They'd think they're saving a life," Claire told him.

"Well, if what you say is true, breaking the law is what they're doing," John said. "Keep me posted, OK? Let me know if there's anything I can do."

"Yeah," said Claire, "I will." She looked at Annie.

"Keep him posted?" Annie repeated after John was out of hearing. "His sister's been kidnapped, and John wants to be kept posted?"

Claire and Annie walked toward the house. Tom stood on the front porch talking to Paul and David. In their SUV, Matt, his wife Mary, and their kids had pulled away, headed for home.

Mark emerged through the living room door.

"Don't answer today," Tom said, starting to sound hoarse. "Just give it some thought." He followed his sons to their vehicles.

It took another twenty minutes before the last of them departed. Greg had gone off to do chores. When Tom stood alone in the driveway, Claire walked toward him. He said nothing. Together they approached a line of Colorado spruce he'd allowed to take up space among his sugar maples.

"Well?" said Claire finally, exasperated.

"Watch your tone, Mary."

"Do you know where Theresa is?" she demanded.

"No, I don't," Tom said. "And neither does your mother. But she tells me," Tom claimed as his face zoomed closer to Claire's, "that Theresa is safe and sound. She's having trouble adjusting to her situation, so she needs some time to settle down."

"That doesn't change the fact—"

"I know all about this sick baby Theresa thinks she doesn't want," he said, "and I'm trusting your mother will help her work this thing out once she's back and her husband gets home. That's what married people do. At least the ones with sense enough to stay married."

Claire felt the blow. "Have you talked to the police?" she asked pointedly.

"Haven't had time nor reason to," Tom replied. "In case you forgot, this place takes the bulk of my energy."

"You're not concerned that Theresa is being held against her will?"

"I trust your mother."

Claire moved closer to him and whispered, "Dad, she's part of a plot. Theresa's a prisoner. Have you asked Mother why Theresa can't come back here to adjust to her situation?" Her father didn't answer. "Did you know your priest was here yesterday?"

Tom looked surprised and shook his head no.

"I didn't think so," Claire said. "The woman you married has helped kidnap your daughter, and you can stand here and say, 'I trust her.'"

"Now you look," Tom exploded. "Theresa's carrying an innocent baby inside her. No one made her get married or get pregnant. Those were free choices she made. We weren't allowed to ask questions about the man she chose to spend the rest of her life with. That's what she said. Well, she doesn't get to ask questions about whether this grandchild of mine has a right to exist. Those are the cards she was dealt."

"It's a crime to kidnap someone," Claire said as calmly as she could.

"You call it kidnapped," Tom replied. "We say she's coming to terms with her situation."

They stared at each other, neither flinching. Claire looked away first and turned on her heel. She wasn't staying, she decided. She'd find a motel, and first thing tomorrow, she'd chase down anybody who could tell her anything useful.

Annie reappeared from the front porch as Claire approached her car. "Take me with you," she begged. "I already put my stuff in the back seat."

Claire shook her head no. "I can't," she said. "You're thirteen years old."

"Fourteen soon," Annie corrected. "And school is out. They won't even miss me."

Claire smiled. "Can't do it, kiddo. Sorry. But you stay on the lookout. Let me know if you hear Mother on the phone with anybody. Make a list of her friends at church."

She pulled Annie's suitcase from her back seat and set it on the driveway.

"Charlie's dad and I just found out Charlie was hurt," Claire added. "He was hurt badly in Afghanistan, and Theresa doesn't even know it."

———•◦•———

Claire negotiated with the front desk clerk for an indefinite stay at a motel next door to the Best Western where she and Woodrow had tracked Lucy Meyer. She hoped she'd see her again.

The discounted room had a standard bed with a badly stained bedspread which she removed and stuffed underneath the frame. The sheets looked clean. She retrieved a bottle of antiseptic spray from her suitcase and sprayed every surface 'til the can was empty. Then she sat down on the room's lone chair to calculate a game plan.

First, she needed a cell phone. She'd stop in at the sheriff's office to see if Antoine Harrison had located hers. If not, she'd have to buy a new one.

She'd also contact the sheriff's detectives assigned to Theresa's case. Then she'd go to the clinic and see Dr. Ryan. After that, she'd drive to Patricia Conroy's house. Claire hoped her high school classmate still worked at the clinic and could tell her something more. Finally, she'd try to locate any church friends of Maureen that Annie could come up with.

Claire arrived at the sheriff's office about eight o'clock Monday morning. It was Memorial Day, so she was pleased and surprised to find that Deputy Harrison was not only working on the holiday but had her phone and Woodrow's too. They were located inside a storage locker at the bus depot, he said. Claire sent Woodrow a text. Hold onto it, he texted back.

For even more good luck, the detectives on the case were in the building and willing to see her. An information officer sent her upstairs to a tiny windowless room where two young men, both clean-cut in dress shirts and ties, sat at metal desks facing each other while sipping coffee out of ceramic mugs. They'd apparently just arrived themselves by the activity on their computers. The one closest to her had a screen saver of a woman in a bikini bottom seen from behind. Claire gave him a look. Blushing, he hit a key, and the screen saver disappeared.

"You're," Claire said, glancing at the paper in her hand, "Detectives Webster and Smits?"

"Yes, we are," said the one with the screen saver, "and who are you?" He motioned toward a wooden chair with a cracked back.

"Claire Haig," she said, "sister of Theresa Haig who is missing and believed kidnapped."

"Believed by who?" asked the other man.

Claire ignored his grammatical faux pas, took a chance on the chair, and sat down.

"My sister's been missing since May ninth. Her name is Theresa Haig."

Detective Webster found the name *Theresa Haig* printed on a manila file and read aloud.

"Deputy Antoine Harrison. Missing person report. Complainants, father-in-law and sister, neither close to subject. Parents not in agreement that subject is missing. Subject may be pregnant. Subject's husband currently overseas in service. Warrant served at farm of Dennis and Mary Lou Peterson, Route 10, Sartell, on suspicion of harboring subject. No evidence recovered. The Petersons deny any contact with subject."

He looked at Claire. "Something you'd like to add?"

"She's still missing," Claire said. "She left behind her wallet, her driver's license, and her cell phone."

"Maybe she went off somewhere with a friend," said Detective Smits. "And maybe the friend's driving. And maybe she just wanted to get away and unplug from the world."

Neither man looked particularly concerned.

"I was hoping you'd know more," Claire added. "I was hoping you'd be searching for her as we speak."

"Look," Detective Webster said crisply, "if the parents don't think she's missing, and we don't have anyone else making a complaint, and you, if I understand correctly, don't even live around here, but you came in last week to announce to the sheriff that your sister's missing, well—" He shrugged.

She didn't like his attitude. It seemed downright hostile, and since they'd never met before and she remained civil, there was no reason for it.

"Doesn't her pregnancy have you concerned?" she pleaded, this time directing her attention toward the other one, Detective Smits, who stood up and walked around the desks to get closer to her.

"Do you know for a fact that she's pregnant?" he asked, thrusting his face down until it was level with hers. He had freckles and horrible breath. She decided to lay it all out.

"Yes. My sister's pregnant with a baby likely to have Down syndrome, and she may be considering an abortion. My theory is that she was abducted because of it, and some of her relatives are part of a conspiracy to keep her out of sight, which is why no one except her husband's family and I are worried about where she is."

Detective Webster laughed. "Well, looks like we're not needed, Danny. She's got it all figured out. Kidnapping and conspiracy and, what else you got going there—child abuse, maybe?"

"You're not acting like professionals," Claire threw back at him.

"Let me tell you something." Detective Webster leaned forward in his chair. "I got three kids—great kids. They mean more to me than anything in the world. And if one of my kids had been born with a purple nose and antennae growing out of his head, I would love him—*just the same.*" He and Claire stared at each other. Neither blinked. "So don't tell me about conspiracies," he went on. "We got just about all we can handle right now, including a hit and run. We're putting in overtime. Sixteen open cases, A to Z. Everything from arson to a vandalized Zamboni. Once we get the hit and run solved, we'll work on your sister's case and all the others, in order of priority."

"Are you suggesting my sister's case is not high in your order of priority?"

He shrugged again. "No. Didn't mean to imply that."

"You didn't have to," Claire said, standing. As she walked through the open door, Detective Webster added, "We *are* working on it."

She was trembling by the time she got downstairs, opened her car door, and sat in the driver's seat. She waited several minutes to calm down.

Her cell phone showed two voice mails, one from Annie, the other from Woodrow. She called Annie first and got the family voice mail. Then she called Woodrow who answered on the first ring.

"How're you doing?" she asked.

"Holding pattern," he said.

"What's that mean?"

"Means I'm ready for Charlie to get here. The logistics are all jacked up, and nobody knows what's happenin'. He may arrive this afternoon or tonight, or maybe not 'til tomorrow. It's drivin' me crazy."

"Where are you?"

"Richmond. I flew in from Birmingham last night." He paused. "How're you doin'?"

"Not well," she admitted. "I struck out with the detectives at the sheriff's office. I don't think they want to find Theresa."

"Why not?"

"This is a Bible Belt too, Woodrow. Soon as I told them Theresa might have been planning an abortion, which somehow I think they already knew, they seemed to stop caring, like they'd just as soon she stays missing 'til she has the baby."

"Guess where you come from an' where I come from aren't all that different," he suggested.

"Maybe."

"So, what's your next move?"

"The clinic. I'm going to talk to Dr. Ryan, whether he wants to talk to me or not, and I'll talk to Patricia Conroy again, if I can."

"Yeah. I owe her work on her car. Tell her I didn't forget."

Claire exhaled slowly, willing her blood pressure down. "Woodrow, I wish you were here," she admitted.

He laughed. "I have that effect on women."

"Call me when you know more," she added.

"Will do."

It was mid-morning, near ten o'clock, as Claire entered the clinic. She asked to see Dr. Ryan.

Dr. Ryan was on vacation, the receptionist said. Another doctor was substituting. Would she like to make an appointment with him?

"No," Claire replied. "Is there any way I can reach Dr. Ryan?"

The receptionist shook her head. Neither Lucy Meyer nor Patricia Conroy was there either. Claire left and drove by Patricia's house. She knocked on the door. Nothing. She waited awhile. More nothing.

Sitting in her car, she googled the FBI and found a link to submit an online report. She typed in Theresa's story and her own name and cell phone. Then she went back to her motel and sent out emails with the basic facts to newspapers and local radio stations. When her phone chimed later that afternoon, it was Woodrow with news about Charlie.

"He's in the burn unit, unconscious, but they say he's stabilized, whatever that means," he said.

"Sounds like a good sign," Claire suggested.

"I spent the last couple hours starin' at his back. It's one massive burn. The back of his head is burned too. They're goin' to have to do grafts."

She could hear Woodrow's rage between the words.

"Wish I could be there," she offered.

"You stay where you are. I need to let off steam, and I don't want to give my mama any more grief on the phone."

"Well then, you'd better tell me everything," she said. She waited a moment. When he didn't speak, she did. "Do they know yet when he might be released from the hospital?"

"Weeks, maybe months," Woodrow said. "He was treated in the field near Kandahar, then they got him to Bagram, and real quick they flew him to Ramstein. At that point he was still critical, but he was breathin' on his own, they said. So, they put him on another flight to Walter Reed, and finally they brought him here."

Claire had no idea where those places were on a map, but she knew where she fit in. She was part of the family that set this whole thing in motion.

Woodrow stopped talking. When he started up again, the emotion had been shoved down. He sounded clinical. They talked for more than an hour, or rather, he talked. None of what he said sounded good.

After the call ended, Claire shut her iPad, pushed her notes aside, and let her mind dwell on Charlie, whom she had never met. Briefly, she was glad Theresa remained undiscovered and therefore untouched by the consequences of decisions other people had made. The kidnappers, whoever they were, wouldn't tell Theresa anything about Charlie. They probably wouldn't want to know themselves.

Claire imagined Woodrow looking at Charlie in his hospital bed, remembering him as an infant, a little boy, a teenager, a soldier, a groom, and now a man deprived of his wife. A long line of Charlies lay unconscious.

2

An FBI agent named Mitchell Gunderson called Claire's cell shortly after she spoke to Woodrow. He worked out of a federal building in Brooklyn Center, about fifty-five miles south of St. Dominic. An analyst would review her information, he said, to determine whether it had legitimate lead value. Then it would be forwarded to a field office or on to another agency, depending on the analyst's report.

"Please take this seriously," Claire implored him. "My sister has been missing for nineteen days. I'm worried sick about her."

"I see that in the form you filled out," he said. "We'll look into it. I can assure you the bureau takes kidnapping very seriously. In most cases, it's prosecuted under state law. But the Federal Kidnapping Act allows us to step in if it's determined that an adult has been taken across state lines. In those instances, we're better able to pursue kidnappers if jurisdiction is divided. We're not talking about a child here, if I understand from what you've provided."

"We're talking about an adult woman who's pregnant," Claire told him, "and I don't know if she's been taken across state lines."

"That casts it in a different light altogether," Agent Gunderson said. "We may want to look at this situation the way we do when we're dealing with a child of tender years. In terms of the law, tender years means any child twelve or under. An unborn child should qualify."

"We just want her back," said Claire. "Her husband will want her back when he's awake." She told him everything she knew.

Maureen had a splitting headache. It moved around like a fish inside her brain, first at the back of her neck, then behind her right eye, then up to the top of her skull.

She didn't know why she imagined a fish. Maybe it was because Father Schmidt had talked about fishing for souls in the previous Sunday's sermon. *Maybe*, she thought, *I've been chosen by God to fish for Theresa's soul. Maybe I've been ordained by Him to use all my might to pull Theresa's soul out of the depths to which she'd let herself sink in her misguided attempt to abort her precious child.*

Or maybe, she thought, *it's her baby's soul I've been sent to save. I'm trying to do that*, she told the Lord in every prayer. *I'm trying with all my might. God help me*, she implored, but there was no answer at the moment. Not in the midst of all this pain. She couldn't understand why He wasn't helping more. Why was He sending *her* a headache? Why wasn't He sending Mary a headache? Or Theresa?

And in particular, the thing that grieved her most, why had God abandoned Tom? *Where*, she begged the Lord, *is the grace I long for Tom to receive—the regenerating, sanctifying grace strong enough to flush away his doubts?*

Tom had become a source of constant stress with his everlasting questions about Theresa. He was angry at Mary for her interference, but he was angry at Maureen too. He couldn't seem to make up his mind which side he was on, and Maureen knew why. Tom's faith was weak. No wonder she had a headache.

Aspirin didn't help. Neither did Excedrin. She'd taken both with her first cup of coffee, figuring if one didn't work, the other would. She didn't eat much at breakfast. Just a muffin to get the pills down. She'd hardly spoken to Tom lately. She didn't know what she could say to him. There was nothing she could say that she hadn't already said to explain away the awful accusations Mary had made about criminal conspiracies and the like.

She tried to push away thoughts about things she could do nothing about—like Annie saying Theresa's husband had been hurt in Afghanistan. What could she do about that, if it were even true? She certainly knew she could do nothing about the law, whatever it was in regard to preventing abortion. She could do nothing to hurry Theresa's pregnancy along. She could do nothing to make other people understand the horror of abortion, if they didn't understand already. Nothing, nothing.

She wondered again why she imagined a fish forcing its way through tiny blood vessels inside her skull. So many things made no sense.

A vehicle drove up the driveway. She heard its tires crunch on the gravel before it appeared, an old-looking, four-door, gray something-or-other that stopped in front of the porch. Tom paid attention to what kind of cars people drove. Maureen did not. She made her way through the hallway and opened the front door. Bright sunshine hit her unexpectedly. She saw two young men get out and walk toward the house and up the porch steps, their light-colored shirts shimmering as they moved. They wore ties and suit pants without the jackets. She tried to greet them pleasantly, wondering if they were salesmen or Jehovah's Witnesses. Whoever they were, Maureen was determined to be brave, to show no sign of weakness in front of anyone. The Lord expected her best effort. No one could know how much she suffered or how worried she was about Theresa.

"Good morning. Are you Mrs. Haig?" asked one of the men. She nodded. "I'm Detective Jeffrey Webster, and this is Detective Daniel Smits. We're with the Stears County Sheriff's Department."

Both of them showed identification. She glanced down long enough to see credentials that looked authentic. So, they were not salesmen.

What were detectives doing here today of all days, she wondered. Wasn't it Memorial Day? No, she remembered. That was yesterday.

Did they intend to arrest her? Was her headache a premonition? Had Mary called the sheriff after she'd barged in on Sunday, and was it the sheriff who'd sent these men with some kind of warrant that had her name on it?

"Could we come inside a moment?" Detective Webster asked.

She nodded, perfectly ready, if that's what God wanted, to be put into handcuffs and made a martyr for the cause of Life. Her headache eased a little as she made that decision. She wouldn't ask to see their warrant. She wouldn't call Tom's attorney, Ben Johnson, to defend her against them. She wouldn't resist in any way. She would bend herself to the Lord's will.

Maureen waved the men inside. Both of them watched her closely. She could feel their eyes. They were probably waiting, she imagined, for some gesture of submission, some sort of confession on her part.

She led them into the kitchen. "Would you like coffee?" she asked, motioning for them to sit down at the table. They seemed amazingly relaxed.

"Sure," the other detective said.

Smit, Maureen remembered. Or Smits. She recalled a Smits family at St. Philomena. She set the coffeepot on the stove so she could make drip coffee, her best brew, pouring extra grounds into the filter. Important moments called for strong, rich coffee. She used arabica beans. No percolator today.

There were chocolate-covered peanut butter cookies in the refrigerator. She put six of them on a platter in the middle of the table and added a pitcher of cream and a bowl of sugar with a silver spoon, as well as cups, plates, regular spoons, and napkins. If they were going to drag her off to jail, she decided, she'd first show them how a gracious hostess entertained her tormentors.

That thought reminded her of Saint Gerard, the patron saint of expectant mothers. She'd been praying to him of late. He was Italian and reputed to have been gracious through all his various trials and tribulations, or so it said in her gilt-edged *Book of the Saints*. He was sweetness and light to a fault, the author claimed, even in extremis.

Maureen was quite sure, with these two nice young sheriff's representatives at her table, that she was in extremis. Yet she couldn't help liking them, especially the one with freckles. He could have been her son.

She scanned the tabletop. The only thing missing was place mats, but her head hurt too much to go find some. *Please, Lord,* she begged, *let this headache go away so I can continue being gracious in my time of affliction.*

"What can I do for you?" she asked. They'd been patient. She appreciated that they hadn't pestered her with questions while she'd prepared the table. She sat down across from them, intending to rest just a moment until the water on the stove came to a boil. She'd turned the burner on high, so it shouldn't be long.

How, she wondered in passing, could she let Tom know if they took her into custody? Maybe these young men would be kind enough to drive around the farm looking for him before leaving the property with her in their sheriff's car. She imagined them putting a hand on her head before pushing her into the back seat. She imagined one of them putting a gentle hand on her headachy head.

"We're here to inquire about your daughter Theresa," said the deputy with freckles. Smits.

"Yes," Maureen replied.

"Some people think she may have been abducted," said the other one, Detective Webster.

"I know that," Maureen said.

"Has she been abducted?" asked Detective Smits.

Maureen contemplated lying. Would the Lord want her to lie? Or, she wondered, should she refuse to answer? What would Lucy Meyer say was the best strategy? Was the Lord in accordance with Lucy? Was He acting through Lucy? So many thoughts swirled in her mind.

She looked at the two men, ready to confess all and let the Lord's chips fall where they may, when the whistle on the tea kettle began to scream. That caused the fish in her head to pound itself with particular ferocity against the top of her skull until she thought for a second she, too, would scream. She shuddered.

"Oh," she said, getting up.

Detective Smits laughed. "That thing makes a noise," he observed.

Maureen nodded, grabbing a hot pad to convey the boiling water to the glass carafe. She made herself slow down, letting the water slide its steamy way into the filter.

"Theresa has . . ." she began.

"Before you go any further," Detective Webster interrupted, "maybe we should tell you what we think."

His remark surprised Maureen. She faced the coffeepot until the last of the water dripped through. No one said anything for almost a minute. That minute seemed an extremely long time, and she wondered why the detective didn't finish what he'd started to say. Finally, she turned around with the full carafe in her hand, ready to pour.

"We think maybe it's just a misunderstanding on your daughter's part," Detective Smits said. "We got the impression that you and your daughter don't get along too well."

Maureen forced a smile. "Which one?" she asked, pouring coffee into both their cups.

"The one that came to see us," Detective Smits answered. He looked at an open notebook. "Claire."

"My oldest daughter is named Mary. I don't know why she calls herself Claire," Maureen said. She sat down again.

Detective Smits smiled. "She changed her name?"

"Not as far as I'm concerned," Maureen said.

"OK, so, it sounds to us as if you and your daughter, Claire or Mary or whatever—you're not getting along, and your other daughter—"

"Theresa."

"Right, Theresa . . . she's where, exactly?"

"I don't know," Maureen replied honestly. "I truly don't know."

"But you'd tell us if you did?" Detective Smits asked.

Maureen looked at him. Was now the time? she wondered. Should she say *no*, she would not tell them if she knew? At that point they'd arrest her, and Tom would just have to deal with the consequences, because she was going to protect Theresa's baby no matter what. Therefore, she would not tell anyone where her daughter was, even if she knew, even under duress, even if it meant prison, she supposed.

"Of course, you would," said Detective Webster. "We just had to ask. I understand your daughter has a special pregnancy going on."

"Yes," Maureen agreed. "It's certainly special."

"We understand that," Detective Smits rushed to finish her thought, "and that's why she needs some space to deal with it. She probably just wants to be alone for a while."

Maureen began to feel a little dizzy.

"So, all we need from you, Mrs. Haig, is maybe a list of who was with you the last time you saw Theresa, before she went off to find some peace and quiet," Detective Webster said.

"We're not making any assumptions," Detective Smits said. "We'd just like to talk to some people and see if we can't get a sense of where Theresa might have gone."

They helped themselves to cookies. "These are really great," Detective Smits said. "Peanut butter and chocolate. There's no better combination."

That's when Maureen realized they were not going to arrest her. She didn't have to tell them anything else. Just give them a list of people who would agree that Theresa went off on her own to think about her situation.

As soon as they left, she'd inform everyone by way of the telephone tree, so the other women who'd helped Theresa would understand that these emissaries from the sheriff's department were not going to get anyone in trouble because they, too, understood what was at stake.

Maureen now knew from the bottom of her heart that the Lord had sent these fine young men, these angels really, to help in this great endeavor of salvation for Theresa and her baby. The Lord had not forsaken her.

Her headache began to ease. The two connected arcs of the Savior's fish had met in her kitchen. That was a story Father Schmidt told often. In early days when Christians were persecuted, if strangers met, one of them would draw half of the fish on the ground. The upper arc. If the other one completed the bottom arc, they would both know they were fellows in Christ. These detectives had drawn the bottom arc, and the fish was satisfied.

Maureen decided to take a nap upstairs after the young men left and she'd finished her calls. By the time she woke, she was sure her headache would be gone.

She wondered where Annie was. Probably off somewhere with a book. That was good. The Lord hadn't wanted Annie to be part of this conversation.

Lucy Meyer's phone played a snippet from Mozart's "Jupiter" finale, interrupting her concentration as she corrected the intern's draft of her remarks at the upcoming 2018 Save Life Convention. They were due at the printer's the next day, May 31.

Lucy deleted every phrase that sounded mean. Personal attacks on women seeking abortions were counterproductive. Moralistic phrasing contradicted the essential argument, which was that *all human life is sacred*. You don't kill someone because he or she's imperfect, because raising a child is expensive, because your romance soured. Pragmatism does not excuse murder.

An RN by training, Lucy had become less nurse than counselor in recent years. She knew antipathy to inconvenient pregnancy led otherwise decent people to make an exception in their own cases, which is to say, to slaughter innocent lives that might become a burden or embarrassment.

Lucy's goal was to save babies by helping mothers make *informed* choices. Theresa Haig's baby was Lucy's child of the moment, a child who would not die on Lucy's watch.

She picked up her cell. The caller was Janet Cahill, a brave woman willing to intervene at the spur of the moment when they had no choice but to move Theresa. Janet Cahill was connected to the Haig family through her daughter Mary who had married Maureen's son Matthew. Janet had offered the use of her family's lake cabin in Mille Lacs County. "What a lifesaver you are," Lucy told her at the time. "I mean that literally."

"What can I do for you, Janet?" Lucy asked now.

"She won't eat," Janet said.

"When did that start?"

"Yesterday. And she's threatening to stop drinking."

"I'll be there as quickly as I can," Lucy said.

In order to convince Theresa that self-abuse wouldn't work, Lucy had to show her why. She called St. Dominic Hospital and asked for a friend who had long been a trusted helper—Betty Maxwell. Lucy and Betty went back twenty years, since the first of six miscarriages Betty had suffered trying to bring a child into this world. Betty would get whatever Lucy needed, and no one at the hospital would make a fuss. Betty knew whom to trust.

Little more than an hour later, the necessary gear in the back of her van, Lucy arrived at the Cahill cabin. Cabin was a misnomer. The Cahills were financially comfortable, and their lake home would be an upscale residence in any city neighborhood. More to the point, it was secure, with acres of woodland attached. Theresa could scream until her lungs ached, and no outsider would hear.

Janet Cahill opened the leaded glass door at the front of the house.

"She's upstairs," she told Lucy.

"Who else is here?" Lucy asked.

"Roberta and Sarah."

Lucy climbed the stairs. The door was unlocked seconds after she knocked. Theresa sat on the bed, her back against an iron-spindle headboard. Both of her wrists were attached to the grillwork. Her feet were tied together with fabric to prevent kicking. Lucy sat down on a wooden chair at the edge of the bed.

"This won't do," she said.

Theresa didn't respond. She didn't even look at her. She stared out the window, which was open, allowing a breeze that made the room feel pleasant.

"I understand you're not eating," Lucy continued.

Theresa said nothing and refused to meet Lucy's gaze.

"In my car I have equipment to sedate you and put a feeding tube down your throat," Lucy told Theresa. "We'll use a nasogastric tube. It will go right into your stomach. You will get all the nutrition and vitamin supplements you need. If you continue to refuse to eat by mouth, the tube will keep you alive. But I'll tell you this: most patients who have a gastric feeding tube are happy to get rid of it. Do you want to put yourself through that?"

Still, she elicited nothing from Theresa.

Roberta Wells, in designer jeans and what Lucy guessed was a hand-embroidered silk blouse, stood against the pale blue wall and looked at Theresa with distaste. Sarah Peters, who had started pro-life work a dozen years ago as Lucy's intern in Minneapolis, wore her usual serene expression.

"Sarah, I have things in the back of the van. Would you bring them in?" She handed Sarah a set of keys.

Roberta spoke as soon as Sarah left. "She's too easy on her," she said.

"That's her way," Lucy replied.

"You know what this one told us when she stopped eating?" Roberta nodded in Theresa's direction. "She said she'll stop drinking next."

"Then so be it," Lucy said. "The feeding tube will deliver enough liquid to keep her hydrated. Has she been sleeping well?"

"She sleeps most of the time. She won't exercise. She won't even walk around the room when we untie her. She also stopped talking."

Sarah came in with a cardboard box she set on the floor.

"OK, Theresa," Lucy said. "Here's the equipment."

She pulled a tube out of the box. "This part will go up your nostrils. It will irritate the nasal lining, and you won't like it at all when the tube goes down your esophagus. I've had a lot of experience inserting one, so you can be sure I'll get it in safely, but it will feel like hell."

Lucy stooped to reach the bottom of the box and pulled out a syringe and plunger.

"Here is a sixty-cubic-centimeter syringe. We'll fill it with liquid nutrition as well as any medication you need. But you'll have to worry about a few things. You may get diarrhea or feel your stomach cramping. The cramps probably won't be worse than a typical period, but the diarrhea can be messy. We'll have to clean you up a lot. Also, we'll need to brush your teeth frequently since you'll probably have some nausea and regurgitation, by which I mean vomiting."

Theresa did not respond, but her eyes seemed more alert. Lucy set the apparatus back in the box.

"Now, do you really want this?" Lucy asked. "Because we will use it. I hope you don't doubt that. We'll do whatever we need to do to save your baby's life."

With a glance around the room, Lucy warned the others to say nothing. Birds called outside the window. Branches stirred, in particular a grove of poplars that formed a wall against the north wind. Cottonwood seed floated through the air, like fuzzy snowflakes, inserting themselves in the window screen. Occasionally, one got in.

"I'll eat."

And that was it. The problem was solved. Lucy looked at Sarah. "Take the box downstairs."

Sarah picked up the box and left.

"I recommend you do some meditating, my dear," Lucy continued. "Think about your baby. Think about your baby's father, and how he will feel if you harm this precious life he helped create. Think about how lucky you are to be able to have a child. Not everyone has that luxury."

She leaned over and gently kissed Theresa on the forehead. Theresa's reaction was swift. Without warning, Lucy's captive turned her face into an image from the wild—eyes slit, nostrils flared, her lips pulled apart not in a smile but a grimace. She emitted an inhuman sound and lunged toward Lucy, who managed to retreat before the prisoner could bite her face.

After that near miss, even Lucy felt the need to hold still and, for the moment, just breathe. She spread her arms, hands leaning back, to tell Roberta not to interfere.

"Have you considered," Lucy went on evenly, once she'd regained her composure, "that *every* baby needs care to stay alive? That's true before birth, and it's true after birth. But the legal system in this country says you can kill before birth. Just think about that! A full-term baby isn't viable. He's still helpless after he's born, but even though he's not viable then, either, the law says you can't kill him. Do you see how absurd that is?"

Theresa did not reply. Lucy tried to make eye contact but failed. Best to allow time for reflection, she thought. She retreated downstairs when Sarah returned to the bedroom.

A new rule would require two people in Theresa's room at all times, Lucy decided, and minders should be rotated frequently so no one would feel overwhelmed by the level of Theresa's resistance on any given day.

"Everyone needs to know that Theresa is dangerous," Lucy told Janet Cahill, who hovered near the front door, clearly unnerved by the sounds that had filtered downstairs.

"No one should get close to her," Lucy added for emphasis.

"What happened?" Janet asked anxiously.

"She's feisty," Lucy said calmly, "and thinking only of herself. It's sad. You'd imagine a woman like Maureen Haig would raise a daughter who understands she's not the center of the universe. But there's so much selfishness in the world."

Janet didn't say anything. Lucy tried to smile reassuringly. "We've got to look on the bright side. If we can get her to twenty-five weeks, the baby should be viable."

"Twenty-five weeks—that's what? The middle of August," Janet pointed out. "It's only the end of May."

"Yes, I know, dear," Lucy replied.

"On the Fourth of July, my husband starts his vacation," Janet continued. "He'll be here for two weeks, and he'll want our friends to fish in the lake with him. There'll be people all over this house."

Lucy froze. "You can't let that happen," she said.

"Well, I can't stop it. What should I say to him? 'Oh, by the way, we have a kidnapped pregnant woman at the lake house.' You think he'll be OK with that? I can tell you he won't."

"He's not pro-life?"

"Of course he's pro-life. That's not the point. We're normal people, Lucy. I thought when you told me about this situation, you just wanted to bring her here for a day or two. But this is beyond anything I imagined. All Dan will see is the liability—"

"So, you're not really pro-life," Lucy interrupted.

"I'm not someone who breaks the law. If my husband finds out, he'll worry about what this could cost us if we're sued. That's how he thinks."

"Oh, my dear, please understand it's worse than that. You are a party to what we're doing. That makes you a coconspirator. You could go to prison."

Janet gasped.

"So," continued Lucy, "we have to make sure the worst doesn't happen. Think, Janet, where can we take Theresa before your husband arrives? Because it's too late for you to walk away. The Lord won't allow it. You need to find us another place as soon as possible."

Claire picked up Annie at the mailbox mid-morning June 4. It was a week to the day since she'd spoken to the FBI, but whatever the FBI was doing, she wasn't privy to it.

In Claire's world, until now, people had believed what she said. But when she talked to anyone who could look into Theresa's disappearance—an investigator at the Minnesota Bureau of Criminal Apprehension, the St. Dominic police, reporters at various newspapers and TV channels—she ran into something she could only call *routine procedural skepticism*, especially when she called people back.

An agent from the BCA had talked to her mother and her mother's friends, all of whom were forthcoming about meeting Theresa on May 9. They all denied seeing Theresa leave the Haig homestead. They didn't know where she had gone, they told the investigator.

Sheriff's department detectives had not been able to confirm a kidnapping, Claire was told. The BCA couldn't locate Lucy Meyer at the nonprofit she'd formerly worked for, nor any nonprofit directors who'd employed her recently. There was some doubt as to whether Lucy Meyer still resided in Minnesota. She had no credit card trail. She seemed to be a person who lived off the grid financially, which was highly unusual, but not illegal. Former coworkers had little to say about her.

On the other hand, no one had found Theresa either, and her father-in-law, Woodrow Cole, as well as Sheriff's deputy Antoine Harrison and Captain Roy Mortensen of the Minnesota National Guard, all confirmed parts of Claire's complaint, though none of them could offer first-hand knowledge of an abduction—if there had been an abduction. It was also suspicious, the BCA agent thought, that Claire's mother wouldn't allow them to interview Claire's underage sister, even with the mother present, and that Claire's father didn't return phone calls and was not around on the morning an investigator stopped by. Neither did he come in to talk voluntarily after they'd sent him a certified letter.

"We're in close contact with the FBI on this," the agent told Claire. "And we'll keep on it. We don't close a case until it's resolved. But at the moment, we're stymied. Some of these women have told us they expect your sister to show up any day."

Claire's last hope was the press. "Today's the earliest this reporter could fit us in," she told Annie as they headed south, adding, "She's not wildly enthusiastic."

"I'm enthusiastic," Annie said. "Driving to the Cities, eating at this famous bistro . . ."

"Cafe Latte's a cafeteria, not a bistro."

"At the same time getting closer to finding Theresa," Annie continued.

They waited in the entry hallway for nearly a half hour before Carole Novak rushed in through the double doors that shielded the cafe lobby from Grand Avenue and its traffic.

"Sorry. I'm on another story and can only stay a short time. Let's grab something," the reporter said, picking up a tray. They moved along the line.

Annie couldn't decide between soup, a sandwich, or one of the fancy salads. There were so many combinations, she thought she could probably eat at this place every day for a year without ordering the same thing twice. She decided on a sandwich on crusty sourdough with a cream cheese-based basil spread. She also ordered a cup of chili and a lemonade. Claire paid for all of them. Ms. Novak found a table and, by the time the sisters joined her, was halfway through her albacore tuna on rye.

The place was hopping. Annie craned her neck to take in the consignment art on the walls. Some of it, like the huge purple- and yellow-polka-dot ceramic pig, was funky. She thought the pig would look great in her dad's office.

"It's not enough," Carole said. "I've gone through everything you sent me, and it's not a story. Not yet at least."

"What more do you want? Tell me what you need, and I'll do my best to track it down," Claire implored.

"Look," the reporter said between her last bites of sandwich, "everything is circumstantial. Your sister here," she nodded toward Annie, "was the last person to see Theresa before she disappeared, but she didn't witness an abduction."

"I pretty much did," Annie objected. "We were supposed to meet—"

"Yes, I know," the reporter interrupted, "but that's all you can say, that you were *supposed* to meet. It doesn't mean she didn't willingly leave with one of those women, none of whom I've been able to reach, by the way. That intrigues me more than anything. When a lot of people slam the door, there's usually a story. I have, what, six names you've given me."

"More than that," Claire interrupted.

"Suzanne O'Brien, Barbara Iverson, and Kathleen Peterson—who you said was Dennis and Mary Lou's daughter-in-law—Dennis and Mary Lou, whose house *you* broke into."

"We knew my sister was there," Claire interjected.

"But you didn't see her. And the guy you were with is unreachable and from out of state. I've tried to call him."

"I'll ask him to get back to you, Carole," Claire said.

"Right." The reporter sipped her latte, shoving aside a plate of crumbs.

"I've also tried to reach Roberta Wells," she continued. "Her husband, David, runs a tech company called . . ." She flipped the notebook page. "Unique

Genetic Solutions. UGS. They're doing an IPO later this summer, and it's attracted some deep-pocket people. If—big if—I could find a link between Roberta and your sister, that might interest my editor. Although—"

"What about the detectives at the sheriff's office?"

"Zip. I spoke to Detective Jeffrey Webster. He wouldn't confirm there was an open investigation, much less what they found. You know how cops are. They tell you what everybody knows from newspapers and TV, and not much more. And what people know about your sister from newspapers and TV is nada."

"Did you talk to anyone at the FBI? Or the BCA?" Claire asked.

"They never comment. Not unless they're making an appeal to the public, which they haven't done so far in this case."

"Did you track down anything on Lucy Meyer?" Claire was practically pleading.

Carole flipped once more through her notes. "Lucy Meyer. Yeah, here. I found a picture of her on a pro-life website. She's a pediatric nurse involved in lobbying, but I couldn't find even a hint that she's done anything illegal. And no one seems to know where she is."

"Did you talk to her?"

"No. She's a hard person to reach."

"Doesn't that tell you something?" Claire asked.

"Not really. The world is full of people who can't be reached or don't return calls. She's probably a busy woman, and I'm just a reporter she doesn't need to talk to at the moment. These local women interest me more. Usually they'll talk enough to at least say sorry, they don't know anything."

"Did you talk to my mother and father?" Claire asked pointedly. "Did you go out to the farm to see where it happened?"

"I did talk to your mother. That's a further complication. She says you've claimed these things at family gatherings, and no one believes you. I offered to come out, but she told me not to in no uncertain terms. I'll tell you this, Claire. Reporters learn to respect people's rights, especially farmers. I'm not going to knock on your parents' door without a clear invitation. There's too many guns out there."

This reporter sounded like someone trying to convince herself, Annie thought.

"She left behind her wallet, her driver's license, and her cell phone," Claire said. "She left them with Annie."

"Yes, I know. But that doesn't prove she was abducted. And since the cell phone's locked, it can't tell you anything. You'd need a subpoena to get into it, and even then, you might not be able to crack it, and if you did, it might not tell you anything. You're going around in circles."

Claire couldn't think of an answer to that.

"I have to go," Carole said as she put her notebook in her shoulder bag and finished her latte. "Thanks for the food. If you come up with something concrete, call me again."

Out she went through the double set of doors, striding down Grand Avenue toward wherever she'd managed to park her car.

"Why did she even come?" Annie asked, eyeing the remains of Claire's abandoned sandwich.

"Free lunch," Claire said.

"Oh." Annie's opinion of the press had just taken a hit.

"After waiting so long for her to have time to meet, this turned into quite a letdown. I expected more," Claire said.

"Speaking of more," Annie mused, "can we order dessert? They have the most amazing-looking desserts."

Claire smiled at her sister. "Of course," she said. "You can't be here and not have dessert." She handed Annie her Visa card.

"I can't believe this!" Annie exclaimed, taking the rectangle into her open hand. "I've never held a credit card before, much less used one."

"Use away," Claire said. "On dessert, I mean. Someone should get what they want out of this."

Annie, about to dash toward the confectionary case, turned back.

"Maybe I shouldn't," she said.

"Go," Claire said.

"It's not fair when Theresa's still missing."

"Your giving up dessert won't bring her back. My alert-the-media plan isn't working, so we need another strategy. For that, at least one of us requires fuel. Go buy some calories."

Annie followed her sister's advice. When she reached the counter, she decided the double chocolate cake looked even more scrumptious than the apple tart, but then she noticed the New York cheesecake with raspberries and vanilla sauce, or—better yet—she decided she shouldn't miss the one with caramel scribblings all over the top.

—◦—

Claire had intended to drop her sister off and leave. But, at the last minute, she didn't stop the car at the driveway entrance. Without a word to Annie, she drove straight up to the house and parked. They got out of Claire's car and went in through the kitchen. Tom stood at the sink, a mug of coffee in his hand, angry as all get-out. Their neighbor's tenant, he informed

Maureen, let his high-powered pesticide drift onto Haig soybeans again, just like last year.

"He says the wind shifted," Tom railed.

"Glad you're both here," Claire said.

"I'm reporting this to the state," Tom announced. "It's already too late to expect a decent yield from replanting that field. He's gonna pay."

Maureen, seated at the kitchen table peeling potatoes, fixed her eyes on her eldest child.

"Without so much as a phone call, without even knocking, you just saunter in and out as you please," she said to Claire.

"Am I unwelcome?" Claire asked.

"You're here one day, gone the next; Catholic one day, a heathen the next; married one day, single the next. I've asked myself a million times where I went wrong with you."

"Guess I fell far from the tree," Claire told her.

"Your father takes two blood pressure pills," Maureen observed, "so I'm not going to fight with you in front of him. Sit down."

Claire nodded.

"I'm gonna call Ben Johnson," Tom declared. "Greg's taking pictures right now." He headed upstairs.

"I've come to ask you one more time: where is Theresa?" Claire said after her father disappeared. Maureen continued peeling, a bowl of scraps in front of her, the peeled potatoes on a platter. She had three to go. "You've talked to quite a few people who are looking for her, I believe," Claire added.

Her mother looked up. "What do you want from me?"

"What did you tell the sheriff's department? And the BCA? And the FBI?" Claire continued.

"Anyone who calls, I tell them the same thing I told you. I don't know where she is."

"But do you know people who know where she is?"

"How would I know what people know but don't tell me?" Maureen asked, her face inscrutable. "Theresa's thinking things out."

"Mother," Claire said slowly, remaining calm, "do you love Theresa?"

"Of course I love Theresa!" Maureen shot back. "I love all my children. I love their precious souls, and I love their future happiness in heaven, and I love their faith in their one true religion here on earth." Maureen had stopped peeling potatoes. She held the peeler upright and used it to gesticulate.

"Theresa's your daughter," Claire emphasized. "Don't you love her more than any religion?"

"No, I do not. My religion means everything to me. No one will ever take my religion away from me."

Claire put her hands on her head, leaned back, and stared at the ceiling.

"Jesus!" she erupted. "Your daughter's been missing for weeks, and all you can talk about is your religion. You're an addict."

"Do *not* take the Lord's name in vain in front of me!" Maureen declared angrily. "I didn't raise you that way."

"What's all this racket?" Tom demanded as he came back into the kitchen. "I could hear you from upstairs."

"I think you two need to face reality," Claire said, trying to regain her composure. "First of all, has it occurred to you that something really bad could have happened? Theresa's pregnant. She could have an emergency. Whoever has her, she's not seeing a doctor. She's not getting checked out at a hospital. She's heaven-knows-where, all alone with people who do not put her interests first, and she's probably desperate to get back home. She's probably worrying about her husband, for one thing. Are you both aware that Charlie's been hurt trying to get home to look for her? *Badly* hurt."

Tom sat down, and for the first time Claire thought he might be giving the situation his full attention.

"What do you mean, *badly* hurt?" he asked.

"He's in a hospital in Virginia with burns on the back of his body and who knows what kind of damage to his brain. And Theresa doesn't even know."

"What could she do if she did know?" asked Maureen.

"She could be there with him!" Claire practically screamed.

"Now, you listen to me, and you listen good," Tom said heatedly. "You don't shout at your mother, not in my house." He nodded toward Maureen. "Your mother's already told you she doesn't know where Theresa is. But if Theresa is somewhere thinking about having an abortion, and she's trying to decide what to do, well, you know where we stand on that subject."

"Indeed I do," Claire said, "but do you know where you stand on kidnapping and criminal conspiracy?"

"What are you talking about?" Tom snapped.

"I told you last Sunday. I'm talking about a crime." Her voice rose. "I'm talking about felony conspiracy to kidnap, felony conspiracy to commit false imprisonment every single day she's held against her will, felony reckless endangerment, especially if something goes wrong and she's injured. If you play any part in a conspiracy, if you even know a crime is going to happen, you're just as guilty as the people who carry it out. You could be arrested. What's more, Theresa could sue you once she gets free. If she died, her husband could sue you for everything you own. Ask your lawyer. Go upstairs and call him again. Maybe he can enlighten you."

"I think you'd better leave now," Tom said quietly. "And don't come back until you can show your mother and me more respect. We don't have to listen to these crazy accusations."

Annie stared at the floor, shaken by what she'd just learned. She didn't even see Claire depart. Never before had she comprehended the meaning of *conspiracy*. She'd known the word *felony* for a long time. But she hadn't realized that being involved in something bad, or maybe even just knowing that it's going to happen, might make someone as guilty as those who actually commit a crime that they maybe don't even think is a real crime.

Now, of course, it all made sense. She imagined her mother getting arrested. She imagined Theresa's husband sending lawyers from Alabama to put her whole family out of their house and off their farm. What would happen then?

She refused to think that far ahead. What did any of it matter if Theresa never got free, if her husband never got to see her again? She was his wife. Annie sometimes forgot that. It made Theresa his next of kin. He would be within his rights to sue her family. She remained in her chair long after Claire left.

Her father went off without saying one word more. Her mother finished the last potato, taking a chunk out of her knuckle with a clumsy move. She had to rush to the bathroom to find a bandage. That was unusual. Her mother must have peeled a million potatoes in her life, but she never cut herself doing it.

———•◦•———

Tom sat on the bed in his underwear. He was not a tall man, but he made up for height with muscle. His legs could hoist a half-grown calf, as he'd demonstrated on many occasions. His biceps bulged. His chest remained as hard and taut as when he was a kid working his ass off for a father who considered praise a poison. Never done, never satisfied. That was the Haig family motto.

Of course, Tom had acquired a bit of a belly over the years, the inevitable consequence of Maureen's talents in the kitchen. There was always a pie or cake around, sometimes both, and they bought ice cream in five-gallon pails from the creamery in St. Dominic. Whenever Maureen noticed his middle getting bigger, sweets would disappear, and he'd endure a month or more without the sensual delight of fat and sugar melting in his mouth. He'd take the deprivation just so long, until one fine day he'd threaten to buy a cake himself. Whether she believed him or not, Maureen would start baking again.

Theirs was a solid union. Tom was too old for her, but it had never seemed to matter. They'd met at a church-sponsored dance with no beer or liquor served, the kind he ordinarily wouldn't have stepped foot in, but a friend of his was looking for a girl who'd left him in a lurch, and Tom went along for support.

Seconds after they walked in, he saw Maureen. Nineteen, golden hair like a halo, thin as a reed and tall, but not too tall. It was her face that magnetized him. There might have been a hundred girls in that hall, but she was the only one who didn't look self-conscious. He knew she knew how beautiful she was. She deserved a younger, better-looking man, but that didn't warn Tom off, far from it. He'd surged through the crowd, stopped on a dime, bowed his head and took her hand to his lips, kissed it, and asked in a whisper, "Can I have this dance?"

Nobody else in the county was smart enough to kiss a girl's hand. He knew that for a fact. They'd consider it "sophisticated," a pejorative to most folk. Plain people don't put on airs. They mind their manners and live a no-frills, salt-of-the-earth life. Tom met that standard among men, but women were different. He had made a study of what the fair sex liked, and they liked it when you kissed their hands. Tom was ready to settle down. He picked Maureen at first sight, and damn it, he would kiss her hand.

She smiled and looked him in the eye as he did it. He practically proposed on the spot, holding off only because he didn't want to spook her. A band on a makeshift stage played the melody to "I Will Always Love You." He hadn't been able to hear the tune since without feeling something of the awe he'd felt the first time he'd met his wife.

Tom's love for Maureen had grown, not diminished, over their years of high fertility and uncertain income. Love is the thing that feeds itself. He saw how she'd supported him through thick and thin, so of course he'd supported her. It was a matter of principle, even about Theresa.

However, Maureen had assured him their daughter would think things over and come back on her own—or call, at least. Where was she? It was damn near the middle of June.

"It's taking too long," he said.

Maureen didn't look at him or respond to his observation.

Tom remembered the day they got married, a cool Saturday in April 1978. Her girlfriends were the bridesmaids, and Tom's brother was best man. Both sets of parents looked none too happy. Maureen's mother couldn't get over the fourteen-year difference in their ages.

"He'll be an old man when you're in your prime," she'd cautioned her daughter right in front of Tom.

"We'll get old together," Maureen had countered. No one could dissuade her. Scarcely a year later, she'd cradled Mary in her arms, their firstborn, a daughter.

Maureen had wanted a son. She'd made that clear to everybody. She said she'd felt in her bones that God would give her a son. Her disappointment was so keen, she cried for weeks after the baby was born and counted herself abandoned, except for Tom.

Tom's mother, Miriam, did most of the diaper changing. She'd washed Mary's little outfits, many of them from her keepsake trunk of things her own daughters had worn. She'd stitched a multicolored quilt to fit the baby's crib. She'd tried to convince Maureen to breastfeed, but in that, she failed. Mary had to settle for a bottle and a mother who felt not much of a bond.

The very idea of suckling an infant seemed an additional humiliation to Maureen. "As if I'm a cow in a barn," she'd said. Tom never understood, but he hadn't argued. He'd stepped in to make things right, fussing over Mary from the day she was born.

For weeks after Mary's birth, Tom's mother did everything. Maureen hadn't the energy to even get out of bed. Later, when she had so many other children and Miriam became too fragile to help much, there was no excuse for Maureen not to rise and shine at dawn.

"I said, this is taking too long," Tom repeated. He hated it when Maureen refused to answer. Two weeks ago, when she'd locked herself in the bathroom after Mary and Theresa's father-in-law barged in, all he'd heard through the door was her crying. Tom was sick of that nonsense.

"You're sitting on the bedspread," Maureen pointed out.

"What?"

"You're sitting on the white chenille embroidered bedspread that I saved for out of my household allowance and bought on sale at Macy's. It's six weeks old and it's been washed exactly once, and I'm not ready to wash it again. Washing wears things out."

Tom got up. "Oh, sorry, madam," he said, "for dirtying your bedspread while our daughter is who-knows-where and in-what-condition and the FBI could come knocking on our door any minute."

Maureen flinched. "Theresa is fine," she said, not meeting his gaze.

"How in tarnation do you know? You have no idea!"

"I *know*," Maureen said, her face set in a way that had once amused him.

"If you know so damn much, tell me where she is, and I'll get her home tonight."

"I know she's OK. I do not know exactly where she is."

"Then you don't know she's OK," Tom shot back. "And you don't know we're not committing a crime."

"That's what you're worried about, isn't it? You're worried someone might arrest us or sue us, and you'll have to pay for it out of the farm."

Tom came toward her and stood within an inch of her nose. He waited a moment before speaking. When Tom was deadly serious, she sometimes had to strain to hear him.

"No, Maureen, I'm not worried about the farm. The farm won't be touched, you can be sure of that. No, I'm worried about you. I'm worried that you've been lied to by some looney-tunes people who talked you into handing over your daughter against her will. If that's not the case, you pick up the goddamn phone right now and call her. You call whoever is with her and tell 'em you want to talk to her right now, and while you're at it, tell 'em I'm coming to get her."

Maureen's eyes filled with tears. "How can I explain this situation to a man who doesn't take his faith seriously?" she implored. "They told me not to call. They'll call me. Theresa's about fifteen weeks along. They need to get her to twenty weeks or twenty-five weeks or whatever it takes so she can't kill her baby. Why won't you see that? You're worried about our daughter. I'm worried about our grandchild. A tiny, defenseless baby!"

Maureen fell against him, her head in the sweet spot on his sternum. He knew she could hear his heart beating. He could hear his heart beating.

"No," he said. "I can't see that. I see outsiders meddling in our family, and I don't like it one damn bit. You call these people tomorrow. You tell them either I sit down with my daughter and talk to her myself, or I'll go to the sheriff and the FBI both."

He turned away, and with an excessive swing, pulled the bedspread off the bed, bunched it up, and threw it on the armchair. He was about to get in between the sheets when he changed his mind and strode toward the door.

"I need a goddamn whiskey," he said, not bothering to pull on a bathrobe.

"Language," Maureen whispered. "Watch your language, please."

Woodrow had become a familiar sight at the laundromat down the street from his motel. He kept to a schedule that included washing his bare-bones wardrobe every third day and the sheets and towels he'd bought for his bare-bones room, twice a week. It was hot and humid both. A man needed to sweat.

He ate every noon in the Richmond VA cafeteria on the ground floor of the Polytrauma System, a sprawling area dedicated to caring for soldiers with injuries to multiple body parts, and in particular, brain injury. Every day he sat alongside Charlie's bed, talked to him, played music—anything

Charlie liked—read from whatever took his fancy at the public library two blocks away, put his mother on the phone next to Charlie's ear so her familiar voice could reach him, and conferred with doctors in the lounge down the hall.

He had breakfast at 6:00 a.m., lunch at noon, and dinner at 6:00 p.m., where he'd grab food at random from the buffet line and eat as fast as possible to get back upstairs.

Every day he ran the distance between his room in the rundown, non-air-conditioned Blue Tree Inn to the hospital wing where Charlie waited unaware of his father's presence. Woodrow clocked his time on a runner's watch. He made the 1,895 yards in just under 7 minutes, 10.4 seconds, and he intended to take a few more seconds off if this waiting lasted much longer. Woodrow had always been a runner. Now he felt not only that his being there, but his running back and forth somehow contributed to Charlie's chances of regaining what he'd lost. He knew it was crazy, but it kept him calm, and he hoped that calm might seep into Charlie.

A major named Newcome was in Charlie's room when Woodrow returned from the hospital cafeteria a few minutes short of 6:30 p.m. on Monday, June 18. He was one of the center's top neurologists, and from the beginning, he hadn't seemed overly optimistic. That day, Newcome shone a light in Charlie's eyes as he had a hundred times before. He wrote something in the chart and turned around as Woodrow sat in a chair on the other side of the bed. The monitors looked the same as they had every other day, beeping and squeaking in what sounded like a primitive chant.

"Would you come down to the lounge with me?" he asked.

"Sure," Woodrow said, standing up.

They walked along the glossy beige corridor, painted the same on all surfaces like a tunnel in a space station. The lounge was small—just a bench and two chairs. The major sat on one of the chairs. Woodrow sat two feet away on the other.

"I'm concerned about Charlie's reaction to stimuli," Newcome began. "I'm not seeing much of a range."

Woodrow drew a deep breath.

"When we put him at a deeper level of unconsciousness, during debridement for example, I expect to see less reaction to any stimuli, and that's what we're seeing. But in between, when we reduce the level, I expect to see more reaction, especially when the stimuli mean something to him. For example, I can't see a difference when you talk to him. We've tested him, looking for responses with various audio and video cues, and they're just not there."

"What does that mean?"

"It can mean many things. We ought not jump to conclusions. But I'm wondering if we could bring in other stimuli. His wife, for example. I see her listed in his paperwork. Looks like he's a newlywed. Could she spend time with him the way you're doing?"

"I don't know where she is," Woodrow said, not knowing how else to put it.

"They're separated?" asked the major.

"She's missing," said Woodrow.

"Excuse me for asking, but is this a Dear John situation? If so, there might be a psychological reason—"

"Hell, no!" Woodrow said. "She's physically missing and has been since May ninth. We think she was abducted. That's why Charlie was in that damn convoy. He got leave to come back and find her."

The major looked at Woodrow, nonplussed. "Sounds like a goddamn clusterfuck."

Woodrow nodded.

"You have no idea where she is? Her relatives don't know where she is?"

"Her sister's looking for her but hasn't found her yet. I keep in touch. They're in Minnesota."

"Was there any trouble between them before she went missing?"

"No, they were fine. She's expecting a baby, and they were both pretty excited. Then she found out something was wrong with the baby, and the next thing we knew, she went missing. Her sister and I think she was abducted to keep her from aborting the baby."

"Jesus!" the major whispered. He stared at the wall. "What about Charlie's mother? Is she in the picture?"

"She abandoned him a couple weeks after Charlie was born. He's met her maybe twice. For all intents and purposes, his gramma is his mama. By that, I mean my mother."

"Could your mother come here?"

"She could, but it's not gonna be easy. She pretty much runs things at home. She talks to Charlie over the phone, though. I put the piece to his ear. He can hear her voice."

The major nodded. "Well, let me tell you how I see the situation. Charlie's back is going to heal. The debridement has gone well. Thing about war is that it's great for medical advancement. We've learned more about burns in the past eight years than we did in the previous fifty. Now—" he paused. "Charlie is going to have scars, but mostly they'll be under his clothes. We can give him, on the outside, something close to what he had going in. We can even transplant hair, so the back of his head looks good. His brain's the tricky part. There aren't any bleeds we can detect, and the inflammation is down. But there's no sign of consciousness or even pre-consciousness."

He paused again, as the two men looked each other in the eye. "We're still in our infancy when it comes to TBI," the major continued. "It would help if Charlie could be coaxed out of unconsciousness. Human will is a big factor in healing, and I've found women can make an enormous difference, maybe because they tend to talk more, especially if they have an intimate history with the patient. They're the ones who might get to him on the deepest level. If you could find his wife, or if you could get his grandma here, that would help. That, and time."

The major stood up, shook Woodrow's hand, and left. Woodrow sat for a moment, trying to suppress his temper. He certainly didn't want to go right back to see his son in the state he was in.

Perhaps, he thought, Rebecca could find someone else to take care of the grandkids and let his brothers run the business so she could fly to Richmond. He knew she wanted to, though she hated delegating power.

He decided to call Claire from a bench outside the building. She answered immediately.

"Where are you?" he asked, too impatient to indulge in idle conversation.

"Just got back to St. Paul. I had it out with my parents this afternoon."

"So, you're tellin' me there's no news since the last time we talked?"

"I'm doing my best, Woodrow. I'm trying to get the press interested and—"

"Charlie needs her here *now*," Woodrow interrupted. "He's still unconscious, and they don't like the way he doesn't react to anything."

"Woodrow, I'm sorry. I'm doing everything I can to find her. Are you in Richmond?"

"Yeah. Outside the hospital."

"And you don't see any improvement?"

"His color looks good. They change the dressings on his back every day. He spends a lot of time on his stomach or even suspended. He's breathin' on his own, so that's a plus. But he won't wake up. His neurologist thinks if we had Theresa here, that would help rouse him."

"Finding her is my full-time job. I've talked to the FBI any number of times."

"I've talked to the FBI too. I feel like we're spinnin' our wheels."

"I'm going to find a way. I promise."

Woodrow exhaled audibly. "Yeah," he said. He sounded as if he were signing off.

"Wait! Something occurs to me . . . Do you have power of attorney for Charlie?"

"He signed some paperwork before he went on his first tour. That might have been part of it."

"Could you use your power of attorney to make a complaint with the FBI on Charlie's behalf? That might motivate them more."

Woodrow didn't respond.

"Are you there?" Claire said.

"Yeah, yeah . . . I'll do it."

———•◦•———

Maureen tried calling Lucy Meyer every morning using the number Lucy had given her in the kitchen the day they took Theresa away. But Lucy's voice mail was always full. Maureen didn't know what else to do. It didn't help that Tom kept pestering her.

Then, one day, she remembered she'd hid Lucy's business card in a compartment in her black leather purse. The card, she saw after retrieving it, was imprinted with Lucy's name, the words *Obstetrics Nurse and Licensed Midwife*, plus an eight hundred number. Just before noon on Monday, June 25, she punched the number into the wall phone.

It rang four times before someone answered. A young woman's voice said, "SAB, can I help you?" There was static on the line.

"I'm trying to reach Lucy Meyer," Maureen practically shouted. "Can you hear me?"

"I can hear you perfectly well," the woman answered in a normal tone.

"I'm trying to reach Lucy Meyer," Maureen repeated.

"May I ask what this is in regard to?"

"I need to talk to her about my daughter, Theresa Haig."

"Would you hold a moment?"

"Yes," Maureen replied. Several minutes passed before the woman came back.

"Are you still on the line, Mrs. Haig?" she asked.

"Yes, I am," Maureen said. Her heart pounded as she heard Tom come into the kitchen from outside.

"I have instructions for you, and I'd like you to follow them carefully. First, I want you to go to a store like Target and buy a phone with prepaid minutes. When you have that phone, I want you to call this number. Do you have pencil and paper?"

"Yes," Maureen said, "but what's wrong with the phone I'm using?"

"Nothing, except that Lucy is not available on that phone."

She gave Maureen a number, and Maureen wrote it down. When she turned around, Tom stood next to the kitchen table.

"What did they say?" he demanded.

"That I need to buy a new phone at Target. It's got to be prepaid. She gave me another number for Lucy."

"Lucy—that's the goofball you've been dealing with?"

"She's a nurse."

"You met her?"

"Yes."

"And now she won't talk to you except on a phone that can't be traced?"

Maureen pulled a chair out from the table and sat down. "That's why I can't reach her?" she asked Tom.

Tom picked up the scrap of paper with the number. "This is what you're supposed to call on the burner phone?"

"I've never even heard of these different phones," Maureen complained. She met his gaze. "Tom, you said call the people who know where Theresa is. That's what I've been doing. This is the first time I got through. But they wouldn't let me talk to Lucy."

"Well then, you'd better go buy yourself a phone the sheriff can't tap. If you need any more proof something's illegal, this is it." He went back out the kitchen door.

Maureen seethed. First of all, she'd been honest with him, and he'd agreed on moral principle that Theresa needed to make up her mind to keep her baby. He just didn't want Theresa's absence to be against the law now that Mary had made such a point of it. As if there were any choice in the matter of what the law said versus what God wanted.

Maureen took her wallet out of her purse, slipped it into the pocket of her dress along with the new number for Lucy, went outside into the too-bright sunshine, got into her ten-year-old Ford sedan, and drove to the Target store at Crossroads Center. Lunch would have to wait.

It took less than ten minutes to find the kind of phone the woman had described, have it rung up, and get herself back to the parking lot. She read the phone's instructions several times, checked the number she'd written down and punched it in, standing next to her car with no one close enough to overhear. She wanted, when she got back, to be able to tell Tom where Theresa was.

Lucy answered on the second ring. "Lucy, this is Maureen Haig. We need to talk . . ." Maureen blurted out.

"Where are you, Maureen?"

"In the Target parking lot. On this phone I just bought."

"It's not a smart phone?"

"It's a prepaid phone. Lucy, where is Theresa?"

Her question met a few terrifying seconds of silence. Then Lucy said, "She's having trouble. Her blood pressure is high. I had to do something, so, I decided this morning to get her a puppy. I'm on my way to pick it up. It was born three weeks ago, a bichon frise. I thought it would help her take her mind off herself."

"My husband wants to talk to her."

"I don't think that's a good idea, Maureen. It would probably raise her blood pressure even more."

"Lucy, he doesn't like it that she's there against her will."

"What did you expect, Maureen? We couldn't convince her. We had no choice. And look at what we've gained. Going on two months more precious time for her baby to grow and not be ripped out like a burst appendix." Lucy sounded angry.

"Tom wants her home. So do I," Maureen insisted. "We know she needs more time to think—"

"She needs two additional months, at least. She needs enough time that she can't find an abortionist," Lucy said, regaining her composure. "Enough time so the baby's viable," Lucy added.

Lucy was right. In her heart, Maureen understood that, even if Tom didn't. They'd come this far. They couldn't afford to let Theresa find some crazy doctor who'd perform a late-term abortion now. But the pressure of a possible criminal situation had somehow appeared. Even Lucy seemed worried about it, with all this secret-phone business.

"A normal pregnancy is forty weeks," Lucy continued after letting her previous comments sink in. "We're supposedly in week sixteen or seventeen, though I have to tell you, Maureen, I think she's further along. It's just a feeling, but I've had a lot of experience."

"How much further along do you think she might be?"

"It's hard to guess without an ultrasound to show us the size of the baby's head. But in any case, she needs more time. We have to give her that."

"I know she needs more time," Maureen admitted. "But she also needs to see her parents. We should be the ones convincing her. She doesn't know that her husband was hurt in Afghanistan. She'll want to see him. And Tom's worried that what we're doing is against the law, and that it's not fair to Theresa. He'll never forgive me if—"

"*Stop*," Lucy said with finality. She let a few moments pass, then returned, her tone conciliatory. "Maureen, do you know much about civil rights?"

"No, but—"

"People who fought the battle for civil rights knew they had to break the law, yet they didn't flinch because they knew right was on their side. And the same with suffragettes. They were put in prison, but they endured because they knew right was on their side—"

"I want to see her," Maureen said as emphatically as Lucy had pronounced the word *stop*.

"Soon," Lucy replied. "Hold off a few more weeks, and I'll arrange for you to see her, I promise."

"Tom too."

"We'll talk about that later," Lucy said.

"I think her father could convince her better than anyone," Maureen argued.

"I don't think she can be convinced. She's unusually headstrong."

"All my girls are headstrong. I've never been able to tell them anything. Boys are so much easier."

Lucy laughed. "Somehow, I doubt your husband is easy."

"No," Maureen agreed. "But neither am I. Lucy, you have to tell us where she is. We have to see her."

"She's safe. For the rest, you need to trust in the Lord, Maureen."

"We have a right to know how she's doing," Maureen persisted. Lucy didn't answer. It took Maureen several moments to realize the line was dead. She stared at the phone, wondering what in the world she would tell Tom.

Then, suddenly, she knew.

She had allowed herself to be caught up in the same foolish panic that gripped her suspicious husband, her sweet, skeptical, doubting-Thomas husband, who, like the apostle, refused to believe what he could not see. Jesus had appeared to all the others. But not to Thomas, who refused to embrace the truth of the Resurrection until he had seen it for himself in the form of Christ risen from the dead.

That's what Lucy was trying to tell her. Keep Tom at bay until we can show him proof of God's will in the form of Theresa's living, breathing baby. Only when he saw that miracle would her husband accept that holding Theresa against her will had been in her own best interest—that what they were doing was right.

"Thomas, because thou hast seen me, thou hast believed: blessed are they that have not seen, and yet have believed."

Maureen knew in her heart of hearts that she and Lucy were standing on the path of righteousness for His name's sake. She had wavered, but Lucy had set her straight.

"Maureen, decline to be interviewed any further. No more phone conversations. Are we agreed on that?" Ben said.

On Thursday, June 28, 2018, Maureen and Tom Haig sat on wooden chairs in front of the desk of Tom's longtime attorney, Benjamin T. Johnson, who maintained a general law office in downtown St. Dominic. Tom had given Maureen two weeks from the night they'd argued in their bedroom to get Theresa home. He'd given her an additional two weeks only because she was positive Theresa was safe and just needed more time to think. But now the two weeks were up, and Theresa was still not back. Tom proposed going to the BCA to talk to the agent who'd sent him a registered letter.

Once upon a time, newly licensed and just starting out, Ben Johnson had been Tom's father's lawyer. Ben was in his eighties now, but he still ran a solo practice, charging an hourly rate below any other attorney in town, and much less than those *mercenaries* in the Cities, as everyone called lawyers in Minneapolis and St. Paul.

"What should we do about the BCA letter to Tom?" Maureen asked Ben.

"Refer the BCA to me, Tom," Ben emphasized. "Keep in mind, you are under no obligation to submit to anyone's interrogation, absent a subpoena." He handed Maureen a half dozen business cards. "Anybody comes around, give them one of these."

Tom interrupted. "This Lucy Meyer won't tell Maureen where Theresa is. Shouldn't we make a point of telling that to these investigators?"

"You can't volunteer her name without involving yourselves—at least Maureen can't," Ben countered. "You were in the house when this person, this Lucy Meyer, injected your daughter with some kind of chemical agent?" he asked, looking squarely at Maureen.

Maureen blushed. She felt as if she were on trial, with Ben Johnson acting as judge and jury. Yes, she had not intervened, she admitted, though she had been dumbfounded. All she knew now was that Theresa was safe. She was being well cared for. She was *not* getting an abortion.

"But you don't know where your daughter is?" Ben asked, again addressing Maureen.

"No, I don't," Maureen affirmed, "and that's what I told everybody who called."

Ben looked stricken. "Did you tell them about the injection . . ."

"No, of course not," Maureen said.

"What did you tell them?"

"I told them what I told those nice sheriff's detectives. That I thought Theresa was with friends, but I don't know where. When they ask about my older daughter, I tell them she's an unstable person, so I don't put much store in what she says. If they ask if Tom and I are worried about Theresa's absence, I say I was more concerned a year ago when she decided to go live in Alabama after she married someone she hardly knew."

Ben looked at her a long moment without saying anything. Then he looked at Tom. Tom bit his lower lip. Ben knew Tom hated to go against Maureen, that he loved his wife more than life itself.

"I'm not OK with any of this," Tom said. "I want Theresa back, and I want her back now. But I don't want Maureen getting arrested. That's why we're here. Can you help us figure this out, Ben?"

"Well, first thing, we've got to get Theresa home," Ben said. "If that means telling the truth to the BCA about how she was taken, or telling whoever else can help us, I think you've got to do that, but not without talking to a criminal attorney first. I'm not a criminal attorney."

Tom exhaled audibly.

"Another thing, as an officer of the court, I have to report to the authorities that there's a possibility an abduction occurred, and that it may be ongoing," Ben explained. "But as your family attorney, I don't have to tell them who informed me about the abduction. That's covered by attorney-client privilege."

"We're your clients on this?" Tom asked.

"You'd better be somebody's clients," Ben shot back.

Maureen shook her head. "I still hope and pray Theresa will come to her senses." Her voice cracked.

"What the hell does that mean?" Tom demanded.

"It means she comes to her senses and lets everybody know she'll have her baby, that she won't try to hurt him. Then Lucy could bring her back to us and we could forget any of this ever happened."

Ben Johnson stood up and walked out from behind his desk. He turned away from the two of them, both still seated, paced a moment, and then turned back to face them.

"You two, Maureen especially, have put yourself in serious legal jeopardy. If the FBI or the BCA, one or the other, talks to enough people to eventually get a judge to sign a warrant, and then if you're arrested and booked, and possibly compelled to appear at a preliminary hearing—well, you're going to need a criminal defense lawyer then for sure, maybe one for each of you."

"Why would I need one?" Tom asked indignantly.

"You've kept quiet, Tom. I know you were hoping for the best and trying to protect Maureen, but the plain fact is, for weeks you've made yourself an accessory after the fact. You'll need someone to defend you too. Now I know a few attorneys here in St. Dominic who do criminal defense, but to be honest, you'd be better off getting someone from the Cities. It won't be cheap, but you've got to do it. I'd suggest you do it before you talk to the BCA or anyone else."

"Are you saying you can't represent Maureen and me both on this?"

"No, I can't," Ben said. "I don't do criminal law. It would be malpractice for me to defend either one of you, especially if the state, or worse, the FBI is involved. They could arrest Maureen before Theresa shows up. Or Theresa could show up and sign a criminal complaint against Maureen. Or maybe something happens to Theresa while she's being held. That's the worst outcome. We've got to think about all those possibilities. You're going to need an experienced criminal lawyer to help you through it." He paused and then spoke again, in a softer voice. "At the same time, I'm telling you to do everything you can to get Theresa back, pronto. Until she's back, your legal jeopardy is the least of your worries."

Tom and Maureen were out on the sidewalk five minutes later, both silent as they made their way to Tom's car. Maureen knew she was testing his limits. Her job all these years, in his mind, had been to eliminate distractions so he could run the farm. She was at fault if her actions increased distractions. Her actions had certainly increased distractions now.

But what could she have done differently? she asked herself. She could not, absolutely could not, have hung up the phone on Lucy Meyer that day when she and Dr. Ryan called from the clinic to say that Maureen's daughter, a Haig child who was also a Catholic girl from a good Catholic family, was maybe going to commit abortion.

Abortion meant kill "a fetus," as they called it in their women's lib brochures, pretending it was not an infant with fingernails and a beating heart and the face of an angel.

Maureen had done the right thing in preventing Theresa from getting into her car with her suitcase all packed to go off and find an abortionist. The sight of her daughter with a suitcase at the bottom of the stairs, and then Theresa trying to get past the women who simply wanted to talk to her, had infuriated Maureen.

How could she have known that preventing an abortion would turn into a criminal offense and start a police investigation? Or that their own small-town family attorney would tell them to hire some highfalutin criminal lawyer from the Cities so they wouldn't get thrown in prison by the FBI?

It was so unfair. She'd always felt that catastrophes were not supposed to happen to decent people who did nothing wrong. They happened to trashy people who did terrible things. She could never, ever have imagined that her favorite daughter would force her into this embarrassing "legal jeopardy."

Tom remained silent as he put the car in gear and drove home. After they turned into the driveway, he finally spoke. "I'm going to ask Ben to find us a criminal lawyer. You're going to do whatever you need to do to get Theresa back here safe and sound. And I mean *now*."

Maureen didn't reply. She knew it was still too early. Tom could hire all the criminal lawyers he wanted, but Theresa should not come back until the danger of her getting an abortion was over.

They needed to trust the Lord to sort this out. Maureen knew that, as surely as she knew that she lived and breathed.

3

Theresa realized immediately that they were lying when they said they'd found the puppy. It showed no sign of hardship. The creature's fur was clean and smelled of shampoo. It definitely arrived with a purpose.

Over the course of her captivity, Theresa had gradually gained a measure of freedom by pretending to accept her situation. Since not long after that revolting day when they'd tied her to the bed, she'd been able to move around the room without interference as long as she didn't threaten anyone. They were always on guard. She knew she couldn't overpower two of them at the same time. Inevitably, if one woman were in the room with her, another stood nearby or just outside the door.

They kept the bedroom door locked with an outside deadbolt, installed by Lucy herself on the second—and now—this third prison cell. Lucy was taking no chances after their one and only physical confrontation, the face-off with the nasogastric tube, an apparatus that still haunted Theresa's dreams. The only response, she'd decided, was to disarm. She became an actress bent on lulling them into complacency.

On occasion, Theresa could hear conversations in the kitchen below by pressing her ear against a vent in the adjoining bathroom wall, something she did in response to any commotion downstairs. When she detected Lucy's arrival one morning with a yipping companion in tow, Theresa figured out the plan—to use this creature, whatever it was, as a distraction to improve her mood, lower her blood pressure, and give her something to love. Theresa steeled herself to resist their machinations.

But her heart melted the moment she saw those tiny paws and wide-set black eyes. Theresa allowed the puppy to crawl all over her. The poor thing, ripped too soon from his mother, was desperate for attention. Out of her own desperation, Theresa gave in, just as her captors expected her to give in on the pregnancy.

She named him Pal. She knew they could take him away at any time—in effect, weaponize him—but she couldn't ignore the fact that Pal gave back every bit of love he got.

Her world had shrunk to the confines of a bedroom and en suite bath. From the windows, she could see grassy marshland beyond a sprawling yard. There were no telephone poles or other utilities. They must be underground, suggesting an upscale location. The furniture looked expensive, as did the embossed wallpaper—cherry blossoms against an aqua background, intense enough to drive an occupant mad.

The meals were getting better. They seemed to be paying attention to what she ate and what she left on the plate. A bag of Taste of the Wild Grain-Free Puppy Kibbles sat on the dresser along with two ceramic bowls—one for Pal's food, the other for his water. She fed him three times a day and gave him plenty of affection, though never in the presence of her jailers, who at least no longer stayed in her room all the time.

Yet, even if the conditions of her captivity had improved, she was as much a prisoner as ever. She knew days were turning into weeks. The boredom was unbearable. She remained passive and mostly silent, waiting for an opportunity to flee.

Lucy did not appear much anymore, perhaps in recognition of the rage her presence provoked in the *patient*, the phrase they used to describe her.

"How is our patient this morning? Look what you have for breakfast!"

At least twice a day, one of them took her blood pressure and wrote it in a notebook, smiling triumphantly when the numbers were good. Her belly was growing. They liked that. They brought her hideous maternity outfits. She had to wear some of them because her own clothes had disappeared in the laundry.

Theresa thought about Charlie all the time. Was he searching for her, or was he still with his unit? If they let her Skype him, she'd wear anything they wanted. That request they ignored. She knew why. If Charlie figured out where she was, he'd come. If he could use some kind of GPS tracker, he could pinpoint this place. The army would charge in, and these women would be arrested.

She began to entertain violent fantasies, especially when they put her arm in the blood pressure cuff, or worse, drew blood. Obviously, Roberta had been trained because in less than a minute she stuck the needle in, got her sample, and covered the entry point with cotton and surgical tape. The procedure underscored Theresa's status as a conveyance to them, a carrier of cargo.

Resistance to their little checkups seemed useless. They threatened to hold her down if she tried, and so she went limp. But she refused to make a fist. If she made a fist, she told Roberta, it would be to give her a black eye.

She instantly regretted that remark. How could she feign lassitude if she let Roberta know how she really felt?

Time dragged on. She imagined Charlie giving her advice. You need to strategize, he'd say. Before a mission, his unit would decide together what to do. She was the entire unit in this situation, a one-person team designed to escape. But how?

She had no descent path. The windows opened, but it was too far down to jump. Tree branches weren't near enough to grab. Casements hugged the house. There weren't any flower boxes or vertical pipes to hang onto. Sometimes Theresa just sat on the bed, feeling helpless. Often, she slept all day, desperate to shut out reality. Charlie's voice came to her in dreams.

"Stop it," he said. "You can't afford to fall apart. Think, Theresa."

Occasionally, she heard muffled voices downstairs and rushed to the bathroom. It was usually Roberta and another of her captors—often Barbara Iverson, a longtime friend of her mother's. She heard Barbara's voice but rarely saw her.

Why didn't her mother show up? Her mother had been part of this plot from the beginning. Theresa imagined confronting her when she got free. If she got free.

"No ifs," Charlie's voice said. "It's not a question of *if.* It's a question of when."

Pal stared at her. Theresa buried her face in the belly of the little beast, and he growled a warning. She turned him over and rubbed her nose in his fur.

"Sweetie," she whispered, "we'll get out of this, I promise."

———•◦•———

Woodrow called Claire the morning Charlie opened his eyes. It had been the glummest Fourth of July Claire could remember, until her phone went off in the late afternoon.

"That's the best news I've heard since Theresa disappeared," she told Woodrow.

"He's not totally back," Woodrow admitted. "He hasn't said anything intelligible, but his brain waves look better, and they think he'll regain full consciousness soon, maybe today or tomorrow."

"You must be so happy."

"I surely am. They said once he's fully conscious, they'll do more brain scans, and if they see what they want to see, they might transfer him to Birmingham."

"What will you say to him about Theresa?" Claire asked.

"The truth. Even when the truth is bad, lies are worse."

"How's your mother doing in that regard? Handling the truth, I mean."

"She's a positive woman, but she asks a lot of questions. I let her know that Charlie's back is lookin' closer to normal. His skin is streaked in places, and they may have to do more grafts, but he's healin' OK. They reduced his pain meds. They had him on fentanyl. We know people whose kids got addicted, and we don't want that to happen to Charlie, so she was glad to hear he's off it. She asked me to send pictures, but I told her not yet. That's Charlie's call."

"Of course," Claire agreed.

"How're you doin'?"

"I'm feeling bad," Claire admitted.

"Isn't feelin' bad normal for you?"

"No," she said defensively. "Normally, I'm fine, as long as my siblings aren't being abducted."

"I gotta tell you, that first day I saw you comin' down the stairs at your school in St. Paul, you looked about as down as a body can get. And that was before you knew anything about Theresa."

"Just what I need," Claire shot back. "You're quite a morale-builder."

"Hey, I'm just relayin' facts . . ."

"Are we working for the same outcome or not?" she interjected.

"Course we are."

"Well, this depressed person is putting posters everywhere, on trees, windows, fence posts . . . And they all have the word *Missing* in ninety-two-point type, with Theresa's picture ten inches high and my phone number at the bottom. The message says *Theresa Cole, wife of a wounded American soldier, is missing and believed abducted. If you see this woman, call the number below.*"

"That sounds real good."

Claire was pleased to hear an apologetic tone. "Annie and some of her friends are helping," Claire told him.

"Annie's a gem," Woodrow observed.

"And since we don't want our posters torn down, we ask permission first."

"But no calls?" asked Woodrow.

"Not yet."

"Your mama still no help?"

"No. Neither is the FBI. I keep calling them. I think they're working on it, but so far, they haven't been able to get anyone to admit that Theresa didn't leave of her own free will."

"Well, keep the faith."

"I'm not big on faith, Woodrow. I can deal with people, facts, and real-life consequences, but so far, the forces of law and order want evidence I can't provide. And the real-life consequences are that Theresa is going to be forced to have a baby she doesn't want."

"Darlin'," Woodrow interrupted, "take a day off and sleep."

Claire forced a laugh. "When all the posters are up," she said, banishing any trace of depression from her voice.

———•◦•———

Maureen invited Ben Johnson over for coffee and a chat. She'd thought about having him come to the house for a private conversation on the previous Friday, the day after she and Tom had met with those lawyers in Minneapolis, but she decided to hold off until Monday. The previous Friday had been the thirteenth of July. Anything that happened on a Friday the thirteenth belonged to the devil, she felt. No one had ever told her such a thing. It wasn't in scripture, as far as she knew. It certainly wasn't in the New Testament or in one of Saint Paul's epistles. But Maureen had always sensed that Friday the thirteenth, like the smoky aura that sometimes appears around a crescent moon on waning autumn nights, or the corpse of a crow laying in one's path, or even a household mishap that resulted in a broken mirror, might signify something not good, something possibly sinister. In any case, such signs called for caution. Friday the thirteenth especially. So, Maureen avoided doing anything she didn't absolutely have to do on Friday the thirteenths.

Ben arrived about two in the afternoon on Monday, July 16. It was the first day of Theresa's nineteenth or twentieth week of pregnancy. Maybe it was even later in Theresa's pregnancy if Lucy Meyer's hunch about her being further along was right. Maureen certainly hoped so.

Maureen's pro bono legal advisor, and her current best friend, came through the kitchen door as she'd suggested. Ben let himself in without fanfare. As usual, Annie was off somewhere reading, probably in her bedroom. Tom was in the pole barn working on equipment. Greg was with him. Zip lay on the kitchen floor, out of the way of traffic, his head on his front paws. He didn't get up when Ben walked in, though he raised his head, thinking perhaps that company meant better tasting food than what lay untouched in his bowl.

"Good afternoon, Ben," Maureen said when he entered.

"Afternoon," said Ben. He looked at her searchingly. "Any word?" he asked.

She didn't have to wonder what he meant. "No," she said. "Which means, I think, that everything is going well with Theresa. Lucy would have let me know if something went wrong. I'm sure of that."

Ben shook his head, but he didn't say anything.

"Won't you sit down," Maureen invited. "Would you like coffee and maybe some pie? I've got apple."

He shook his head again. Maureen sat beside him at the kitchen table. "Ben, I just have to talk to somebody about this mess we're in, Tom and me. I got another call from the BCA this morning. It was for Tom, really. I referred them to you, like you said."

"Yes, I know. I got that call too. I referred them to your new attorneys."

"You mean those people in Minneapolis, Webster and Arnold and something?"

"Webster, Arnold & Anderson, yes."

"We went to see them last Thursday."

"I know," Ben said. "Tom called me after."

"It was awful, Ben."

"Well, I'm sorry, Maureen, but you needed—"

"Everything about it was horrible. The traffic going into the Cities. The way people drive. It's so congested. We got lost. We had to drive around the block a couple of times before Tom could figure out where to park. You know, you can't just park on the street. You have to find a ramp, and it needs to be the right ramp, or you don't know where you are when you come out."

"Maureen, I don't—"

"And then once we got in there, Ben, it was like nothing you've ever seen. Money, money, money, that's all I could think. We came out of an elevator into this huge open space in a building called LaSalle Plaza, or something like that, and it was thirty stories high. You could see the sky straight up from indoors. There was marble everywhere and a fountain like a waterfall. Their office was almost to the top floor." Ben sighed. "When we got inside, before we even saw a lawyer, they made us fill out forms. Both of us."

"I probably should have gone with you," Ben said.

"I wouldn't have wished it on my worst enemy," Maureen told him.

"Well, Maureen—"

"We each had to hire our own lawyer," Maureen said. "Separate lawyers. After we filled out all their forms, we got what they called a *free consultation*, but it was nothing but them listening to us, then telling us we had to have two separate lawyers, but first we had to give them a retainer. Five thousand dollars each for a retainer, Ben. I just sat there next to Tom, and I thought he'd explode. He wrote out two separate checks."

"I'm sorry, Maureen." She waited. He had no further excuse. So, she went on.

"They wanted to take us into separate rooms, but Tom said no, that they should help us together. So, there we were with two of them in one conference room, all of us sitting there, and one of them said that what they mainly cared about is keeping us out of prison, that they're helping us only so that we—Tom and I—don't get arrested for lying to the FBI. I asked them, don't they care about the baby, that we do everything we can to save Theresa's baby, so he's not born too soon? and the one lawyer just looked at me as if I were crazy. And then he said, 'No!' That their concern is for me. And then Tom said he thought maybe they should hire a private detective to find Lucy Meyer, to make her tell us where Theresa is, and the other lawyer said we were not supposed to have anything to do with Lucy Meyer and were not to try to find her."

"What else did they say?" Ben asked.

"They gave us this." Maureen handed him a paper she had folded inside her pocket.

Ben took it, unfolded it, and read aloud. "Title 18, United States Code, Section 1001 makes it a crime to knowingly and willfully—(1) falsify, conceal, or cover up by any trick, scheme, or device a material fact; (2) make any materially false, fictitious or fraudulent statement or representation; (3) make or use any false writing or document knowing the same to contain any materially false, fictitious, or fraudulent statement or entry; in any matter within the jurisdiction of the executive, legislative, or judicial branch of the United States."

He nodded.

"There's more on the back," Maureen pointed out. "But what it comes down to is that I could go to prison if I told the FBI something I knew wasn't true. That's what they said. They don't care why or what it means to Theresa's baby. They don't care that Tom has the same opinion about Theresa and her baby and that he was just trying to support me doing the right thing. All they care about is whether I lied to the FBI, and I'm not even sure anymore what I said, so how do I know if I lied?"

Maureen stared at the stove. Ben reached over and put his hand on hers. "I know," he said. "This is hard on you both. I hope you haven't talked to anyone . . . official . . . since the last time we talked."

Maureen shook her head, indicating no, she hadn't.

"Did they want Tom going into the BCA?"

"No. They said not. They don't want either of us talking to anybody without them there and without them setting it up in the first place."

"So, you haven't tried to reach Lucy Meyer again?" Ben asked. "Even on one of those burner phones Tom said you used?"

"I know the lawyers said not to, but I tried anyway. It didn't matter. The number doesn't work anymore. And I don't have a new number to call."

Ben nodded. "Maybe we should have some coffee and pie," he said.

———•◦•———

Her hearing grew progressively more acute in captivity, as did her other senses. Theresa could watch the temperature rise or fall outside in the relative tumescence of grass. She could feel the velocity of the wind. She could see the imminence of a storm. She could tell by looking out the windows what time it was within about fifteen minutes, an intuition confirmed by casually asking anyone who entered to check their watches, since Pal needed to be taken outside three times a day.

Roberta Wells—the woman's last name came to her one morning—wore an Apple watch on her wrist, an obviously expensive bauble she enjoyed showing off. It had GPS capability plus its own cellular connection which meant, Roberta pointed out pridefully, you could text or make phone calls, no phone required. Pride goeth before a fall, Theresa recalled, imagining ways she could take that watch off Roberta's wrist and use it to call for help. A 911 operator would know via GPS exactly where she was. Theresa plotted escape schemes, seeing them play out in her mind's eye.

Eventually, Sarah began to appear later in the morning, sometimes not before mid-afternoon. The day came when Theresa no longer heard Suzanne O'Brien's car. It was old and rumbled distinctively. The other women also helped sporadically, and then, not at all. Even Lucy came to the house less often. Theresa knew Lucy's car well since it emitted a squeak when the brakes engaged. No squeak, no Lucy. Also, its doors slammed as if a latch were loose. Theresa guessed it was a cheap rental or something on loan.

Roberta's car, on the other hand, whispered sweet nothings as it crawled across the gravel behind the house, an area Theresa couldn't see. Roberta's car doors shut like heart valves. A woman who wore an expensive watch probably drove an expensive vehicle. People like that were not accustomed to violence, and Roberta seemed too manicured to be an effective warrior. Sometimes she wore high heels and a dress that looked as if she were on her way to a cocktail party, suggesting she ricocheted from warden to luxury wife. She was also a woman who saw the inside of a gym on a regular basis and likely had a trainer. But had her trainer taught her how to fight? Charlie had taught Theresa.

Unlike Roberta, Theresa could determine when their struggle would take place. Imagine a choreography of altercation, Charlie had instructed her back in Alabama. "Think of it like dancing, smooth and deliberate."

Theresa had been loath to learn. He'd led her to his favorite spot, a clearing with tall pine trees surrounding them in every direction. She'd worn the pale-yellow dress Charlie liked, the one with an embroidered bodice and the hint of a ruffle for sleeves. It was a blue-sky day, she remembered, and the late autumn had a pungency that reminded her how short their time together would be. Charlie's next deployment loomed. She didn't want to be sensible. She wanted the magic to go on and on.

He'd insisted she learn self-defense techniques. She'd resisted. Neither could have anticipated how desperately she'd need those skills.

First, the open hand strike. Use the heel of the hand to target the head, back or front, and do it hard. Aim for the eyes, cheekbone, or back of the neck. Theresa thought she could accomplish that move, although the longer she had to deal with these women, the less violent she felt. They were control freaks, but not evil. To take advantage of the hand hit, she had to summon rage against Roberta, and it wasn't there. Anger and frustration, yes. Maybe rage would appear in the heat of the moment.

Second, a kick to the groin—a good maneuver when you're wearing athletic footwear, like the Nikes Theresa had on for her appointment with Dr. Ryan. They had a reinforced leather toe. Lucy had been careless enough not to confiscate them.

She plumbed her subconscious, searching for everything Charlie said. At first, she remembered only one moment.

"Sir, request permission to take a break, sir!" She'd rubbed her face in his shirt and grabbed him by the waist.

He'd kissed her ear. "You're not taking this seriously," he'd whispered.

"Oh, yes, I am," she'd replied. "I'm seriously in love with you."

He'd laughed. They'd held each other. Longleaf pine seeds had whirled to the forest floor around them, gliding softly to earth, eager to germinate, and oh, so filled with promise. She'd wanted that moment to last forever.

But all too soon, they were back to demonstrations of Charlie's tactics, the most important of which was to strike one's opponent repeatedly in quick succession, without slowing or stopping until the opponent was completely incapacitated. She'd forgotten the details and needed to dig them out.

Theresa explored her memories, mentally and physically reenacting the ways her hands and feet should move. She reached deep inside to find the requisite energy. She was tired and needed to remind herself that Charlie was out there worrying, trying to find her, maybe the whole US Army was trying to find her. She had become plunder in the abortion wars. She was enslaved. Her body had been wrenched out of her control, and she was going to get it back. She would kick and scream her way to freedom. Imagining such a scenario, Theresa experienced a flash of fury. Then she waited.

Pal could sense the change. He looked at her from the pillows on the bed, head up, eyes fixated on her stance, alert for her to strike. She knew when Roberta would come to take Pal for his walk. Pal knew when Roberta would come. When Roberta came up the stairs, she would not know that today Theresa was ready, because today, for the first time, Theresa was sure Roberta was alone in the house. For once, she had no helpers. That meant it was D-Day. Theresa knew she might only have this one chance.

The door opened. Theresa stood in the space behind it. Roberta entered, and before she could close the door, Theresa was there, punching Roberta in the back of her neck. She kneed her in the tailbone, and as Roberta screamed and fell, she came down on top of her, pulling Roberta's head up by the hair, and slamming her face as hard as she could on the floor. She twisted Roberta's right arm behind her back and smashed the hard sole of her foot on Roberta's ankle. No one came to Roberta's rescue. No one stood in the hallway. Pal whimpered and ran under the nightstand, his little head pushed down to make himself a ball.

Theresa was already out of breath. Her middle had never felt so heavy or so stretched. When Roberta started to get up, Theresa decided to run. She grabbed Pal from his hiding spot, gave Roberta a parting stomp on her back, and rushed into the hallway.

Before she reached the kitchen, she realized what a mistake she had made by not locking Roberta inside, the way they locked her inside, the key all the time remaining in the exterior of the door. Also, she'd forgotten to take Roberta's watch. It would have been so easy.

She looked around frantically for the key fob to Roberta's car. There was a Lexus parked outside, and a purse on the kitchen table. She turned the purse upside down. No key fob fell out. She started to open a zipper compartment when she heard Roberta drag herself to the top of the stairway, apparently able to move.

Theresa ran outside. With Pal in her arms, she hurried down a driveway to the front of the house and along the narrow road that linked the site of her captivity to who-knew-where. She was running on a gravel pathway barely wide enough for two cars to pass, both sides of the road lined with sporadic grass and drainage ditches. There wasn't another house in sight. She'd been so counting on other houses nearby.

"Pal, why didn't you warn me?" she whispered. Pal remained silent, his body trembling in her arms. Theresa supposed he'd been so terrified by what he'd witnessed in the bedroom, he was now afraid violence might be visited on him.

"You're OK, darling," she reassured him, kissing his head as she ran.

She was perhaps a quarter of a mile along, the late morning sun on her back, when pain hit her like bullets entering her rib cage, ricocheting up and down from her shoulders to her knees. She looked around. There was no place to hide or even to rest. Knee-high reeds rose out of damp soil as far as the eye could see, riven by channels of clear, blue water. It was beautiful, but desolate. The only dry spot was the road itself. She wished for someone's car to appear, a kind stranger's car, but it didn't happen.

Theresa stopped several times, and every time the pain eased momentarily and started again yards later. She kept running when she could, as long as she could, pausing in between to breathe deeply. The pain wasn't going to end, she finally realized, and slowed her pace. Pal wriggled out of her arms.

This is what came of no exercise for weeks. She had to keep going. Pal followed her, picking his way among the gravel stones. He wouldn't let her pick him up.

Then she lost her balance on the edge of this road in the middle of nowhere, falling sideways and rolling down an incline. When she reached the soggy bottom, a cramp in her stomach prevented her from getting up. Her breath came in gasps. There were no other sounds, except her gulps for air and the caws of nearby crows.

No sounds, that is, until a car came into view on the road. Roberta, from behind the wheel of her Lexus, emerged but left the car running. She opened the back door. Theresa saw it all in slow motion and tensed her body for another battle, expecting retaliation, but instead Roberta, limping, dragged her up the incline toward the vehicle. She lifted, tugged, and pushed Theresa inside.

Theresa was in too much pain to protest her renewed captivity. Roberta's face was bloody and already starting to swell. Roberta said nothing to Theresa, but she left the back door open long enough for Pal to approach, scooped him up, and deposited him on the floor of the Lexus. Theresa thought Roberta would return her to the house. But that didn't happen. Roberta punched two fingers at the phone on her wrist and told someone on the other end that she had a woman in labor and would be there soon.

She was in labor. That hadn't occurred to her. Was she having a miscarriage? Theresa was half-conscious when they arrived. Medics lifted her out of the car, put her on a gurney, and hurried her inside the building. She saw the words *St. Dominic Hospital* on a sign next to the ER entrance as she flew by.

4

Claire had decided to extend the radius of her search an extra twenty miles east of St. Dominic, roughly in a line toward Taylors Falls. It was the twenty-sixth of July. She'd just left the print shop when her cell phone vibrated. She checked the screen. St. Dominic Hospital. In seconds, her heart accelerated from nothing to full throttle.

"Yes?" she answered quickly.

"Is this the party who put up posters about a missing woman?" a voice inquired.

"Have you seen her?"

"I think so. We're talking about a woman named Theresa, but your poster said her last name was Cole. This woman has a different last name, and she—"

"If someone told you her last name is Haig, she's the same person," Claire got out. "Is she at the hospital now?"

"Yes," said the voice.

"Who are you?" Claire asked.

"I'm an ER nurse at St. Dominic's. She's upstairs, in obstetrics."

"What's her condition?"

"I can't tell you that. I'm not even supposed to tell anyone she's here without her permission."

"I'm her sister."

"I'm calling because the poster said she was abducted. She was brought in about twenty minutes ago. The person who brought her in is here also. I'm not sure if there was an accident or what. I'm going to call the police."

"I'll be right there."

Claire phoned Annie. Their mother was at a funeral lunch, Annie said. Their father was somewhere on the farm.

"Let him know Theresa's found," Claire said. "She's in the hospital."

"He wears a pager now. I can beep him," Annie practically shouted in her excitement. "Is Theresa OK?"

"Call him right away. I don't know how Theresa's doing."

"I'll bring her pouch along," Annie suggested.

"Good idea," Claire agreed.

Traffic was moderate. Claire drove the speed limit but no faster. She didn't want to get picked up for speeding today of all days. The signal lights on the main drag took longer than usual, but once she turned north, she zipped along, arriving barely fifteen minutes after getting the call from the nurse. It felt like an hour.

She hurried toward the building until something stopped her. A patient had just come outside in a wheelchair pushed by an orderly. A limousine waited against the curb, twenty feet from the entrance. The person's nose and one side of her face were bandaged. On impulse, Claire used her cell to take a photo, in case it was someone involved in Theresa's abduction. Then she continued inside to the same reception desk she remembered from the night of Woodrow's concussion, reminding her that she should call him before heading upstairs. She punched in Woodrow's number.

"Yeah, hi Claire," he said, pleasantly.

"Theresa's at St. Dominic Hospital."

"You're there?" Woodrow asked.

"I'm in the ER. Theresa's upstairs somewhere. I don't know yet how she's doing."

"Hold on," said Woodrow. She could hear him in the background, probably talking to Charlie. She couldn't hear Charlie, though. In a moment, Woodrow was back. "I'm comin' up there," he said. "Can you meet me at the airport?"

"Sure. Let me know when."

"I'll do that," he said. "Call if you find out more." Abruptly, he was gone.

Next, Claire rushed upstairs to the obstetrics ward and tried to inquire at the desk. Only one nurse was working the station at the moment. Claire finally got her attention and the briefest scrap of information. Her sister was in a labor and delivery room. Claire couldn't go in there unless expressly authorized by the patient, she said. She could take a seat in one of the waiting areas. Even the hallways leading to the delivery rooms were off limits to anyone not on staff, particularly in regard to a critical patient. Claire understood what the nurse wasn't saying.

"My sister's a missing person," Claire protested forcefully. "I have to know she's all right."

"She's not a missing person now," the nurse replied. "I can tell you this much: she's in labor, and you need to stay right here until we can get her stabilized or she delivers her baby. If you try to get past this desk, I'll call security."

Claire paced the floor as people came and went: nurses, orderlies, a few who might have been doctors, all of them ignoring her. She couldn't say how much time went by, but finally, unable to stand it anymore, she went back downstairs and exited the elevator as Stears County Deputy Antoine Harrison was about to step in.

Each seemed startled to see the other. "My sister's upstairs," Claire blurted out, "and she's in labor. I think they're trying to stop it."

"That's what I heard in the ER," he said. "A woman brought her in, and someone recognized your sister and called police. They had it out on the scanner."

"This might be the woman who brought her in," Claire said, pulling out her phone to show Deputy Harrison the photo she'd taken in the parking lot. Only half of the woman's face was clearly visible, but Claire hoped that was enough to identify her.

"She was leaving when you took this?" Harrison asked, examining the photo.

"Yes. Just as I was coming in. She looked in pretty bad shape."

"Do you know who she is?"

"No," said Claire, "but I'll bet Theresa does."

Harrison nodded. "I called my contact at the FBI," he told Claire. "They should be sending someone over, once your sister's able to talk."

"What about the detectives on this case?" Claire asked. "Smits and that other one?"

Harrison shook his head. "I wouldn't count on them," he said. "Not for attribution, but my advice is, deal with the FBI. They're your best chance to figure this out."

Claire nodded. Just then, Tom and Annie arrived. Tom's clothes were dirty, and his forehead displayed a streak of grease at the hairline. Annie was wearing a pair of ratty blue jeans and carrying a small black pouch.

"Where is she?" Tom asked, out of breath. He ignored Deputy Harrison.

"Upstairs in obstetrics," Claire told him.

"Let's go," Tom said, heading toward the elevators. The first one to stop was crammed with people on their way up from the underground parking ramp. Rather than wait for another elevator, Tom forced himself in.

Before leaving, Deputy Harrison asked Claire to let him know when the

FBI showed up. Annie and Claire joined Tom upstairs a few minutes later as he engaged an obstetrics nurse.

"She's in labor," said the same nurse at the obstetrics desk. She told Tom exactly what she'd told Claire.

"Her father should be able to see her," Tom insisted. "She's been missing."

"You can't see her *now*," the nurse repeated. "We're trying to slow her contractions. If we could delay the birth even a day, it would be a plus for the baby."

"What if you can't delay it?" Tom pressed angrily.

"Try to calm yourself." With that and a censorious look, the nurse left to deal with someone else.

The last thing one could tell Tom Haig was to calm himself, Claire thought. She put her hand on her father's shoulder. "I called Woodrow," she said.

To Tom's puzzled look, she added, "Charlie's father. He's on his way here. I'll pick him up at the airport when he gets in."

"Why isn't Charlie coming?" Tom demanded.

"Charlie's in a military hospital. He's badly hurt. Remember? He can't travel yet."

"Oh," Tom muttered.

"I'm so glad Theresa's back!" Annie exclaimed. "But I'm scared she's having her baby too soon. I hope she's going to be OK, Claire. I just hope everything's going to be OK . . ." She was breathing rapidly, shifting her weight back and forth from one foot to the other. To Claire she seemed on the edge of a panic attack.

"Do you think there's something else we should do?" Annie looked at Claire rather than her father. "What else should we do?"

"Be quiet is what you should do," Tom said.

Hospital personnel moved past them toward a room down the hallway that they guessed held Theresa and her doctors. Someone pushed a cart in the same direction. Someone else told them to clear the area. An orderly pulled a mobile IV around the corner, skirting the three of them, his face a blank.

"This is a goddamn nightmare," Tom moaned. He looked around. "Where's your mother?"

"At church," Annie told him. "A lady died."

"A lady died?" Tom repeated sarcastically.

"It was a lady who had pneumonia."

"Who dies of pneumonia in July?" Tom asked, not expecting an answer. "You two go get her," he added.

He looked hard at Claire, who clearly did not want to leave. "Can you do that for me?" he snapped.

The last thing Claire wanted to do was leave the obstetrics ward at that moment. They were probably yards away from where Theresa lay on some kind of birthing table. She was probably getting an intravenous drip to slow things down or stop labor altogether. Claire had heard that doctors could do that. She wanted to search the internet to find out more about how. She wanted to sit next to Annie and put her arms around her and comfort her. She wanted to do anything but go fetch her mother.

But she couldn't say no to Tom. That had always been her problem. Growing up, Claire wouldn't say yes to her mother's nonsensical demands, but she'd always found it hard to say no to this worried, gruff man whose face and character informed everything she was. Her first memories were of Tom playing with her as she scrambled across the floor to outrace him. Even when they fought, she never doubted he loved her. He'd made her feel safe. It had taken Theresa's kidnapping for her to stand up to her father, but she couldn't say no to him now when he was in pain.

"Yes, I'll get her," Claire replied.

"I'll come with you," Annie said quickly. They headed for the car without speaking. Claire checked her phone to see if there were any messages from Woodrow. Nothing yet.

When they arrived at St. Philomena, the funeral lunch was in full swing. A wall of the dining room entry was filled with memorabilia and a greater than life-size portrait of an elderly woman. They saw their mother from a distance in the open kitchen, filling baskets of rolls and bowls of carrots, mashed potatoes, gravy, and coleslaw. Broasted chicken legs, wings, and breasts were flying out on big white platters. Pitchers of lemonade and pots of coffee had been set on paper-covered trestle tables in the dining hall. People seated on folding chairs were busy filling glasses and coffee cups in their vicinity. The mood was festive. Claire and Annie rushed past the hugs and chatter, making their way toward Maureen, whose face told them she'd known at first glance that something awful had happened.

———•◦•———

"Maureen, I'm so sorry. We underestimated the lengths she'd go to."

Lucy Meyer stood over Maureen, who sat on a cushioned bench in an open area near the obstetrics desk. The skin at either side of Lucy's eyes stung with salty tears she couldn't stanch. She'd been beside herself for the last half hour.

"I am so, so sorry," Lucy repeated. A paper cup in her right hand, Maureen remained motionless. "May I sit with you?" Lucy asked softly.

Maureen nodded. "I can't drink this," she said, indicating her almost-full coffee. Lucy took the cup, walked to a plastic-lined waste bin in a corner, and let it drop in.

"No one t . . . tells me anything," Maureen stammered when Lucy came back and sat beside her. "I made Tom take Annie home. I'm staying however long it takes. I need to know if Theresa's going to—" Her voice cracked.

"She's in tough shape at the moment," Lucy acknowledged as an expectant couple entered the area, the woman bent over in distress. Nurses rushed toward them.

"What do you know?" Maureen asked anxiously.

"One of the ER nurses told me Theresa had fresh bruises all over her body. Roberta brought her in. Roberta's in bad shape too. She's got cracked bones in her face from Theresa slamming it into the floor in the house. Her husband came and took her to a private clinic. He wouldn't let them treat her downstairs. I don't know how she managed to get your daughter here."

Maureen gasped.

"Roberta said Theresa ambushed her when she came to get the dog for his walk," Lucy continued. "She was crying so hard, I could barely understand her. She blames herself."

"Is Theresa's baby going to be OK?" Maureen asked.

"I don't know, Maureen. No one does. Theresa told one of the nurses to just get it out of her, so now they're thinking she might have tried to force a premature birth. She told them she fell down a hill. Maybe she threw herself down. Maureen, I have to tell you—I've never, in all my years, met a pregnant woman who would assault someone the way she did."

Unable to speak, Maureen shook her head, bent forward and began to sob silently, with great heaves, her face in her lap.

"At the moment, she's lost," Lucy went on. "More lost than we'd imagined. But that doesn't mean we can't still help her, especially if the baby can be saved. We mustn't give up, Maureen."

"How did I go so wrong with her?" Maureen managed to get out before another wave took hold.

"There are a million ways for things to go wrong between a mother and her daughter. Don't blame yourself," Lucy said, placing her fingers on Maureen's wrist. Her pulse was steady, she noted.

Twenty minutes later by the cheerless clock on the wall, Maureen sat up and wiped her face with crumpled tissues. "Will you stay with me 'til it's over?" she implored.

"Of course, I'll stay with you," Lucy assured her. "I'll stay all night if need be."

It was cold in the room, typical of hospitals. Lucy took off her sweater and wrapped it around Maureen's shoulders. Maureen let her head fall on Lucy's chest. Lucy braced it with her other hand.

"Why wouldn't you let me see Theresa when I called?" Maureen asked.

"That was a mistake," Lucy acknowledged. "I realize now I should have let you talk to her. I made a lot of mistakes, Maureen. I should have made sure Roberta had someone with her every single minute, no exceptions. It's just that Theresa seemed to be settling down the past few weeks. We thought she was out of the woods. Her attitude had improved so much."

Maureen didn't respond. She raised her head from Lucy's chest and stared blankly at the wall. Lucy searched her mind for some better way to comfort her. "People get through things," she told Maureen. "Even terrible things like this—I think the Lord sends these moments as a test."

Maureen murmured something unintelligible.

"I was even younger when I got pregnant myself, Maureen. I was barely fifteen, and I thought it was the end of the world. I wanted my baby gone too, just like Theresa."

"Theresa doesn't know what she wants," Maureen whispered.

"I'd been infatuated with a boy who said things he didn't mean. He begged me and flattered me until I gave in to him, and then later on, he wouldn't even talk to me."

Maureen pulled herself upright.

"When I told my parents, they were upset, of course. At first, I thought it was out of concern for me, which they hadn't shown a lot of before. They made some phone calls the night I told them, and the next day my mother called the school and said I was sick, and then she took me on a drive in the country."

Maureen closed her eyes.

"She wouldn't tell me where we were going. All she'd say was that I was a child, too young to have a child myself. She said a doctor would examine me. But when we got there, it wasn't a doctor. It was a woman in a kitchen who gave me pills I thought would put me to sleep. But I stayed awake the whole while. The woman put a cloth in my mouth. And all that time my mother stood by the table, looking at me as if I were the vilest thing on earth."

"What does any of that have to do with Theresa?" Maureen interrupted.

"Theresa will find out, Maureen, as I did, that an experience like that doesn't go away. Everything we ever do is inside us. A trauma involving another life stays just below the surface. It did for me. I think, for the rest of her days, whether her baby survives or not, Theresa will remember that hillside, just as I remember lying on a table in somebody's kitchen."

"I suppose she will," Maureen said.

"I understood later that my mother's main concern was her own reputation. What would other people think when they found out? The same ones who helped my parents find an abortionist would likely turn around and tell their hairdresser and their neighbor at the wash line. My mother got looks at the grocery store, she said. It wasn't about me or the baby for her. It was about what the town thought of us, which was why my family moved away."

"If Theresa tried to force a premature birth," Maureen said, "and that gets out in St. Dominic—"

"If gossip gets out, it's nothing, Maureen. Nothing compared to the life of the baby inside her. Nothing to her relationship with you, and yours with her."

Maureen's face contorted. Lucy could envision more sobbing ahead.

"Maureen, from ancient times, there have been two kinds of people. Those who've murdered and those who have not. It's very, very important for Theresa to be innocent of murder. For her sake. For her baby's sake. Maureen, put all your energy into praying that Providence will help us again. And in the meantime, do everything you can to support Theresa. Help her understand that you love her no matter what."

"I'm so mad at her," Maureen got out in a whisper.

"You can't afford to be mad at her. You need to remember who you are, what kind of mother you are."

"My girls don't listen!" Maureen insisted. "I can't make them listen."

Lucy put her arm around Maureen and gripped her tightly. "Maureen, you stay here and try to calm yourself. Let me find out what's happening."

She let go of Maureen's shoulder and stood up, her gaze fixed on the obstetrics desk. Just then, a man and woman came in. Lucy could tell at a glance that they weren't expectant parents. The man wore a navy-blue suit and held a notebook and a pen in his left hand. He showed a leather-encased ID to the nursing staff. The woman wore tailored black pants and something whose profile distorted the side of her jacket. Lucy wondered if it were a weapon. She knew that only law enforcement officers on an active investigation were allowed to carry a gun inside a hospital.

She sat down again, quickly. The man and woman were having an intent conversation with the staff, one of whom picked up a phone.

"Maureen, I hate to break a promise, but I'm going to have to leave you."

"Why?" Maureen looked up at her, startled. She didn't want Lucy to leave.

"Those two at the desk—they may be a threat to my work."

Maureen spent a long moment staring at the obstetrics desk.

"I'm so sorry," Lucy said, kissing Maureen's forehead. "But I can't stay with you now . . . I'm so sorry, Maureen. Please try to hold yourself together . . . and remember what I told you."

With that, Lucy stood up again and steered herself briskly toward an open elevator. She disappeared as the doors closed.

———•—•—

Maureen stared ahead, unable even to pray. She had never felt so disconnected from everything around her and so helpless to make things right. She understood that it all went back to Theresa's initial defiance of the Lord's will. Her daughter had resisted God's grace, and that meant that she—Maureen—had failed as a mother in the most significant moment of her life.

She'd known for weeks that the mission to save Theresa's baby was in jeopardy, and that it was a far more serious jeopardy than all this legal mumbo jumbo people talked about. She knew her daughter was obstinate, self-centered, and too in love with herself to put her child first. That's why Theresa had to be in a safe place where she could think long and hard, reflect on her situation, and with the help of the Holy Spirit, gradually open herself up to God's beneficent grace.

As a woman who put religion first, Maureen recognized the most transcendent truth of the New Testament, namely that there is no greater struggle in the universe than the battle between the Lord Almighty and Lucifer, a battle that had raged since the ninth of May inside Theresa's ungenerous heart. She knew Theresa's confinement couldn't be allowed to end yet, because the Lord had not yet won. Even if the doctors could stop Theresa from having her baby that very night, how could they prevent her from doing harm to the unborn child tomorrow or the next day? God didn't want Theresa wandering about, susceptible to the devil. Of that Maureen was sure.

"Excuse me, ma'am," someone said. Maureen looked up. A man in a dark blue suit bent over her, his features doughy behind black-framed glasses. She saw a baby face with a nose that barely registered, so snub did it seem. His mouth was small too. A baby's mouth.

Baby was all Maureen could think about. She wondered, vaguely, where Lucy had gone. She was quite sure Lucy Meyer had been beside her a moment ago.

"What?" she got out, blinking to see better. Her eyes felt moist, as if wet air were raining on her face.

"Ma'am, this is Mitchell Gunderson," said a woman beside the man. The woman looked young too, though not as young as the man. "My name is Ramona Eggers. We're with the FBI, and we're looking into the disappearance of Theresa Cole. We believe she's your daughter."

The woman was short and wore a man's style of clothing, black trousers and a matching jacket with silver buttons. She opened a small black leather case, revealing a gold-colored badge on one side, and an identification card with her picture and FBI in large letters on the other. The picture hardly looked like her. Maureen studied it closely. Then she looked at the woman who stared back as if Maureen were a specimen of fish to be dissected.

Fish again. Thinking of a fish had of late become a sort of amulet. Maureen imagined the Lord sending her the image of a fish whenever she needed help.

"What do you want?" she asked irritably. It was not the time, she thought, for these civil authorities to interfere in private matters. She and Tom weren't supposed to speak to them, in any case. That's what their Minneapolis lawyers had told them.

"We'd like to talk to you about your daughter," the other one said—the man Maureen recalled was Mitchell Gunderson. That name rang a bell. She thought she'd spoken with him on the phone. She hoped she hadn't lied, since lying to the FBI was apparently a matter of huge importance.

Maureen shook her head, making her refusal clear. "My daughter is in crisis right now. She's in premature labor."

"Ma'am, could we go somewhere to talk?" the woman asked. "There's a room down the hall that we're told we can use."

"I'm not going anywhere with you," Maureen said.

"Then we'll need to talk to you here," Mitchell Gunderson warned.

"Can't you see this is not the time?" Maureen cried out suddenly, drawing the attention of people nearby. "My daughter is maybe having her baby tonight, a baby she shouldn't have for months. It's too soon." Maureen began to cry. Her face fell forward into her hands. She let it fall as her body rocked up and down, her sobs growing in intensity.

The agents looked at each other, waiting for Maureen's distress to cease. Mitchell Gunderson walked a few yards away and pulled a chair from a row of them, hauled it into close proximity with Maureen, then found another chair and did the same for his partner. The two agents sat facing Maureen. Others in the vicinity moved away, as if tacitly giving the three of them some privacy. Maureen continued to cry. The agents continued to wait.

Finally, Maureen looked up, her emotions spent. She saw that they were still there, waiting. Crying didn't get rid of them. They remained in her way. She couldn't even get off the bench she occupied.

"Would you mind," she said, looking hard at Agent Gunderson, "going over to the desk and asking the nurse in charge if there's been any change in my daughter's condition?" Maureen was quite sure he would not refuse, and she was right. He got up and walked toward the desk. When he came back, he smiled slightly.

"She said your daughter's labor hasn't progressed. That's good news, I gather, but she's not authorized to share it with me. She did, though, for your sake."

What did that mean, she wondered. Was she supposed to be grateful to him for doing something she could have done herself if he hadn't blocked her way?

"Ma'am, what was your daughter doing before she came here?" asked the other one, Ramona Eggers. The woman's name came back to Maureen as if God had sent it.

"I have no idea, Miss Eggers," she said. She said *Miss* rather than *Agent* to irritate her.

"Do you know the person who brought her into the ER today?" Agent Gunderson asked. "Her name is Roberta Wells, we're told. She was in bad shape, bad enough to be admitted, but she insisted on leaving the hospital."

"I know her," Maureen confirmed. "She's a parishioner at my church. That's St. Philomena Catholic Church here in St. Dominic."

"She's on a list we got from the sheriff's office, the list of women who were with your daughter the day she disappeared," Agent Eggers said.

Maureen stared at her. "People don't disappear," she said. "We're not ghosts. My daughter was seen by those women because they were in my home for a meeting, and they saw my daughter there. Roberta Wells is active in my church, and she was one of those women."

"When did *you* last see your daughter?" Agent Gunderson pressed.

"I don't remember," Maureen said. "She comes and goes. My husband and I agreed not to interfere with Theresa's comings and goings when she came to live with us during her pregnancy."

"When was that?"

"Earlier in the spring. Late March, I think. I don't remember the exact date. I've already told you all this, I'm sure."

"No, ma'am, you did not," Agent Eggers said.

"Ma'am, have you talked to Roberta Wells since she brought your daughter here?" Agent Gunderson asked.

"No," Maureen said.

"Then how did you know your daughter was here?"

"My other daughter told me. My daughter Mary."

"How did she know?"

"I have no idea. Are these questions over?"

"Mrs. Haig, we've tried to reach Roberta Wells," Agent Eggers continued. "She's not responding to our calls, and she wasn't home when we went to her residence. No one was home there. We couldn't reach her husband, either, and he's not responding to our messages. Do you know where they are?"

Maureen looked at the agents in turn. She shook her head in despair.

"I'm not supposed to talk to you," she said, suddenly recalling the attorneys' strict instructions. "I don't know the answers to your questions, and I just can't deal with you tonight. All I can think about is my daughter."

They looked at her. "We'll be back tomorrow, then," Agent Eggers said. They both stood up.

"We'll want to talk to your daughter as soon as we can," Agent Gunderson continued. He spoke more kindly than his partner, Maureen felt. "As soon as she's able," he added.

She could almost tolerate him, Maureen decided. But not the other one, the FBI woman who looked at her with such suspicion, as if she had done something wrong.

⸻•◦•⸻

When the two agents were truly gone, Maureen approached the obstetrics desk. "Has there been any change?" she asked. She knew the nursing staff recognized her by now. She didn't have to tell them Theresa's name or that Theresa was in labor in a room down the hall or that she, Maureen, was Theresa's mother.

The RN at the desk said she would try to find out. It was a new person, Maureen noticed. The nurse returned minutes later. From the look on her face, Maureen could tell the news was grim.

"She's been sedated," she said. "They're giving her antibiotics intravenously, as well as steroids to speed up the baby's lung development. We think the child will be born tonight. There's only so much we can do to slow it down."

The nurse put her hand around Maureen's upper arm. "We're doing everything we can," she said and squeezed gently. Maureen nodded. She looked around, wondering what to do with herself, where to go, unwilling to return to the bench against the wall. Then she noticed a sign pointing in the direction of a family lounge down a different hallway. Maureen followed it.

There were two people inside when she entered: her daughter and Charlie's father. Incredibly, Mary and this man sat together in one of the wide chairs, Mary bent across his lap, her head on the opposite armrest, the man with his head back, both of them asleep in what was surely an unseemly intimacy for strangers.

What kind of girls have I raised? Maureen thought again. Her middle daughter refused to accept the precious gift of life God had given her because it wasn't perfect. Her first child, divorced and calling herself by a new name, had turned into a complete mystery. Among them, only Annie remained normal.

Maureen left the family lounge, returned to the obstetrics desk, and found it unoccupied. She decided that was another sign from God, and so searched down the forbidden hallway until she finally found the door to the only room that mattered in this hospital. Through a narrow window, she could observe figures behind a curtain, five or six of them crowded around a patient she knew to be her daughter. She couldn't actually see any part of Theresa. Yet she was sure her daughter lay inside on a birthing table, attached to a fetal monitor, to a blood pressure machine that tracked her heartbeats, and to something that could give her oxygen. The room was filled with ultramodern medical gadgetry—all of it designed to perform miracles—if miracles were needed, and if the Lord allowed them.

She leaned against the wall. Her grandson, if he survived, would be born too soon, with the odds stacked against him. Maureen wanted to welcome his unique, beautiful self into the world. She interceded for him, moving her fingers on rosary beads in the side pocket of the dress she'd worn to the funeral lunch.

Something finally happened at 2:40 a.m. The door to the room opened, and a flurry of obstetrics people rushed out, pushing and pulling a wheeled bed down the long hall past double doors that led elsewhere—to another delivery room, or maybe, Maureen worried, to an operating room. The people wheeling the bed hardly noticed her. Even Theresa didn't see her. Theresa's eyes were shut. Her face looked white.

Terrified, Maureen hurried back to the family lounge. It was the only place she could think to go because the double doors that closed behind Theresa informed the public in no uncertain terms, *Hospital Personnel Only.*

In the lounge, Charlie's father was awake, Mary still sprawled on top of him. Maureen met his gaze.

"I think they just took Theresa to have her baby," she said.

Maureen's voice woke her daughter, who pulled herself upright, revealing a face marked by the armrest and a frightful halo of hair.

"What's happening?" she asked.

"Your sister's having her baby," Maureen replied, coldly.

"Where?"

"Down the hall," Maureen said.

"Will they let us know when the baby's born?"

"I certainly hope so," Maureen said. She noticed Charlie's father looking at her, alert and calm, saying nothing. Why was he even here? she wondered.

According to the birth certificate, at 2:57 a.m. on Friday, July 27, 2018, a live baby boy was born to Theresa Haig Cole and Charles Harrison Cole at St. Dominic Hospital in St. Dominic, Minnesota. Maureen, donning a hairnet, gown, and face mask, having washed her face and arms thoroughly, was allowed into the delivery room a few minutes later. She promptly gave the nurse her input on the newborn's first name.

"It will be Patrick," she said, when the baby's mother failed to answer the question.

"I can type that in provisionally," said the nurse. "But we'll have to confirm it with the mother when we bring her the birth certificate to sign later on today. The child's legal name has to come from her."

"That's fine," Maureen said. "Just put down Patrick for now. She can change it if she wants."

Maureen and the nurse both looked toward Theresa, waiting for her to say something. She said nothing.

The nursing staff cleaned Theresa on the table, and none too gently, Maureen observed. The infant, on the other hand, was taken with utmost care to an area behind a screen and placed inside a glass-topped carrier whose cover remained open as a doctor inserted an intravenous tube into his tiny arm and a second tube for breathing down his throat. Patrick didn't cry even before the tube went in. His skin was a mottled red and purple, and so thin, you could see blood vessels pulsing underneath. His eyes were closed, and he had no eyelashes that Maureen could discern. But he had fingernails, translucent, perfect fingernails, and though the shape of his face had the flatter look associated with Down syndrome, Maureen could sense by the typical Haig stubbornness of his expression that he was strong and would survive.

"We're concerned about jaundice," one of the nurses said, though Maureen couldn't see any yellow in the baby's skin. "We need to get him under lights."

Maureen was not allowed to hold him. For now, she couldn't even stick a finger into the little opening in his glass house, but they assured her that, pending his mother's permission, later on she could touch him.

He weighed one pound and thirteen ounces, and they guessed he had been born somewhere between the twenty-sixth and twenty-seventh weeks of gestation, meaning that Theresa was indeed further along than she'd told Dr. Ryan on the day of her clinic appointment. Lucy was right about that.

But there was something else that concerned everyone more than the jaundice, more even than the long time Patrick took between his inaudible breaths—something having to do with his heart.

The nurse asked Maureen to leave the room. Maureen looked toward the birthing table. Theresa's face was turned to the wall. She still hadn't said anything. Maureen was afraid to approach her.

Outside, she found Mary and Charlie's father. She told them what she knew. Mary wanted to go in, but a nurse stood with her back to the door. Then the door opened, and an orderly wheeled the baby in his glass box down the hall in the direction of the neonatal intensive care unit, a locked wing of the building, someone said, where relatives couldn't follow until authorized.

In any case, they would need an imprinted wrist band before they could see the infant. They were told they shouldn't even be where they were without it, much less enter the NICU. Theresa would be taken to a room of her own shortly. In the meantime, relatives of the mother were advised to go home, shower, and put on clean clothes to minimize risks of contamination. Security for the NICU would be even tighter.

Once the last of the hospital personnel departed, Mary and Charlie's father went into the room anyway. Maureen followed. She wanted to hear what Theresa had to say.

Theresa lay on the table, staring at the ceiling. She was covered by a white blanket. Her face was bruised. Bloody sheets overflowed a plastic bin alongside the table.

"Theresa, can we do anything for you?" Mary asked, stroking her sister's arm.

"It's a little late," Theresa said sarcastically. "You could have rescued me weeks ago. That would have helped."

"Your sister tried," Charlie's father said. "Believe me, she tried."

"Oh, really?" Theresa responded in a voice that suggested skepticism.

Maureen, from the other side of the table, looked at her daughter and felt mainly shock and dismay. It seemed clear that Theresa was going to blame other people rather than herself. Maureen retrieved a handkerchief from her purse, but she was determined not to cry.

"This is a restricted area," announced a nurse in the doorway. "You can visit once the patient is settled in her room, as long as you keep your voices down. But please leave this room *now!*"

Maureen walked out first and made her way down the hallway, not knowing where she was headed, her face in her handkerchief. She needed to find the chapel.

Before Claire and Woodrow could follow, Theresa grabbed Woodrow's arm.

"Where's Charlie?" she asked urgently.

"He's back in Alabama," Woodrow whispered, leaning toward her. "And he needs you. He asked me to come here and find you."

"Why didn't he come himself?"

"He couldn't. I'll explain later."

"I want to leave right now. Will you take me?"

"Soon as they discharge you, I surely will," said Woodrow. "I'll get you back to Charlie as fast as possible." He patted Theresa's hand.

"Will you do something else?" she pleaded.

"Anything, sweetheart."

"They gave me a puppy. He was in the car when they brought me here yesterday. It's a silver Lexus, and it belongs to a woman named Roberta Wells."

Claire reached into her pocket and pulled out her phone. "Is this Roberta Wells?" she asked, showing Theresa the photo she'd taken.

"Yes!" Theresa replied emphatically, meeting Claire's gaze.

"I saw her leaving the hospital in a limousine when I got here," said Claire.

"You think her car is still in the parking lot?" Theresa asked.

"I'll look," said Woodrow.

A security guard tapped on the door. "Folks, you need to leave. I'm told you've been warned," he said.

"Yeah, we're going," said Woodrow. He squeezed Theresa's hand. "We'll be back, darlin', soon as they get you settled."

She squeezed his hand in return.

Claire couldn't figure it out. True, Woodrow seemed to have charisma and she did not. But there had to be more to it. In her search for whom to blame, Theresa chose only other women— their mother in particular, but also herself—the sister who'd spent weeks searching for her. All she could think about was her husband.

She walked with Woodrow downstairs and through the sliding glass doors to the parking lot. In the middle of the night, there weren't many cars in the vicinity. Doctors and hospital personnel used a separate underground area. Only patients and patients' families parked on the asphalt expanse in front of them. They spotted the silver Lexus right away. Someone had moved it close to the building after the owner abandoned it at the ER entrance, and whoever had done that maybe hadn't noticed the puppy.

The Lexus was locked. They could see the puppy curled on the floor in back. Whether it was asleep or dead they couldn't tell. There was no sign the little fellow was breathing. Three of the car's windows were shut, but the fourth was down a few inches. Unfortunately, that wasn't enough to reach in without unlocking a door. Besides, the Lexus probably had a security system that would have to be turned off.

Claire and Woodrow hurried back to the ER reception desk, where Woodrow explained the situation to the woman on duty. She found the Lexus key fob in the locked lost and found drawer and called security to open the car.

The guard walked briskly outside with Woodrow and Claire, opened the car, allowed Woodrow to remove the puppy and made a point of relocking the car. Back at the ER desk, he copied information from Woodrow's driver's license onto a form and made Woodrow sign for the dog.

The woman at the desk handed Woodrow a bowl of fresh water. He set the bowl on the floor, and the puppy buried his face in it.

"Sorry, but you'll have to take him outside," she told them. "Only service dogs are allowed inside."

"We'll do that," Woodrow assured her, adding, "you're a kind lady." He grinned at her, and she smiled back.

"I try to be," she said as he and Claire left.

"Wish I had your talent for getting people to help," Claire noted as they walked away.

"I'm sure you have talents of your own," Woodrow quipped.

——•◦•——

The beaming attendant brought Theresa a breakfast tray from the cart in the hallway. She was young, scarcely twenty, Theresa guessed, and one of the few friendly staff she'd met.

"Here you go," the attendant murmured, lowering the tray onto Theresa's lap. Theresa felt a pain in her midriff where the tray touched, and she flinched.

"Oh, I'm sorry. Did I hurt you?" the attendant asked, alarmed.

"I'm just a little sore," Theresa said.

"You have quite a few bruises on your face and arms."

"I fell down a hill," Theresa told her.

"You're probably anxious to see your baby . . ."

"No," Theresa replied. "Could I ask a favor, though? Could I borrow your cell phone?" Minutes later, Theresa searched the internet until she found information on something she'd heard about: the Minnesota safe haven law.

A parent who is unable or unwilling to care for an infant can, within seventy-two hours of birth as determined within a reasonable degree of medical certainty, give up custody of the newborn by bringing the newborn to a hospital and leaving the newborn with a hospital employee on hospital premises, providing the newborn is in unharmed condition.

That's what Theresa remembered.

The hospital must not inquire as to the identity of the mother or the person leaving the newborn or call the police, provided the newborn is unharmed.

Within twenty-four hours of receiving a newborn, the hospital must inform the local welfare agency that a newborn has been left at the hospital but must not do so before the mother or the person leaving the newborn leaves the hospital.

Theresa was eager to leave the hospital. However, she first took a moment to examine her breakfast tray. Under the cover was a bowl of hot oatmeal with raisins, a box of 2% milk, a glass of orange juice, a small pastry, a large red apple, and a cup of black coffee with a tiny carton of half-and-half. Hunger set in suddenly.

As she was eating, a woman in a blue suit walked in with a clipboard. "Good morning," she said, "My name is Eleanor Reston from hospital admissions. We see you have not been formally admitted. I can help with that."

Behind Eleanor were Claire and Woodrow. They had cleaned up from the night before.

"Did you find Pal?" Theresa inquired.

"If you mean the pup," said Woodrow, "we sure did."

"It's not visiting hours," Eleanor Reston told them. "You'll have to come back later in the day. Six to nine this evening would be fine, but do not try to bring any puppies in here, please. For patient safety, animals are not allowed in the hospital."

Theresa looked at Claire. "I gave my purse to Annie," she said. "It has—"

"Oh, that's right," Claire said, "it was in the lounge. I put it under the chair." She rushed off to get it.

"She left my ID in a lounge overnight!" Theresa said indignantly.

"Don't worry, she'll find it," Woodrow told her.

Claire was back within a minute, clutching the black pouch. She handed it to Theresa, who said nothing as she took it, examined its contents, and looked up at Eleanor.

"I want to see a hospital administrator," she announced.

"Someone can come up later in the day," Eleanor replied. "Now if you'll show me a form of personal identification. A driver's license will do. And your insurance card, so we can get the process started."

"First, I want to see a hospital administrator," Theresa said.

Eleanor met her gaze. "There's an administration meeting this morning, followed by the monthly board meeting. I doubt anyone can get to you before mid-afternoon."

"In that case, you can admit me mid-afternoon," Theresa countered.

Eleanor stiffened. After a moment she said, "I'll see if I can find someone," and left the room.

Theresa looked probingly at Claire. "What are you doing here?" she asked.

"Hey," Woodrow said, taking Theresa's left hand, "I want you to know Claire's been workin' her tail off tryin' to find you. I'm sure it felt like nobody was lookin', but she *was*, believe me. We just didn't have the right information."

"Woodrow got his head bashed in by the butt of a rifle," Claire informed her sister. "We followed Lucy Meyer to a farm near Sartell. It belongs to some relation of ours. Woodrow went through a basement window and—"

"That was *you*," Theresa said.

"Just so you know," Woodrow told her, almost in a whisper as he leaned over. "We were tryin', sweetheart. We really were. But they moved you, and we couldn't find out where."

"What did Lucy Meyer tell you?"

"Nothin'. That woman's slippery as an eel," Woodrow said.

"Woodrow got a concussion," Claire added, "Then when Charlie—"

"What about Charlie?" Theresa's eyes went wide.

"Good morning. I'm Gloria Kooning. I'm told you need to see an administrator." A fifty-something woman in a flowery violet dress and matching earrings stood in the doorway. "Seems to be quite a crowd for nine o'clock in the morning," she added. "How did you get in here? These are not—"

"I'm giving up the child I had last night," Theresa interrupted her. "According to the safe haven law. I'm giving it up."

Gloria Kooning looked at her. She didn't move or say anything.

"Here's my driver's license and my Tricare card," Theresa went on.

She handed the cards to Ms. Kooning, who continued to look at her, not saying anything. "You delivered your child here last night?" Ms. Kooning asked, finally.

"Yes," Theresa said.

"Now you want to surrender your child to the hospital?"

"Yes," Theresa repeated.

"Just a moment," Ms. Kooning said, nodding for emphasis. "Just a moment, please. I'll look into it."

Before leaving, she turned to Woodrow. "You shouldn't be in here," she told him.

"These are special circumstances," Woodrow said, meeting her gaze. "It's a delicate situation, as you can see."

"I'll be back shortly," Ms. Kooning said, and left.

Woodrow and Claire glanced at each other, then at Theresa, who began crying between gulps of oatmeal, tears running down her cheeks amid gasps for breath. Her head fell back against the pillow.

"Charlie" was the only word she managed to get out.

Woodrow stroked her damp forehead. "We'll figure this out, darlin' . . . I swear we'll figure this out. You need rest now."

"No," Theresa said. "I'm rested enough. I want to get on the road right away. I need to be with Charlie as soon as possible."

Woodrow stood next to Theresa, holding her left hand. Theresa stared off into nothing. When she focused again, her mother stood in the doorway. Theresa wondered what she had expected. All those weeks when she'd wanted to confront her mother, Maureen hadn't come. Now she was here every time Theresa looked up. Everyone was here. Why weren't they here before?

"Your son," Maureen got out, her face contorted. "You can't give up your son." She had cleaned up too. She wore a different dress than the one she had on yesterday. Her hair was combed, and she'd applied lipstick.

"He's not my son," Theresa replied, her composure back. "It wasn't my decision to have him. You decided. You and your maniac friends. You and Lucy Meyer. Her vigilantes kidnapped me, with your help, and now you can deal with the consequences. Your baby is going into foster care, to some complete stranger, and there's nothing you can do about it. I'm going home to Charlie."

Maureen leaned against the door frame, unable to speak. She had been so sure that once Theresa saw her child, love would conquer her doubts as it conquered every other mother in the world. Theresa would see how wrong she'd been the very first time she looked into her baby's eyes, and she would be grateful to Maureen for having prevented the horror of an abortion.

But apparently Theresa still felt otherwise, even now, showing a hardness of heart Maureen would not have believed possible. Who can reject her own flesh and blood once he's been born? A drug addict, someone mentally ill, a selfish trollop? Theresa was none of those things. She had been loved. Maureen didn't understand why Theresa couldn't give love in return.

"You can't mean that," Maureen said, but even as she spoke, a part of her feared Theresa did mean it. She decided not to cross the border between the hallway and her daughter's bedside. She could see it wouldn't be a debate she could win, not at the moment. Maybe Theresa would change her mind after the shock of delivery wore off.

In part, Maureen blamed Lucy, who had abandoned the original plan to convince Theresa, not force her. Maureen had trusted Lucy, and now Lucy kept saying 'I'm sorry, I'm sorry.' What good did sorry do?

Without another word, Maureen went down the hall and back through the locked doors she had talked a staff member into letting her bypass. She reached the elevator where she pushed the button for the first-floor lobby. She had promised to let Tom know how things were going. Now she wondered how she could tell him.

Maybe she wouldn't have to tell him, she thought. There was still a chance Theresa would regain control of herself and claim her son, perhaps later today.

——•◦•——

Woodrow was tempted to follow Maureen and do his utmost to bridge the chasm that had opened between his daughter-in-law and her mama. If Theresa went back to Alabama, she would be reunited with Charlie, but she would still leave part of herself in Minnesota. She would have to explain to Charlie how she had abandoned their firstborn in a hospital without either one of them even seeing their son.

On the other hand, Charlie needed Theresa beside him as soon as possible. It might take too long to sort out matters in Minnesota.

In the end, Woodrow didn't follow Maureen. He turned back to comfort his daughter-in-law. Claire stood next to her sister, though he noticed she didn't touch her again.

"She still thinks she has a right to control me," Theresa told Woodrow, her eyes brimming. "I almost hate her."

"She is difficult," Claire said quietly. "But children love their mothers no matter what. It's a force of nature."

"Not for me, it's not a force of nature," Theresa replied. "I want Charlie. I love Charlie. The rest of the world can go to hell as far as I'm concerned."

Theresa pulled her body to the edge of the mattress. She slipped barefoot to the floor and began rummaging in a cupboard beneath the metallic table beside her.

"They cut off the dress I was wearing," Theresa informed them. "All I've got is this stupid gown with the back open. Nothing to wear out of this place!" She returned to the edge of the bed.

"I have a dress at the motel," Claire replied, not taking her eyes off her sister.

"Is that where you're keeping Pal?"

Claire nodded. "We bought him puppy food. He's got a water bowl. He's fine."

"Will you get me that dress *now*?" Theresa persisted.

"OK," Claire agreed. With that, she left the room.

"What about Charlie?" Theresa demanded as soon as her sister was out of sight.

"You better get back in bed, at least 'til she returns," said Woodrow. "Then I'll tell you 'bout Charlie."

"I'll sit here." Theresa plopped into a chair.

Woodrow talked slowly, minimizing what Charlie had gone through. Theresa bent at the waist and cried into her lap. He stopped talking and let her get it out, hoping she'd release as much pain as possible before she and Charlie were reunited. The more emotion discharged in Minnesota, the less she'd have to tamp down in Alabama.

It took Claire almost an hour to return with a loose-fitting dress and a scarf that could double as a belt, plus some lightweight leggings she'd purchased on the way back.

"I checked us out of the motel," she told Woodrow. "The puppy's in the car with the windows partly open. It's even hotter than yesterday, but I found a spot in the shade."

Theresa went into the bathroom to put on Claire's dress. She still looked a sight when she came out. Her hair needed shampooing. The bruises on her face were starting to turn purple. Claire was four inches shy of her sister's height, so her dress barely reached mid-thigh on Theresa. The leggings made it look like a long blouse. That was OK with Theresa, who sounded almost serene when she said, "This will do for now."

They took an elevator to the first-floor admissions desk where Theresa asked if there were anything she needed to sign before leaving.

"Are you authorized to leave?" the woman behind the desk asked.

"I'm leaving," Theresa repeated.

"Let me talk with the attending on your floor. Where were you?"

"Room 509."

"Your name and birth date?" Theresa gave her the information. "I see here in your file that someone from the FBI wants to interview you," the woman said when she'd finished making notes and having Theresa sign various forms. "They'd like you to call as soon as you feel well enough to talk to them. There's a card here . . ." She handed Theresa a business card. *Mitchell Gunderson*, it said. Theresa glanced at it but made no effort to take it. Woodrow reached past her and took it instead.

"I'm sure she'll call them when she's ready," he told the woman behind the desk.

Ten minutes later, a young, harried-looking doctor came out of the elevator and approached the desk. He seemed tired. His white coat had dark specks on one sleeve. He flipped through the pages of a chart he must have retrieved from the foot of Theresa's bed.

"I feel fine," Theresa told him.

He stopped flipping and returned Theresa's determined gaze with a pleading expression. "Please let me examine you, Ms . . ." He looked for the name. "Mrs. Cole."

"How long will that take? I don't want to go back upstairs."

Woodrow leaned toward her. "Let him make sure you're OK," he whispered.

The doctor shot him a look of gratitude. "There's an exam room down the hall, on *this* floor," he said.

A half hour later, the three of them were finally outside with a sheaf of instructions and orders to call 911 if Theresa experienced any bleeding, fever, or pelvic pain.

Woodrow opened the door of Claire's car so Theresa could climb into the back seat. Pal yelped as he jumped into her lap. Theresa fastened her seat belt, cooing at her small companion. She winced several times at the kicks he doled out.

"Sure you're OK to travel?" Woodrow asked Theresa.

"I'm fine," she said.

"Can you two spend a few nights at your place in St. Paul?" Woodrow asked Claire.

"Why do we need to spend time in St. Paul?" Theresa objected.

"We need to check out this car for the trip, for one thing, and make sure we've got everything we'll need packed inside, and at the same time let you get some rest after all you've been through."

"You need more clothes too," Claire reminded her sister.

"I'm staying here," Woodrow added. "There's things I've got to do."

"What things?" Theresa demanded.

"Patricia Conroy," Woodrow said.

"Who is Patricia Conroy?"

"She gave us information about Lucy Meyer," Claire told her sister. "Why do you need to see her?" she asked Woodrow.

"Promised I'd fix her car," he replied.

"*Now?*" both sisters responded.

"I may not be back. Now's the only time I got."

"It could take days to fix her car," Claire pointed out. "I don't think you owe her that."

Woodrow put his hand on Claire's knee. "I promised. Man's word is the measure of his character. We still believe that in Lafayette County."

"What's the point of my leaving the hospital today if we can't go straight to Charlie?" Theresa interjected.

"Don't worry, sweetheart. We'll get you there soon as we can," Woodrow said.

Claire dropped him in front of Patricia Conroy's house, and the sisters continued to St. Paul. Woodrow would make his own way to Claire's apartment, he said. They were not to worry.

Just shy of ten o'clock, Woodrow walked up Patricia Conroy's driveway. The vehicle was still on blocks, covered by the same blue tarp. It was wet from an early morning shower.

He didn't have to knock on the door. Ms. Conroy stood behind the screen, a spatula in her hand.

"That to swat me?" he asked, grinning.

"Making pancakes," she replied, smiling back.

"I'm here to fix your car," Woodrow said.

"You are?" She sounded surprised.

"You gave us vital information. In return, I promised to get your wheels back on the road. Got any tools?"

Ms. Conroy invited him inside. "'Nuff pancakes for two," she said. "Come on in."

"Kind of you, ma'am." He sat at her kitchen table.

"You're welcome to look around the garage," she allowed, setting a pancake on a plate for him. "That's real maple syrup in the pitcher. Help yourself. Coffee too. I don't usually make a big meal before I go to work, but today I was feeling sorry for myself. As you can see, I made too much batter."

"Thank you, ma'am," he said as he dove into the pancake. Woodrow hadn't eaten much in the past twenty-four hours.

"The garage is a mess. There's a toolbox belonged to my grandpa on a workbench in the back. Don't know what's inside."

"I'll look through it," Woodrow said. "And I'll have to find parts," he added. "What you got for a vehicle again?"

"'98 Volvo," she said. "Inherited from my grandparents. This was their house. They always kept their car in decent shape, but I haven't done a lot to take care of it since."

"Meaning, I'd guess, you haven't done more than drive it and buy gas?"

She laughed. "Pretty much. My boyfriend—ex-boyfriend—said a lot needs fixing."

"Willin' to trust me with your credit card? For the parts, I mean."

She exhaled and thought about it. "Just for the parts?"

144

"Yup. I'll give you all the receipts."

She thought for a moment. "The card's got a $5k limit."

"I'm hopin' it won't need that much. Where's the nearest Volvo dealership?"

Patricia didn't answer for a while. But then she announced, "I'm going to take a chance on you." That settled it. The dealership, it turned out, was three miles away, a parts store was less than two. Patricia gave him spare keys to the house, the garage, and the Volvo. "I sure hope you can be trusted," she told him.

Woodrow nodded.

"By the way, I don't work at the clinic anymore. I'm doing intake at an urgent care center. Noon to midnight. I get there on the bus, plus a mile walk."

Woodrow turned to leave.

"Just so you know, I left of my own free will," she added. "I wasn't fired." Woodrow wasn't really listening until she added, "Dr. Ryan resigned. He's gone from the clinic. He's leaving town, I think."

———•◦•———

The Volvo needed transmission work and a complete brake job. It also needed new shocks, an oil change, a warning light replaced, and new tires. Nonstop, with the right tools and a bay to hoist it up, Woodrow could finish in two to three days. But he had other things on his agenda. He called Claire at the end of the afternoon. "I'll try to get back by Monday. Might be late. Might be Tuesday," he told her.

"Theresa wants to talk to Charlie," Claire replied.

"I'd rather she not call him. Charlie can't speak well enough. My mother is with him now, and he can hardly have a conversation with her face-to-face. I think it's better if Theresa waits 'til she's there in person."

"It's all she can talk about," Claire persisted.

"Tell her, as sweetly as you can muster, that Charlie would be embarrassed if he couldn't make himself understood over the phone," Woodrow said. "A man needs to feel in charge at least of himself."

"I'll tell her as sweetly as I can muster," Claire said. "As sweetly as I always say things."

"Don't get in a lather . . . It's just that I noticed you two aren't exactly—"

"Close?"

Woodrow laughed. "Do your best. If she's still upset, tell her to call me."

He stopped at the parts store, and they put him with one of the owners who leased a bay attached to the warehouse next door. He agreed to rent it out for two hundred fifty dollars. Woodrow bargained him down to one hundred seventy-five and got him to throw in the tow. He called around to salvage yards and hired a salvage yard helper to fetch what he needed and bring the parts to the warehouse bay.

Woodrow worked until after midnight using tools on a pegboard in the bay. He carefully cleaned and oiled them before he put them back. When the owner returned to lock up, he shook his head in disbelief. "Not many mechanics work nonstop that long," he said, "not even on their own vehicles."

The transmission repair was far from done. Woodrow guessed it would take at least another day. "How about another hundred dollars to cover the cost of Sunday through noon Monday?" he inquired.

The owner laughed. His name was George, and he'd run his shop for thirty-eight years. He didn't usually rent to strangers, he said, especially not to a guy who wasn't even local. But he liked Woodrow for some reason, and there was nothing he needed to get done on the Lord's Day of rest, so he agreed to one hundred fifty dollars, but Woodrow had to be done by Monday, 7:00 a.m.

"Sooner," he added, "if I need it for an emergency."

Ten minutes later, Woodrow called Patricia and gave her an update on the Volvo. She offered to let him spend the night on her sofa, and he took her up on it. She allowed him to use her shower, after which he went out like a light, waking at six to the smell of bacon.

"This is Southern-style hospitality," he told her over breakfast.

"We can be hospitable in the North too," she said, adding, "Besides, you're fixin' my car."

They ate pretty much in silence until Patricia swallowed hard, and said, "There's something else."

"What?" he inquired. He had to get going, so his 'what' sounded a bit impatient.

"Before I left Dr. Ryan's practice, I saw those posters around town about Mary's sister, the one they said was abducted. So, my last day I looked into the computer at the clinic, 'cause her sister had been Dr. Ryan's patient. And there was no record. Her file was deleted from the computer. And so was any contact information for Lucy Meyer. It was all just . . . gone."

Woodrow flinched.

"Theresa's file was there in May," Patricia continued. "I know 'cause I saw her workup, and I was the one who filed her test results. Then the whole shebang disappeared. It wasn't even in the appointment diary."

Woodrow nodded. "I've gotta get going," he added. "Much obliged for the information. I'll be at the hospital awhile and then in the building next to the parts store. Your car is in a bay there. It should be out by sometime on Monday."

He wiped his hands on a napkin and started toward the door.

"Are you planning to live in Minnesota?" Patricia asked as he left.

He turned around. "No, ma'am. I'm headed back to Alabama in a few days."

"I've never been to Alabama," she remarked as the door swung shut.

———•◦•———

Early Sunday morning, Woodrow ran the distance from the parts store bay to the hospital entrance. It was nine and a quarter miles. He used the lobby restroom to wash up before presenting himself to the lady at the front desk. He needed to meet his grandson.

The receptionist told him where to get his visitor's bracelet, sanitary gown, and face mask prior to entering the NICU. When he got beyond the locked doors, he found Annie in the hallway looking through a glass wall at the bank of incubators. Only three seemed to be occupied. The distance and angle were too great to see much of the babies. One plastic dome held his grandson, but Woodrow couldn't tell which.

"Hi," Annie said, smiling shyly.

"Hi yourself," he replied. He put his hand on the back of her neck and squeezed. She giggled.

"He's in the one on the right," Annie said, reading his mind. "We've been in there, Mother and me. I mean Mother and I. Only one of us at a time, though. They let me stay five minutes, but my mother they gave longer."

Woodrow nodded. His grandson's first domicile stood on wheels like a trolley, and it had an undercarriage that held rectangular boxes, one about two-thirds the size of the other. Most of it was gray or transparent plastic, but the focal point had to be the blue boat that held the baby. Like a submarine periscope, a pole sprung up at one end with a screen attached.

An RN came out to check his bracelet. "The Haig/Cole baby," she said.

Woodrow shook his head in the affirmative, fighting tears. He hadn't thought being here would affect him so much.

"Have you seen him before?" the nurse asked.

"No," he said, smiling at her. "First time."

"You may be in for a shock. You've washed thoroughly, using the antiseptic soap and lotion on *all* exposed skin?"

"Yeah, I was real careful about that."

"Are your vaccinations up to date?"

"Yes, ma'am."

"Do you have a cold or feel one coming on?"

"No, ma'am," he said, smiling.

"Good. Put this on, and I'll take you in," she continued, still not smiling back. She handed him a sealed packet containing a hairnet. He put the hairnet on, even though his hair was short and shampooed that morning.

They went inside. The RN explained that at twenty-four weeks, a child's lungs are not developed enough for him to breathe on his own so he needs a controlled environment. He was what they call a micro preemie, born at less than twenty-six weeks–though he might be twenty-six weeks or even twenty-seven weeks old. They couldn't be entirely sure.

Woodrow didn't hear the rest because he was looking down at Charlie's son. The tyke's chances weren't the greatest, Woodrow understood. But he could also see the grit in the little fellow's face, or what was visible of it.

This baby was a Cole. Like Charlie, he'd make it back to Lafayette. He would walk someday. He'd laugh. He'd get rid of all those tubes and wires and rise up out of his submarine and become whatever he was capable of being.

When Woodrow returned to the hallway, he saw Maureen standing next to Annie.

"You're still in Minnesota," Maureen observed.

"Yep. Had to meet my son's son since—"

Maureen cut in, "There's a meeting on the second floor in a half hour." She looked at her watch. "Twenty minutes, actually. Being a grandfather, you should be there. We need to determine who'll have temporary foster custody. That's what they call it."

She put her hand around Annie's upper arm and pulled her along through the NICU doors that locked automatically from inside whenever anyone left.

Woodrow took off his sanitation gear, dumped it into a bin, then followed Annie and her mother to the elevators. Annie made eye contact and smiled once they got inside. Maureen stared over his shoulder at the elevator wall.

———•◆•———

The second-floor conference room had a long, glossy mahogany table with accent strips of zebra wood and walnut. *Pricey*, Woodrow thought. This was no poor man's hospital. The table could easily fit twenty people. Around it, padded navy-blue chairs moved on wheels over a flat, blue-speckled gray carpet. A display monitor covered most of one wall. Woodrow sat down as Maureen, Tom, and another man came in, choosing seats across from him in the middle of the table. The extra man was elderly, maybe eighty, Woodrow guessed, but he detected a sharpness behind the old man's eyes. The man stood, reached across the table to shake Woodrow's hand, and said, "Hi, there. Name's Ben Johnson. I'm here to advise the Haigs."

"You're a lawyer?" Woodrow asked.

"Yup," Ben Johnson said.

Woodrow nodded, wondering if the chips were stacked again him. Against Charlie too, he thought, given that Theresa didn't want to raise the baby.

A storm of people entered, took chairs, and introduced themselves. Chief Hospital Administrator Laura Himley. Hospital attorneys. Some kind of outside attorney. Pediatrics doc named Lennox or Lenix, something like that, plus Stears County Child Protective Services Director Beverly Hagen, and finally a young woman with carafes of coffee and ceramic hospital mugs on a cart.

After the introductions and the coffee pouring, Beverly Hagen took the lead.

"We're here at the invitation of St. Dominic's to lay out the situation regarding the Cole infant," she began.

"His name is Patrick," Maureen interrupted loudly. Tom patted her hand.

Ms. Hagen cleared her throat. "The child," she continued, "has been turned over to St. Dominic's at the request of his mother under the Minnesota safe haven law, which allows surrender of a newborn to a hospital within seventy-two hours of birth, no questions asked."

The pediatrician coughed and cleared his throat. His fingers strummed the table as Beverly went on.

"Child Protective Services was called, per state law, and now the newborn, who is also a premature infant . . ."

"He's a micro preemie," the pediatrician corrected.

"A micro preemie," Ms. Hagen repeated.

"Born before twenty-six weeks," the doctor added. "Under two pounds. High risk."

Ms. Hagen nodded.

"Pessimism is uncalled for," said Maureen, still seated. "Patrick's a baby. He's not a *micro* preemie." Tom squeezed her hand again.

"In any case, the newborn is in this hospital. After signing his birth certificate, his mother surrendered him, and he is now under the jurisdiction of the Minnesota Department of Human Services and Stears County Child Protective Services and will remain so until a suitable home can be found, and by that, I mean temporary foster care until a court can determine—" Ms. Hagen said.

Woodrow stood up. "Excuse me, ma'am. I'm Woodrow Cole, and my son Charles Cole is the father of this baby. My son is currently being treated for injuries that occurred in Afghanistan. He is now recoverin' in Birmingham, and it will take some time before he is able to resume normal life. In the meantime, I'd like to point out that he has not, as the baby's father, surrendered parental rights or anythin' else. Before you start talkin' about a 'suitable home,' I think you might keep that in mind." He sat down again.

Ms. Hagen nodded. She cleared her throat.

"Does that mean," she asked Woodrow, "that you are asserting Stears County should not have temporary legal custody of this child while he's being cared for in this hospital?"

"I don't know what my son wants," Woodrow replied. "But you should remember that he has signed away nothin', given up nothin'. In the meantime, while he's recoverin', his baby needs that NICU you've got, and my son is grateful for it."

"We *do* know what we want," Maureen interjected, standing this time. "As Patrick's grandparents and the ones who know his mother better than anyone, we'd like to raise him in the home where his mother was raised. We want to adopt him, unless his mother changes her mind. We don't want him going to some redneck place where they can't take care of him."

She glared at Woodrow, whose nostrils flared. He felt a prodigious measure of sympathy for any child of Maureen Haig.

"And," Maureen continued, "I think we should arrange for transport immediately to Children's Hospital in St. Paul. People at my church have been telling me what miracles they perform there. I talked to one of their hospital's administrators last night. I think it's where Patrick should be treated."

Ben Johnson leaned over and whispered something to Tom, who rose just as the pediatrician also stood up.

"My wife is getting ahead of herself," Tom said emphatically. "Adoption is not something we need to talk about right now. It takes a lot of thinking to figure out how to deal with this situation."

The pediatrician intervened. "Sit down, everyone, and let me explain a few things." He wiped his brow with a tissue from a box on the table and tossed it on the floor.

"First off, our NICU facility is outstanding. You can't find better anywhere in this state, in the entire Midwest as a matter of fact . . ." He paused briefly. "Mrs. Haig," He turned his focus to Maureen, who had resumed her seat. "Moving this child would be risking his life at the moment of his greatest vulnerability. You're gambling with his life if you think moving him would help. It would probably *kill* him."

Beverly Hagen looked troubled and was about to say something when the doctor resumed. "If you had any idea what it takes to save a micro preemie— the team, the talent and training, the experience, the constant monitoring, the interventions, the knowing what needs to be done immediately . . . If you understood the added stress on the infant's body if he's moved—on his heart and lungs especially—if you'd ever seen an infant with RDS because there's not enough surfactant, or with a PDA that won't close on its own, or any one of a number of other issues that require intervention that can't wait—" He stopped to take a deep breath, then concluded, "Well, you wouldn't suggest such a . . . such a wrong-headed thing as taking him out of here." He looked as if he wanted to strangle Maureen.

Laura Himley, the hospital administrator, cut in before anyone else could. "Indeed, our patient has a difficult road ahead of him," she said. "We need to keep him at St. Dominic long enough for him to leave the incubator. That may be months from now. In the meantime," she continued, looking at Maureen, "he needs time and love and good medicine that we can provide. Moving him would be dangerous, as Dr. Lenix has made clear. I would add that Dr. Lenix is one of the finest neonatal physicians in the Midwest. He has extensive certification in neonatal medicine and specializes in cardiac care for pediatric patients. I can explain in more detail if you'll come to my office, Mrs. Haig."

Woodrow got the impression this administrator put out a lot of fires.

"Our attorneys," Ms. Himley continued, "would not want any of us to be liable for what might happen if a micro preemie is moved. I'd also like to remind everyone that this baby is in St. Dominic Hospital at the request of our county social services agency. Under the safe haven law, the mother has relinquished custody of the child not to any relative or other individual but to our county social welfare agency, as the state statute stipulates. The safe haven law says nothing about the rights and responsibilities of the baby's father. They are yet to be determined. In the meantime, the county holds temporary legal custody. No one should presume any other rights at this time, and that includes relatives on both sides."

Ms. Himley stopped talking. She seemed to anticipate more questions. But no one else had anything to say. After glancing at his pager, Dr. Lenix left the room.

Woodrow checked out Maureen's expression again. She stared back at him. It might be a bad idea to leave Minnesota, he thought, since returning to Alabama meant ceding the field to her and whatever decisions she might try to make about his son's baby. But he had to get Theresa back to Charlie. He didn't want her traveling alone on a plane.

The meeting seemed to be over. People departed in twos and threes, Tom looking the most disgruntled. As Woodrow turned to follow, he saw that Annie had snuck into the room and sat unnoticed, slunk down in a chair at the far end of the table.

A half hour later, a bus rumbled its way down the street in front of the hospital as Woodrow contemplated whether he had enough wind to retrace his previous run. He'd need seven to eight additional hours to finish repairs on the Volvo. Running back would be faster and give him more time to do the work, but he was well past his glory days. If an occasional ten miles was achievable, two in one day might stretch his ability to accomplish much else.

That made it a challenge, he thought. He'd decided to let the bus go without him when he saw Annie. She had just exited a parked white Cadillac and was walking toward him. Her mother lowered the vehicle's front window and yelled something, but Annie kept walking. On the other side of the car, Tom Haig stood with his lawyer.

"I just talked to Mary—I mean Claire," Annie announced on arriving in front of Woodrow.

"How did you manage that without a phone?"

"Got one!" she exulted, pulling it out of her jeans. "It was a surprise present from my dad for my fourteenth birthday. Mother didn't even know he was getting it."

"Congratulations," Woodrow said. "Claire say how Theresa's doin'?"

"She's sleeping a lot," Annie said quickly, adding, "Claire says you're all going to Alabama soon. I thought maybe I could come along. It's summer, so I wouldn't miss any school."

"What do your parents say?"

"I haven't asked them yet. What would *you* say?"

"That you need your parents' permission."

The Haig vehicle—a vintage four-door Cadillac in prime condition—drove up with Tom at the wheel. The rocker panels had been replaced, Woodrow noticed, and the front passenger door was not original either. Its shade of white was slightly brighter than its surroundings, though you had to look closely in bright light to notice. There wasn't a scratch on it that Woodrow could see. It was waxed to perfection. The chrome gleamed. Tom was a man who loved cars.

"Annie, get in," Tom yelled.

Woodrow thought they'd drive off, but to his surprise, Tom got out, came around to the front of the car, and offered his hand.

"I liked what you said back there," he told Woodrow. "About your son's rights. I want you to know my wife's heart is in the right place, but I don't think she's thought it through. If you and your family lay claim to this child, I'm not going to oppose you."

Woodrow shook his hand. "We don't know yet what Charlie wants or what he'll be capable of once he's out of the hospital."

"Understood. Can we drop you anywhere?" Tom motioned toward his car.

"That'd be mighty kind," Woodrow said.

"Get in the back with Annie. Seems she can't get enough of you."

"She's a nice kid."

"Yeah," Tom said, "with crazy ideas."

He dropped Woodrow in the alley behind the auto parts store.

———•◦•———

Tom drove home at high speed. Ben waited on the porch.

"Thanks for stopping by," Tom said to him. "Let's brew us some coffee."

He made it. He didn't ask Maureen, who was still in a sulk from the hospital, and he certainly didn't look forward to the conversation they were about to have, which was why he wanted his lawyer there to reinforce what he needed to tell his wife. He put out mugs, poured half-and-half in a creamer, and laid spoons and place mats on the table—all things Maureen would normally do.

Maureen was last through the door. She set her purse on the counter, and as slowly as she could, took a cherry pie out of the pantry and placed it in the center of the table within everyone's reach. She opened the cupboard and half-heartedly retrieved dishes, forks, a stainless-steel pie server, and a knife Tom kept well sharpened. She hunted for clean cloth napkins in the living room hutch, found four matching ones, and put them alongside the pie.

Annie sat at the end of the table, having poured herself a glass of water. Tom filled the coffee cups.

Tom and Ben talked about the weather and how well Tom's soybeans were doing. They speculated about the price he'd get. The prices for both corn and soybeans had dipped drastically since new tariffs went into effect. Everybody hated the tariffs.

During a pause, Maureen broke in. "I'm set on adopting our grandson," she announced, "unless, and I mean only unless, Theresa takes hold of herself and reclaims her child."

Tom took a sip of his coffee and set the mug down. Ben hadn't touched a thing yet.

"That's not the way it's going to be," Tom said flatly.

"Do you think I'm going to let my precious grandson be swallowed up by those heathens in Alabama?" Maureen asked angrily.

Annie stiffened. "They aren't heathens," she asserted. "Woodrow isn't a heathen . . . and even if he were a heathen, so was Voltaire."

They all looked at her. Tom said harshly, "Go to your room or outside. This is no conversation for kids." When Annie hesitated, he added, "Get going!"

Annie retreated to the back stairs where she could still hear what was said.

"Why are you so set against it?" Maureen implored her husband.

"It's not our job. It's Theresa's job and her husband's job. Do you know what it costs to raise a sickly kid?"

"What does that matter?" Maureen retorted, her voice rising almost to a screech. "We've got so much land. If we need money for Patrick, we could sell a few acres and not even miss it."

At the word *sell*, Tom's face reddened. "You, my darling, have nothing to sell," he said.

"What are you talking about?" Maureen retorted.

"Sell needs ownership," Tom replied. "You sell what you own. As far as this farm is concerned, you own exactly nothing."

Ben winced. "That's not the way I would have put it," he observed.

"I own half of everything," Maureen insisted. "Half this house, half our land, half our crops, half our animals. We share fifty-fifty. That's what marriage is about."

"No," Tom said quietly. "This farm we live on is in a trust my father set up after his father died. I am the trustee, but I have never owned it. The trust owns the land, the crops, the animals, the barns, even this house. I draw a salary from the trust, and I make decisions concerning the farm until our sons take over, one of 'em at least. So, bottom line, this farm is not yours to do anything with, much less waste its value on a baby who would suck us dry with medical bills."

Tom paused. "Tell her, Ben," he said sharply. Ben did not speak. "Where the hell is my backup?" Tom demanded.

Maureen looked at their lawyer, bewildered, before turning back to her husband.

"You want to pile one failure on top of another! Our failure to raise a daughter who would never abandon a child God gave her. And now you want us to fail to rescue our own grandchild?" Her voice breaking, she paused a moment for breath. Tom and Ben said nothing.

"Theresa was automatically excommunicated when she chose to have an abortion. That she was unable to commit her sin is beside the point. She tried! She failed only because wiser heads intervened. So then, with no way to kill her child once he was born, she abandoned him instead. We can't repeat her mistakes. God would never forgive us."

"Tom is right about one thing," Ben said when he thought Maureen had

154

finished. "The farm is in a trust." He looked at her sympathetically.

"I have no idea what that means. What is a *trust*?" Maureen demanded.

"Tom should have told you years ago," Ben said. "This is the kind of family secret that tears people apart. To Tom, this farm is a living thing, a link from generation to generation. To you, Maureen, it seems more like a family resource to be tapped in case of emergency. But that's not the way its ownership is defined. Maureen, a trust is a vehicle set up to protect assets so they're not available to be taken out except by the trustee. That's not you. You can't sell any part of it."

"I had no idea," Maureen said quietly, on the verge of tears again. "Honestly, it's just one thing after another. I don't understand your legal mumbo jumbo, Ben. But I do know this. If Tom and I abandon our grandson, then we are worthless. Patrick needs to be baptized and raised in our faith. *Our* faith! Anything else, we'll have behaved no better than Theresa. We'll have abandoned our religion along with our grandchild. I will not do that. My religion means more to me than anything in this world . . ."

"That right?" Tom interrupted. "You love your religion more than me? More than your children? More than this life we built together?"

"More than anything," Maureen repeated.

"And you think your religion gives you the right to make other people do what you want?" Tom continued.

"To do *what is right*," Maureen countered. "I have an obligation to see that what is right happens."

"And if it doesn't happen just 'cause you want it? You can't treat people like livestock you have control over and tell me, my goddamn religion says it's right!"

"My religion is your religion too," Maureen yelled at him. "It's *your* way to eternal life."

"Eternal life," Tom scoffed. "When you're dead, you're dead. You're like a little kid, Maureen. I'm the only grown-up on this farm."

Another silence stretched. Husband and wife beheld each other as strangers.

"I've known you both a long time," Ben said, looking back and forth between them. "As a friend as well as your attorney. I like you both. You're thinking on different wavelengths is all." Neither of his clients said anything. "Folks, I think you need to contemplate this matter long and hard before you decide anything. Husband and wife conversations are not my bailiwick. I've got nothing to contribute when it comes to psychological matters, or religion, or any of those aspects of life."

Neither Tom nor Maureen replied. Ben stood up to leave.

Annie stayed where she was, perched on the bottom step of the back stairs, where the tip of one of her shoes was still visible from the kitchen.

"When you're dead, you're dead," she whispered. "Hamlet made it sound a lot more complicated."

Carole Novak parked her dusty Kia in front of Claire's duplex. Moments later, Claire and Woodrow pulled up behind her.

"A semi dropped him on I-94 at Lexington Avenue," Claire told Carole as she approached. "He met the driver at a pit stop in St. Dominic, and she just up and offered to make a detour and give him a lift to St. Paul."

Claire and Carole exchanged a wry look.

The afternoon was pleasant, just shy of eighty degrees. Claire suggested they sit on her porch overlooking the street. Most of the houses in the neighborhood had flower displays in their front yards: daylilies, coneflower, veronica, daisies. They calmed the spirit. Except for the cars and utility wires, it might have been a hundred years ago.

Claire led Carole out to the porch, abandoning Woodrow in the living room. Then she went back inside and reemerged with a tray holding chilled glasses and a pitcher of lemonade. Carole pulled out her notebook and voice recorder.

The porch's furniture included a white wicker settee positioned against the wall it shared with the house. It looked comfortable, padded by thick blue and white cushions, but Carole took one of the hard pine chairs facing it, guessing that Claire would want to sit beside her sister on the settee. Claire had warned her on the phone that Theresa was fragile, angry, and suspicious of just about everybody.

When Theresa followed Claire outside, for the first time Carole met the woman who, supposedly, could back up Claire's version of the putative crime, a crime neither the sheriff's detectives in St. Dominic nor the police department would admit had actually happened.

Claire's sister had been crying. You could tell she was pretty beneath the bruises and blotches on her face and arms. At first glance, Carole had taken them for tattoos, but she realized now they were the result of a serious altercation.

Unfortunately, the father-in-law, Woodrow, came out of the apartment and joined them on the porch. He looked like he'd just had a shower. Carole found his presence annoying and hoped he wouldn't say much. Theresa set herself at the end of the settee closest to Woodrow. She held a white puppy in her lap.

Carole knew from experience that interviews went best when the number of participants remained small, focused, and—except for the reporter and her subject—silent. The ideal setup was interviewer and interviewee, and no one else.

"Woodrow," Theresa said, ignoring the others, "have you spoken to Charlie?"

"I talked to my mama this mornin'," he replied. "Charlie's still not too good on the phone."

"Oh," said Theresa, tearing up. "He can't talk?"

"He can talk fine. But it's easier for him when the person is sittin' right there."

"So why did it take you so long to get here?" she accused.

Woodrow's reply seemed apologetic. "Made a promise," he said. "We were so desperate to find you, I'd have given just about anythin' for the information we needed. To tell you the truth, though, the only thing I regret was the lack of reconnaissance when we tried to rescue you. I went on a mission unprepared. No excuse for that."

"It's OK," Theresa said. "I've been feeling faint the last few days, and I needed to sleep. But I don't want to waste any more time."

"Theresa, would you mind if I record our conversation?" Carole asked, impatient with all this off-point conversation. "I wouldn't want to misquote you."

Theresa looked at Carole. "Who are you?" she asked.

Carole lowered her voice. "I'm a reporter with the *Minneapolis Free Press*. I'd like to write a story about what happened to you."

Theresa hesitated. "I'm not sure I want a story in the newspaper," she said.

"How about doing the interview today, and then you can decide later if we can quote you in print?" Carole suggested. "In the meantime, I might be able to check what you tell me against what other people say . . ."

Theresa nodded. Carole took that to mean she could use her digital voice recorder.

"So, can you tell me about the day you disappeared?"

"I went to see my obstetrician . . ." Theresa began.

She recounted everything: the clinic visit, Lucy Meyer's intrusion into Dr. Ryan's office, the test results she didn't get to see, the ambush at her mother's house, the women in her mother's living room and how they talked to her . . .

"Did you get to know these women during the weeks they held you against your will?" Carole asked.

"Roberta Wells and Sarah—mainly," Theresa said. "There were more in the beginning, but at the end it was just those two."

"What about Lucy Meyer? Did you get to know her?"

"She's a monster," Theresa said.

"How many different houses were you held in?"

"The first one was a farmhouse. The second was on a lake. The last one was in some kind of marshy area. I don't know where it was, but it must have been close to the hospital because it didn't take us long to get there."

"Tell me about Roberta Wells. She's the wife of David Wells, whose company will do an IPO in a few weeks."

Theresa nodded, answering questions for more than an hour. No one interrupted. Carole used her cell phone to photograph Theresa with the puppy.

"What do you think motivated these women to abduct *you* in particular?" Carole asked.

Theresa shrugged. "I think they're always motivated."

"What do you mean, *always motivated*?"

"Like in a cult. Anyone thinking about abortion could be a target."

"They can't be pleased with the outcome," Carole noted. "I mean when you consider the difference between what they intended to accomplish versus what they actually accomplished."

"You'd have to ask them," Theresa said coldly.

"I thought maybe you had some idea—"

"Well, I don't," Theresa snapped.

"I understand," Carole replied. Theresa stood up. Woodrow stood too.

"Maybe you should call it quits now," he told Carole in a voice that sounded like an order. Carole hesitated, then turned off her recorder. Claire walked her to her car.

"Given what she's been through, I think she needs some space," Claire advised. "Let things settle down."

"Stories don't wait for things to settle down," Carole said. "Just the opposite."

———•◦•———

Theresa stretched out on Claire's bed. It was still mussed from a nap she'd taken earlier with Pal snuggled beside her. The bedroom door was closed. The atmosphere was calm, quiet, dim. It was a relaxing place where she'd slept for most of two days.

Claire's bedroom faced north so the midsummer sunshine didn't stream in. The curtains stirred in a slight breeze. Her cell phone lay on a table next to the bed. Theresa picked it up and punched in the number on the business card she'd propped against the alarm clock. The clock read 4:47 p.m.

She half-hoped she'd get a voice mail this late in the afternoon so she could simply leave a message, but a man answered.

"Mitchell Gunderson," he said.

"Mr. Gunderson, I'm Theresa Cole. You left your card for me at St. Dominic Hospital. I'm the—"

"I know who you are, Mrs. Cole."

"You're with the FBI."

"Yes, I am. We've been very worried about you, Mrs. Cole. How are you?"

Theresa laughed, and even to herself, she sounded bitter. "I've been very worried about me too," she said. "I'm doing better now. Still not a hundred percent, but at the moment I'm more concerned about my husband than I am about myself."

"Where are you, Mrs. Cole?"

"I'm at my sister's apartment in St. Paul."

"I'm in Brooklyn Center. I wonder if we could get together, maybe tomorrow, either in St. Paul or here at the bureau."

"I'm leaving town tomorrow morning," Theresa said.

"You are?" He paused. "May I ask where you're going?"

"Alabama," she said. "I need to be with my husband."

"Mrs. Cole, I'd be willing to come to you. I could drive over and be there about an hour from now, depending on traffic."

"That's why I'm calling. To be honest, I don't think there's anything I care to tell you."

He paused. "Mrs. Cole, may I ask outright, were you kidnapped last May? Were you taken by force and kept in captivity?"

Theresa waited, breathing deeply before she answered. "As soon as I answer that question, things will happen, won't they?"

"What do you mean?"

"I mean you'll open a case. I'll become part of an investigation."

"You're already part of an investigation, Mrs. Cole. You've been part of an investigation since your sister reported you missing."

"Well, the fact of the matter is, I've decided I don't want to be caught up in that. Correct me if I'm wrong, but I'm guessing you'd need me to cooperate if this investigation goes any further. I'd be expected to do things, say things, show up and testify and deal with all kinds of people. It will get—complicated, since I'll be in Alabama, and you'll be in Minnesota, and there'll be hearings and depositions and I don't know what all."

"Criminal cases can get complicated, yes, Mrs. Cole. That doesn't mean they're not warranted. That doesn't mean we don't try to see justice done if someone has deprived a person of liberty. The government can't allow people

159

to be taken against their will."

"Yes, I understand that. But what if I tell you how it feels from my point of view? I just spent part of this afternoon going over it all for the first time since I got free. It was like reliving it. And in a way that was good. It helped me turn the corner a little, at least. But right now, I have to tell you, my husband needs me more than I need to get some kind of revenge for what people did to me. I can't afford to spend the next, I don't know, umpteen days or weeks going over and over what happened this summer while my husband is trying to recover from what he's been through. And I don't even know yet what all he's been through. I haven't seen him since before it happened."

"I know your husband was wounded in Afghanistan, Mrs. Cole, and I was very sorry to hear that. I can understand he's your first priority, but at the same time—"

"At the same time, I can't talk to you right now. That's what I'm trying to say. I'd like you to take this case, or whatever you want to call it, I'd like you to put this investigation on hold."

"It doesn't work that way, Mrs. Cole . . ."

"Well, tell me this—if I don't meet with you, if I don't swear to some kind of statement, and cooperate with your investigation starting right now, what happens then? Can you compel me to do something?" She heard silence from the other end. She waited.

"What happens then," Mitchell Gunderson said, "is that the bureau can't proceed. We need your testimony. We need you to tell us what happened so we can investigate further and ultimately present a case to a jury. That's how our system works. If a victim won't come forward, it makes it very hard for us to do our job, and it makes it hard for us to prevent a similar crime from happening again."

"I understand that," Theresa said. "Believe me, I'm not making light of this. It was a horrible ordeal. I can't begin to tell you, and I don't even know how I'll feel about it tomorrow or the day after. But right now, at this moment in my life, I need to be with my husband, and I cannot—I just cannot spend time dealing with the FBI. No matter how important it is. My husband is the person who matters now. Not what happened to me." She could hear his steady breathing. "I'm sorry," she said.

"May I call you later on?" he asked. "Say, in a week or so?"

"I'll be at this number," she told him. "But honestly, I don't know that I'll feel any differently."

Woodrow had to see his grandson again. Elena, the cute NICU nurse now on an afternoon shift, agreed to a Zoom session. Woodrow sat on Claire's porch, communing with the littlest Cole, a doll-like bundle the size of Woodrow's hand.

The nurses were calling him Patrick, even though the name on the birth certificate had no legal significance. Whoever got ultimate custody could name him whatever they chose.

For the moment, though, Maureen had outsized influence, since she was in St. Dominic, and everyone else was not. When Theresa signed the birth certificate, Woodrow figured she probably didn't bother to change the name put down the night before because she didn't care. Woodrow didn't care about the name either. He was just glad the county welfare people had temporary legal custody, so Maureen couldn't assume anything more than she already had.

He wished the screen on his cell phone were three times bigger. The staff had put a sign on the front of the incubator, "Patrick Haig/Cole." The baby's bottom half was mostly diaper, with two little sticks, each leading to a tiny foot.

It made him look all the more like a minuscule space visitor. He had a tube in his mouth connected to a ventilator that breathed for him. They would eventually replace it with a mask attached to his face but not yet, Elena said. He had an IV line stuck into his umbilical stump to mimic the womb's nutrition. He had stickers attached to wires on his chest, his feet, both wrists, his arms, and his little legs, none of which moved. He seemed frozen in place. The sight of him warmed Woodrow and chilled him at the same time. He was profoundly grateful that people like Elena hovered over Charlie's son, watching for any sign of distress and ready at any moment to call in the medical equivalent of the Marines.

"His grandmother had him baptized last night," Elena informed him. "Her priest performed the ceremony, using an eye dropper. They were quick about it . . . just a few seconds with the canopy up. We're not supposed to allow that sort of thing, but his grandmother practically begged the shift supervisor, and she's a devout Catholic herself. I hope that's OK with you."

"I don't mind," Woodrow said. "Long as it didn't cause any harm. How's he doin' now?" He tried to keep his tone upbeat.

"We're watching a number of issues," Elena said. "The biggest are his eyes, whether his sight will be OK, plus whether there's any bleeding on his brain, and third, how his digestive system functions. But we shouldn't get ahead of ourselves. We need to take it one day at a time."

"Could you point your phone at him again?" Woodrow asked.

She did, and Woodrow looked for any sign of movement. The infant's chest rose and fell in slight undulations, almost imperceptibly. His tiny fingers were still. His booties didn't move either, his toes hidden inside. But he was pink. Pink was good.

Elena promised they could stay in touch. She had to end the call because someone else had come into the NICU. "Sorry," she said, and was gone.

Woodrow sat on the wicker settee, the last image of his grandson stamped on his mind. Carole Novak had left an hour earlier. Theresa was inside with Pal. Claire walked onto the porch.

"Someone check out your car?" he inquired.

"My mechanic worked on it this morning. Nothing major, nothing like what you did for Patricia Conroy."

"That sticks in your craw, don't it?" Woodrow asked.

"Well, it seemed excessive," Claire replied. "You spent three extra days in St. Dominic fixing a car for a woman you don't even know."

"So what?"

Claire laughed. "The men I've known are less profligate," she said.

"Profligate . . . don't think I ever been called that before. I'd say it was plain decency, given what she did for us. Your objectin' makes me wonder what's a decent man in your book?"

Woodrow leaned back against the cushion behind him, absentmindedly reaching into his pocket for cigarettes that weren't there.

"I'm the last person you should ask," Claire said.

"Why?"

"I don't generally trust people, especially men. So, I'm not on the lookout for decency."

"Ever been in love?"

"Oh, yeah. Worst mistake of my life. I found out what men are really like after I married Rob."

"That mean you're done with the lot of us?"

"Show me a man who doesn't take what he wants and tell a woman he's doing her a favor in the process, and I'll show you a better actor than most. There is a war between the sexes."

Woodrow smiled. "Well, you know what they say about that particular war . . ."

"What?" Claire asked sarcastically.

"It'll never be won . . . too much fraternization with the enemy." He smiled again, hoping to lighten the mood.

"That's a bad cliché, don't you think?" Claire retorted.

"It's the plain fact of the matter . . . And speakin' of plain fact, I see how it is 'tween you and Theresa. As I recall, you didn't come to her weddin' either. Why's that, I wonder?"

"She didn't invite me," Claire replied, a tremor in her voice.

That possibility hadn't occurred to Woodrow. He looked away, so as not to embarrass her.

Claire changed her tone a moment later. "I suppose you'll want to leave bright and early?"

"I'd say five, six at the latest," he answered. "But it's your car. By rights you set the schedule."

"We'll leave at seven," Claire decided, opening the porch door. "I'm too old for five or six."

Woodrow shook his head. He didn't much like it when a woman called herself old, especially if she wasn't. And in his experience, hardly any women called themselves old, even the old ones.

5

Claire's 2010 Jeep Commander drove more like a toy than a real vehicle, in Woodrow's opinion. An imitation Cherokee, it was all right angles and cut corners and about as comfortable as a stagecoach. He wondered aloud how she'd kept it going for ninety-five thousand miles.

"If you're trying to goad me, it won't work," Claire informed him.

"No, ma'am. I'm tellin' you the god-awful truth."

Claire drove the first two hundred miles. Woodrow felt antsy sitting in the passenger seat with a woman at the wheel, but there was nothing he could do. Her vehicle, her rules. In the back seat, Theresa listened to music on Claire's old iPod, noise-cancelling headphones over her ears, Pal asleep on her lap.

Woodrow kept alert for ticking noises, warning lights, water leaks, and turn signal malfunctions. He didn't want to get pulled over by a state patrol officer, and he certainly didn't want to deal with a breakdown, given he was bereft of tools at the moment.

They stopped often, mainly so Theresa could walk around and Pal could relieve himself. Theresa had him on a pink leash she bought at a convenience store, as if a self-respecting male of any species should have to tolerate a pink leash. Woodrow didn't make a point of it. You couldn't joke with Theresa.

Every time they slid into a gas station, Woodrow lifted the hood and looked for trouble. Worst case scenario, this piece of shit broke down far from a repair shop. He thought about that possibility but didn't want to spook Claire by saying it. The mission was to get Theresa back to Charlie. Two hundred miles in, Claire let him drive.

Behind the wheel, Woodrow glanced at her from time to time and saw the tension in Claire's face. Every time they stopped, she felt her sister's forehead. Both of them kept a lookout for hospital signs and stuck to the freeways. Woodrow made mental notes of mile markers and ramp exit numbers.

They'd departed St. Paul a little after 7:00 a.m. on Tuesday, July 31, and arrived in Birmingham by late afternoon on Thursday. Theresa didn't seem worried. She wasn't bleeding, she'd said nonchalantly. That remark worried Woodrow all the more.

———•◦•———

Theresa tried not to dwell on Charlie's injuries as they headed south. She struggled to put what happened to him out of her mind, which meant what Charlie suffered came over her in waves, minutes apart, like contractions birthing a whole new couple. Their days of bliss were over. They were sober people now.

At least she knew the truth. At least Woodrow had been the one who told her. His voice and cadence reminded her of Charlie. He was of, for, and from Alabama, a place that had no connection whatsoever to her mother.

Charlie's family had embraced her from the first time he took her to Lafayette. They'd met accidentally at the airport in Atlanta. She'd been on a layover with friends coming back from Cancun.

Who stops in the middle of a concourse to help a handsome soldier pick up paperwork he'd dropped on the floor at the very moment she walked by? A tourist on the cheapest flight possible, she absolutely had to reach St. Dominic in time to put herself together for a new job that started the next day, yet she ended up throwing her ticket away and ditching the job.

Her friends thought she was crazy, but how they'd envied her! She and Charlie spent his leave getting to know each other. His family put her up.

Charlie proposed when his leave was over and he had to report back to his base. He got down on one knee their last afternoon, putting his great-grandmother's ring on her finger, a sapphire in a white gold setting that his grandmother had saved for the next generation. Theresa wore it back to Minnesota, where her family seemed less than thrilled to hear she would marry a stranger. Her mother was particularly upset, assuming, Theresa suspected, that she and Charlie had already slept together, and possibly conceived an out-of-wedlock child. Charlie and Theresa had not slept together. But Theresa would never share with her mother what she and Charlie did or did not do.

At Theresa's insistence, Woodrow stopped at a mall in St. Louis where she bought a tea-length summer dress with butterflies embroidered on a field of white muslin. It had long sleeves that would cover up what remained of the bruises on her arms. She'd wear the dress when she saw Charlie again, and it would erase time, put them back in that forest clearing where he'd proposed. The closer she got to Alabama, the more she assured herself that Charlie would be on the mend by the time she arrived and his injuries would have no long-term effects.

During their last stop, about twenty miles outside Birmingham, Woodrow took Theresa aside while Claire, having filled the tank, went into the station. Claire wouldn't let Woodrow pay for gas.

"Can I say something without hurtin' your feelings?" he asked.

Theresa grew tense. "You can try," she said as Pal licked her arm. "Depends on what it is."

"It's about what you tell Charlie. I know this sounds like I'm interferin', and I guess I am. You and Charlie have your own way of communicatin', and you can probably read his mind and explain things to him better than anyone. But sooner or later, he's goin' to hear the whole story of what you went through, the birth and all, and you surrenderin' the baby." Woodrow paused. "Sooner is better than later. It should all come out. And comin' from you is better than from anyone else."

Theresa's face remained impassive. "I'm not going to argue about it," she told Woodrow.

"It's not about arguin'. It's about sharin'," Woodrow said. "You need to bind each other's wounds."

Theresa nodded. "I can do that," she said.

Claire came out of the station, and they all got back in the car.

"In less than an hour, Charlie and I will be together," Theresa announced as she read the mileage signs, her tone livelier than at any time on the trip. Pal jumped around in her lap, his front paws climbing up her shirt until his nose nuzzled her throat.

When they finally pulled into the patient parking lot, Rebecca Cole stood in front of the VA hospital to meet them. Charlie's grandmother—Woodrow's mother—had embraced Theresa from the moment Charlie brought her home. Theresa had returned the favor. She liked everything about Rebecca, who was about as unlike her own mother as a woman could be.

Woodrow had called Rebecca from their last stop. The area was busy with men in wheelchairs or on crutches, orderlies and relatives helping them. Theresa grabbed the plastic bag that contained her new dress and got out of the Jeep's back seat, just as a hospital employee rushed by, narrowly avoiding a collision with the car door. Pal barked to protest her departure.

"Where can I buy some makeup?" Theresa asked Rebecca as soon as they'd hugged.

"There's a gift shop inside," Rebecca said, still embracing her grandson's wife. "But you look lovely, darlin'. Charlie's goin' to go wild for you just as you are."

"No, I've got to cover the marks on my face," Theresa insisted. She turned back to Claire. "Can you keep an eye on Pal?"

"Sure thing. I'll wait over there." Claire pointed toward the edge of the VA building where a line of ironwork benches beckoned from the shade of several dogwood trees.

Rebecca led Woodrow and Theresa inside where they saw just how over-crowded a military hospital can be. The chairs in the waiting area were all taken. Kids ran in circles, bumping into people. Some patients and their caretakers had to sit on the floor.

Charlie had been doing well all week, Rebecca told Theresa as they head-ed toward the gift shop where Theresa picked out a bottle of foundation, setting powder, lipstick, an eyebrow pencil, and a pair of earrings.

"He's tickled pink you're on your way," Rebecca said. "Here, let me get that." She paid for Theresa's items, and the three of them hurried toward the elevator, took it upstairs, and walked down the corridor.

"Where can I change?" Theresa asked, looking around at the doors.

"In here." Rebecca indicated a restroom around the corner and went in with her.

Woodrow waited in the hallway. *Bet Charlie's pulse goes up every time someone mentions her name*, he thought. Meaning her new outfit was over-kill. All that really mattered was that she walked through the door. *Semper Fi.*

Woodrow hadn't felt that way about a woman for a long time, though he had to admit, Theresa's sister was growing on him.

Theresa emerged wearing her new dress and a pair of skimpy sandals she'd borrowed from Claire. She wanted to go in to see Charlie alone, she said, so Woodrow and Rebecca waited in the hallway. When she didn't come back out, they figured the reunion was going well, and they let them be.

Rebecca suggested they find Theresa's sister, who was still outside with the puppy, and then get something to eat in the cafeteria. Dogs were allowed in that part of the hospital, if they were on a leash, an orderly told them.

Pal was hungry. Inside the cafeteria, he behaved as long as Claire fed him bits of meatball. She kept him on her lap.

"You're not goin' back to Minnesota in that contraption," Woodrow in-formed her after he'd finished his hamburger. She looked at him, a forkful of salad on its way to her mouth.

"I won't allow it," Woodrow added.

"What are you talking about?" Claire asked. "You have no right to criticize my car. It's none of your business."

"It's more a soup sandwich than a car," Woodrow returned.

"I don't appreciate being lectured about a vehicle that got us here, didn't it?" Claire said. "It's really none of your concern what I drive home."

Rebecca looked back and forth between them, a smile on her face.

"Sorry to interrupt," she said, "but I haven't been formally introduced. Where are your manners, Woodrow?"

———•◦•———

Claire hadn't intended to feel comfortable in Lafayette, a town named, one assumed, for the marquis who was such a help to General Washington during the American Revolution. As she recalled, there were many Lafayettes in the country, but this one had welcomed Theresa to its bosom. It had become part of the Haig diaspora, if she could use such a ponderous term to describe her family's scattering.

Entering the Heart of Dixie state on their way to Birmingham, she'd noticed the flags right away. At a highway rest stop, a horizontal red cross on a field of white flew next to the American flag, the two at approximately the same height. The state flag may have even been an inch or two higher. A granite plaque at the base of the installation read, *Alabama We Dare Defend Our Rights.*

What rights did that mean? she wondered. The bill of rights? Equal rights between men and women? Civil rights? The right to vote? The right to enter family-planning clinics? The rights of all children to an equal education? The rights of the individual, including those incarcerated in Alabama's notorious prisons?

The South felt like a foreign country to Claire, and she was determined not to like it, despite the beauty of the countryside they passed through as Woodrow drove her car home. Close to their destination, they rolled by cotton fields, goat farms, big country houses alongside modest ones, and, to Claire's surprise, numerous dark outcroppings tinged with rust, as if the bowels of the earth had risen to the surface.

"Coal runs naked in Lafayette," Woodrow remarked. "No need to dig for it."

"In some places," added his mother.

"Fossil fuels should be left in the ground," Claire observed. "They poison the earth when they're excavated, especially coal."

Rebecca agreed. As they'd approached what Woodrow called the family's "pine plantation," its size surprised Claire, not just the main homestead but barns and outbuildings perched on a hill that rolled down to a narrow creek. The word *plantation* was jarring.

"There's a waterfall 'round that bend," Rebecca informed Claire, "and it's pretty to look at, but don't you go wadin' anywhere near 'cause you'll lose your footin' on the rocks and the rush of those waters'll pull you under. It's darn cold, too."

That's the feeling Claire got about this whole, unfamiliar place—beautiful and perilous. She intended to head back to Minnesota after a good night's sleep, more than satisfied to see her sister finally free and reunited with her husband.

A wooden bridge led to the front of the Coles' main residence, a multi-story pitched roof structure with functional white shutters and an eight-foot entrance door, also painted white. Claire was relieved to see no Confederate flags outside. A crowd of children stood on the porch. One, a tall boy with his left arm in a sling, walked to within a foot of her after she got out of the car, inspected her minutely, and asked, "You be a Yankee, ma'am?" He looked like a smaller version of Woodrow.

"Yes, I am," she told him. "And I might be dangerous."

"I doubt you're dangerous," he replied laconically. "Or my uncle wouldn't a brung you."

She laughed. "I'm Claire," she said and held out her hand. "Happy to make your acquaintance."

"Jeremiah," he replied, shaking it. "Pleased to meet you, ma'am."

He smiled Woodrow's smile, looking her up and down as if trying to decide if she'd been pretty back when she was young. Claire felt herself flushing. Just then the front door opened and out came a dog that rushed past on his way to Woodrow. On arrival, the creature stood on his hind legs and threw his entire weight at his target, almost knocking Woodrow to the ground. Woodrow grabbed the animal's front paws and let the dog lick him.

"This here's Koda," Woodrow told Claire. "He adopted me when he was 'bout a year old."

Koda weighed well over a hundred pounds, Claire guessed, a Labrador from the general look of him, but there was husky in him too, evident in his glowing green eyes.

"Somebody shot him when he was a pup," Rebecca added, a little slower to exit Claire's vehicle. "Woodrow spied him from the highway, draggin' along a frontage road with his right hind leg bleedin'. Woodrow got off the highway, tracked him down, and brought him home. He's been a member of the family ever since."

Claire eyed Koda warily as he came to sniff her.

"Koda still has pellets in his leg," Jeremiah informed her.

"Woodrow's my oldest," Rebecca told Claire, gaining her stride as they approached the porch. "Jacob, my second, is father to Jeremiah here. Jeremiah's going on fifteen. His older brothers are Waylon and Anthony. Rory, my third son, is four years younger than Woodrow. Rory has Grace here, who's also fifteen; Lorene, thirteen; John, ten; and Peter, eight. Finally, there's my son Lewis, six years younger than Woodrow, and here's his sons: Matthew, who's twelve; William, nine; and Brady, seven." Rebecca reached out and tousled Jeremiah's hair. He laughed, unembarrassed.

"Jeremiah has a habit of fallin' out of trees," Rebecca added.

"Twice," Jeremiah admitted. "My fault both times."

"I'll be eleven pretty soon," John remarked as they bustled inside.

The kids set out plates, cutlery, cups, and glasses on a table adorned with a blue-and-white checkered cloth. Claire recalled her mother had one just like it.

"Woodrow's brothers and the older cousins are plantin' today," Rebecca told Claire. "On this plantation we replace what we cut."

"I'm not with 'em only 'cause of my accident last week," Jeremiah informed her. "My dad don't want me on the crew until my arm is healed. Otherwise, I'd be out there."

Claire nodded in sympathy.

"It was my fault," Jeremiah said again. "My mind gets to wanderin', and then I get sloppy."

"Maybe your mind is trying to tell you something," Claire suggested. "Maybe you're not a tree-climber by nature."

Jeremiah didn't have an answer to that.

Inside, the Cole house looked even older than it did from the outside. A beamed ceiling hovered over cooking, dining, and social space, all in a single room. Books lined the walls on either side of the fireplace. The furniture appeared handmade and many times refinished. The floorboards were original, judging from their wide, worn planks and forged nails.

There were no Confederate flags to be found, but numerous antique rifles were mounted horizontally on just about every expanse above shoulder height. She assumed Woodrow kept them in fire-ready condition.

"I hope having me here is not an inconvenience," Claire said to Rebecca.

"Being Theresa's sister makes you family," Rebecca replied, "and family is never an inconvenience. Now you come on upstairs and tidy up. I don't imagine my son stopped for rest and refreshment as often as he should have."

They went up the stairs together, with Rebecca's arm around her shoulder. Claire recalled the way her mother had greeted Woodrow on the Haig front porch, as Annie told the story. In the realm of hospitality, it was Coles:

one, Haigs: zero.

When she came back downstairs, Claire saw that Rebecca's grandchildren had laid out a a cream cheese-and-fruit dip, a basket of hush puppies, grits topped with butter and brown sugar, buttermilk biscuits, a pitcher of gravy, a platter of thinly sliced ham, and raspberry cobbler in a casserole. They poured drinks from jugs of sweet tea and lemonade. Jeremiah kept catching Claire's eye and grinning. She wasn't sure if he liked her or just found her peculiar.

Claire helped with dishes afterward. Then, she dug out her computer, found a quiet place in a corner of the living room area, and went online to review the courses she'd set up for the fall semester. It took several minutes to realize they weren't there. She called Linda Ryan in admissions.

"Claire! Don't tell me you didn't get the letter?" Linda exclaimed.

"What letter?" Claire asked.

"It went out in late June, just before the deadline. Gist of it is they're folding remedial courses into adult education. Public school teachers will handle them from now on. They got a grant from the state."

"I have a contract!" Claire protested.

"Yes, I know. But it had a clause that lets them do this before June thirtieth. I'm sorry you didn't get the letter. There was a severance check inside." She paused. "Claire, this was entirely a financial decision. It's no reflection on you or the other instructors."

"They told me last year I could teach a literature course in the spring," Claire protested, a catch in her voice.

"I'm sorry," Linda said.

She may have been sorry, but Linda's commiseration did little to soften the blow. Claire was officially unemployed, uninformed about it for most of the summer, and now faced an unexpected job search.

In a daze, she walked toward the open kitchen and sat at the table across from Woodrow's mother, who had busied herself matching pairs from a mountain of laundered socks.

"You look like someone died," Rebecca remarked.

"That's what it feels like," Claire said, moving her hands to the back of her neck, as if her head might fall off.

"What happened?"

"My job's gone. My toehold in academia."

"You mean back in Minnesota, you're out of work?"

"Seems to be the case," Claire acknowledged.

"Well, that's a setback," Rebecca said matter-of-factly. "But you know what we say 'round here about a setback? You just might turn it into a setup."

Claire tried to laugh. "A blessing in disguise?"

"Could be," Rebecca said.

"It sure doesn't feel like it," Claire said. "I let mail sit unopened, wasting time I could have spent lining up a new job."

"You weren't wastin' time. You were searchin' for your sister."

Claire nodded. Woodrow's mother was right. Finding her kidnapped sister was more important than being employed. The thought gave her comfort, but only a little.

She had taken to Rebecca right away. In her late sixties, maybe early seventies, neither tall nor big boned, the Cole family matriarch nevertheless loomed large wherever she stood. Her untreated gray hair, tied in a bundle at the nape of her neck, suggested an independent personality, yet when she looked at someone, she gave that person her undivided attention. Claire concluded that Rebecca was the reason the male contingent of this clan seemed comfortable around women. She decided to take her advice and let the news from back home settle before making decisions about what to do next.

As the week went by, Claire's panic began to fade. Staying with the Coles provided a pleasant respite, full of big breakfasts and long walks around the property. The Cole estate, four hundred sixty acres, was covered in pine, including trees centuries old. Every year the family planted more than they harvested. The oldest stands they left alone.

Southern yellow pine and eastern white pine grew well in Lafayette County, Rebecca explained, but they could be unstable in high winds, especially during the spring. The soil was sandy, and trees put down widespread, shallow roots. Without a deep tap root, fragile anchorage was a fact of life. Woodrow's father had been killed by a falling pine as he searched for his dog in a windstorm.

"We tread a narrow path," Rebecca explained. "Lookin' at our timber, the house, equipment, an' all my worker bees—the whole family works—you might think we're rich. But even when things go well, bad luck can take us down, 'specially if someone gets hurt or acquires some disease."

They passed numerous cabins. The Coles built them for hunters. With dense forest came animals, and with animals, a source of supplemental income. In season, the family sold permits to people who knew how to shoot, could pass a test, and were willing to abide by limits. For a fee that included lodging in one of the cabins, they could track free-roaming turkey, whitetail deer, mallard duck, and occasionally wild hog, all of which graced the Cole table on a regular basis. One of Rebecca's four sons accompanied the hunting party to make sure nobody aimed in the direction of the house. Rebecca kept the kids inside those days. The walls of the house were thick, built to keep arrows and musket shot out. They kept out stronger stuff now.

Rebecca's daughters-in-law had part- or full-time jobs in town. Rebecca was the family's day care provider during the summer, and homework tutor after school started. Claire pitched in on the tutoring, since Rebecca insisted the grandkids catch up on what they'd forgotten during the summer. Muggy August days went by in a pleasant fugue, though occasionally Claire reminded herself, "I need to get real and leave."

———•◦•———

Two weeks after Patrick's birth, the Haigs still didn't have word one on whether the baby's father intended to exercise his parental rights or even whether his paternal rights could be terminated. It was possible the state wouldn't allow it, Ben told them. He wasn't sure, since family law lay outside his area of expertise.

Maureen and Tom knew Theresa had reached Birmingham, where her husband was being treated for burns. She hadn't called home. They only knew she was there because the baby's great-grandmother, Rebecca Cole, had phoned the Haigs twice. Both times she'd spoken with Maureen, who told Tom word for word everything she said.

It would be a long haul for Charlie. Theresa was entirely focused on his recovery. So far, Theresa hadn't mentioned the baby. No one in Alabama knew about the child, and if Rebecca had her druthers, no one would.

Maureen complained to Tom that Rebecca kept using phrases like "the baby," or "the child," while Maureen more precisely referred to "her baby," meaning Theresa's. Let there be no doubt. Patrick was Theresa's newborn son. By every moral, legal, and social standard, an infant belongs in the care of his mother, Maureen told Rebecca plainly. She explained it all to Tom, who made no reply.

For her part, Rebecca said she expected the two families could work it out together with "open hearts and minds," whatever that meant. Maureen didn't care for Rebecca at first, but she warmed to her as they talked. She tried to explain to this lady—whom she had met only once at Theresa's wedding—that Patrick needed to grow up in the place he'd been born. Besides which, he wasn't going anywhere for the next three to four months, according to the doctors at St. Dominic's.

Maureen asked Rebecca to have Theresa call her, but it didn't happen. Theresa had no interest in talking to her mother, she said by way of Rebecca. Maureen blamed Mary, who seemed also to be staying with the Coles in Lafayette. She couldn't imagine what kind of place it was, or why Mary would remain there when she had a job waiting in St. Paul. Maureen didn't ask to speak to Mary, and Mary didn't call her, which was just as well, Maureen felt.

Who would or would not talk to Maureen was not an issue as far as Tom was concerned. Once Charlie had completely recovered, he could convince the administrators at St. Dominic and the people at Stears County Child Protective Services that his family, without any assistance from the Haigs, ought to be the ones to raise Patrick in their own fashion—even if Patrick's mother felt no love for him, had abandoned him at birth, and neglected him all these weeks.

"And," Tom pointed out to Maureen, "Patrick going to the Coles might be the only way to bring Theresa and her baby into their rightful relationship."

"You're telling me the Coles are likely to get Patrick if Charlie wants custody," Maureen lamented. "Then they can raise him any way they want, even as a heathen."

"That's the least of our worries," said Tom.

Rebecca kept calling. The hospital let Theresa stay with Charlie in his room, she said. There was no sign of bleeding in his brain. The swelling was gone. His vision was almost back to normal, and his headaches had become infrequent and less intense. His memory was better. Overall, the doctors were pleased by his progress, some of which they attributed to his ability to sleep a lot in the beginning, and the rest to the calming effect Theresa had on him.

"He didn't smile 'til she got there," Rebecca said. "Everybody noticed the change right away."

Maureen's most recent conversation with Rebecca took place a week later, after the doctors sent the patient home to Lafayette. Charlie and Theresa moved into a cabin on the Cole property. Rebecca was jubilant.

"Your daughter's been a godsend," she told Maureen.

"She hasn't been a godsend to Patrick," Maureen told her.

———

Ten minutes after eight on an overcast August morning, Ben Johnson stopped at the entrance to St. Dominic's NICU to talk to Tom and Maureen. The three of them were scheduled to meet at eight thirty in the hospital's conference room with St. Dominic's chief administrator and the head of Stears County Child Protective Services. Ben suggested they speak privately beforehand in a lounge around the corner from the NICU.

"I'd caution you both to listen carefully to what is said at this meeting and to hold back saying anything yourselves," Ben told them.

Tom squeezed Maureen's hand.

"The thing is," Ben continued, "what we want carries very little weight as long as Patrick's father is in the picture."

Maureen and Tom said nothing.

"The second thing you need to understand is the difference, assuming Patrick's father does not want physical custody, between formal adoption—which is the long-term goal—and temporary foster care."

"Temporary foster care?" Maureen repeated.

"The choice would be telling them you're aiming for outright adoption down the road, or just asking them for temporary foster care with you as foster parents," Ben explained. "Temporary foster care is preferable, in my opinion. It's the only thing available now, anyway, and it gives you flexibility in the future. Once an adoption takes place, you're trapped until the child ages out. Now, hold on—" he said in response to the look on Maureen's face. "By trapped, I mean you can't alter the situation even if it's untenable."

"There's nothing untenable about Patrick," Maureen declared, "whatever *untenable* means."

"Look, Maureen, we don't know how serious Patrick's disabilities might be, how expensive his needs will become in the future, or what complications might arise."

"Patrick is not going to have complications, and even if he does, we will never walk away from him," Maureen protested.

"An adoption cannot be undone," Ben pointed out, "not without a judge signing off, and a judge is not going to sign off unless he or she feels there's a better option for the child. Which often there is not."

"So, you advise we ask for temporary foster care. No talk about adoption," Tom said.

"Yes," Ben confirmed. "Once you adopt, the child's problems become your problems. Though the county may help, and the federal government would likely subsidize the process of adoption."

"What you're saying is immoral," Maureen interjected. "Of course, Patrick's problems are our problems."

"On the other hand," said Ben, "if you petition for temporary foster care and later decide you want to adopt, you'd be in a good negotiating position regarding how much financial and medical help you'll get from the county and state, and remember, that aid typically lasts only until the child is eighteen or maybe twenty-one if you apply for an extension. After that, it's a whole new ball game."

"Ben, you're supposed to be helping us," said Maureen. "Temporary foster care is not in *Patrick's* best interest . . ."

"Be quiet and listen," Tom admonished her.

"I'm trying my darnedest to help," said Ben. "These are complicated issues, Maureen, and I'm not a family lawyer. But I do know that foster care means Patrick's problems belong to children's services, and they pay you to help them, with you having the right to walk away if you need to."

"It's cruel," Maureen said hotly. "It's unchristian."

"Temporary foster care sounds sensible to me," Tom said.

Ben strode toward the door. "Let's pick up our discussion after the meeting. The important thing now is that we stay calm, and you let *me* do the talking," Ben said, looking squarely at Maureen, who refused to meet his gaze.

Downstairs in the same second floor conference room where they'd met previously, the three entered to find the hospital's administrator, Laura Himley, flanked by the same two lawyers she'd brought with her last time. Beverly Hagen, the child services lady, sat to the left of Laura.

Maureen gathered it was not expected to be a long meeting: no coffee.

"Mr. Cole is not joining us today?" Laura asked.

"He's back in Georgia," Tom said.

"Alabama," Ben corrected.

"Right, Alabama," Tom conceded.

"My clients have been in contact with the Cole family," Ben added.

"As have I." Beverly brandished an envelope.

Maureen almost jumped out of her seat.

"On Thursday the ninth . . . in other words, yesterday," Beverly continued, "the department received an insured, registered letter from the Coles' family attorney attesting that Staff Sergeant Cole is the biological father of the child born to his wife, Theresa Cole, on July 27, 2018, but that he has chosen to surrender his rights to physical custody of the child at this time."

Maureen's heart leapt. A boulder had been removed from the front of a deep, dark cave, and Patrick was, in a way, resurrected. He would grow up in Minnesota. That's what the letter meant.

"In the same envelope was a separate letter from Rebecca Cole, who is Staff Sergeant Charles Cole's grandmother and the baby's great-grandmother," Beverly said.

Maureen held her breath.

"Rebecca Cole wrote, 'To whom it may concern, I have not met him, but Patrick Cole is in my heart and in the hearts of our family here in Lafayette. There are many among us who can love and care for him and give him every opportunity to thrive, and in that endeavor, we wish to let you know that we are willing and able to take him to our bosom.' She included a list of other family members and their relationships to the Cole baby."

Beverly paused again.

Maureen felt her teeth grinding top on bottom so hard her jaw hurt. Tom squeezed her hand.

"The letter concludes 'Should you need any of us to appear in person to discuss the baby's future, kindly let us know and we will come to St. Paul. Respectfully yours, Rebecca Cole.'"

Beverly added, "I think she means St. Dominic."

No one spoke for a while.

"The way it stands, Stears County retains legal temporary custody," Beverly concluded. "The county has placed the child under the care and concern of St. Dominic Hospital for as long as he needs to be in the NICU. In the meantime, we will be looking at alternatives for permanent custody in the future, including the baby's biological father, should circumstances change, as well as his mother's extended family, and the extended Cole family. I should add that federal guidelines on the application of safe haven laws require the state in question to make every effort to maintain family connections, if possible."

Maureen reached past Tom to tug on Ben Johnson's sleeve. "Should we say something about adoption now?" she whispered urgently.

"No," Ben said.

"I understand there is additional information regarding Patrick's medical condition," Beverly added.

Maureen didn't like the sound of that.

"It appears Patrick will require a surgical intervention," Laura said. "It will be performed by Dr. Lenix. The county has given its approval, and the surgery is scheduled to take place on Monday morning."

"What kind of surgery?" Maureen demanded. She stood up, unable to sit any longer.

"It's to correct what's called a PDA," Laura replied. "I'm sorry Dr. Lenix couldn't be here with us today to explain the procedure."

"What's a PDA?" Maureen insisted on knowing.

"A PDA is a congenital heart defect, technically called patent ductus arteriosus. It's common in premature babies, but Patrick's heart is the size of a walnut, so there's added risk. Not doing the surgery is riskier, however. We really have no choice but to go ahead as the county has instructed, given the facts at hand. I can assure you our surgical team has done this surgery many times."

"How often does it turn out well?" Maureen asked pointedly.

"I don't have that information at the moment," Laura responded, "but I can tell you we are very optimistic."

Her optimism did not console Maureen. Everyone else looked impassive, unable, or unwilling to react. Patrick's maternal grandmother felt a sudden urge to talk to Patrick's paternal great-grandmother, who might be the one person on earth who could appreciate the extent of the panic she felt.

Monday morning. Heart surgery. "Can I watch?" Maureen asked.

"Through a window or something?"

"I'll look into that," Laura said.

———•••———

At 6:00 a.m. Monday morning, August 13, Maureen and Annie stood at the nurse's station outside the NICU, hoping they could observe Patrick's operation. Maureen hated that it would take place on the thirteenth of the month.

Another bad omen occurred when Dr. Lenix refused to let her watch from behind the glass observation wall. It was his policy, a nurse said. He believed in tight control, personally approved every member of his surgical team, took offense when a team member left or got sick, and rarely, meaning never, allowed outsiders to view a surgery. He played chamber music at low volume during procedures, critical or not, and permitted no unnecessary conversation. Total focus, zero distractions.

Omens came in threes, Maureen believed. The third bad omen had yet to happen. She asked a nurse about the odds of the PDU going well. It's a PDA, she was reminded. The procedure closes a connection between blood vessels near the heart that should have closed off at birth. But in Patrick's case, that hadn't occurred, even after they gave him medication. So, they had to do what she called a surgical ligation. Patrick would be much better after the operation, the nurse assured her.

It was Maureen's longest morning in recent memory. Her usually chatty daughter had nothing to say, which was a blessing. They sat together in a family lounge, the TV near the ceiling set on mute. It should go well, she reminded herself over and over. At nine o'clock Laura Himley came in, smiling broadly, and Maureen felt a surge of relief.

"He's back in the NICU," Laura said, "and he's pinking up beautifully. We've had him under observation since the surgery finished, and I'm told his vitals are good."

"Can we see him?" Annie asked.

"Yes, but one at a time," Laura cautioned.

Annie went in first while Maureen called Rebecca. She'd promised to call her as soon as possible, and it pleased her to honor her promise to the Coles, if for no other reason than to demonstrate that the Haigs also had *open hearts and minds*. Perhaps Theresa would be there to appreciate the effort her mother was making. Perhaps Maureen could talk to Theresa directly and gauge her reaction.

Maureen and Rebecca spoke briefly. Theresa was not there, Rebecca said. She was with Charlie about a ten-minute walk away. Claire entered the room halfway through the conversation, and Rebecca handed her the phone. Maureen didn't have much to say to her oldest daughter except to tell her that Patrick was doing well and that she wanted to talk to Theresa.

———•◦•———

Carole Novak had made separate flash-drive copies of two portions of the audio file she'd recorded during her interview with Theresa Cole in St. Paul. She'd priority-express mailed one segment to David Wells—the one that had to do with his wife, Roberta's, link to Theresa.

Her initial impression on the day of the interview was that Theresa didn't have the grit she saw in Claire, but later she felt Theresa might be the stronger of the two, which was why Carole had kept her questions short. The portion of the interview involving Roberta Wells came across as particularly intense.

On August 20, a sunny Monday morning, Carole drove north from downtown Minneapolis to St. Dominic's warehouse district to meet with David Wells in person. He was president and CEO of a startup called Unique Genetic Solutions. His executive assistant had contacted her earlier in the morning to say that Mr. Wells would make time in his schedule if she came to see him that same day. Carole had no idea what to expect.

UGS occupied the entire sixth floor of the building. A receptionist finally ushered her into Wells' corner office at about two o'clock. She'd waited more than an hour in the reception area for him to get back from a meeting. Their appointment had been for one o'clock, but he didn't seem to consider it much of a priority.

Floor-to-ceiling windows on two sides flooded the interior with light. The glass was smudged, though, and the other walls, recently papered in a pale-green grass cloth, hadn't been wiped clean since the paper was hung. A light fixture wasn't connected. Stray wires hung loose. Blue tape indicated where artwork should be placed, art that obviously hadn't arrived yet. His office was a work in progress.

Carole could smell organic compounds off-gassing from the carpet. She was taken aback by the strength of the odor. It seemed strange that a health-related company would tolerate toxic fumes even briefly if its employees were exposed. Their presence suggested a rush to move in. She wondered if David Wells was too engrossed in his upcoming IPO to pay attention to the details of things happening around him, including what his wife was doing in her abundant free time.

Her biggest questions concerned whether he had been familiar with Roberta's attitudes on abortion before the kidnapping had taken place, and how much he had known about her involvement with Lucy Meyer and Lucy's guerrilla campaign to "save all babies," no matter the cost to a pregnant woman's liberty.

When she walked in, Carole had immediately noticed two upholstered wingback chairs in the UGS company colors—mint-green and white. They stood in front of the main piece of furniture, Wells' modern mahogany desk. She wanted to position herself in one of those chairs and whip out her notebook, or better yet, her recorder. Wells sat behind the desk, his back straight, his expression distinctly unfriendly. He didn't even get up to greet her.

"This conversation," he announced even before she could introduce herself, "is off the record."

She nodded, reluctantly. "And it won't be taped on any device," he added.

"No," she agreed again.

His stare was meant to be unnerving. Carole had learned negotiation techniques as a child, taking in kitchen table debates among her father and his colleagues in the labor movement. She knew how to steel herself.

"You've listened to—" she began.

"Yes, I've listened to your excerpt," he interrupted, "and I find it offensive that you would send something like that to my office when you must know in a few days my company's public offering will hit the market. I have to wonder if that's part of a strategy." He didn't invite her to sit down.

"I simply want to give you and your wife an opportunity to respond before this story appears," Carole replied. "I'd like to know whether you and Roberta discussed her attempts to prevent an abortion, and whether you were aware that she and the pro-life activist Lucy Meyer had orchestrated the kidnapping of a woman named Theresa Cole. Theresa's voice is the one you heard on the tape. Lucy Meyer is—"

"When would this story appear, if your editor prints it?" Wells interrupted again.

"I can't say at the moment."

"This week?"

"It's the paper's policy to give persons involved in our reporting a chance to tell their side. If you or your wife wish to comment, now is the time."

"Let me be clear. Neither I, nor my wife, will cooperate with you. Do not contact either of us again. If you attempt to do so, I will involve my attorneys, and you and your paper's publisher will deal with the consequences. Do you understand?"

"I understand you have no comment at the moment," Carole said evenly. "But should you change your mind, please let me know. You have my card.

A story doesn't go away because it's upsetting, Mr. Wells. I'm giving you a chance to respond, a chance to get your and your wife's statements on the record. You should consider taking it." She put out her hand to shake his, but he ignored it. Reluctantly, she left his office.

Outside in the building's parking lot, she stood next to her car and considered whether she'd added anything of value to what she already knew. She turned her recorder on and talked into it, listing a series of impressions that might be of use later.

Feeling hot, Carole removed the suit jacket she'd worn inside the air-conditioned building. Her bare arms immediately felt as if they were burning. She rued the fact that the meeting had been so short after such a long drive. What had she learned, really?

She'd learned that David Wells was very worried. Her editor would probably get a call from his attorneys within the hour. That's how worried he was.

Her next stop was the Haigs' farm, a short detour on hope and a prayer, but this time Carole had lucked out. When she'd phoned from her paper's parking lot in downtown Minneapolis before leaving for St. Dominic, Maureen Haig had agreed to see her, and she'd sounded almost friendly.

———•◦•———

Mrs. Haig opened the front door of the farmhouse, as Annie, the kid from the cafe, lurked in the background.

"Hi," she said. "My name is Carole Novak from the *Minneapolis Free Press.*"

Maureen nodded, then opened the door wider and invited Carole inside. "Just so you know, I'm determined to get information, not give it," Maureen said, leading the way to her kitchen. Annie followed.

"Thank you, Mrs. Haig. I won't take much of your time." Carole caught Annie's eye.

"Sit down." Maureen gestured toward a chair at the kitchen table. Annie took the chair next to it. "I'm making coffee," Maureen added.

Carole did not pull out her notebook. She left her recorder in her pocket. Theresa's mother was tense enough already, she decided. An enticing aroma filled the kitchen as Maureen's coffee dripped into a glass carafe. Maureen sat at the table, facing Carole.

"You've talked to her?"

"She talked, and I listened for about an hour," Carole told her. "Of course, she's pretty much in shock about everything that's happened."

"She's in shock? We're *all* in shock," Maureen said, adding quickly, "Do you think she's coming out of it now?"

"I think she's struggling. It's a lot to process," Carole said.

Maureen took umbrage at that. "First off, *process* is not a word we use in this house," she told Carole. "Meat gets processed. People have things happen to them, or they decide to do things, but here we don't process. What does that even mean?"

"I'm sorry," Carole said, regretting the expression.

"Is there a chance, once she's done *processing*," Maureen continued sarcastically, "once her *processing* is finished and out of the way, that Theresa will regret her decision to abandon her son? Do you think she'll come back for him?"

The question stunned Carole. "Based on our talk, I'd say she's angry about being kidnapped," she told Theresa's mother. "She was kidnapped, wasn't she?"

The coffee had stopped dripping into the carafe just a moment before. Maureen got up and filled two mugs. She set one in front of Carole. She didn't offer milk or cream to dilute it, and Carole didn't request any.

"Can I have coffee too?" Annie asked loudly.

"Shouldn't you be doing homework?" Maureen retorted.

"Mother, it's summer," Annie said. The formality of *mother* struck Carole.

"Theresa described being kidnapped," Carole picked up where they'd left off. "She has a really good memory for detail. She talked about the puncture wound she felt before she passed out. The various houses she was kept in. Her confinement inside a bedroom with no access to the outdoors. The way her kidnappers prevented her from contacting her husband or anyone else. That's what made her most angry. Being cut off from her husband."

She watched Maureen Haig's face change. "We didn't handle it the best," Maureen said softly, looking down as if speaking to herself.

"How would you have handled it, if you could do it over again?" Carole inquired.

"I don't know. Lucy went too far, I think. She's admitted she made mistakes."

Carole silently rejoiced. "Lucy Meyer is a strong woman from what I hear," Carole said quietly. Maureen didn't reply. "People say she's dedicated," Carole continued, "and sometimes dedicated people go too far."

She had no idea what people said about Lucy Meyer. None of the pro-life organizations she'd called would even admit to knowing who Lucy Meyer was.

"Do you think there's a chance Theresa will come back for her son?" Maureen asked again, looking hopeful.

"She's your daughter, Mrs. Haig. Your guess is probably better than mine. Would you like to listen to a part of the interview I recorded? It has to do with what happened in your living room."

Maureen shook her head. "I don't want to hear Theresa complaining as if she's the only one who matters," she replied. "I want to hear Theresa admitting there's another person involved, a person whose life depends on her. I want to hear Theresa say she's sorry, not that she thinks everyone else should be sorry."

Carole nodded.

"She thinks only of herself," Maureen continued. "Lucy was right about that. If Lucy's method was wrong, her heart is in the right place, and so are the hearts of all of us who helped. Patrick is the one whose life matters most. Why can't Theresa see that?"

"You call the baby Patrick?" Carole asked. She wondered who gave him that name. Theresa hadn't mentioned it in the interview.

Maureen stood up. "I think you'd best leave now," she said. "I've got supper to prepare."

Rising reluctantly, Carole reached into the left-side pocket of her trousers, retrieved the flash drive containing the snippet she wanted Maureen to hear, added a business card, and placed the two items in the middle of the table.

"You might want to play this on your computer," Carole told Maureen. "I'd like to get your reaction. In any case, I can come back for it."

Maureen gestured impatiently toward the kitchen door.

Carole left, feeling dismissed. Today wasn't the first time in her career she'd felt pushed out, and it wouldn't be the last. She had to walk around the side of the house to reach her car.

Once inside, with the engine turned over and the air conditioning running on high, she recorded impressions for a good five minutes. Then she pulled out her cell phone, hoping the sheriff's detectives would be back at their desks and willing to talk. She ended up with their voice mail, again.

Lafayette was a place where locals moved at a slower pace than Claire was used to. They smiled and opened doors for ladies. They called her "Miss Claire."

The town square centered on a domed courthouse a bit grand for the size of the community. Beyond the square, she and Woodrow had lunch in a restaurant one afternoon, or more precisely they sat outside the restaurant on a veranda overlooking a pond. The only discordant note for Claire was

Woodrow asking questions she didn't care to answer. Woodrow could be an open book all he wanted. It wasn't her style.

Yet the pure fact of the matter was that she hadn't left Alabama because of Woodrow. In the wake of Theresa's abduction, an idea had taken root and was now as tall as her dad's corn in September. There seemed to be no way she could banish it.

She had begun to imagine Woodrow as the father of a small child. Her small child. It was a fantasy, a gossamer dream. He was in his late-forties, she guessed. She was thirty-nine. They were both a bit old for parenthood. They hardly knew each other.

Besides, she had no reason to believe he wanted to become a father again. Were they even compatible? They disagreed a lot. But she liked him, she had to admit, and the like was getting stronger every day.

"What's going on? You look like you're about to ask me something," Woodrow drawled.

"No." She shook her head. "I'm just thinking."

"Thinkin' 'bout what?"

"Nothing in particular." Claire shrugged. She could tell he didn't buy that.

Their meal looked like something out of a magazine—a platter of crab legs surrounded by a spicy tomato coleslaw and a basket of hot cheddar biscuits with honey butter on the side. Woodrow described Charlie's progress. His optimism was infectious. She enjoyed the pine-scented air on the veranda, the breeze, the zesty food, and Woodrow's mellow voice.

That evening, curled in an armchair in the third-floor bedroom at the back of Rebecca's house, Claire relived their time together, noticing in retrospect how Woodrow had done all the talking. She'd just sat there like an audience waiting for Godot.

Her room nestled beneath a pointed eave overlooking the wash lines and a vegetable garden. Woodrow slept one floor down. Evidently, he had no interest in climbing the stairs, in coming to her, so she told herself to suppress her delusions and be done with Alabama.

But no sooner banished, her delusions reappeared. She found him attractive. He wouldn't be like Rob. She thought he might find her attractive. But he'd said or done nothing to indicate it.

As the night grew still, having itself fallen asleep while she remained well beyond the reach of Morpheus, Claire decided she needed to hear the word *no* loud and clear. Then she could leave.

She tiptoed toward the front of the house and down the staircase to the second floor. Woodrow's door was slightly ajar. She pushed it open further and ventured inside. The room was dark except for moonlight that filtered through the curtains. She couldn't detect any breathing and wondered if he was even there. Half-turned to go back upstairs, she heard his voice.

"Now don't tell me you finally found some gumption 'n' then you turn tail and run."

"I found gumption? What about you?" she whispered to the barely discernible figure in the bed.

"I been waitin' for consent," he said.

Beverly Hagen sat on the sofa in the Haig living room, having deposited several pamphlets on the coffee table.

She and Lucy had failed to convince Theresa to do the right thing, Maureen thought to herself, and now it had come to this. It had come to the Haigs and the Coles fighting over a baby as if he were a football.

Patrick was now a ward of Stears County. He was in the temporary foster care of Stears County, and as the county's child protective services director, Beverly controlled his fate. Maureen had tried to—how did someone put it on the telephone tree?—oh yes, she'd tried to *bond* with Beverly.

But the woman would not allow Maureen to get close. She'd told Maureen on several occasions that, as a professional advocate for this baby, she could not form personal relationships that might influence how she handled the process of deciding what would be in the child's best interest.

There was a likelihood, Beverly informed Maureen, that the court would appoint a *guardian ad litem* for Theresa's child. A motion was scheduled for the next day, in fact.

The Haigs had not been informed about any court motion until this very moment, Maureen pointed out. Ben Johnson had not been aware either, he said. At Maureen's invitation, he had come to the Haig farm today and now sat in one of the wing chairs facing the sofa.

Maureen had brought in a tray of lemon ricotta cookies interspersed with slices of banana bread, along with her silver-plated coffeepot, a tiny carafe of half-and-half, a sugar bowl, forks, porcelain plates, cups and saucers from her alternate set, and tiny silver spoons. She had decided not to use her rosebud china, substituting the Tiffany pattern with blue fruit and flowers. Blue would be calming, she thought. It might lead to better understanding.

"What does that mean, guardian ad litem?" Maureen asked Ms. Hagen, sitting next to this woman who had more power over Patrick than anyone else.

"It's the usual procedure in a case like this," Beverly explained, "as I'm sure you've heard." She nodded toward Ben.

"It is the usual procedure," Ben agreed, "but I've checked with the court every day. There's nothing on the calendar."

"The judge just agreed this morning. We're recommending Aaron Short. He's an experienced family law attorney who's served as a child's guardian on previous cases. It shouldn't take more than a few minutes of the court's time."

"Of course, I'll be there," Maureen said. "I'm not sure about Tom."

"Mrs. Haig and I will be there," Ben concluded. "I know Aaron well, by the way. He's a good man."

Ms. Hagen nodded. "In addition, you should know I got a call from the NICU this morning. Apparently, Patrick has a new issue. He's already receiving antibiotics for a blood infection, as you know." She looked around the room.

"Yes, we know," Maureen urged, anticipating further information.

The expression on Ben's face suggested he had not known.

"His blood pressure, platelets, and both his white and red cells have all been low since yesterday. This morning, Patrick's physicians saw evidence of a bacterial infection in the trachea tube they put in to give him oxygen. They've got him on some new medications. The NICU staff can tell you more."

Maureen felt a dull ache begin in the back of her head. She leaned against the sofa, willing the discomfort to subside so she could concentrate. Headaches were becoming all too common, and she wondered why the good Lord sent them. To test her resolve, she thought.

"I'm sure the guardian ad litem will want to hold off on any status changes until Patrick is ready to leave the NICU. That will be awhile," continued Ms. Hagen. "In the meantime, the county is dedicated to doing everything possible to help him get through this first stage of his life, but–"

"But–" echoed Ben.

"Our resources are not infinite. Even with the state's help, a few cases like his can break the bank. In most situations, the county doesn't have a choice. We bear the burdens, by which I mean the public does, because these are our children. But in this situation, there is a choice. He is as much a child of Alabama as he is a child of Minnesota."

"I don't understand," Maureen interjected. "Don't you think we can do a lot more for Patrick here than they can in Alabama?"

"I don't know," Beverly said. "I haven't studied Alabama's programs. But you must understand that even with state help, his care has cost the county more than any child in recent memory. At some point in our deliberations, we need to include the reality of the county's limitations."

Maureen felt dumbfounded. *Dollars and cents, that's all people cared about.*

"At this point, the unknowns exceed the knowns," Ms. Hagen summarized. "We don't know how much function he will attain. We don't know his IQ. We don't know the extent of his emotional stability in future years. I ask you to have patience with the process but try also to realize that there aren't perfect solutions to every problem."

She rose. "I'm leaving you brochures that explain the programs available in Stears County. Pay particular attention to the disability services program."

Beverly seemed ready to depart. Reluctantly, Maureen walked her to the door.

When she returned to the living room, she looked at Ben. "Can you explain what that woman said?" she asked him.

"County budgets are stretched," said Ben, helping himself to a cookie and pouring his first cup of Maureen's rich coffee.

"Everybody's budget is stretched," Maureen said sarcastically.

"Now, calm down," Ben responded, motioning toward the sofa. "Sit," he added.

"She seemed to be hinting they'd just as soon send Patrick to Alabama once he's out of the hospital," Maureen observed.

"She was more than hinting," Ben said. "But remember, she's just one cog in the wheel. There's also the guardian ad litem. Aaron Short will be the person whose opinion we need on our side—that is, if you and Tom can get yourselves on the same side."

Ben took another cookie for the road. "You know, Maureen, my wife was a wonderful woman, and I miss her every day, but she couldn't bake worth a darn. It always surprises me that Tom keeps the weight off when he gets goodies like these."

Maureen smiled. "Take a bunch," she said. Ben did, and she watched him drive away with satisfaction on that score, at least.

Thank goodness, she reminded herself, that they had Ben Johnson to advise them, even if custody disagreements weren't his specialty.

Of course, if Theresa hadn't tried to get an abortion in the first place, if she'd been willing to carry Patrick full-term and let him be born when he should have been, then none of this would be necessary. Maureen couldn't get over that simple fact.

———•◦•———

Since she'd made it back to Charlie, Theresa had learned a lot about the intersection of scar tissue, connective tissue, collagen, cartilage, and bone. In Birmingham, they'd allowed her to dispense with the nurses and massage

Charlie's back herself, modeling the flesh beneath her hands with generous applications of prescription cream. Her fingers moved gently but firmly over his blue-and-purple skin, sensitive to the slightest indication Charlie felt pain. From the day of her arrival, she was the only person he'd allowed to touch him. Before, the nurses had applied cream several times a day. Theresa applied it constantly, all day long. Her fingertips became as soft to the touch as Pal's fur.

She'd snuck Pal into Charlie's room. Charlie was lucky to have nurses who went gaga over him, enough to allow a few deviations from the rules. It seemed to be a peculiar Cole charm, something that ought to be marketed, Theresa thought. She smuggled Pal out for walks whenever he pushed his nose against the door. No one accosted her going in or out.

Charlie would tease Theresa when she got back, wondering what put a smile on her face. His teasing became a trigger for gymnastics calibrated to minimize contact between Charlie's back and anything but air. They made love in his hospital bed, with the door locked and the curtains tightly drawn. The joy of reunion was a potent medicine. Pal slept in a corner and took no notice.

Pal hadn't taken to Charlie right away, but now he loved him. He could leap from floor to chair to Charlie's lap in seconds, and he made Charlie laugh. Theresa's spirits soared when Charlie laughed.

She continued the massages after she and Charlie returned to Lafayette. The nurses had given them six cases of the cream. It was expensive, they said, and impossible to duplicate on your own. The bottles inside held a cup each, good for maybe a day at Theresa's pace.

A nurse admitted that the cream was not so much prescribed as pilfered. One of Charlie's doctors seemed intrigued by the possibility of faster healing if Charlie continued to receive several times the massage routine in the protocol. The staff took pictures of his back every day and asked Theresa to continue.

Once home, the two of them settled into a hunter's cabin that looked as if it had been aired out, swept, and scrubbed with a toothbrush. An enormous bouquet greeted them on the counter—roses from Rebecca's garden, delphinium, painted daisies, Queen Anne's lace, a few stalks of bee balm.

A small refrigerator held Charlie's favorite foods. The bed was only standard size, but it had a feather mattress and pillows and a quilt that appeared to be handmade and looked as if it had never been touched. In a peculiar way, this was the honeymoon that hadn't happened for them. They listened to the sawing of crickets at night and the rumble of frogs. In the evening they ate dinner with the rest of the Coles, but otherwise Charlie and Theresa spent their time alone with each other, except for Pal who sauntered in and out as he pleased.

For her part, Theresa began to feel native to rural Alabama, despite the heat, and had no regrets regarding her decision to leave Minnesota. Mostly, she tried to forget the world she'd left, lest it raise her stress level, and that in turn raise Charlie's stress level. Charlie needed to stay relaxed. His blood pressure was back to normal, and she intended to keep it that way.

Charlie had not asked Theresa anything about what she'd endured, not about the kidnapping, the birth, or giving up the baby. She'd asked him if he had questions, and he'd said, "Not questions, but I have an ear. When you want to talk, I'll listen." But she had not yet reached the point where she could talk about it, even if Charlie's father said she ought to.

Theresa did get occasional voice mails from the FBI—though not from Mitchell Gunderson, the agent she'd spoken to before leaving St. Paul. These were from a woman, someone named Ramona Eggers, who asked her to call back anytime day or night. Agent Eggers made it sound urgent, but so far Theresa hadn't called her. She didn't even listen to the entirety of the messages. She wasn't ready.

Sometimes she thought Rebecca stood on the precipice of a question. Rebecca never said so outright, but Theresa sensed that, kind as she was, Charlie's grandmother did not totally embrace her. It galled her that Rebecca seemed to embrace Mary. Or rather, *Claire.*

6

Carole Novak got a tip from a court recorder. David and Roberta Wells had filed for divorce. Suspecting a connection between the abduction of Theresa Haig and the Wells' marital breakup, she tried to reach Roberta. Failing that, she called anyone who might be connected to her. Most people said they knew nothing; a few knew what Carole already knew; several, including the receptionist at St. Philomena, wouldn't discuss the matter or pass her on to anyone who would, and two women said to be at Maureen's house the day of Theresa's abduction—Helen Swanson and Barbara Iverson—hung up on her. She also called Liz Mueller, the friend of Roberta who worked at the clinic where Theresa had received prenatal care. Liz Mueller's voice mail was full. As usual, the sheriff's detectives assigned to Theresa's case did not return texts or voice messages.

As a last resort, Carole decided to contact Annie Haig, someone she'd hoped not to bother since Annie was, after all, a child.

Annie knew nothing about Roberta Wells' divorce. She had not overheard her mother on the phone with any of the church ladies recently. But she was up in her room or out of the house a lot during the summer, reading books in her favorite spots, hiking, and keeping a journal with her most private, intimate, elusive thoughts. Annie believed thoughts had to be recorded immediately so they wouldn't vanish like the hummingbirds she watched flitting from flower to flower in the hanging baskets on her family's front porch.

Getting a call from Carole Novak thrilled her to pieces. "I'll do what I can to get you more information," she promised Carole, trying to sound like an adult. An hour later she set the afternoon mail on the kitchen table. Her mother was home for once.

"What are you doing?" Annie started, knowing full well what her mother was doing. She had just taken a Bundt cake out of the oven and put it on a rack to cool, then loosened the aluminum foil wrapping from a package of cream cheese on the counter, gestures so synchronized they seemed part of a single act.

"There's a funeral tomorrow," Maureen replied, not looking up as she took a bowl out of the cupboard. "I don't really know the family, so I'm just making the one cake. You're in charge of putting supper on the table."

That was no surprise. Lately, Annie was in charge of putting lunch on the table most days and supper half the time. Her mother prepared meals ahead so the work involved was minimal.

"They told me not to come to the NICU so often," Maureen complained. "The more problems Patrick has, the more they discourage visitors. It interferes with their precious schedule. I think they don't want us to know when something goes wrong for fear we'll blame them."

Annie needed to steer the conversation toward Carole's questions. "Mother," she began slowly, as if cogitating a matter that originated in a deep recess of her brain. "Can I ask you something that's spiritual and practical both?"

It was the perfect way to put it. Annie knew the word *spiritual* would command her mother's attention.

"What?" Maureen asked, glancing quickly at Annie.

"Well, I'm wondering how a Catholic family can have a divorce, since the Church doesn't allow it?"

"What brings this on?" Maureen asked sharply.

Annie knew her mother hated talking about divorce. "Three girls in my class had their parents get divorced last year. Now it's on the news that your friend Roberta Wells is getting a divorce. How can that be?"

Maureen looked down as she eased the lemon cake from the Bundt pan onto an oversize white plate. She dropped the softened cream cheese into a bowl, added half a cup of whipping cream, a quarter cup of sugar, and a teaspoon of lemon extract, and stirred furiously until the frosting turned smooth as satin. Lemon Bundt cake with lemon cream cheese frosting was one of the Haig family's favorite desserts. Annie got up and opened the cutlery drawer, extracting a demitasse spoon which she dipped surreptitiously into the bowl of frosting.

From the floor, Zip watched her movements. An intelligent fellow, he knew his best chance to get some of this fabulous white stuff lay in petition by eye contact. Annie was well acquainted with the strategy. He stood up on his haunches and smiled, holding her gaze all the while. She grinned back at him, took half the contents of the tiny spoon into her own mouth, and applied the remainder to her finger which she held out toward Zip, who licked it until her finger was thick with his saliva.

Her mother was not watching. Normally, she got mad when anyone fed Zip from a finger, cutlery, or plates reserved for humans. She frosted in deft swishes, and when she was finished, put a plastic cover over the cake to protect it. Maureen had a whole shelf of plastic covers for church food.

Annie washed her hands at the sink and then sat across from her mother, who was staring into space as if she were hypnotized.

"What's the matter?" Annie asked, startled. There had been no hint of frozen stiff syndrome a moment before. Maureen continued to stare at nothing while Annie sat there, not knowing whether to leave or what to say if she stayed. Finally, Maureen's eyes came back into focus, and she looked at her daughter, an expression of horror on her face.

"I feel so responsible," Maureen got out.

"Responsible for what?" Annie asked.

"For Roberta. I was the one who called her after Lucy Meyer phoned me from the clinic. I invited her and the other women to come over and talk to Theresa. I set it all in motion. Now Roberta is paying the price."

Annie realized she had drilled into a dike. She regretted saying anything, that's how huge her mother's pain looked from across the table.

"David Wells was nothing when she met him," her mother charged. "Her family money made his success possible. Now he's divorcing her." Maureen looked at Annie sharply. "Are you sure? Where did you hear it?"

Annie scrambled to find an acceptable explanation. She couldn't reveal that she had found out through a Twin Cities reporter, especially one her mother had met and didn't trust.

"It's on the internet," Annie said. Surely at this point, news of the Wells' divorce was on the internet, since Roberta's husband ran some kind of famous company.

"What did they say?" her mother asked.

"I guess their lawyer went to the courthouse today?"

"Here in St. Dominic?"

"I think so. I can't exactly remember."

Maureen shook her head.

"Maybe you should go see her and try to make her feel better," Annie suggested.

Maureen shook her head. "She's visiting a relative in Québec." She rose from the table, removed her apron, and took the covered cake to a table in the entryway, returning briefly for her car keys.

"I'll be at church just a moment, then the hospital," she said. "Pork chops are in a pan in the fridge. They're cooked, so they just need heating up. Vegetables are in the pan too. I'll call to let you know when I'll be home."

Annie listened to her mother's car departing.

Now came the hard part, deciding how much to share. She had fulfilled her mission, but was it a right and noble mission? Or was it an act of betrayal?

It seemed to have been a summer of betrayals. First, the church ladies taking Theresa hostage, which was betraying Theresa's rights as a citizen in a free country. Of course, before then, there was the betrayal at the clinic where the doctor shared Theresa's information with outside people. Then the church ladies getting Theresa into such a lather that she ended up having Patrick too soon.

After Patrick was born, Theresa abandoned him. That was a major betrayal.

And now the only person who admitted she felt responsible for doing anything wrong had just walked out of the Haig kitchen not knowing that her daughter was about to spill the beans about her friend Roberta to a reporter! Would that make *her* a complicit link in the chain of betrayals?

Annie needed to take a walk before supper so she could sort out the pros and cons of the matter. She considered sharing one thing only with Carole and not saying who told her. For example, as rumor had it, that Roberta Wells was in Québec.

That might satisfy Carole, spare her mother, and prevent Annie from falling into ignominy as a full-fledged, no-question-about-it snitch.

———•◦•———

Woodrow had been besotted once before, instantly. As a scientist might explain, the embryonic moment is decisive. He loved a girl the moment he beheld her. A *coup de foudre*, Claire called it after he shared the story of Josie, who was Charlie's mother.

Josie Singleton sat at a desk close to a second-floor window in his freshman history class. The morning sun danced in her hair. She wore a gold necklace and a white blouse and had the most perfect profile he'd ever seen. He wanted to pick her up and carry her away, caveman style. He wanted to whisper all kinds of poetic things to her and make her love him back the way he loved her. Instead, he stood there like a buffoon until the teacher pointed out that he was the last student on his feet and would he please sit down.

No one knew Josie's high school years would be her apogee, a fleeting effervescence of champagne in bourbon country. She liked taking risks and took them often, careful to surround herself with friends who'd shoulder the blame if things went wrong. She lost acolytes from time to time but was always on the lookout for new ones. Even her residence in Lafayette turned out to be short lived. But who recognized impermanence in 1984, when Woodrow and Josie and most of their classmates turned fourteen?

She rarely gave Woodrow a glance. He must bide his time, he reckoned. He thought about her constantly but kept his distance and let other boys make ill-fated advances. He would be the one she could never quite figure out. He would be the one who seemed to pay no attention to her until she couldn't stand it anymore.

His first year of high school ended with no progress, but Woodrow remained steadfast, even when Josie was sent by her parents to live with a cousin during the summer. If she had not come back, he might have lost his determination, eventually. But she did return, as did his ardor, and the cat-and-mouse game recommenced, only this time he sometimes caught her looking at him.

Three years later their story was over, and she was gone for good. She wanted a beautiful life, she said. Seventeen was too young to be a mother. She put their infant in his arms. Her parents didn't want him. So, Woodrow could take Charlie and raise him up, or she would put the baby out for adoption to unknown parties and let fate decide what would become of him. Those were the only choices she'd allow.

Woodrow tried to talk her into getting married. He'd join the military, and Josie could live with him on base. There were lots of benefits for families. They'd make it work.

"You wouldn't even be an officer," she'd told him. "We'd be nobodies. I won't settle for that."

They were still a couple in the spring of senior year. He got to take her to prom, even though by then she was "starting to show." Her parents were so humiliated, they wouldn't allow her to leave the house after graduation, given she'd become the talk of the town. Charlie was born in late September, and a week later Josie left Lafayette for good. In the years that followed, Woodrow refused to fall in love again. It was a question of operational risk assessment. The risk had seemed too high, until now.

Claire didn't remind him of Josie, but how much he thought about her reminded him of how he'd felt in those dizzy months when he'd first discovered love. Woodrow had wanted Josie heart and soul, and it ended with a knockout punch. Now he wanted Claire, but it was different. His feelings for Claire had crept up on him, little by little, and, funny thing, it was the way they fought that excited him the most. She wasn't in love with herself. She didn't insist on winning every time. She fought fair. She looked him in the eye. She made arguments that he could counter. Most of all, she let him enjoy their fights. They were fights without rancor and without grudges afterward.

Of course, he gave in a lot, as he had with Josie. He'd stopped smoking from that first time she'd objected. He no longer used profanity in her presence. Well, hardly ever. Without apology or explanation, he'd consigned his Confederate plate to the bottom of his toolbox. He'd waited for Claire physically—never touched her until the night she came to him.

Yet, Woodrow knew something was missing. He even knew what it was. He wasn't essential to Claire. He figured she'd say no for sure to any outright marriage proposal. He could hear her saying no in his mind. He imagined after she said it, she'd disappear as fast as she could.

So, he decided to bide his time. Maybe Claire was still too wounded from her first marriage, he reckoned, like he was still wounded by Josie. If he told himself the absolute truth, he knew for a fact that the ones we've loved live on inside of us, like bone and marrow, part and parcel of who we are until the day we die.

He shared none of this with his mama, but he got the impression Rebecca knew that he and Claire were sleeping together, and if so, he knew she felt it was their business, not hers, so she kept quiet about it and did not venture upstairs.

———•◦•———

Early in the morning on the last day of August, a phone call from the NICU informed Maureen that Patrick had a new infection. When Annie walked into the kitchen a few moments later, Maureen removed her apron and washed her hands at the sink.

"I need to get to the hospital right away," she said. "You handle breakfast. And clean up afterwards. I don't want to come back to a single dirty dish."

Maureen rushed up to the bedroom and put on fresh clothes, not bothering to make sure things matched. These emergencies never ended. They scared her to death.

Patrick had a revolving "care team," a cadre of specialists whose photos and job descriptions were in a folder Maureen took everywhere. Her grandson's problems were many, interconnected, and difficult to manage. In his first weeks—Patrick had passed his four-week mark last Monday—his life itself was still not a certainty.

When she'd asked Laura Himley what percentage of babies born this early survive, she was told it was more than 90 percent. "Every day his overall chances go up, but we still need to manage the complications with both the prematurity and the Down syndrome," Laura said.

More than 90 percent should have reassured Maureen, but it didn't. Sometimes she could feel the blood pounding in her temples, not only when she was in the NICU looking at this sweet helpless child, but in the wee hours when she'd wake up in a sweat, even on cool nights. It reminded her of menopause. She'd walk to the windows and look out at the fields, trying to regain a sense of calm from the breeze that wafted in, the sight of fireflies in the distance, the trombone of frogs in a pond not far from the house.

The tubes they stuck into Patrick, the stickers all over his skin, the ventilator that wouldn't let him swallow or drink, all those invasions had to be painful. There was a tiny window in his incubator through which the NICU staff allowed Maureen, after she'd scrubbed with soap and antiseptic, to introduce a finger and gently stroke Patrick's palm. Every single time, Patrick responded, grabbing on as she sang a hymn like "Rock of Ages." Protestant melodies had great power, Maureen felt, and she did not resent their provenance.

Patrick's lungs worried his care team. They were not taking in enough oxygen, his pediatric pulmonologist told her on Patrick's four-week birthday. She called it *respiratory distress syndrome.* Maureen thought in a whole month, they should have solved it. But apparently not. His lungs had not had enough time to mature before he was thrust into the outside air, and there was no easy remedy. It was Theresa's fault.

A baby's lungs did not mature, as the doctor put it, until week thirty-six in the womb. Patrick should still be inside Theresa getting the oxygen he needed from the placenta. But the placenta had torn catastrophically, which was the reason for the premature birth.

The pulmonologist talked on and on about a substance called *surfactant* that Patrick's body was not producing in sufficient quantity. They were giving him some kind of synthetic surfactant. Patrick still needed the ventilator, but they wanted him off it as soon as possible so he wouldn't develop pneumonia.

It was all so complicated. Maureen read through the brochures about potential problems for micro preemies until she couldn't read one more word. The doctors were experts. Let them figure it out. Their faces and names began to blur.

All Maureen wanted was to put her finger in Patrick's palm and pray for the day he'd come off the contraption that breathed for him. She said the rosary as she sat by his side in the NICU. She prayed to Saint Philomena especially. She prayed to Saint Anne, the mother of Mary and grandmother of Jesus, the saint for whom Annie was named. She prayed to the Virgin herself. Her job was to be there, to pray and make sure God did not give up on Patrick.

Despite morning traffic, Maureen reached the hospital before seven thirty. The NICU staff often worked ten-hour shifts, and the doctors were constantly on call. She wanted to get there while the ones who had seen Patrick's new crisis develop were still available to talk to her. All she knew when she entered was that he had an intestinal infection of some kind.

A nurse stood over Patrick's incubator, checking his indicators—temperature, humidity, oxygen, air pressure, brain activity, signs of apnea, and on and on, reciting each in turn and saying, *"Good"* to let Maureen know. Maureen hovered until the nurse finished and looked at her, smiling broadly.

Smiles were reassuring. She motioned for Maureen to step a few feet away. She thought babies could sense what people were saying and whether it boded well or not.

"He has a new infection?" Maureen whispered.

The nurse nodded. "We noticed it about three o'clock this morning and called his GI specialist. That's Dr. Branson. He put him back on antibiotics and five hours from that point, they seem to be working." She paused. "I can put in for overtime and stick around, if you like."

Maureen nodded. This nurse, Elena, was the one she trusted most, though they all seemed competent. She wondered what the staff thought, seeing only one of Patrick's relatives caring enough to check on him and witness his struggle up close. She could hardly wait to embrace him skin-to-skin when he finally left the NICU, when the outer membrane of his body was strong enough not to tear like tissue and his lungs were developed enough for him to breathe on his own.

Meanwhile, Patrick's mother was nowhere in sight. Patrick's mother didn't even want to talk to Maureen when she called down to Alabama. Maureen decided to phone Rebecca when she got back to the farm and ask again to talk directly with Theresa. She had also begun to write letters.

———•◦•———

Roberta Wells, née Roberte Bouchard, whose recorded ancestry reached back to the mid-seventeenth century, had not only an aunt but numerous uncles, cousins, friends, and acquaintances in Québec.

Like most people she knew, Carole Novak lived paycheck to paycheck. She couldn't afford a flight to Québec to search for Roberta. There was only one alternative. She had to somehow get her subject to talk on the phone.

She wrote a formal letter and sent copies to Roberta Wells at the addresses of possible relatives in Québec, adding "Personal and confidential. Please forward" at the bottom of each envelope. The letter promised Roberta new information. It included Carole's phone number and email address.

Of course, there was no response. Carole considered calling every Québecois named Bouchard one by one but held off. It would be better if the connection were initiated by Roberta herself.

Just when she got out of the habit of checking every half hour, she found an email from Roberta Wells on the first of September, a warm and cloudy Saturday morning. Would she care to talk off the record on Zoom?

They set it up. A minute before ten o'clock, Roberta Wells walked into view using a cane for balance. Carole hardly recognized her. They'd never met, but she'd seen photos. Six weeks after the violent struggle that led to the premature birth, the woman on the computer screen looked gaunt. Her face still showed some bruising under her eyes and on one cheek. She seemed seriously depressed.

"You have information?" Roberta began.

"I'm not sure how much you know about what transpired since the end of July," Carole began, "but first let me introduce myself. Carole Novak from the *Minneapolis Free Press.*"

"Yes," Roberta nodded, sounding tired.

"As you know from my letter, I'm a reporter," Carole continued. "I'm going to share what information I've been able to gather . . . which is something reporters don't usually do, but in this case, I feel you need to know what happened in the aftermath of Theresa's getting away from you."

Roberta nodded again.

"Has anyone been in touch with you about the baby?" Carole asked.

"No," said Roberta, whose face lit up for the first time. "How is he?"

"He's holding his own. It's been a full five weeks since he was born, and they are taking very good care of him at the hospital. It will be a while, though, before he's released."

"But he's going to be OK?"

"No one can say for sure."

Roberta started to cry. "We didn't—" She took a deep breath. "We didn't mean for him to be born so early. That was the opposite of what we wanted."

"What was your plan?" Carole asked gently.

"To buy him more time. She would have aborted him."

"And you couldn't allow that."

"Just because he wasn't perfect!" Roberta got out in a sob. She struggled to regain her composure.

"You loved him, even though he wasn't your baby," Carole suggested.

"I couldn't get pregnant. We tried for years. And to see another woman throwing a baby away because she didn't want the burden—"

"Life changes dramatically when any mother has a child. If you add in the challenges of a diagnosis like Down syndrome, it can be overwhelming," Carole said.

"She could have found help. I wished that baby had been mine. I would have done everything I could for him."

"But, of course, you and your husband have the means to do a lot more for a child with Down syndrome than a woman like Theresa."

"What does that matter? You think a poor woman's baby is worth less than a rich woman's? What does a baby care about money?" Roberta looked less depressed than angry now.

"Do you regret anything?" Carole asked gently.

"I regret not succeeding," Roberta said.

"May I ask why you are in Québec? If you were in St. Dominic, you could probably visit Patrick. I'm guessing they'd let you, with his grandmother's permission."

"His name is Patrick?"

"Yes. For now. That's what Theresa's mother calls him."

"How much does he weigh?"

"I don't know. The nurses in the NICU could tell you. Their machines measure everything."

"That's good. I'm glad. But I can't come back to St. Dominic. Not yet, at least."

"May I ask why not?"

"David doesn't want me there. David," she laughed bitterly, "he certainly wouldn't want me talking to you."

"I'm only looking for background information," Carole interjected. "I won't quote you going forward unless we agree that you're willing to go on the record."

"I can't go on the record. I've signed things."

"Are you going through with the divorce, you and David?"

"Yes, apparently."

"Is it because of what happened to Theresa?"

"That was the end for David. I didn't tell him while it was happening because I knew he'd blow up."

"Would you yourself want to adopt Patrick, should the opportunity arise?" Carole asked.

Roberta didn't answer. Carole waited. "I promised not to interfere with the baby. I promised in writing," Roberta said. She started to cry again.

Carole waited a long time. When Roberta finally straightened herself and wiped away her tears, Carole tried another tack.

"Can you tell me anything about Lucy Meyer?" Carole held her breath after she posed the question. It might be a deal breaker.

"I didn't know Lucy before," Roberta replied matter-of-factly, her composure returning. "She came to St. Dominic after Dr. Ryan called a national organization. Lucy took charge of everything. She was the one who called Maureen Haig, and then Maureen asked the women in our group to come to her house that day."

"That day, meaning May ninth."

"Yes. Maybe. I don't remember the exact date."

"You mentioned a group. What group?"

"The group at our clinic. We called it 'Pregnancy Options,' and it was doing well at first. We got plenty of donations. But then these internet trolls started posting about us and after that we had a hard time getting pregnant girls to come in."

"Trolls posting where?"

"I don't know all the places. Agnes Olson monitors them. They claimed all we offered were diapers and car seats, but no financial help for the baby's future. As if that were some kind of justification for abortion. It got so bad we knew we had to do something more proactive."

"Did you decide to abduct Theresa as part of something more proactive?"

"No!" Roberta replied angrily. "That just happened. Dr. Ryan called Lucy to come to St. Dominic, and Lucy met Theresa and realized she was likely to abort her baby, so Lucy called Maureen."

"How did Lucy know Maureen?"

"I imagine Dr. Ryan gave her Maureen's number."

Carole sensed that, as long as she asked questions, Roberta would answer. "When did you decide to get involved?"

Roberta looked nonplussed. "I was already involved. We have a telephone tree. We talk to each other all the time, and suddenly here was something we could do to save a child."

"But you didn't convince Theresa," Carole said.

"No. She was stubborn. Finally, Lucy had to give her a sedative."

"When did you decide to do that—to give her a sedative?"

Roberta shrugged. "It just happened."

"You mean Lucy Meyer decided alone. It wasn't a group decision."

"We didn't discuss it beforehand."

"How did Maureen react?"

"I think she was surprised, like the rest of us. But once Theresa was unconscious, we all agreed to take her someplace safe."

"Where was that?"

"I don't know. We went to a farm owned by someone related to Maureen. Later we had to move again, twice, and it was a nightmare both times. She wouldn't come willingly so Lucy had to slip sleep aids into her food. Even then, it took three or four of us to transport her."

Carole stopped for a moment to absorb the casual way Roberta spoke about behavior she didn't seem to connect with anything criminal.

"Do you regret getting involved?" she asked.

"I told you before. I only regret that we failed."

"You saved Theresa's life, Roberta. She and the child might both have died, if you hadn't managed to get her to the hospital in the end. You did that despite your own injuries. That part wasn't a failure."

Roberta didn't say anything further.

Carole wanted to foster future conversations, so she promised to share anything she could find out about how Patrick was doing and whether his mother contemplated coming back for him. She asked if she could she take a screen shot. Roberta shook her head no and turned off Zoom.

———•◦•———

Theresa received a letter from her mother. Rebecca passed it to her at lunchtime when the mail arrived.

"How could you do this to your infant son who wants only for his mother to hold him?" Theresa read. Maureen had added, "If your baby dies because you abandoned him, it will be entirely your fault." *Entirely* was underlined.

She threw the letter into a burn barrel set on a concrete square about fifty yards from the house. She lit subsequent letters on fire and tossed them in unopened. Whenever a new one arrived, Rebecca handed it over matter-of-factly as she sorted through advertising flyers, correspondence with hunters and timber customers, utility bills, government notices, Charlie's VA statements, and various paperwork addressed to Woodrow.

Theresa knew her mother called Rebecca frequently and in the course of their conversations asked to speak to her middle daughter. She told Rebecca she didn't want to know anything that "got said," as Charlie put it.

Apparently, things got said in the South but not necessarily repeated. It seemed a function of the region's gentility, a quality Theresa began to recognize as armor. Everyone in the Cole household was polite to a fault, except Jeremiah, who sometimes couldn't hold back.

Under the gentility was steel. The South was only in part the easygoing place she'd thought it was when she and Charlie fell in love. For one thing, the Cole family seemed a clan separate from the rest of the community. People in the surrounding area knew them well enough, Woodrow especially, since he fixed their machinery. But relations were cordial, not warm. Rebecca explained the difference. Cordial was a willingness to tolerate but at a skeptical distance. Warmth was the basis of friendship. The Coles were too careless of social strictures to warrant warmth. And they had a reputation for not being Christian, which people obliged to them refused to believe.

There were more churches in Lafayette than in any place Theresa had ever been. You couldn't go a mile without driving past one. Grace Church of the Nazarene, Kings Baptist Church, Abundant Life Church, the Church of God, New Liberty Free Will Church, the Original Church of God, Calvary Baptist Church, the Church of God of Prophecy, and a dozen more.

A family without a church got noticed, a shopkeeper told Theresa when she asked. They all knew Rebecca, Woodrow, and Charlie, and they had nothing personal against them. But how can you trust a man to repair your truck if you're not sure he's godly? Some folk demanded to know outright whether Woodrow was an atheist, and he always answered "No, sir," without going into detail. That was enough to satisfy the denizens of Lafayette County for business dealings—but only for business dealings, and only because Woodrow was so darn good at figuring out the cause of mechanical troubles.

Theresa felt she was treated with genuine warmth whenever she went into town. She was a Northerner who had chosen to follow her husband to Alabama. Theresa's husband had been injured in Afghanistan, and she was tending to him the way an army wife should. Moreover, they were a beautiful couple, still newlyweds and besides, people could see the love in Theresa's eyes, they said. It helped that she was blond and cute as all get-out, one admirer told Theresa.

Rebecca had cautioned Theresa not to mention to anyone that she had left a child behind in Minnesota, nor that she had been kidnapped.

"Folks won't understand," Rebecca said. "They'd hold it against *you*, not the ones that took you. In Alabama, we dare to stand up for our rights. That's what the monuments say. But first those rights have to be granted by other people, meaning white Baptist people. No one comes out and says it, but that's the way it is."

Theresa nodded. "I understand perfectly," she said.

At home, she and Charlie were still settling in. Theresa tended a garden in the early morning since the summer heat made physical work after ten o'clock oppressive. She rubbed cream into Charlie's back after he exercised, spraying it first with aloe vera that she kept in the refrigerator. They both took Pal for walks. She rubbed more cream on Charlie's back when they returned.

She knew how hard it was for him. He needed to protect his skin under cloth thick enough to prevent the sun from penetrating the shirt on his back. He couldn't be exposed to direct sunlight on any part of the "affected areas" where scarring met the grafts. Charlie felt frustrated that his recovery wasn't complete.

"It will never be complete in terms of sensitivity," his army dermatologist told him. Charlie didn't want to hear that, nor did he want any psychological help. He was still determined to heal enough on his own to get back to his unit and keep his army career on track.

Theresa said nothing when he talked like that. She had read enough to know how unlikely it was that he'd ever be fit for combat again, and secretly she felt glad about that part. But she wasn't going to be the one who said it.

In her way, she was itching to get back to some kind of normalcy too. However, the Cole dominion was no longer the place they needed to be. "Claire" was there, for one thing. She'd never get used to that name.

Theresa remembered when she was little and sat on a pillow at the supper table to make her face higher so she could see what was going on while everyone listened to Mary. Mary talked a lot. Their father let her get away with murder, her mother said. Mary's attitudes were a bad example for the boys as well as the girls. Mary ignored their mother and carried on all the same.

It was as if they lived in a country with two competing systems of government—their mother's dictatorship and their father's democracy. Their mother demanded quiet and submission. Their father gave free rein to any opinion, no matter how raucous, unless it defamed their mother. Theresa's father loved a good argument.

Mary and Theresa were fourteen years apart. By the time Theresa was old enough to understand what unusual words meant, Mary was close to leaving. When she departed, it scared Theresa immensely. She was only eight, but already she knew that Mary was essential to things getting talked about. Otherwise, life was full of secrets and prohibitions, with no one to explain it all.

———————

On the Tuesday after Labor Day, a letter addressed to SSgt. Charles Harrison Cole arrived from the US Army. It announced his doctors' affirmation of medical readiness to enter the Wounded Warrior Transition Program. Four words that said, essentially: come to a meeting where we'll decide if you're fit to remain in active service.

There was no choice in the matter. Fort Benning was the closest option, so they scheduled the interview there. Charlie was advised to bring along a set of civilian clothes in case the decision involved immediate separation. Theresa insisted on coming too. The meeting would take place on Wednesday,

September 12, if that were convenient for Charlie.

Fort Benning was 229 miles away on the Alabama/Georgia border. They decided to drive. The first-class airline ticket the army sent Charlie could be cashed in for more than enough to pay for gas, meals, and a motel, if needed. His uncle Lewis offered the loan of his almost-new GMC Terrain. It had a V6 and all-wheel drive, and its powerful air conditioning would keep Charlie cool no matter the heat outside.

They left early Monday morning, taking a direct route through lush Alabama hill country. For a while they got stuck behind a convoy of logging trucks, but mostly it was pleasant. Theresa drove half the time and urged Charlie to get some sleep. But he couldn't sleep.

Charlie knew the base well since it was where he'd trained for the infantry. In uniform, he looked like any other soldier. Theresa got some stares though. She could see the look of pride on Charlie's face when they passed by men who gave her a long, up-and-down appraisal.

"I don't think that's allowed anymore," she pointed out.

"What's not allowed?" Charlie asked with a straight face that didn't quite succeed.

"Sexual harassment by leer. Where do I file a complaint?"

"Don't know," said Charlie. "Haven't had cause to file one myself."

His mood was improving. They decided to look around at off-post housing in the area, just in case. It was a sweltering day, but they saw three places in Columbus, including one she loved.

"Even if they let me stay, it might not be here," Charlie pointed out.

"But maybe it will be," Theresa replied.

Neither slept well that night. Charlie's back ached, and he couldn't find a comfortable position. Twice she sprayed his skin, applied the medicated cream, and bandaged it again. He fell sound asleep around four o'clock, but she had to rouse him from a nightmare at dawn. He wouldn't talk about his nightmares, and she didn't ask.

Theresa had to remain outside the office while Charlie met with a colonel at ten o'clock. She couldn't see inside since the blinds were drawn. When Charlie came out less than twenty minutes later, his face was inscrutable. She briefly met the colonel, and then they left the building. Charlie was still in uniform.

"Let's eat," he said, as they stood outside.

"What happened?"

"I know a good place."

His idea of a good place turned out to be a Ruby Tuesday, and his idea of a good lunch was a toasted bun and hamburger smothered in ketchup, onions, and mustard with dill pickles and french fries. There was nothing—

absolutely nothing—on the menu that Theresa thought she could tolerate, but she ordered a lemonade and biscuits with honey on the side, just to have something in her stomach.

"No gravy with the biscuit?" the waitress asked.

"No gravy," Theresa affirmed.

"Biscuits come with gravy. Honey will be extra," she was told.

"Fine," Theresa said.

The waitress departed.

"Well?" she asked Charlie, who seemed amused about the biscuit and gravy thing.

"There's basically three options after an injury," Charlie explained. "Going back to my unit, they knocked out first thing. The army thinks I can't take the heat."

"And the other choices?" Theresa prompted.

"A full medical discharge with benefits—lifelong."

She could see on his face that wasn't what he wanted.

"And . . ."

"And they offered to let me try out as a drill instructor. Here at Benning to start. If I can handle the heat, they'll send me to Fort Jackson for the training. Three sessions, twenty-two days long. And then, I hope, we'll be back at this post for good." He grinned.

"Do you think you can do it?" She returned his grin.

"I don't know. But I hope so, 'cause I took that option."

"Don't I get a say in the matter?" His gorgeous long-lashed eyes twinkled like the old Charlie. "Yes, ma'am. If you want to nix it—"

"I thought you said you already took that option."

"They're lettin' me talk it over with you before I sign."

She laughed. "How big of them."

"I'd be training to instruct in the same place and the same way I went through basic myself," he added, leaning toward her, "and I'd get paid enough, especially with spousal support, so we could afford to live off base. We'd essentially start over."

Theresa found his enthusiasm contagious. As much as she had needed to get out of Minnesota, they needed to get away from Lafayette and create a place for themselves.

"Let's rent that little house," she said.

"Don't you want to look around more?"

"No. I can already see us in that house. And the sooner we get settled, the better."

"Yes, ma'am," Charlie said, looking pleased. "But there's something else I gotta do."

He'd turned somber and looked at her without blinking, the slow gaze he'd shown in the beginning when their story was about how much he adored her.

"What?" she asked.

"I need to visit Minnesota."

His words hung in the air. She knew what they meant. He would see the baby for himself, the baby she had signed away, the baby who never seemed to disappear entirely from her life.

He broke their stare finally, glancing down at his plate.

"Theresa, darlin', I have to see my son," he said, looking back up.

"You understand," she replied, "he's not *my* son."

Charlie nodded. "I understand. I know what they did to you. But I still got to see him."

Theresa took a long time to respond.

Recently, she'd told him everything she could remember, every detail she hadn't blotted out, just as Charlie's father had recommended. Charlie hadn't prodded her. He'd waited until she was ready. They'd talked for hours. She'd seen on his face how deeply it affected him.

"They had no right," he'd said.

"No, they didn't," she'd agreed. "But I've been thinking about it since, and I realize now that I should have told you. I shouldn't have decided on my own to drive to St. Paul and have an abortion before you even knew. That was a decision you had a right to be in on."

He'd nodded. "I'd have liked to mull it over, at least."

"I'm sorry, Charlie."

She had hoped that discussion put an end to it. But now, facing him across a narrow table in a restaurant, she knew it still wasn't over. She and Charlie both were tethered to Minnesota, no matter how much she wanted to cut the connection.

"And when you see him, what's going to happen?" she asked. "Are you going to say, *wait a minute, I want him back*?"

"I won't do that. I know the price of it would be losin' you, and that price I am not willin' to pay."

Again, they looked at each other without saying anything, until at length she whispered, "So you're planning to just look at him and walk away?"

"I have to see him."

"You say that now, but in my mind, I imagine you'll want to transport him here once you've seen him."

"He's in a damn incubator. He can't be moved. He's got an infection," Charlie said impatiently.

"How do you know that?" she asked.

"My grandma," he said.

"So! My mother talks to your grandma, and then your grandma talks to you, and now they've got you feeling you have to see him. What happens after that? I need to know, Charlie."

"Nothin' happens after that. I come back home to you."

"Because if you do bring him here, the army might have to rethink the offer they made, when they find out you have this distraction. You told me once the army hates distractions."

"I must have been a distraction to my dad, but he kept me anyway."

"You didn't grow up on a base. Your grandma raised you."

They looked at each other. Neither spoke, until Theresa nodded and said, "You do what you have to do."

After they left Ruby Tuesday, they drove straight to the real estate company handling the place they wanted. By the end of the afternoon, it was settled. The house was partially furnished. They could buy some sheets and spend the night in Columbus before heading back to Lafayette first thing in the morning.

There wasn't a lot of conversation on the way back. Charlie played bluegrass on the radio as he drove, and Theresa kept her eyes shut, pretending to sleep.

———•◦•———

"It's less than a day to Minnesota if we drive straight through," Woodrow said. "I want you to come."

"Why?"

"You know the terrain. You know the people. Charlie's out of his element up there, and so am I."

"You seemed to get along just fine last May."

"It's not a question of gettin' along," he interrupted. "It's a question of feelin' comfortable. Seemed like folks were messin' with me up there every time I met 'em."

Woodrow stroked the sides of Claire's neck.

His fingers were callused. He smelled of Rebecca's homemade soap, a concoction his mother scented with pine and tobacco. Claire hadn't liked the aroma the first time she got close to him in the cafe at MSU. Then, he was just a strange man with a Southern accent. But in the past three months, his physical presence had become as essential to her as breathing, and things she'd found off-putting before had melted into the natural order.

"Do it for me," he said.

She was reluctant to put herself back in the place where Mary grew up. She wasn't Mary now, but forced into a room with her mother, she would surely revert to Mary.

"I've never met Patrick," Claire pointed out.

"So what?" asked Woodrow. "You can see him or not, as you choose."

Twice she'd peered over Woodrow's shoulder when he'd Zoomed with the NICU in St. Dominic. Both times, she had to look away. The infant's plight left her feeling "zero at the bone," a line from Emily Dickinson that rushed at Claire the first time she'd encountered Patrick. She didn't want to get any closer.

However, if she turned Woodrow down now, there'd be a barrier between them. Everything paled next to that.

"Twenty hours max to get there," Woodrow promised. They'd stop for gas, food, restrooms, and repairs if necessary. He put a bag of tools in the trunk and assigned three-hour shifts at the wheel. Charlie drove the first one. Woodrow next. Then Claire. They took Claire's new car, a used Mercedes Woodrow had found and fixed up to replace the Jeep.

"We'll leave at 6:00 a.m.," Woodrow said, and that's what they did, departing a half hour before sunrise on Saturday, September 15. While one of them slept in the back seat, the other kept the driver alert. Woodrow brought along a box of CDs, mostly country and bluegrass. Claire didn't much care for the places they stopped to eat, so they bought fruit and yogurt at local stores or whenever they pulled off for fuel.

At one thirty Sunday morning, Woodrow turned the Mercedes into the parking lot at the patient and family entrance to St. Dominic Hospital. The sky was clear, but there was too much ambient light to see any autumn stars. Charlie got out first. Claire was still asleep in the back seat. Woodrow had neglected to wake her for her final shift.

"Big place," Charlie said. He stretched and stared up at the building, wondering what part of it held his son.

"Want to go in now?" Woodrow asked.

"Think we should clean up first," Charlie said.

He felt nervous as all get-out. He had planned to drive to the hospital and head straight to the NICU, but now that he was actually standing outside, another reality set in.

No matter how much he worked it over in his mind, he couldn't get past the simple fact that, for Theresa's sake, he had to give up custody of his firstborn son, and he would have to do it in front of his father, a man who'd refused to give him up when his mother didn't want him. He'd asked himself a thousand times, did that make him a lesser man?

Woodrow drove to a motel whose sign flashed a neon arrow down the street. He rented a room with two double beds.

The motel looked modest but clean. Woodrow roused Claire, and the three of them lumbered inside. Claire took a hot shower. Then Charlie a cold one. Finally, Woodrow.

Charlie watched his dad lie next to Theresa's sister in the bed closest to the window, his father's arm around her waist. He was glad for them. Charlie's lifelong belief had been that his mother was irredeemable. She had broken the iron law of womanhood when she'd rejected her firstborn son. He'd blamed her for rejecting his father too. He felt his father deserved a better woman, one who would measure up to the decency of a man he had always admired, even at a distance when his father was deployed somewhere overseas and the only communication between them was by APO mail. He'd lived for those letters. His father was the only parent he'd recognized.

Once when he was twelve, his natural mother had asked to meet him, but he wouldn't allow it. The way he saw it, she was dead.

Maybe that was unfair. It had never occurred to him before that his mother, like Theresa, might have found herself in a situation that terrified her. Maybe she'd done things in the heat of the moment, like Theresa did when she turned their baby over to the county. Maybe what seemed like something a woman decided when she didn't give a damn was, underneath, something she did in panic when she was under fire.

Charlie had been under fire. He knew what it was to make decisions in the second-by-second chaos of an ambush that came out of nowhere. He knew terror. In a firefight, a soldier has to rely on his training. Nothing else will help him. A new mother doesn't get that. Nobody trains a girl to get pregnant at seventeen the way his mother did, just like nobody trained Theresa to get kidnapped and make her way out of a hostage situation and have a baby right after and act as if any of it had been her own doing. He was startled by his thinking.

They had breakfast at six o'clock in a coffee shop nearby. It was seven thirty on Charlie's watch when they handed their photo IDs to a security clerk in the hospital. Charlie was already approved to see Patrick, since his name appeared in the computer as the baby's father.

He felt as if he were heading into combat as the elevator took them up to the NICU. Elena, Woodrow's Zoom enabler, strode briskly toward them outside the entrance. Woodrow introduced her to Charlie and Claire.

"There's someone else who would like to meet with you if you have time afterwards," Elena told Charlie.

"Who's that?" Charlie asked.

"Beverly Hagen, the head of Stears County Child Protective Services. She wanted to be notified if the baby's father ever showed up, so I called her when

I heard you'd come in."

Charlie nodded assent. He looked at conversation with this county woman as basic reconnaissance. Any information he could get from her would inform future decision-making, he felt, and was information he could take back to Theresa.

He and his father washed up and put on masks and gowns before they followed Elena through the NICU's inner doors to where Patrick's incubator stood. Elena assured them he was doing fine this morning.

"I'll leave you alone for a bit," she said before departing. Woodrow stood next to his son a few moments, then pulled a few feet away.

Charlie stared at his boy. He had worn a lot of gear in Afghanistan. *Battle rattle*, they called it. On top of his camouflage, he put on IOTV body armor every morning. That was his Improved Outer Tactical Vest, an enhanced version of the old army vest. The new one let him add soft armor panel inserts as well as ballistic plate inserts in the front and back, plus it had side plates and collar and groin protectors. The next items he put on every morning were his elbow and knee pad set. They didn't weigh much. Of course, he wore basic mountain combat boots and his bulletproof tactical helmet with night vision goggles, aiming laser, and a communications headset, as well as goatskin Lomax gloves. His sunglasses were designed to deflect shrapnel. On top of all that, he wore a load-bearing vest with pouches for magazines, grenades, a first-aid kit, and canteens, as well as a CamelBak bladder he filled with one hundred ounces of water before heading out every day. On his back, he wore a rucksack with a whole lot of other stuff including MREs (Meals Ready to Eat).

With the average daily temperature hitting ninety-seven to one hundred nine degrees Fahrenheit in high desert country, Charlie had to put all that gear on his body, hating the seventy pounds it added to every step, and hating how hot it made him feel. He put it on anyway because he knew it might save his life. He knew it might bring him back to his family and back to Theresa. He knew battle rattle was worth the aggravation.

Now he saw an infant encased in battle rattle of his own, fighting a war on terrain other people had put him in. He knew his son didn't volunteer for the life he clung to. He didn't sign up for this. Charlie counted the attached electrodes on his boy's skin, electrodes attached to wires attached to monitors that flashed numbers on a screen. The numbers pulsed, as if speaking, indicating to NICU nurses whether his son's heart was beating the way it should and whether his breathing was too rapid or not rapid enough, and whether his body temperature was holding steady. He saw the apnea monitor set to signal an alarm if his son's breathing stopped. He saw the arterial line that monitored blood pressure and blood gases. He saw the central line that channeled medicine and nutrition into his child's body and let the nurses draw blood without piercing his son's delicate membranes every time. He saw the CPAP machine that sent air and oxygen to his son's lungs through endotracheal tubes. He saw the urinary catheter that went into his son's bladder. He saw Bili lights to treat jaundice. They weren't on, so the baby's liver must be working right, he figured.

Charlie didn't think this speck of a child would be able to leave his war's theater anytime soon. He tried to remember how long it had been. Since the end of July, he recalled. This innocent baby came into the world and had suffered seven weeks of hell so far because some demented oxygen thief of a pro-life nut job stuck a needle into Theresa's arm. If he had that woman in a rifle scope right now, he knew what he'd do. He'd frag the bitch to pink mist.

———•◦•———

Woodrow thought he knew what Charlie was thinking—Woodrow was thinking the same thing. He got close to the incubator again, made eye contact with Elena as soon as she returned, then looked at the port on the side of this elaborate glass box that kept his grandson alive.

"Would you like to touch him?" Elena asked Charlie between ventilator breaths.

Charlie nodded. Elena cleaned his hand and in particular his index finger with antiseptic wipes and guided it to the port. Woodrow stayed silent, watching.

Charlie's son grabbed the finger. Charlie stood motionless, then leaned over to examine more closely what could be seen of his child beyond the tubes and gizmos. The baby's eyes were closed. They did not open for this father-son moment.

After a while, Elena said the nursing staff needed to tend to him now, so Charlie and Woodrow would have to leave. Charlie seemed not to hear.

"We have to let go now," Woodrow whispered.

Charlie nodded and pulled his hand back. When he did, the boy's eyes opened. They all saw it. Charlie's son was conscious. His previously placid face contorted as his fingers grabbed the air, trying to reconnect with the finger Charlie had taken away. His little face reddened and the edges of his mouth, firmly attached to the breathing tube, twisted in what seemed a vain attempt to make a sound he could not make with lungs not yet ready to function as they should.

"He's mad as hell," Woodrow said to Charlie.

"Got every right to be," Charlie returned.

"Your being here tells him something," Woodrow said.

"Tells him what?" Charlie asked, anger in his voice.

"Tells him you care," said Woodrow.

"And what will my leaving tell him?" Charlie asked. "I promised Theresa I'd come back without him."

"We'll figure it out," Woodrow said.

"He doesn't know that," Charlie replied. "He doesn't know he'll ever get out of there."

———•·•———

It was the same room where they'd met in July, the day after Charlie's son was born, and the two women were the same decision-makers who seemed to hold the baby's future in their hands. Woodrow knew he should trust them. They were probably well-versed in what needed to be done. But he felt antsy in the North, which was why he'd wanted Claire to come along. Anxiety gripped him when it came to questions about this child, whose untimely arrival had pierced his heart like nothing since the birth of his own son twenty-nine years earlier.

He noticed the doctor was new. The hospital's chief administrator, Laura Himley, introduced Dr. Peter Calloway as the leader of Patrick's neonatal pulmonary team. Woodrow wondered how many teams Charlie's son had working to keep him alive with all that high-tech equipment in the NICU.

The three of them—Woodrow, Claire, and Charlie—had been asked to come to the conference room on the hospital's second floor. Woodrow doubted Charlie was fit to talk at the moment, but his presence was specifically requested.

Claire seemed worried. "You doin' OK?" Woodrow asked.

"I'm imagining Patrick's incubator strapped into the back seat of the car on our way home," she said, "and it gives me the willies."

Woodrow shrugged. "No time for fantasy. We need to deal with facts."

Claire looked at him strangely. Apparently, that's what Haig women did, Woodrow surmised. They stared and went silent when they didn't like a situation.

"You remember Beverly Hagen, Stears County Child Protective Services director," Laura said, nodding toward the other woman.

"Beverly asked for this meeting," Laura continued, "so I'll turn things over to her."

Beverly cleared her throat. "Perhaps we should start with Dr. Calloway," she said. Dr. Calloway remained seated.

"Well," he began, "I have to tell you the entire NICU is in love with Patrick. The little guy's a fighter, and we are fighting right alongside him. We monitor everything day and night, and while he's nowhere near able to leave the NICU, nor is he out of danger, his health is improving. Right now, he has an intestinal infection we're treating with antibiotics. He continues on the ventilator. We'd like to wean him off for the sake of his lung development, but for now he needs it. His previous infections have cleared up, including the one in his bronchial tube. He seems alert. We're a little less concerned about his vision and hearing then we were a week ago, but he's not out of the woods on those fronts either. His heart surgery was a success. However, he isn't gaining weight. That and the intestinal infection are our principal concerns at the moment." Dr. Calloway paused. "I know parents and grandparents don't like to hear this, but we are taking Patrick's progress one day a time."

Just then his pager beeped. He checked it and stood up. "I'm sorry, but I've been called upstairs," he said. "Not for Patrick, though. As I said before, he's doing well, and we're all optimistic."

Dr. Calloway excused himself again and left the room. A few seconds later, Charlie followed him.

Beverly seemed taken aback by Charlie's departure. "We thought your son and his wife might have changed their minds regarding custody," she suggested, addressing Woodrow. "That's why I asked for this meeting."

"No, ma'am," Woodrow told her, "not that I'm aware, they haven't changed their minds. But Charlie sure is glad to finally meet his son."

"Well, just so he knows," Beverly returned, "nothing's set in stone yet. A judge will still have discretion, and your son could reassert his right to legal and even to physical custody when the time comes for discharge from the NICU."

Woodrow nodded. With Charlie gone, the meeting seemed to be over. Claire looked relieved, he thought.

———•◦•———

"Mind if I walk with you?" Charlie asked Dr. Calloway as he caught up with him.

"No problem," the doctor replied, briskly climbing stairs.

Charlie peppered him with questions. What was his background? How much experience did he have working on preemies? Could he describe Patrick's biggest risk? What odds would he give for Patrick to come through everything as if he hadn't been a preemie?

Dr. Calloway, it turned out, had been born and raised in Stears County on a farm near Cold Spring. His brother Eric had arrived prematurely and had the genetic defect for cystic fibrosis. Eric was three years younger. He'd died when his older brother was nine.

The family had been in and out of hospitals innumerable times during the six short years of Eric's life, so his older brother Peter got used to being in medical settings and paid attention to what was being said, what treatments the doctors performed, what equipment they used. He'd asked the nurses all sorts of questions. At Eric's funeral, Peter had decided he'd become a neonatologist someday and save kids like his brother.

"Cures are harder than I thought when I first got started. But we keep pushing the age back, saving younger and younger preemies," he said.

"Give me your honest opinion," Charlie asked. "What are the odds for Patrick?"

"Better than they were," was all Dr. Calloway would say.

Tom paid Ben Johnson a monthly retainer. But lately his old friend and family attorney acted as if he worked solely for Maureen. That had to stop. Ben knew full well that he and his wife were at loggerheads about this kid. Tom had enough to worry about. He didn't need to torture himself with Maureen's money pit of a noble cause.

Ben arrived around noon. Maureen made ham and cheese sandwiches, slicing into a loaf of freshly baked whole-wheat bread. She served them with heirloom tomatoes and a spicy mustard sauce she'd invented. On the counter sat a banana cream pie. Lunching with Tom and Maureen was better than any restaurant, Ben always claimed, which was why he preferred to come to them rather than have them to his office.

"Got any pickles, Maureen?" Ben asked suddenly. "I know you can a slew of dills every fall. You're famous for 'em."

"Oh, gosh. Sorry, my mind's elsewhere these days!" Maureen exclaimed, rushing out of the kitchen. Tom stared at his lawyer.

"I didn't ask you over here to eat pickles," he told him.

Ben smiled with no apparent comprehension.

"Here they are," Maureen announced, returning with a mason jar. "I knew you were partial to dills," she added as she pushed it across the table toward Tom.

"Open that, please," she said, in an altogether different tone. Tom twisted the jar's lid until the cover loosened. The way Maureen sealed these things, she could never get them open on her own.

Ben plucked a pickle with his fingers.

"Hope you don't mind," he said to Maureen, who shook her head.

"There's so much vinegar in the juice, it doesn't matter," she said, "especially since they won't be around long."

"Thing is," Ben observed between bites of his sandwich and his pickle, "there's always an atmosphere of impending doom at the county. Now I hear they had three caseworkers quit at the same time—right when Bev Hagen's worried her budget won't stretch to fit the county's costs this year. She's not taking it well, I can tell you."

"How does losing three people affect our grandson?" Maureen inquired.

"It doesn't directly," Ben said. "But it makes her job harder. Meanwhile, she's got personal problems. Can I tell you something in strictest confidence?"

"What?" Maureen asked. Tom felt more annoyed than ever.

Ben looked closely at Maureen.

"Yes, yes," she said. "I'll be careful not to share anything personal—except of course with people I really trust."

Ben sighed. "Truth of the matter is her husband took a job in the Cities."

"So, she's moving?" Maureen exclaimed.

"No," Ben replied. "He's moving, and she's staying put."

"He's leaving her?" Maureen gasped.

"Looks like. In any case, she's not herself these days."

Maureen's eyes blurred. "I hate hearing someone's been left in the lurch by her husband," she told Ben. "It happens even to women at church who've never done a wrong thing in their lives." With that, she abruptly left the room.

"She's gone upstairs to call her friends—find out what they know," Tom told Ben.

"So much for strictest confidence. Guess I shouldn't have mentioned Bev's private life. Unprofessional on my part. This situation with the baby is getting to me too."

"Maureen will be fine," Tom insisted as the doorbell rang.

He got up from the table and walked toward the front of the house, exclaiming "Now what?" to no one in particular. He opened the living room door to find the Coles on the porch—Theresa's young husband and the husband's father. Beside them stood his oldest daughter.

"Good afternoon, sir," Charlie said. "I wonder if I could speak with you and your wife."

"My wife's upstairs gossiping in strictest confidence with her closest friends," Tom said matter-of-factly, stepping aside so they could walk in.

Theresa's husband appeared nonplussed. Apparently in the South, one doesn't mention a spouse's eccentricities to guests. Tom didn't care. This whole situation was taking too long to fix, and he was sick of it. Maybe, he thought, Theresa's husband had come to announce he wanted custody of Patrick after all.

"Come in, come in," he added graciously, leading them into the living room.

"So, this is where it happened," Charlie said.

"This is where what happened?" Tom asked.

"The hypodermic needle they stuck in Theresa," Charlie responded.

"What are you talking about?" Tom inquired again, his hopes dwindling.

"I wanted to see the place where it all began," Charlie said.

Woodrow put his hand on Charlie's shoulder. "We've just been to the park where Theresa went to think before she was kidnapped," he explained. "Claire knew where it was. Charlie here is tryin' to understand what his wife went through."

They were interrupted by footsteps on the stairway. Tom's heart sank when he saw Maureen. She wore socks but no shoes. On her face was the splotchiness that comes from letting feelings run amok.

Ben Johnson approached Woodrow. "This might not be the best time," he said.

Charlie walked up to the sofa but didn't take a seat.

"Right here," he remarked, looking down. "Theresa sat in the middle with women in front of her, and a woman close on each side. And somebody jabbed her with a hypodermic needle that put her out. That what you remember, Mrs. Haig?"

Maureen's hand went to her throat. "That was later," she said. "And no one intended—"

"But y'all did it," accused Charlie.

Ben intervened. "Charlie, may I call you Charlie?"

"Sure," Charlie said. "We're family, right? Theresa's my wife, and Patrick's my son. Though Patrick's not the name we might have given him. It was foisted on him, the way Theresa havin' him was foisted on us."

"Charlie," Ben said quietly, "we can't look for a winner here, none of us, least of all Patrick, who's the most innocent of all. But we shouldn't look for a villain either. We're at the point we're at, and the best thing we can say is that it's complicated. In my experience, when a situation is complicated, the wisest course is to search for compromises everyone can live with. Blame is a waste of time."

Charlie didn't seem interested in what Ben had to say. He kept his gaze on Maureen. Woodrow stood at his back, with Claire beside Woodrow.

"Do you know what a fetus looks like at twelve weeks?" Charlie asked Maureen.

"He looks complete." Maureen didn't flinch.

"He's two inches long!" Charlie cried.

"Two inches of humanity," Maureen replied. "Two inches that already are a formed child. All its organs—"

"Two inches is the size of Theresa's smallest finger from nail to knuckle."

"What difference does size make?" Maureen raised her voice.

"Half an ounce," Charlie said, moving closer to her. "You took control of my wife's entire body 'cause you thought half an ounce of her belonged to you."

Charlie had gone too far in Tom's opinion. He stood next to Maureen and put his arm around her. "You won't threaten my wife in this house, in front of me. No, sir, you won't," Tom said.

"I'm not the one issuin' threats, Mr. Haig. It was my wife they threatened. They took her by force. Tell me, sir, what would you do if somebody took your wife by force?"

Unable to answer, Tom stared back. He and Theresa's husband were inches apart. Woodrow gently nudged Charlie away.

"Patrick wasn't Patrick when you stuck that needle in my wife," Charlie continued. "Keepin' the pregnancy or not was her decision. She was the only one who had a right to make it."

"Mr. Cole, what must your family think, your friends and relatives, knowing what Theresa wanted to do with your baby?" Maureen demanded. Her previous upset banished, she sounded sure of herself.

"My kin mind their own business, and they don't stick their noses in ours," Charlie snapped at her.

As Charlie spoke, Maureen drew herself straight as a pencil. "I feel sorry for you, Mr. Cole. Your wife tried to kill your son, and failing that, she gave him away. He'll go to strangers, she said. To tell you the truth, I'm ashamed to call Theresa my daughter. For you, I just feel *pity*." She accentuated the last word.

"I can see," Charlie retorted, "you're a woman doesn't respect borders. No use talkin' to you about anything."

———•◦•———

"Now I understand why Theresa won't speak to her mother," Charlie said to Ben as the two men left the house and stood for a moment on the porch before continuing in the direction of Claire's car.

Charlie leaned against the Mercedes, thankful it stood in the shade. His back ached. He was going to have to toughen up if he wanted to make the grade at Benning.

"This is hard on everyone," Ben said.

Charlie looked around the farm. The air was redolent of harvested hay. The fields were lush. It wasn't nearly as hot here as in an Alabama summer. The winters saw plenty of snow, and the houses sat on basements. A bundled-up state, in other words. He guessed Northerners couldn't take as much heat as Southerners could, but they had cold down pat.

"That woman, Theresa's mother, I 'spect she could stand over the body of a stranger she shot for wanderin' into her yard, and sure as tarnation she'd find a way to absolve herself and bring God into the mix," Charlie observed.

"She's in pain," Ben replied. "People in pain lash out. I've seen it many times."

From the comfort of the shade, Charlie watched his father and Theresa's dad come out on the porch. They were close enough to overhear.

"You got something to say to me in private?" Tom asked Woodrow.

"Yes, sir, reckon I do."

"Have to do with Patrick?"

"No, sir. It's about your eldest daughter." Woodrow paused a moment before resuming, "The Southern tradition is to request permission from the father of a woman you'd like to marry. Well, I've been courtin' your daughter Claire awhile now, and I plan on proposin' when I get the feelin' she might say yes. I wanted you to know that."

"Claire?" Tom sounded incredulous.

"Yes, sir."

"You mean Mary. I don't have a Claire."

"I know her as Claire," Woodrow said.

"Yeah? Well, whoever she is, you saw the way she was inside. Not a word to say to us. That's not my Mary. The Mary I remember talked things out. Talked 'til she was blue in the face. But then she left my house. She went off and got married, and then she got divorced before the ink was dry, and now she's got herself a new name. It's no wonder she's driving her mother nuts. Now you come along–"

"Well, sir, maybe now is not the right time to ask."

Tom looked him in the eye. "There's no right time for you to be askin' to marry the sister of your son's wife. There's no right time for that in my book."

"I'm sorry to hear that. I was hopin' for your approval, sir," Woodrow persisted.

Tom shrugged. "Hope what you want. I'm hopin' you'll take Theresa's baby to Alabama soon as he's out of the hospital."

With that, Tom went back inside.

Theresa decided to use the time Charlie was gone to feather their nest at Fort Benning, and Rebecca agreed to come along, delegating business authority to Jacob in her absence. Woodrow gave the go-ahead to use his pickup to transport whatever furnishings Theresa selected from the multitude of old stuff in the Cole attic. Rebecca gave Theresa free rein.

So Theresa picked her way through drop cloths and cobwebs as Pal sniffed the floor, intoxicated by the scents of whatever creatures had recently prowled this vast, previously unexplored terrain. Theresa found two bureaus of drawers, a rocking chair, a small kitchen table and four side chairs, a pine nightstand for one side of the bed and a rosewood table for the other, three landscapes Rebecca had painted long ago, a full-height mirror, and twelve place settings of bone china Rebecca had inherited from her great-grandmother.

"Take this silver too," Rebecca offered, opening a drawer in a walnut hunt board.

Theresa picked up a fork. "It's heavy. This is solid silver!" she exclaimed.

"Goes back to the old South," Rebecca said. "That silver passed through generations of my family on my father's side. I always thought it was tarnished."

"Silver can be cleaned," Theresa observed.

"Not tarnished by the air," Rebecca said. "By the blood that bought it. I've been lookin' closer at my family tree, ever since my mama died. There's rotten timber, I can tell you."

Theresa seemed startled. "Oh," she said, adding, "are you sure Charlie and I should take it? Someone might steal it."

"Take it," Rebecca insisted. "If somebody steals it, good riddance." Theresa didn't know how to respond, so she said nothing. "By the way," Rebecca added, "I hadn't thought to tell you before, but I do appreciate your sister gettin' Woodrow to take that Confederate plate off his truck. I think he got so tired of the way outsiders look down on Southern boys, the plate was his way of sassin' back. I always hated it."

"I can't take credit for what Mary—I mean *Claire* does," Theresa said.

"Have to tell you, she reminds me a good deal of you and you of her," Rebecca continued. "You're cut from the same cloth. Too bad you're not close."

Theresa smiled wanly at Rebecca. When Charlie brought his bride home to Lafayette, she'd imagined melting into his family like butter in a frying pan. And she probably would have, had she not felt panic at the thought of living with people she didn't know without Charlie around. Instead, she'd made the colossal mistake of going back to her parents' farm when Charlie deployed.

Mary would not have been naive enough to think their mother would respect her as the grown-up, independent, married daughter she was when she returned to St. Dominic, pregnant, anxious and missing Charlie so badly.

Theresa had assumed on a practical level that there would be better pre-natal care in Minnesota than in Alabama, and that her longtime clinic in St. Dominic would be closer to where she lived. Only three doctors practiced in Lafayette, and none of them were obstetricians. The local hospital was small, and according to Rebecca, it didn't have enough nurses. Charlie's grand-mother had agreed that the hour and a half drive to Birmingham was too far for routine appointments. Even Tuscaloosa was forty-five minutes away because of all the congestion at the university. St. Dominic seemed the logi-cal choice, and so Theresa answered in the affirmative her mother's frequent exhortations to "come home."

As Charlie pointed out later, she might have had a harder timer in rural Alabama getting predictive prenatal tests, much less ending the pregnancy. But she would have had Rebecca to help, not Maureen sabotaging her decision.

Sometimes Theresa's fingers would go to where Lucy Meyer's needle had stabbed the muscle in her upper arm. Out of nowhere, she would feel a prick at that specific spot. It was probably her imagination. But every time, it seemed as if it were happening again. She associated the feeling not with Lucy Meyer, whose face she tried to blot out, but with her own mother.

Mary would have recognized the situation for what it was and, in similar circumstances, would not have put herself in their mother's clutches. She would have left St. Dominic the way she left her husband. The breakup of Mary's marriage had always been a mystery, but Theresa's bet was that a day had come when Mary learned that Rob was cheating. Mary had proba-bly packed her suitcase on the spot without ever looking back, whereas she couldn't see disaster coming if it sounded its horn like a freight train. After she'd left Dr. Ryan's office, if she'd kept driving to St. Paul without stopping at the farm, how different things would have been. There was no logical reason to hold that against Mary, but somehow, Theresa did, especially now when her sister, obnoxiously reborn *Claire*, had established herself in the Cole homestead and seemed to have taken first place in Rebecca's heart.

"We can't get it all in." Rebecca stood on the front porch with her grand-sons. Theresa had made her way down to the kitchen with a reluctant Pal squirming in her arms. She watched as Charlie's cousins, Waylon and Anthony, rearranged the bureaus back-to-back to make space for the table set on its side.

"Not even close," shouted Waylon. "No way y'all can fit this in without crackin' something."

"Should we rent a U-Haul?" Theresa asked, not knowing what else to suggest.

Anthony and his brother guffawed.

"I don't imagine we've ever rented a U-Haul, given all the vehicles this family owns," Rebecca observed. "We're going to need help, though. Can both you boys come along to Fort Benning?"

"Probably," Anthony said. "I'll call Dad."

Woodrow's brother Jacob gave his sons permission to take the rest of the day off and use his own Chevy Silverado for the trip. Technically, the whole family worked for Rebecca. Theresa knew Jacob would have given his boys permission to do just about anything Rebecca wanted. Out of respect, they always asked anyway.

An hour and a half later, the furniture was packed tightly in two vehicles with scarcely an inch to spare.

"When we leavin'?" Waylon asked.

"Lunch first," Rebecca said.

They ate quickly, washed up, and got set to go. At the last moment Rebecca found a spot for a box of kitchen gadgets and some clean rags. They drove nonstop, Pal on Theresa's lap, and arrived in the vicinity of Fort Benning around five o'clock.

Since the boys intended to bring the Silverado home that same night, they insisted on unloading everything immediately and putting it where Theresa wanted. They left without supper.

"We'll get something on the way," Waylon promised.

"That's eighteen for you," Rebecca said as they drove off. "Just out of high school and not a care in the world. I just hope they slow down when it gets dark."

"I felt that way, not a care in the world, up until last May when my carefree days came screeching to a halt," Theresa said.

"Any regrets?" Rebecca asked.

"I regret trusting my mother."

"But do you regret anything about the baby? You know, Woodrow has a mind to adopt him."

"That's Woodrow's decision," Theresa said. "Nothing I can do about it."

"Meanin' you don't want him?"

"Meaning that baby is not mine. I've decided to put the past to rest and

222

live in the present."

"Honey, as William Faulkner once wrote, and we all been repeatin' ever since, *the past is never dead. It's not even past.*"

"It is for me," Theresa returned. "I'm just so tired of thinking about it."

Rebecca nodded. She and Theresa fell asleep on the queen bed that came with the house. The mattress and box spring were worn out, so buying replacements was the first item on Rebecca's shopping list.

It was nine o'clock the next morning before they woke. Theresa was shocked by how late they'd slept.

"I guess exhausted bodies take what they need," Rebecca said.

She'd brought along a dozen eggs, some of her brown nut bread, blueberries, and coffee. They looked around the house in the light of day as they ate at the kitchen table. Pal enjoyed crumbs of the nut bread. Theresa had forgotten his kibbles.

"Place needs a good cleanin'," Rebecca pointed out. "Any objection to workin' on a Sunday?"

"None at all," Theresa agreed. She'd been trying lately to affect a drawl, drawing out words at the end of a sentence to give them a Southern lilt. Rebecca gave her a strange look.

"Then let's get goin'," she said.

Inside the bureau drawers Rebecca had packed two pails, bottles of soap, brushes, and towels. They scrubbed the walls, floors, and ceilings, moving from room to room until the whole house smelled of soap and disinfectant and the dust and critters were gone. To keep away from all the commotion, Pal napped at the far end of the porch.

They cleaned the inside of the refrigerator with diluted bleach, washed drawers that pulled out, polished cupboards and furniture with lemon oil and used a lemon spray on the windows and doors, sliding them up and down, opening and closing sashes, oiling hinges as required. The tile in the bathroom took the most time. The heat felt oppressive. It was ninety-two by two o'clock, and the humidity kept rising.

"First thing I'm gonna get is an air conditioner," Theresa said.

"You'll need permission from the landlord," Rebecca advised. "And you'll have to mind your p's and q's to get it."

Rebecca suggested they buy Theresa some new dresses, calf-length, full-skirted, and flowery, and a wide-brimmed hat, with shoes to match. And that she wash her hair and let it fall to her shoulders in all its golden glory.

"They won't be able to resist you," Rebecca said. So that's what she did on Monday morning. Theresa walked up to the front door of her and Charlie's new landlord, pushed the doorbell, and handed the wife a sprig of daisies mixed with yellow roses she'd bought at a local mini mart. Like so many people she'd met in Alabama, they were gracious. They were in their seventies, she guessed, and long retired.

Of course, they wanted to know where she came from. She accentuated that she was not from a big city. She came from a farming community in Minnesota. Just a country girl herself. They had tea and trimmings. The lady, it turned out, made small individual cakes every day so there would always be something fresh and delicious on hand should company come to call.

When Theresa asked if they would consider letting her put air conditioners in two of the windows, they readily agreed. She told the landlady she and her husband would install them carefully, and they would leave them behind if they departed. She explained Charlie's injuries and why he needed a cool environment at night to rest and prepare for the rigors of the next day. Theresa left feeling elated.

It occurred to her as she walked away that if she had not matched a preapproved template—stylishly attired, blond, and beautiful—things might have gone differently. But she no longer cared about ifs. Theresa had decided to deal only with reality henceforth, like Mary did.

When she got back to the house, she found out that Charlie had phoned Rebecca. He, Woodrow, and Claire were going to clean out Claire's apartment, Rebecca said. They were putting Claire's furniture in storage and letting the landlord know she didn't plan to renew her lease. When they were finished, they'd return home. Charlie said he'd call Theresa when he found some private time, as soon as he'd settled down from his Minnesota experience.

Rebecca didn't say what she thought he meant by *settled down*, and Theresa didn't speculate.

The next day, Theresa called the information office at Fort Benning to inquire about civilian jobs on post. She wrote down contact numbers and figured out where to go to interview. She'd wear one of her new outfits again.

Rebecca planned to rent a sewing machine, buy fabric, and work on curtains. Serene, Theresa said. White would be best. She wanted Charlie to come home every night to a place of solace, sweetness, and joy.

———————

The morning after they returned from Minnesota, Woodrow located a 2017 VW GTI for sale by owner. He and Charlie headed out to see it. Charlie was eager to find a vehicle and drive it to Fort Benning. He'd talked to Theresa twice and said he couldn't wait to get back to her.

The two walked around the pearl black GTI looking for dents or rust. They took it on a twenty-minute test run. Woodrow inspected the vehicle's internal components as well as he could without hoisting it. The odometer said sixty-nine thousand miles; the seller was asking $21,000 in cash or certified check. It was still under warranty, but only for a bit.

The owner was an insurance executive who bought and sold cars as a side gig. He was the buyer of choice in the area if anyone had to raise money fast. All sales were final. Every vehicle had a clear title, and he would stand behind that, but there were no refunds possible for any other reason.

Charlie switched his attention momentarily to a 2018 Havana Red Genesis G80 parked near the GTI. The sign in the window said $39,900, a lot more than Charlie aimed to pay. It had forty-five thousand miles. He was about to turn away on price alone when Woodrow intervened.

"Let me have a look," he said.

An hour later, Charlie drove southeast in the Genesis on his way home to his wife. Woodrow headed back to Claire, who'd been still asleep when they left.

Woodrow had stashed a wad of hundreds in his pocket. He'd bargained the owner down to $38,900 and paid the difference in cash to get the Genesis near what his son expected to pay for the GTI. Charlie looked stupefied, and for a moment Woodrow thought he'd turn him down. They had a conversation a few paces away.

Woodrow felt good being able to help his son. He knew Charlie wouldn't have accepted it from anyone else. When the seller went back inside his house, and Charlie was set to leave, Woodrow asked if he expected a skirmish about the baby once he reached Fort Benning.

"Nope," Charlie said. "We'll be OK."

"I hope so," Woodrow told him. "She's your wife. You cling to her."

It was not his place to say. Ordinarily, Woodrow would never intrude on another man's private relations, least of all his son's. But he also understood the power of that little guy in Minnesota, his body all tangled in tubes and his face tethered to a contraption that breathed for him. He wanted to assure Charlie that the family would look out for Patrick, and that he and Theresa should concentrate on healing each other. But he couldn't quite put it into words.

"Have a safe trip," he added, his right hand on Charlie's shoulder.

"Yes, sir," Charlie said. A minute later, he was a dot surrounded by dust on a gravel road, headed toward Georgia.

—•◦•—

Woodrow spent the drive back to Lafayette strategizing. A lieutenant he knew in the corps once told him to always look at the whole chessboard before making a move. Woodrow tried to do that. Around ten, he walked into the kitchen and found Claire scrubbing carrots and potatoes. He washed up from the road and joined her at the sink.

"You find a car?" Claire asked.

"We sure did."

"Charlie like it?"

"He didn't go for the one we went out to see. Picked something else."

Claire nodded, patting another Idaho potato dry. Woodrow peeled it. He knew she liked chunky mashed white potatoes and smooth gravy, hold the onion and garlic. Woodrow enjoyed potatoes any which way a cook prepared them, providing they had enough salt. Of course, his preference was for sweet potatoes.

"There's some things I'd like to talk over," he said when Claire looked up.

"That sounds ominous."

"Time we get 'em straight."

"What exactly needs straightening?" she asked as she washed her hands.

"What we expect from each other."

Claire pulled a towel from a drawer. "Now's good," she said.

Woodrow made coffee. He needed a jolt. As it started dripping, he joined her at the circular pine table Rebecca's grandmother long ago saved from a fire. It had scorch marks on top. Rebecca rarely put a cloth on it. "Don't cover up history," she decreed.

Claire gave Woodrow a smile he couldn't quite interpret. "I don't need coffee," she said.

He waited until he'd filled a mug for himself, then sat next to her.

"Over the years, quite a few women been willin' to jump into bed with me, but I never found one I wanted to spend my life with. Not sure if that was bad luck or bad salesmanship," he began.

"I'd say you're pretty good at salesmanship," Claire observed. "How many times have you put your heart and soul into it?"

"Just Josie," he admitted. "Before you."

"You still think about her?"

"Nope."

"Why'd you give up on her if she was the one you wanted?"

"She gave up on me. Affection is never even, Claire. Somebody always wants more, and that person is likely to get hurt."

"Do you regret that you didn't keep trying?"

"Nope."

"Are you afraid I'll disappoint you, like Josie did?"

"Josie and I never talked anything out. We were young and didn't have expectations as much as hormones. Both of us made—lookin' back—I guess you'd call 'em unwarranted assumptions."

"Do you think we're making unwarranted assumptions?"

He sighed. "I think we need to say out loud what we're after, and we need to say it *now*, at the beginnin'."

She didn't reply, so Woodrow continued, sipping his coffee. "I think we could make a go of it together, but I've got to be honest with you, Claire. Wouldn't be fair to tell you later."

"Tell me what?" She sounded alarmed.

"I 'spect your mama'll wanna keep Charlie's baby," he said. "I got to tell you, I don't like that idea one bit, and I'm gonna fight it every inch."

"How is our making a go of it connected to Charlie's baby?"

"There are people willin' to do hard things." Woodrow pushed his mug away. "And then there's people who talk a good game but hunker down soon as the shellin' starts. Your mama's got the fightin' spirit, but I don't think she's got the reserves. And she might not know it, but she can't raise that child alone."

Claire looked at him with wide eyes.

"Your daddy's not gonna help," Woodrow continued. "Plain truth is he doesn't want the child around. And your little sister's just a kid. As for those church ladies, they're gonna cut and run 'fore too long."

Claire shrugged. "I have no idea what any of them will do," she said with a catch in her throat. "What's it got to do with us?"

"Raisin' this baby might be tough, and if it is, it never stops. I was readin' up on it, and they say it takes a toll on people, 'specially someone like your mama. She's not young."

"And we're young? Tell me outright, do you plan on the two of us taking responsibility for Theresa's child?"

Woodrow grinned. "That's the beauty of it. We got a lot of people in this family, and we're good-hearted. I think we can divvy it up."

Claire shook her head. "They've told you that? Your brothers, their families, and Rebecca?"

"We tell each other a lot of things without exactly puttin' them into words."

"Well, put this into words for me."

Woodrow grimaced. "Fine. I figure for us, you and I, to get Charlie's baby one way or another. And I want to marry you. Two separate things, but they need to work together."

"You want to marry me?"

"Yeah. Didn't I just say that?" Woodrow stroked her arm. "Don't we make love every chance we get?" he whispered, leaning his head to touch hers.

"Unless, of course, you agree with your father. He seems to think it's not fittin' I marry you, given my son's wife is your sister."

Claire didn't pull her arm away. Good sign, he thought, as his brother Jacob walked in, letting the screen door slam behind him.

Rebecca wanted that screen door to slam. Woodrow had offered to fix it a thousand times. A person could be almost anywhere in the house and know someone entered the kitchen by the reverberation.

"Sorry to interrupt," Jacob said, looking at Woodrow as he poured himself a cup of coffee. "But we got an order's gonna take three days nonstop. I talked to Mama. She'd like you to help."

"No problem," Woodrow said. "I'll be there shortly."

"Charlie get off all right?"

"Yeah."

Jacob nodded and left, taking the mug with him.

"I'm glad he interrupted," Claire remarked as Woodrow's brother drove away. "It gave me a chance to think about what to tell you."

"Go ahead."

"All right. First off, my father doesn't get a say on whom I marry, if I marry anyone. That's my call. I don't believe in subjecting major decisions to a vote, especially major decisions on the man I love and choose to spend my life with. Love is too rare for that."

Woodrow liked hearing those words. He'd been worried that when the time came to ask Claire to marry him, some part of her might feel the way her father did.

"But secondly, I have to tell you, I'm scared stiff of this baby. He'd need so much. I'm just getting my head around being with someone." She took his hand in both of hers. "Woodrow, I've been alone for so long, and I'm accustomed to the freedom that comes with it. This child would—" Words failed her. Claire got up and poured a glass of lemonade from a pitcher in the refrigerator. Then she sat down again.

"If we got custody," Woodrow mused, "we'd change his name. Charlie wouldn't have called his son Patrick."

"Charlie's not the one aching to take him on as a day-to-day responsibility," Claire pointed out.

"Maybe Rufus," Woodrow suggested.

"Be serious!"

"I am."

"You really think your extended family can pull together to help us care for a child who's probably going to need watching every minute of every day for the rest of his life?" she asked.

"Won't know 'til we try," Woodrow said. "I just thought you should understand what I'm aimin' for—what I hope you want too. And that's to be a part of this family, not some guest who wanders in and out when she's in the mood, all the while talking 'bout her personal freedom."

Claire sighed. "There's more I've got to say," she told him.

"Well, fine. Spit it out. Get it all out, now we're at it."

"All right," she said again. "I'll tell you. I want to have a child of my own before it's too late, and I can't think of any other father for that child. I want you . . . and nobody else."

Another grin appeared on Woodrow's face.

"But Charlie's child with all he'd need . . . I wonder if you've thought through just how enormous an impact that would have, not just on me, on everybody," Claire said.

"It's a lot to ask," Woodrow admitted. "But darlin', don't make assumptions. He's a baby now, and he'll grow into a little boy with feelings like anyone else. We can't know at this point how it'll be. He might not be much trouble at all. We won't know 'til it happens."

"Suppose I had a condition before accepting you?" Claire interjected. "Suppose I wanted us to live somewhere else? Would you give up this world you're comfortable in?"

"I'd be loath to leave," he admitted.

"Yet I'm supposed to take a chance on something just because you want it? Because you're a man, and I'm a woman and that's the way it's always been? Is that how you're thinking?"

"A family pulls together, men and women both," Woodrow replied. "Otherwise, it's not a family."

"What this amounts to is you forcing me to choose between the man I love, who comes with a weight the size of a mountain, or going away on my own and giving you up."

"It would tear me apart if you went away," he said, staring at the burnt spots on the table.

Since it seemed Claire had nothing more to say at the moment, he went outside, gently closing the screen door behind him.

7

Elena gave two weeks' notice so she could follow her husband to Minneapolis, where he'd found a better job. Her last day would be September 28, a Friday. She felt bad about not seeing Patrick through to discharge, she told Woodrow, but under the circumstances there was no alternative.

"Family comes first," Woodrow said.

Elena told Woodrow that she had some good news. Patrick was coming off his breathing equipment that very afternoon. He'd been on both a mechanical ventilator and the high frequency oscillator. His BPD—bronchopulmonary dysplasia—had lessened, thanks to the medication they were giving him. His gastrointestinal problems seemed to have cleared up, too, at least for the moment. If all went well, she'd Zoom with Woodrow again later in the day so he could see Patrick breathing on his own. More of him would be visible without all that stuff in the way.

There was a possibility of a collapsed lung, but she said not to worry. They would deal with it if the need arose. The nursing staff continued to monitor his blood gases. Oxygen levels that were too high or too low could indicate new problems with his heart, kidneys, or even his eyes. In addition, Patrick kept trying to pull his tubes out. He moved more than he had in the past. His eyes were open a lot. He loved to hold Maureen's finger, or at least Elena said she thought he did, given the ferocity with which he grabbed on.

She knew she'd given Woodrow a lot of information in one burst, too much to take in quickly, given his long-distance love affair with Patrick. Only Maureen, who visited every day, could match Woodrow's level of concern, she said.

There was also a county social worker who came in several times a week. She reported directly to Beverly Hagen. In addition, Patrick now had a guardian ad litem.

"His name is Aaron Short," Elena told Woodrow. "He shows up frequently, and he asks the doctors all kinds of questions. The staff likes him," she added.

"I haven't met him," Woodrow said. "What do you know about him?"

"Not much, but he seems nice."

———•◆•———

Woodrow left a message for Ben Johnson later that day. Ben didn't get back to him until mid-evening, just as Woodrow was finishing repairs on a buncher that had to be operable first thing in the morning.

"Charlie's baby get all those tubes out?" Woodrow inquired straight off.

"They tell me he did," Ben said. "And he made the transition pretty well, I hear. He's got an official guardian now. Were you aware of that?"

"Yeah," Woodrow said. "Fellow named Aaron Short."

"That's right," Ben said. "I've known Aaron for thirty years. He'll do a good job helping the court decide what should happen for the little fellow."

"Why didn't you get this guardian ad litem thing?" Woodrow asked.

"That would have been a conflict of interest, since I do legal work for Tom's corporation. Issues that have to do with the farm, mainly. Commodities contracts, land disputes, anything involving subsidies or regulations. Those are my specialties. I don't practice family law, and even if I did, I couldn't represent the Haigs' interests and their grandson's too. Now it seems that Maureen wants to take Patrick's care on herself, if the court allows it. Tom's not happy about that, but I don't think he's going to stop her, not in the short term at least. Unless Theresa changes her mind. That's what Maureen says. I hope you don't mind my calling Charlie's baby Patrick, by the way."

"What I mind is Charlie's baby going to Maureen Haig."

"That's a question for a court to decide," Ben said. "The guardian ad litem will have input, of course. But the bottom line is that the child's best interests have to come first."

"Is it in a child's best interest to go to the woman who had his mother kidnapped? You tellin' me a judge would sign off on a kidnapper getting custody?"

"Nobody's established in court that there was a kidnapping," Ben said. "Maureen's talked to investigators. But she hasn't been charged with a crime, Woodrow. Far as I know, Theresa hasn't spoken to anyone in law enforcement."

"It happened, Ben. If you're going to represent the Haigs, you'd better look into that part of it."

Ben made no further comment, but he did tell Woodrow how to reach Aaron Short.

⎯⎯•◦•⎯⎯

Aaron Short had been practicing general law in the greater St. Dominic area for almost as long as Ben Johnson. The men knew each other, but their paths did not often cross in the courtroom, since Aaron's cases tended to involve divorce and child custody while Ben handled mainly farming matters. Neither man had set out to limit his legal experience to one area or another. It just evolved that way.

Courts in Stears County had picked Aaron Short as guardian ad litem on numerous occasions over the years. Aaron had a seemingly gentle disposition, but underneath his country lawyer demeanor lay a "tough old buzzard," as one judge called him. When his client was a child, Aaron fought with particular vigor. He hated bitter divorces where children were involved.

Aaron was a lifelong "bachelor farmer," a phrase he'd heard used by the radio humorist, Garrison Keillor. He lived with his longtime partner, Roger Eusted, on a ten-acre hobby farm that Roger had turned into an apple orchard. It was a pleasant life, except for the grinding of Aaron's teeth at night when a custody case went bad. Roger kept asking Aaron to retire, but that day had not yet arrived.

Woodrow called Aaron Short as soon as he'd hung up with Ben. He tried to introduce himself, but found he didn't have to explain who he was.

"Your grandson's doing really well," Aaron said. "They tell me if his improvement continues, he could be released by late October, or maybe early November. That's five to six weeks from now."

"That's real good news," Woodrow said.

"Now, as you may have heard," Aaron continued, "it's my job to make a recommendation to the court regarding who gets temporary foster custody once Patrick is out of the NICU."

"You got a recommendation in mind?" Woodrow asked.

"My mind is totally open at this point. No preconceptions. But as you may also know, in cases like your grandson's where the mother has relinquished custody under a state's safe haven law, the federal government through its Social Security statutes requires me to explore every avenue to preserve family connections. So, if I may ask, is there any indication your son and his wife have changed their minds about custody?"

"I don't think so," Woodrow said. "I can ask again, but I don't think his wife wants to raise the child."

"Then I have to look at family alternatives," Aaron cut in. "Can I further ask, are you and your family disposed to have him live with you and grow up in Lafayette? I'm talking long-term, after temporary foster care has ended. Ultimately, the court will want to find a permanent home for your grandson."

"Yes, sir, we are disposed to have him grow up here in Lafayette. We certainly are."

"In that case, I'd like to talk to you and your family face-to-face. How would you feel about a visit?"

"Anytime. We'll lay out the welcome mat," Woodrow replied.

"Well then, I think I'll schedule a flight to Birmingham," Aaron said.

"That's great. I'll pick you up at the airport," Woodrow offered.

"No, uh, I'll want to look around and get a feel for the area first. I'll rent a car and drive out to your property, if that's OK with you."

"It sure is," Woodrow said. "Whenever you want, you just come on out."

———◦•◦———

The first weeks of October are a sweet time to find oneself in Birmingham, Alabama. Frost won't arrive before December, and the temperature rarely climbs over eighty or dips below fifty. Wisteria and jasmine turn yellow-gold on iron wrought archways, and ceramic pots of gardenia dot front lawns with fragrant white blossoms determined to hang on as long as possible. Aaron Short was so informed by his seatmate on Delta Flight 2791, an elderly resident of Vestavia Hills, a suburb just south of the city.

"I've lived in the vicinity of Birmingham all my life," she said, "and I wouldn't feel at home anywhere else. For an avid plantswoman like me, it's a paradise."

"A plantswoman!" Aaron repeated. "Then I expect your own garden is a work of art."

"I've won awards," she confided. "More than my share."

Outside the airport, a cool mist still hung in the air, though it was near noon by the time Aaron retrieved his luggage. His flight had taken four and a half hours, including a stopover in Atlanta. He rented a car, drove into the city, checked into the Redmont Hotel, took a two-hour nap, and spent the rest of the afternoon and early evening investigating facilities.

The university hospital had a Women and Infants Center that was open twenty-four hours a day. It was big—four hundred thousand square feet—and equipped with the latest technology, enthusiastic nurses, intensive at-risk infant care, private NICU units, and empathetic doctors. A hospital representative gave him a pile of brochures and business cards to pore over. Back at his hotel, he fell asleep without eating and awoke in the middle of the night with no idea where he was.

He spent the following day at a branch of the Birmingham Public Library. Aaron wanted to know the history of the university hospital, its reputation, policies, staffing levels, and skill in handling difficult cases, and he wanted it to come from a neutral party with no particular ax to grind. The library staff found a retired nurse who volunteered twice a week in the new health information section. Everything she told him sounded good.

Early Thursday morning he made his way to the Lafayette County Child Welfare office. It was a letdown. The director wasn't in. Two staffers holding down the fort either didn't know or didn't care to say how the county would handle medical care for a high-risk preemie with Down syndrome who was still in the NICU in a hospital in Minnesota. In fact, Aaron would have to say his questions left them agape.

Finally, he looked at available medical facilities in Lafayette. There were two family clinics and a rehabilitation center. The main clinic was open most days of the week until 6:00 p.m., but it closed on Sundays and had abbreviated hours on Saturday. So, a child's level of risk depended somewhat on when a crisis occurred.

He drove onto Cole property around noon two days after arriving in Alabama. Rebecca came out to greet him. The family matriarch was the only one at home apart from the dogs, an old German shepherd retired from police work, and Koda, Woodrow's mixed-breed Labrador rescue. Koda almost knocked Aaron over.

Rebecca told Aaron her boys were out cutting timber, Woodrow included. She invited him inside and watched him size up the place. His eyes seem to linger longest on the books that lined the floor to ceiling shelves. "Some go back a hundred fifty years," Rebecca told him, "mostly on my family's side, not the Coles."

He moved in closer to examine the titles.

"My late husband's people were what we call *ne'er do well*," Rebecca reported, "by which I mean they'd not much to say for themselves until Preston had the brilliant idea of proposing to me. I was twenty-two at the time, and good looking back then. S'pose most twenty-two-year-olds are good-looking. The clincher was that I came with property, a whole lot of it from my father's estate. He'd died not long before, and my mother didn't want to bother herself with business, so I was his one and only heir."

"I can see that proposing to you would be a brilliant idea on your husband's part," Aaron said with a grin.

"Knew I'd like you," Rebecca replied.

Aaron looked up as the kitchen door slammed. It was the older Haig girl, he guessed, the one his friend Ben Johnson called *Claire, not Mary*. She wore a straw hat and a loose cotton dress with sleeves to her wrists. In her arms she carried a basket of vegetables. Rebecca introduced them.

A half hour later, Woodrow came in, and the four had sandwiches and chilled cucumber soup for lunch at the kitchen table. Aaron wanted to meet the whole Cole clan, but these three mattered most.

"First off," he said, "I got a favorable impression of Birmingham and what it has to offer a child like your grandson. If the boy lived in Birmingham, I'd feel comfortable he'd get the care he'll need."

"I gather that means you wouldn't be pleased to see him growing up in Lafayette," said Woodrow.

"It's not ideal," Aaron agreed. "In the immediate vicinity, there's no medical facility open for emergencies after six o'clock, and you'd have a long drive if he needed specialized intervention."

"There's the university hospital at Tuscaloosa," Woodrow pointed out. "It's closer than Birmingham."

"Hadn't thought of that," Aaron said.

"I'll take you there," Woodrow suggested.

Aaron agreed. "But first let me ask, what would be your primary objective in having your grandson live with you?" He scanned their faces one by one.

"To love him," Woodrow replied. "Love him enough so he'll feel good about himself and the world he lives in."

"Love is necessary, no question," Aaron said. "I know what it's like when people are only fighting to win for the sake of winning or to prevent the other party from winning."

"We're not thinking in terms of winning," Woodrow said.

"What about you two?" Aaron asked, looking in turn at Rebecca and Claire.

"I agree with Woodrow," Rebecca said. "There's plenty of love in this house. I've got a big, empty bed. My great-grandson can sleep in a crib beside me, and I'll hear if something goes wrong. But I'm getting old. There'll come a time when I can't pick him up, and if he acts out, I'll likely not be able to handle him."

"So, what happens then?" Aaron asked. He looked back and forth between Woodrow and Claire.

"I'd be willing to help," Claire said, "but I don't want to be the one responsible for him."

"I appreciate your honesty," Aaron said. He looked again at Woodrow.

"Woodrow knows he'll take the brunt of it," Rebecca said. "With a child like Charlie's son, somebody's got to sacrifice his life. He's as much a cause as he is a baby, and Woodrow's going to have to dedicate himself to that cause, since he's determined to have him."

"Are you OK with that assessment?" Aaron asked Woodrow.

"I have to be," Woodrow said.

"He might become a handful as he grows up," Aaron pointed out.

Woodrow nodded. "I understand that. But you need to understand that he's my grandson. We don't abandon kin in this family."

"You'll need backup," Aaron said. "More than Rebecca or Claire. That has to be worked out."

Another silence ensued.

"I'll be lookin' for someone," Woodrow said, finally.

Aaron nodded.

"You know, we keep seeing the downside of this," Woodrow added, "but we tend to ignore the upside. He might fit in just fine."

Aaron nodded. He noticed that Rebecca and Claire didn't chime in, though, and surmised that they remained wary of how it would all turn out.

Rebecca brought a plate of ginger snaps to the table, along with a pitcher of cucumber water poured over ice that cracked emphatically in the space between cold and colder.

"If you could stay a while longer, we'll introduce you to the entire family," Woodrow suggested.

"I'd like that," Aaron agreed.

After lunch, Woodrow led him around the property. He met the other brothers, saw the muscle and endurance that growing timber required in this part of the country, sensed the family pride and solidarity. But would it be enough to give Charlie's son a decent life, he wondered, assuming the child wouldn't suffer from overwhelming physical and mental limitations?

He stayed two more days. Before leaving, Aaron asked Rebecca for a look at the family tax returns. He suspected the state and county in this region might be strapped for funding, maybe more so than in Minnesota, and he wanted to know if the Cole family could afford to raise the child mostly on their own.

These situations could become a mess if a family didn't pull together over the long haul. Claire's hesitation bothered him. But Aaron didn't share those concerns with the Coles yet. He was still in the information-gathering phase of his journey south.

Dr. Michael Ryan had lost a child to abortion. It happened when he was a first-year resident at a regional hospital in Milwaukee. His fiancée, a fellow resident, got pregnant. They'd been careless, fatigued from work. Their shifts had been long. It was both their faults; it was nobody's fault; it just happened.

He wanted to get married and have her take a year off to deliver the baby and breastfeed. After that, he was certain his mother would assume daytime care and even nights when necessary. However, two years after *Roe v. Wade*, Cheryl had another option, and she took it. Michael would never forget the fury he'd felt when she got back from Chicago and told him. She hadn't even had the decency to let him know in advance. She'd killed their child by unilateral decision in another city in another state and informed him matter-of-factly in the on-call room the following day. He had rarely felt such an urge to violence. The hardest thing he ever did was to unclench his fists as he looked at the expression on her face. There wasn't a trace of guilt or regret. They didn't even know whether the child had been a boy or a girl. It was too early to tell.

Of course, they were finished after that. For the rest of their residency, he could barely stand to look at her. A year later, she took a fellowship in Colorado, and he never saw her again.

When the doorbell rang in 2018, Michael saw a young woman on his porch who might, for a split-second, have been Cheryl in 1985. She was the same height, and wore the same haircut. Even her body language mirrored Cheryl's. Or did he imagine it? Some days, he saw Cheryl everywhere.

"My name's Carole Novak," the woman said, extending her hand. "I'm a reporter with the *Minneapolis Free Press*. I wonder if you'd let me ask a few questions."

Michael was tempted to get rid of her. He knew what it was about—the Haig girl who'd delivered prematurely. That baby lay in the NICU now, a preemie without a good prognosis. He wasn't sure of its gender. The memory of the mother's attitude disgusted him.

His lawyer had advised him not to talk to anyone. His malpractice agent would throw a fit if he knew. This reporter was probably a feminist who'd portray him as the bad guy. He should slam the door in her face.

But he'd always regretted not hearing Cheryl out. It had taken him years to realize he needed to understand *why*. He'd asked himself over and over: what would induce a good woman to do such a hideous thing?

Dr. Ryan had been getting ready to leave St. Dominic for a job in a health-care facility in another part of the country—somewhere no one had ever heard about what happened to one of his patients the previous May. And here was this woman who looked like Cheryl.

———•◦•———

Carole had positioned herself in her pale-blue Kia under the low hanging branches of an Amur maple tree across the street from Dr. Ryan's house. About six o'clock, his black Ford sedan pulled into the driveway and disappeared inside the garage. She waited a few minutes before getting out of her car to approach the 1920s' style bungalow. It sported a realtor's *For Sale* sign halfway between the front door and the sidewalk.

Inside, the walls of the house were bare. Carole suspected they'd been recently painted a recommended shade of pale gray that continued from room to room throughout the interior. If photographs, diplomas, or paintings had once adorned the walls, all traces had been removed.

Before venturing to interview Dr. Michael Ryan, she'd researched his background. Born into a politically conservative family, he'd had a rural upbringing in Ripon, Wisconsin. He went to medical school at the U in Milwaukee. His internship and residency occurred at St. Luke's Medical Center. He was divorced and had no children.

"Would you like coffee?" he asked as she took a seat in an armchair next to an empty wood-burning fireplace.

"I'd prefer tea, if you have it," she replied. "Herbal."

He nodded. "Think I've got some chamomile."

"Perfect," she replied, trying to sound cordial. Ten minutes later, they sipped tea together. "I'm wondering," Carole started, putting her cup down gently on a glass-topped oval table, "would you mind discussing what happened to one of your patients? Theresa Cole came to your office on May ninth of this year and—"

"You've talked to her?" he asked.

"Yes."

"When was that?"

Who was interviewing whom, Carole wondered. "In late July, after her child was born prematurely."

He was silent for a moment, his face half-turned away.

"Can you tell me—"

"We need to set some ground rules," he broke in.

"What kind of ground rules?"

"Well, for one thing, I don't want to be quoted."

Of course, he didn't want to be quoted. Had she run into anyone willing to be quoted?

"All right," she agreed, grudgingly.

"I also want a tit-for-tat. I tell you something, you answer my question."

"That depends on what you ask me."

He nodded. "My first question has to do with Mrs. Haig's—"

"Mrs. Cole," Carole corrected. "Theresa Haig is married to Army Staff Sergeant Charles Cole."

"That's right," he recalled. "My question has to do with Mrs. Cole's motivation. She seemed upset when I told her that her child might not be typical. Did she tell you what her intentions were after she left my office?"

"You thought her intention might be to have an abortion," Carole suggested.

"That's what I feared."

"I'd have to listen to the tape again to determine whether she referenced abortion at that time."

"You recorded your conversation with Mrs. Haig—I mean, Mrs. Cole?"

"Yes."

Dr. Ryan removed his black plastic glasses. Carole remembered that in the interview, Theresa said he took off his glasses during her clinic visit. Did that mean something? He returned the glasses to his face. "Are you going to tell me whether she was planning to have an abortion?" he asked accusingly.

"If I recall correctly, she didn't say she was thinking about abortion when she left your office," Carole said, "but I can't know for sure."

"What would have been her motivation for an abortion?"

"Again, I don't know, but my guess is that she didn't want to raise a baby with Down syndrome."

"I never told her she might have a baby with Down syndrome," he insisted.

"I believe someone told her," Carole recalled. "Possibly Lucy Meyer."

"She was ten to twelve weeks pregnant by her estimation. At that point, her baby's brain and spinal cord were fully formed. His face showed expressions. His electrical system could be measured. Even at ten weeks, he was recognizably human."

"I doubt she was thinking about fetal development," Carole ventured.

"There's no other way to think about a baby in utero!" he said angrily.

Carole felt embarrassed for him. She'd never met a doctor who sounded so emotional about what was, in essence, someone else's personal decision. "We're speculating here," she pointed out. "Perhaps she didn't want her life changed to the extent it would have been—"

"Did she want her baby's life ripped to shreds by an abortionist?" he interrupted. "Ripped to shreds, as if it were nothing. People aren't nothing,

Miss Novak."

"I doubt Theresa thought her pregnancy was nothing, Dr. Ryan." Carole spoke softly, hoping that would calm him. But it didn't seem to have any effect.

"Sometimes, Miss Novak, people can't understand an experience unless it happens to them. So, I'd like to ask you, just for a moment, to try to picture yourself as that fetus—which you once were. All of us once were. Now, if your mother had taken mifepristone at ten weeks, followed two days later by misoprostol, violent contractions would have torn you away from the uterine wall and expelled you. You would have died. If you were too developed for medication to work, you'd have been vacuumed out. Either way, *you*—Miss Novak—you would have become medical waste. Your brain would have shut down. Your nervous system would no longer have sent signals. You'd have become *nothing*, Miss Novak, and you wouldn't be here today asking me questions. I want you to picture that in your mind."

He picked up his tea and took a few sips before returning his gaze to her. Something told her that her reaction mattered enormously to him. Otherwise, he wouldn't be breaching patient confidentiality in talking to a journalist. He seemed desperate for someone to agree with him, or at least to follow him down the path he'd taken.

Why not, she thought. Maybe she'd be able to write more accurately about a doctor who would egregiously betray his professional responsibility if she first tried to understand what circuitous route his mind had taken prior to inviting a kidnapper into his clinic.

She closed her eyes and thought about being the tissue expelled during an abortion. She imagined a blob of bloody material vacuumed out of someone's body and deposited into a small metal container. She could see the scene in her mind's eye, but she didn't feel anything. She opened her eyes. He was watching her facial expression. She suspected that he thought the idea of being aborted had the power to terrify her.

"I can't identify with the blob of tissue you described," she told him simply. "I'm sorry. It doesn't resonate with me."

"It doesn't resonate," he said sarcastically. "It doesn't *resonate* . . . Well, then, let me ask you, Miss Novak, can you imagine being laid out on a mortuary slab? Can you see yourself naked, lying on a stainless-steel bed? It's raised several inches on the sides to capture any runoff from your body. There are holes in the basin to allow fluids to drain away. You're dead. First thing that happens is a forensic pathologist plucks out your eyes. Later he makes a Y-incision to open your breastplate. One by one he removes your body's major organs: your heart, your lungs, your liver, your stomach, your spleen . . . He weighs each organ and examines it. He'll remove your brain next. Your brain is very, very soft tissue. It's beautiful. It's the universe of your life experience. To enter your brain, Miss Novak, he makes a cut across the crown of your head, sawing from the bump behind one ear to the bump behind the other, cutting bone but leaving soft tissue intact. Then after your brain is removed, it's dissected before it's sliced for samples or preserved in a jar. Or maybe it's discarded. Treated as medical waste along with the rest of your body. Parts might be sold for experiments. Or your body might end up in a landfill or an incinerator." Dr. Ryan stood up and looked at her, his gaze downward as if she were indeed lifeless on an autopsy table.

Carole noticed that his hand trembled so much, he had to put his cup of tea on the glass tabletop. She was fascinated by the picture he had just painted for her benefit. All those macabre details. He had to have rehearsed his description of a body on a slab over and over again to transmit it to her now without missing a beat, like some cranky old professor in front of a blackboard.

"Does any of that *resonate* with you, Miss Novak?" he asked.

"Yes," she said, meeting his stare. "It's chilling." She refused to blink.

Carole had been present at crime scenes. She'd viewed dead bodies in the morgue and studied evidence photos. He was taking the wrong tack if he thought he could frighten her with enumerations of procedures she'd seen before.

What he had done was give her insight into his own psychology. Theresa had trusted this man. That meant Theresa hadn't had a clue what lay beneath the surface.

He was a human being in deep, searing pain. Carole suspected these images of death were the first thing he saw when he woke in the morning and the last thing he witnessed at night. They were his life. In her opinion, he had no business practicing medicine.

But, of course, she couldn't prove anything of the sort. She didn't have what he'd said on a recording device. She couldn't quote him. In terms of her work, this meeting with Theresa's doctor was useless.

"Let me tell you something else, Miss Novak," Dr. Ryan went on, sitting down again. "Let me inform you that there is no difference between the death of a fetus and the death of a fully formed person. Each is the extinction of a universe of life experience. The death of the blob of tissue in a metal receptacle is as awful as the death of an adult body on a mortuary slab because they are separated only by time. One is a future life lived. The other life has already been lived. They are equal in value, since time lived doesn't signify worth. Time itself is an illusion. But the murder of a human being is not an illusion. It happens every day. Theresa Cole was on the verge of committing just such a murder, and she needed to be stopped."

"So, you stopped her?" Carole asked him quickly, meeting his eyes again.

He leaned back in his chair. "No," he said emphatically. "It was not I who stopped her. Fate intervened."

Carole exhaled, frustrated. What could she do with *fate intervened?* How could she prove that Lucy Meyer responding to his summons was not *fate?*

"It's my turn now," she said. "May I ask you some questions?"

What did he know about the abduction Theresa described? Did he plan it in concert with Lucy Meyer? How did he come to know Lucy Meyer? Did he expect Theresa's case would be reviewed by a medical board? Was he prepared for criminal charges if they came?

Her questions were pointless because he wouldn't answer them, not even indirectly. He rambled instead, telling her things about his ex-wife, about the medical establishment, about the laws of the state of Minnesota. Tyranny of the system, he called the law. He described a long-ago girlfriend named Cheryl. By the time he stopped talking, he seemed calm and exhausted.

Carole realized then that he hadn't invited her into his house to allow her to interview him or even to help her understand his point of view on abortion. He had invited her in so that he could vent.

She left his home feeling stymied, but with one certainty. Dr. Michael Ryan was a heartbroken man. When he had said early on that people couldn't understand an experience unless it happened to them, that was real. It was the crux of the matter. She was sure that at some point, he'd had a personal experience with abortion. Maybe his ex-wife had aborted a child before he could stop her. Possibly these images he'd tried to force on her—the aspirated fetus, the body on a mortuary slab—were his way of punishing a woman, any woman, by making her share his pain. Or maybe the images he conjured were part of an endless cycle in which he visualized an abortion beyond his preventative powers.

That brought the issue back to control. If an abortion had occurred in his personal life because Michael Ryan was unable to stop it, was he heartbroken because of the abortion itself, or because of his powerlessness? Could his ego not bear it?

None of these questions gave Carole a handle on the feature article she wanted to write. Her editor didn't think much of her efforts so far and had suggested she move on. She worked on other stories. Yet she couldn't make herself stop poking and probing this one.

———•·•———

When Beverly Hagen was a child, she and her sisters went fishing with her grandfather during the summer. He took them out on the lake at the family cabin, always on a calm day, always with life preservers strapped snugly around their torsos.

"Don't rock the boat," he'd say if one of them tried to stand up. Their grandfather took safety to extremes. He'd spent forty-five years in the Merchant Marine and had seen Lake Superior at its fiercest. Where water was concerned, he anticipated the worst.

"It's possible to shore up a ship against a wind from one direction," he'd told them in one of his stories, "but when the wind comes from every direction, hurling a vessel against all sides of the sea at high speed, the surges slam into the hull and break it apart, especially if the hold is void. Always remember: You gotta have cargo or you're doomed in a storm. Don't rely on water alone."

The Stears County Child Protective Services director had been fond of her grandpa's stories and recalled them at the oddest times. She knew she was relying on water alone—well-intentioned promises without the budget to back them up.

Rural America was hollowing out, as the sociologists put it. No matter how well he knew his land or how hard he worked or how rich his soil, a farmer like Tom Haig could lose what he had in a disastrous season or two. How would an infant like Patrick fare then? Bev believed the Haigs would already have signaled to the court their ultimate intention to adopt Patrick, had the farm economy remained strong.

She expected Tom Haig, Ben Johnson, and Tom's wife, Maureen, at her office that afternoon. Tom had requested the meeting. She hoped that he and Maureen had reached a decision. Bev opened the file on the case of Patrick Haig/Cole and started a new page, headlined Monday, October 15, 2018. She looked at her watch. 2:20 p.m. They'd be here any moment.

Bev wondered if they realized the financial drain Patrick's care had become for the county. One day in the NICU costs $3,000, but that figure was theoretical because it was just the base rate. There were so many things the daily rate did not cover. Some days, his care was in excess of $7,000. Other days it was as high as $11,000. Patrick had so far spent eighty-one days inside a NICU incubator. Bev had been going over bills and demanding explanations from the hospital all that time.

Her assistant ushered in Tom Haig, who came to her office in work clothes. They were reasonably clean, at least. Ben Johnson followed shortly after, wearing a dark blue suit with the jacket over his arm. She'd known Ben for many years and liked him well enough, but her heart sank when the Haigs asked him to represent them. Patrick's expenses were going to suck up resources for years to come. Ben had probably advised his friends to let her department bear the brunt by prolonging the county's role in temporary foster care.

"Where's Maureen?" she asked as the two men took chairs in front of her desk.

"She's not coming," Tom said.

Ben looked surprised. "Why not?" he asked.

"Why not is because I'm trying to prevent her from taking on something she can't handle," Tom said. "She's in way over her head thinking to raise a kid like this. At our age, she shouldn't have to raise any kid. Our parenthood days are finished. That's why not."

Ben shook his head. "Tom, you can't decide things behind her back."

"Yes, I can," Tom said emphatically. "She's not going to ruin her health doing something somebody else should be doing. End of conversation."

Bev looked at Ben. If Tom Haig said no to Maureen's desire to adopt Patrick, then the county had little recourse but to look at the child's paternal grandparents, that is, if Aaron Short recommended them and if they were willing.

"Well," Ben said, "our problem is that Patrick will likely need care for a long time, maybe all his life, and he's going to need to live in a place that has access to high-quality programs. I think Patrick should remain in Minnesota, if not with the Haigs, then with a foster family in St. Dominic. Would you have an alternative family, Bev?"

Beverly Hagen leaned across her desk.

"A good foster family that would care for a special needs child on a long-term basis is a treasure," she said. "Such people exist. I worked with one for many years. But they moved to Minneapolis when their last foster child graduated from high school. They're too old now to foster Patrick. I've looked around in the area, believe me, but I can't find anyone like them at the moment. And, of course, I have to mention, the law prefers we find a home with a family connection."

"Just so you keep in mind it's not going to be us," Tom said.

"Patrick's a baby no one's prepared for," Ben observed. "A lot of people wanted him born, but now that he's here, we don't see those people queued up to take him into their own homes."

"Maybe they got too much common sense," Tom suggested.

"I don't know about that," Ben said, "but I think I'll talk to Maureen and find out who among those in her faith community might be willing to consider it."

"No, you won't," Tom said loudly. "You're not saying word one to Maureen. She doesn't even know about this meeting."

"I don't think you get to tell me to whom I can or cannot speak, Tom.

Maureen knows the people involved in making sure he wasn't aborted. Those are the people likely to step up now."

"Ben," Tom said, standing suddenly, "you work for the corporation, not for Maureen. From now on, you stay away from Maureen, or so help me, I'll meet you behind the barn, and I don't give a damn how old or decrepit you are." He started for the door.

Ben remained seated. "That so?" he said.

"Yeah, that's so. I'm not paying any bills for legal work you do for Maureen from now on. You got that?"

Ben nodded. "Makes sense," he said, "given your animosity toward your grandson."

Tom put his hand on the doorknob. "I got no animosity. I'm just not gonna let this misery fall on Maureen." He opened the door.

"Where should I send my file on Patrick?" Ben inquired. "Maureen will need another lawyer, I expect."

"Dump it in the trash," Tom replied, a second before he shut the door behind him.

———•◦•———

Woodrow could scarcely find the hours in a day to answer all the calls he got.

"Boom in prices on pulpwood and saw timber," he told Claire the first morning. "That always brings in fly-by-nighters. Those boys go from farm to farm offering to harvest those itty-bitty stands that big outfits won't touch. Usin' some truly half-assed equipment, I might add."

"Mm-hm," Claire responded, half asleep.

"Course no one talks about equipment when they're offerin' a sweet deal. Folks sign contracts on the spot."

"Sorry," Claire murmured, now awake.

"Then when their equipment breaks down, as it surely does, and if'n they can't fix it themselves, they look around for mechanics."

"Like you," Claire murmured, turning the pillow to its cooler side.

"I'm recommended more than most. It's good money, cash in advance. I don't work no other way. But I hate to leave you so early in the morning, darlin'."

He finished dressing, kissed her forehead, and was gone. The birds were stirring. Claire tried, but she couldn't go back to sleep.

When Woodrow came home the second Saturday night, about ten o'clock, he announced that the outside harvesters had finally departed, and that he, and more than one customer, hoped they'd never show up in Lafayette again.

"It was a mess," he said, pouring himself a shot of Jack Daniel's in the kitchen. "Pine not marked for cuttin' got felled, fences got ripped and no one's payin' to put 'em back together, and this morning 'fore dawn they rolled over a dog in their vast carelessness."

"*Great Gatsby*," Claire noted.

"What?" Woodrow asked.

"*Vast carelessness* is a phrase from *The Great Gatsby*. At the end of the novel."

"Thank you for that," he threw at her, plainly annoyed. "I'm sure the boy who lost his dog will want to make a note of it."

Claire looked at him, stunned. Her remark may have been stupid, but Woodrow didn't snap like that, ever. She must have conveyed the hurt she felt because he came over to where she sat and put his forehead against hers.

"I'm sorry, darlin'. These last two weeks have made me unfit for human companionship."

She rubbed his head. "Better sleep it off, then."

The following morning, sitting on the edge of the bed, he stroked her face. "Don't you think I see how antsy you're gettin'?" he asked as her eyes struggled to open. "I halfway expect you'll up and leave me one of these days."

"You think I'd have a baby without her father beside me?"

For a long moment, Woodrow looked into her face, searching for confirmation. "You're pregnant!" he declared triumphantly.

Claire nodded. "I took the test after you fell asleep last night."

"So why do you look so glum?"

"I'm just scared about how it'll all turn out."

"We'll be takin' a leap of faith together," he said.

"I'm not big on faith, Woodrow."

"Then why'd you let yourself get pregnant?"

"Excuse me! You had something to do with it."

"Sure, but I'm ready and willin' to stick. You talk like you're halfway out the door."

She shook her head. "That's not true. But I worry about you wanting to take on Charlie's son too."

"A baby's got a right to a father and a mother livin' together to raise up what they brought into this world. Charlie's baby didn't get that, and I think it's a damn shame."

Claire stroked Woodrow's callused hand. "You, my darling, are inclined toward grand gestures," she said. "It's one of the things I love about you. You look for opportunities to do things other people think are not practical.

When Theresa disappeared, you rushed to Minnesota, and then you rushed back for Charlie when he got hurt, and now you're rushing to find a way to give your grandson a decent life."

"What's wrong with that?"

"A decent life may not be in the cards for him. We might end up miserable, all of us. And maybe someday there'll be talk of asking *our* child to take care of Charlie's son after we're gone."

"Or we'll make other provisions," Woodrow countered. Claire didn't blink. "I don't see we got a lot of options," Woodrow continued. "You want your mama to raise him? You think she could handle it? Or you want him to go to some institution where they change his diaper once a day and let him lie alone the rest?"

"I want a reasonable life for us," Claire insisted.

"Far as I'm concerned, reasonable starts with us gettin' married and havin' a smidgin of faith in the future. We'll deal with the rest as it comes, includin' Charlie's son." He kissed her forehead. "We're havin' our own child, Claire," he said soothingly. "Glory be, we're waitin' on a newborn babe who ties us together . . . That's something you'll hear a lot in these parts . . . Blessed are the ties that bind."

"They didn't bind when Theresa had Patrick," Claire replied.

"I know," Woodrow sighed. He held Claire's face between his hands and kissed her. The turmoil inside her died down, but just for a moment.

——•◦•——

"Two more weeks? Is that for sure?"

"Nothing's for sure where Patrick's concerned. It's a guess," Aaron said.

Aaron Short was the one who dealt with the "team" now. They told him everything. Maureen was lucky to get scraps of information, even from Dr. Calloway. She had taken to waking in the middle of the night, often from nightmares that Patrick had gone to someone else, or worse, that he'd succumbed to mucus in his lungs. His lungs still weren't developed. Apparently, lung development took place at the very end of a normal pregnancy. Theresa's pregnancy had been anything but normal. She was as pig-headed as her father, ignoring her health and the baby's when she'd tried to run away. Patrick was paying the price.

Maureen had hoped her little prince would start to breathe normally after the endotracheal tube had been pulled out. This week Patrick had acquired some new syndrome, or maybe it was an old syndrome that got worse. They'd been giving him surfactant from the start, a nurse told her, so Patrick's lungs wouldn't collapse. Now he'd developed a condition called breathing distress syndrome, so they'd inserted prongs in his nose again. He kept trying to get rid of them. She took that for a good sign. He was aware. He was feisty. He broke her heart.

Maureen wanted Patrick home with her. She had it in her mind that if she held him in her arms without all those machines hissing away and hospital employees darting their plastic-covered hands in and out of his incubator, moving him this way and that, if he were free of it all, then finally he could feel her love and devotion. She knew God wanted him home with her. She could feel it when she prayed. Her devotion to Patrick came with God's grace.

As a consequence of God's grace, she had for this child a wellspring of love that had not existed for her own children, even the boys. All eleven had been born healthy and full-term, starting with Mary who had cried all day and half the night. Maureen had been so disappointed in Mary.

She would not be disappointed in Patrick. Patrick would make up for what he had lost in his bad start, and he would excel beyond other supposedly normal children if he were given lots of time, attention, and support. He would get all those things and more from her.

"Have you made your decision?" Maureen asked Aaron as they had lunch at a restaurant he favored. She'd asked for this meeting. It was the first time she'd had a chance to talk one on one with the person who would have so much to say about Patrick's future. She'd wanted to ask Aaron Short questions without Tom in the room. She'd been furious when she found out that Tom told Ben he couldn't help her anymore.

Aaron put down his fork before answering. Maureen had eaten about a third of her tuna salad in the first few minutes after the waitress brought it. She didn't want any more. Aaron had ordered an oversize plate of meatloaf and mashed potatoes, both bathed in a pungent red sauce. His entree came with a white roll that he smeared with the establishment's signature apple-cinnamon butter. He'd requested apple pie with homemade vanilla ice cream for dessert.

"I go wild in restaurants. Roger has me on a diet at home," he'd informed Maureen when they first sat down.

Maureen could see why his partner had him on a diet. Aaron Short was a stout man who, unfortunately, wore extra pounds around his middle. She doubted he did much physical work in his law practice, other than hoisting files out of a cabinet and walking across the street to court. She was trying very hard to like him, despite his personal lifestyle, of which she had to disapprove. Her approval or disapproval of his moral choices meant nothing, of course, compared to the fact that he held it in his power to influence the court. That was all she could afford to think about.

"I'm still gathering facts," Aaron said. "A decision is not imminent. But I'll tell you this. Despite what you may have heard, the baby's father is not out of the picture. I know he signed a letter of intent to relinquish custody. In my opinion, that doesn't mean squat. I've been practicing family law for three decades, and I've seen what judges think about fathers who try to walk away from their children. In this instance, technically, the safe haven law protects the mother—not the father. Especially since the county may want the army to help pay for the child's medical bills."

Maureen lost the ability to breathe. She opened her mouth to let in more air, desperate to regain the power to protest. "How would that work?" she finally got out. "Could Patrick's father get custody of him without Theresa being involved?"

"I don't know," Aaron said. "It's a complication. If the mother won't allow the child in the home, and he's on active duty, he might not get physical custody. But he could be required to pay child support."

"Oh," Maureen said dismissively. Child support was not her worry.

"Meanwhile, Bev Hagen hasn't been able to find an acceptable temporary foster family for him. He'll need one as soon as he's released from the hospital, so that's my number-one concern right now."

When he saw the expression on her face, he put up his hand, splaying his fingers to stop Maureen from interrupting. "Maureen, I have to look at this holistically."

"Holistically?" Maureen had no idea what that meant, but she found it increasingly annoying when people, especially staff at the hospital, used technical words they expected her to know. She couldn't be assumed to understand unless they spoke in plain English.

"I'm sorry," Aaron said. "I mean I have to look at the big picture, now especially, since your husband has made it clear he doesn't want you to take on the job of caring for Patrick. He thinks it'll be too much for you, and frankly, so do I. You're fifty-six years old, Maureen, and Patrick's not an ordinary baby."

"All the more reason Patrick needs someone who loves him more than an ordinary baby," Maureen lashed out. "As if," she added, "there's such a thing as an ordinary baby."

"What I mean is, I don't think one person your age will be enough," Aaron responded calmly, lowering his voice almost to a whisper. "Patrick is fragile. He will have a lot of physical problems. He'll need to be back at the hospital or in a clinic frequently for years to come. You can't do it alone, Maureen. It bothers me that your husband doesn't support you in this."

Aaron finished his meatloaf and mashed potatoes while Maureen thought about what he'd said.

She wouldn't be alone. She had to make him understand that. From the first, saving Patrick had been a team effort. It would be a team effort in the future. Maureen didn't think Aaron realized the combined strength of the women of St. Philomena.

"You're warriors," Father Schmidt had once told the congregation right from the pulpit. "Warriors banded together in the service of the Lord."

That was the truth. Warriors had saved Patrick before he was born. Warriors would save him now.

"I'm on three committees at church," Maureen told Aaron. "The fundraising committee, the environmental committee, and the funeral lunch committee. I have about fifty friends among them. I'll have so much backup, Patrick won't be without someone to give him whatever he needs for a single minute of the day." She nodded at Aaron emphatically.

Aaron sighed. "I'm sure you have a lot of friends, Maureen. In fact, I know you do. But it's not something minor you're asking of people."

He pushed his plate away, having sopped up every last drop of sauce with bits of his buttered roll. Their waitress returned briefly to exchange it for a smaller plate with the apple pie and a baseball-sized scoop of ice cream.

"Then there's the question of how he got here," Aaron said after a long silence.

"What do you mean, how he got here? He's a gift from God," Maureen retorted.

"There are rumors going around, Maureen, and if they concern this baby, they concern me. I haven't been able to determine anything conclusively, but I have a source at St. Philomena—I won't say who—except to tell you this person says some of the ladies there have been bragging that they're responsible for this baby being born. Maybe they're the same ladies you're thinking about to help you take care of Patrick."

Maureen looked at him. She said nothing.

"I can't get anything out of the sheriff's department, but I've usually found, Maureen, that where there's smoke, there's some kind of fire. You know as well as I do that Stears County is about as pro-life as pro-life gets. So, I'm going to ask you outright. Did you or any of those ladies you're counting on at your church have anything to do with your daughter going missing in the weeks before this baby's birth? The Cole family seems to think so. Your oldest daughter agrees with them. They told me outright that Theresa was kidnapped. Not *maybe* kidnapped. Definitely, they say. So, I'm asking you right now before our talk about temporary foster custody goes any further . . . Maureen, did a kidnapping or anything like a kidnapping happen to your daughter Theresa, and if it did happen, were you involved?"

Maureen breathed in deeply, stifling a sob that rose almost to her throat.

She fought for time. *Lord, give me strength,* she prayed, *to meet Thine enemies in Thy Name. Yea, though I walk through the valley of the shadow of Death, I will fear no evil, for Thou art with me. Thy rod and Thy staff they comfort me . . .*

She couldn't remember the rest. Something about heads anointed with oil and cups running over.

As a Catholic, Maureen hadn't been encouraged to read the psalms as a general practice. It wasn't like the rosary. The mysteries of the rosary she knew by heart. She could recite them backwards and forwards. But she wished now that she'd memorized the psalm about strength in the valley of shadows because she needed that kind of strength. She needed to follow the path of righteousness as long as it led to Patrick's salvation. Patrick's salvation had to come first. For Patrick's sake, she would fear no evil.

"The court will need to know the truth," Aaron Short went on. He kept his gaze on her. "No judge is going to let you take your grandson home, even for temporary custodial care, if he thinks there's any possibility you were involved in kidnapping his mother."

Maureen let more time elapse. Finally, she spoke with anger in her voice. "Theresa went somewhere to think, Aaron. I don't know where she went. But I do know that only Theresa is responsible for Patrick's premature birth. Whatever else you heard, just put it out of your mind."

Aaron Short blinked. Just once, he blinked. Maureen forced herself to smile at him. "We're on the same side," she said.

"I know," he replied. "But I had to ask. I'm sorry to have accused you, Maureen." When the check came a few moments later, Maureen grabbed it.

Charlie took pride in his ability to withstand adversity. *Bring it on!* was a motto he'd adopted at the age of eight, followed later by the old British maxim: *Never complain, never explain.*

His first few weeks at Benning were intense. No one else thought it particularly hot, but the sun bored through his shirt. Within a half hour of a drill's start, his back and shoulders throbbed as tissue swelled and sometimes popped under the pressure garment the doctors insisted he wear. He took the pain. He did not visit the infirmary. He didn't ask for medication. He obeyed orders and performed his job to the best of his ability. Currently, his job was to train for the fitness test. Whenever his captain asked, he said his back was fine.

Only Theresa knew the truth, and only when he got home for the night. And even then, he pretty much tried to shrug it off. His gorgeous wife tended his blisters with antiseptic after he'd removed his clothes and showered. She rubbed in cool cream, bandaged his back, and overall made him feel like a kid again.

As a real kid back in the day, he wasn't fit for the army. He drank in high school, shrugged off his father's advice, hung out with idiots, and ate junk food. He'd hated his mother.

Hating his mother became a full-time job. Working with his uncles was something on the side, something he'd do just until he figured out where to point his future. The hours were long, especially in trimming season. Charlie built muscle. He looked the best he ever would, as he'd clearly seen in the mirror. Nineteen is a man's physical peak. At nineteen, the drink and poor diet didn't seem to affect him at all.

Not long after his twenty-second birthday, as Charlie watched some of his pals detour into drugs and absentee fatherhood, he stopped drinking and ate what Rebecca put in front of him. He pulled books from the shelves in the living room—Hemingway, Melville, Faulkner, Conrad, Orwell, even the ancients like Homer, Herodotus, and Marcus Aurelius.

It was the beginning of his real education. About the same time, he decided to make the army his career. He survived basic training at twenty-three, acquired better friends, and discovered his passion. Charlie loved the US Army, and he believed the US Army loved him. At the end of basic, his drill sergeant told him he was the ideal recruit.

Theresa tried to follow Charlie's lead. Few things rose to the level of crisis, he told her. The world is full of obstacles, but they're problems that can be solved if a person puts his or her mind to it. Within a week after he reported for duty, Theresa found a job on base. Good civilian jobs on base were said to be hard to come by for army wives whose husbands weren't commissioned officers, but that generality—true or not—exempted Theresa. As she described her interviews, Charlie could imagine how it went. She'd have walked in dressed in one of her Southern belle outfits, wearing those five-inch heels that brought men to their knees, smiling in the friendliest way. They'd decided on the spot that they'd have to hire her for something.

Charlie knew Theresa noticed the way most men looked at her. They fantasized about her, married or not, but he also knew that in her opinion, no man would ever measure up to him.

Theresa's job turned out to be counseling army brats. She worked in a four-person office, helping adolescents make the transition to a new base. But her focus remained on Charlie, which was where he needed it to be. At thirty, with burns on his back, he was lucky to become a DS candidate, even considering he had nearly five years of combat rotation. Admission was a high honor, he told Theresa, and meant a lot of people must have talked him up, since he was pretty much damaged goods. She hated it when he said things like that.

Their life had settled into a pleasant routine when, on the second to last Friday in October, about six o'clock in the evening, Woodrow phoned. He had news, he said, and Charlie immediately thought it had something to do with Patrick. Instead, it was a wedding invitation.

Claire had agreed to marry him, Woodrow announced, and he wanted Charlie and Theresa to come for the wedding if Charlie could get leave. November 21, the day before Thanksgiving, they'd exchange vows in the forest clearing—the same place all the important moments in the Cole family were made official.

Charlie congratulated his dad. He'd do his best to get leave, he said. Theresa stood nearby, looking puzzled. When he told her, she recoiled.

"That's grotesque," she said.

"Grotesque?"

"Yes!"

"Honey," he pointed out, his hands on her shoulders, "grotesque is part of the South. Don't you know that? Ever read Flannery O'Connor? And look at Faulkner's people. I could give you a thousand examples but none of it matters. Only thing that matters is the feelings people have. If my dad and your sister love each other, that is *not* grotesque."

Theresa pulled away. "I didn't expect this," she said vehemently. "I'd just about forgotten Mary's in Alabama. Why didn't she go back to Minnesota? Now she'll be what? My mother-in-law? *I can't believe it*!"

"Hey," Charlie said, trying to take her back into his arms.

"No," she objected. "Let me be. I'm going for a walk." She grabbed a shawl and rushed outside. Charlie watched her march down the road. There was a park she liked about a mile away. He'd give her some space, though it bothered him. A beautiful woman out alone after dark? *Hell*, he thought, before deciding to follow her.

As he kept Theresa in sight, Charlie thought about their baby. Sometimes in quiet moments, day or night, he conjured back that incubator and his tiny son inside. *Now that was grotesque.* The marriage of his dad to Theresa's sister seemed pretty damn normal by comparison.

8

Theresa's son left the hospital on October 31, a Wednesday.

In his preliminary report, Aaron Short had recommended that Maureen be allowed to care for Patrick as a temporary foster parent. There weren't other good options, he told the court. Beverly Hagen agreed. With Ben Johnson's pro-bono help, Maureen had submitted a written care plan, including the names of church-affiliated volunteers who had offered logistical backup. In special consideration of Patrick's fragile status, Chief Hospital Administrator Laura Himley had agreed to increase supervision beyond what would be considered normal for a newly released preemie. Aaron would make frequent visits, as would a county social worker. A two-way video connection had been installed in Maureen's bedroom and would be used as necessary for conferences with hospital staff.

"This is probationary," Aaron warned Maureen. "Normally, it takes a year to be certified for foster care. What the court is doing for you is exceptional."

Maureen thanked him effusively.

She had prepared for Patrick's arrival by cleaning every inch of the house, most particularly the master bedroom that would become Patrick's de facto nursery. She machine-washed the curtains and all the linens, scrubbed the floors, sprayed Lysol on any surface Patrick might touch. She bought an ample supply of disposable surgical masks at a medical supply store and planned to require anyone near Patrick to wear one. She put Annie to work cleaning after school and on weekends.

That Wednesday, the bus let Annie off in front of the mailbox, as usual.

She extracted a mass of envelopes and catalogs, noticing a thick letter from Alabama among them as she ambled toward the house. The yard was full of cars. It reminded her of the day the church ladies kidnapped Theresa.

Inside she saw the same women, newly arrived with food—most of them desserts, it seemed. There were a few casseroles, though.

"I'll put it all in the freezer," Barb Iverson told Annie.

"We're waiting for the go-ahead from your mother," interjected Suzanne O'Brien. "Those of us who've had flu shots at least two weeks ago will get to see Patrick today. I was just telling everyone that we need to wear face masks."

Several of the attendees had already left, Barb announced, out of fear they might have something that could infect Patrick.

Rosemary Schmitz was blunt. "I don't do face masks," she said. "They make it hard to breathe."

"So, how do you feel about having Patrick home?" Suzanne asked Annie.

"Maureen is being extremely careful," Helen Swanson cut in. "I think it's excessive, but there you have it. He's her baby."

"Actually, her grandbaby," Suzanne corrected.

"Patrick cried all the way home, so Maureen's first priority is getting him calmed down," said a blond lady whose name Annie couldn't remember.

"I told her that," Mrs. Swanson noted.

"Well, babies cry," Irene Overdale said. "It's totally normal. New parents get used to it, and so will we."

"My mother is not a new parent," Annie pointed out. "She's—"

"Don't sell your mother short," Barb Iverson admonished. "She's got the angels on her side."

Annie nodded.

After the last of the church ladies finally departed, Annie went upstairs. Patrick was awake, screaming as Maureen rocked him. His tiny fists were clenched, and his knuckles had become white dots. For a split second, Annie thought her mother was going to assign the child to her, an eventuality she didn't think she could handle. He sounded like a jet engine.

"Can you put supper on the table for your father and Greg?" her mother asked. "I forgot to make something ahead of time."

Annie agreed, afraid otherwise her mother would hand Patrick over to her.

She debated getting one of the casseroles out of the freezer, but they weren't very large, so she decided, since her dad and Greg had big appetites, to make the meal herself. It should be something substantial and impressive, like a beef stew. *How hard could it be?* she thought. She found a pot in the cupboard and a two-pound package of stew meat in the refrigerator, as well as plenty of carrots, celery, onions, and a hard white thing. Rutabaga, she guessed.

Cutting some of the vegetables turned out to be difficult. She had to use the sharpest butcher's knife and be very careful how she held it. But she succeeded, with no finger damage.

Next, weren't there potatoes in a stew? she wondered. She found three in the vegetable bin and peeled and divided each into four pieces. She added a pound of mushrooms after brushing them clean. Her mother's stews always had mushrooms.

She dropped it all in the pot, covered the contents with cold water, and set it on the stove at medium high, stirring occasionally. Tom and Greg came in an hour later and washed up at the sink. The stew was boiling nicely. *It should be ready*, Annie thought, though she suddenly recalled that her mother's stews required sides like biscuits and a salad. There wasn't time, however, so the stew would have to do. She used hot pads to lift the cover and a ladle to get it into bowls, one each for Tom, Greg, and herself. It looked oddly mushy. She hoped that wouldn't matter. At least it was thick.

Tom eyed his bowl as the steam rose, waiting until it had a chance to cool. Annie made a mental note: *do not serve food straight from a boiling pot.* After he tasted the stew, he looked at her. He didn't say anything.

"This is horrible," said Greg.

"What do you mean?" Annie demanded, knowing darn well what he meant once she'd tasted it herself.

"You made this?" Tom asked gently.

"Yes," Annie admitted.

"Did you put salt in it?" he continued.

Salt! She hadn't thought about salt. Wasn't salt supposed to be bad for you? "No," she said.

"Did you put *any* spices in it?" Tom asked.

"Just vegetables and meat."

Greg laughed. Annie glared at him.

"Stop that," Tom said to Greg. "Your sister is doing the best she can." He turned his attention to Annie. "Didn't your mother teach you how to cook?"

"She just asked me to make supper." Annie got the words out, on the edge of crying, which she decided she would not permit herself to do. "I didn't think it would be so hard."

Tom sighed. "We're all going to have to make adjustments," he said. "I'd hoped this day would never come."

"In the meanwhile, this stuff's not fit to eat," said Greg. "Can I order pizza?"

"No, you can't. Get the saltshaker," Tom told him. "And pepper. Then shut up and eat."

They ate in silence. Annie wanted to bring up the subject of the letter from Alabama, still unopened on the counter, but she was afraid, given her bad stew, that it wasn't the right time. The letter stayed on her mind, though. Finally, after she'd served the sour cream raisin pie Barb Iverson brought over, she handed her dad the envelope.

"Looks like it's from Claire," she said.

"You mean Mary," he replied.

"Yes, Mary. Aren't you going to open it?"

He looked at her, impassive.

"Please," Annie begged.

Tom tore open the envelope, took out a sheaf of papers, and read. Annie could see the missive was handwritten in black ink on expensive linen stock. There were three pages, each covering one side only.

"Your mother's not going to like this," Tom said when he'd finished.

"Can I read it?" Annie begged again.

Her father hesitated before nodding. "Might as well. You'll find out soon enough."

Annie grabbed the letter. Even Greg looked interested. She'd half expected something terrible had happened. The truth set her mind to rest. There would be a wedding in Alabama. Claire and Woodrow were getting married. Woodrow would become her, what? Her brother-in-law? She couldn't stifle her excitement and grinned at her father.

"A wedding!" she exulted, returning to the letter for more details.

"Whose wedding?" Greg inquired.

Annie read on. It would be the day before Thanksgiving, in a forest, in the open air. Would they come?

Would they come? Of course, they'd come. What an idiotic question. Then she saw her father's expression and realized it was not an idiotic question.

"Your mother going all the way down to Alabama to see your sister married to a redneck sharecropper—or whatever he is—in the middle of the woods, not even in a church?" thundered Tom. "And she does this now when we're dealing with Theresa's sick kid! Shit!" He pounded the table.

Annie had seen her father pound his fist on the kitchen table many times. It didn't usually mean much, but this time she thought it might. And he *never, ever,* used the *s*-word in the house. Not that she could recall.

"Aren't we going to the wedding?" she asked meekly.

"Aren't we going to the wedding?" Tom bellowed. He was really angry now. "No, we're damn well *not* going to the wedding. I don't know what Mary's thinking, sending us a letter like that!"

"I want to go to the wedding," Annie wailed.

"Well, you can forget it," Tom said. He left the table and headed upstairs.

Greg looked at his sister. "You really thought they'd go? Are you crazy?"

She paid him no mind. Luckily, she lived in a family of eleven children, and all but two were gone from home. For sure at least one of her older brothers would want to drive to Alabama to see his sister get married.

"You've got a little crying machine there, don't you?"

On her first NICU discharge visit, Alice Mollen stood looking at the two of them, a morose Maureen in the rocking chair and a bawling Patrick in her arms. The infant lay swaddled in multiple layers of cotton designed to keep him calm. Calm he was not.

Alice served on the environmental committee at St. Philomena. A mother of twelve, Alice was also a pediatric RN at St. Dominic and had raised her own child born with Down syndrome. She knew how to advise Maureen without alarming her.

Now that the time had come to bring Patrick home, Maureen was terrified. Patrick resembled none of her other babies. When they'd thrown tantrums, she'd put them in their cribs and left the room. Of course, they'd had the advantage of a healthy birth to a mother who didn't reject them. That made all the difference.

Maureen used the NICU-recommended bottles and the NICU-recommended powder shipped from Europe for Patrick's formula. Supposedly, the product came from the milk of cows that grazed on picture-perfect farms where they didn't use pesticides, and the air was pure, and the mountains in the distance made the cows feel contented, or so she'd joked to Tom.

She knew the formula manufacturer left out high-sugar ingredients like corn syrup, and added good things like probiotics. She knew where to get the right diapers and wipes. She washed her hands constantly and made sure everyone who encountered Patrick did as well.

Each morning, Maureen set up the day's formula on the kitchen counter, ready to be made liquid by the addition of purified low-fluoride bottled water, as the NICU staff suggested. Maureen took all her advice from them.

Patrick had met the requirements for release from the hospital even before they let him go. His size had increased steadily; he could maintain his temperature; he sucked vigorously on the nipples of his bottles; he had no tubes in him anymore; there was no sign of infection; and he weighed over five pounds. Maureen was particularly proud of that last statistic.

Aaron Short stopped by frequently, usually around mid-morning.

Maureen introduced Aaron to Alice Mollen the first time their paths crossed, just as Patrick unleashed another fit, struggling to free his arms from the fabric that bound them. Maureen gave Patrick everything he could possibly want: repeated diaper changes, nourishment, comforting swaddles . . . Still, he cried day and night. She couldn't figure out why.

"Don't you worry," Alice soothed, bending over Patrick. "Babies outgrow this howling, all babies including kids with Down syndrome. My Marissa was a preemie too, and after I took her home, I swear she screamed for seven months straight. It was like she blamed me. But look on the bright side—he's exercising his lungs. He'll be healthier for this hullabaloo."

As time went on, Maureen realized she needed to take full advantage of her helpers and trust in the Lord for everything else. Barb Iverson took charge of the schedule and came herself for part of every Monday. Irene Overdale showed up twice a week. Helen Swanson promised to stop by frequently but couldn't be more precise because she was the church choir director and also met with private students. Agnes Olson volunteered for an hour or two on Wednesdays, Rosemary Schmitz on Thursdays, and Liz Mueller on Fridays. Suzanne O'Brien said she'd pop in whenever needed, just call.

Since Tom had decided to sleep on a makeshift bed in his office, Maureen asked Annie to move into the master bedroom with her, the two of them taking turns whenever Patrick woke and needed comforting. Most nights Maureen handled the first shift from after supper until about two o'clock. Annie took over until she had to get ready for school at seven.

For Annie, the only bright spot on the horizon was Claire's wedding, except that she wasn't sure anymore how she'd get to it. She'd called her brothers but mostly talked to their wives. Matthew's Mary said they had Thanksgiving plans with her parents. Mark's Debbie said they weren't going to Claire's wedding, period, without giving any excuse. John's Amy said their baby was too young to travel. Paul, David, Andrew, and finally even Luke said they didn't want to drive to Alabama, and besides, they'd already been to one of Mary's weddings.

Desperate, she typed the departure and destination cities into Google on her cell phone. She couldn't drive. It would be dangerous to hitchhike. Amtrak was too expensive. Finally, a bus schedule popped up.

The bus, of course.

—•—•—

"Woodrow Cole, folks say you don't believe in the Lord God Almighty . . . That true, Woodrow?"

Woodrow peered over his reading glasses at Leona Dunwoody, a long-ago classmate and high school friend of Josie's. She was now a judge's clerk in the Lafayette courthouse. Leona probably knew everything he'd said and done in Josie's presence during those angst-filled years of first love.

He removed his glasses and grinned at her. "You joshin' me, Leona?"

"No, sir. I want an answer."

Leona might have been pretty but for proportion. Her eyes were dots on an unusually wide white face. They looked like black peas floating in cream soup with red pepper mixed into the broth, the red being Leona's constellation of freckles.

"Well, Leona . . ." He leaned over the counter. "Fact of the matter is, I do believe. Far as I'm concerned, your sweet smile is proof aplenty of the divine."

Leona blushed. "Oh, my hind foot!" she exclaimed.

"Admit it, Leona, you got a soft spot for me," Woodrow teased, his eyes glued to hers.

"Nothing of the kind," she countered, reddening more. "Now what're you here for?" She turned her gaze on Claire. "You're with him?" she asked, less pleasantly.

"Yes," Claire said.

"Well, honey, you don't look or sound like a resident of this county."

"I'm from Minnesota," said Claire.

"Minnesota!" Leona exclaimed. "Sweden of the North!" She turned back to Woodrow and read the application he'd filled out.

"I can't hardly believe it," she said.

"Believe it. We aim to get married." Woodrow took Claire's hand and raised it with his own to the marble slab that separated Leona from the public.

"Then you'd better understand somethin'. Judge Loring don't officiate at weddings anymore. You'll have to find yourself a genuine preacher . . . Are you even baptized, come to think of it?"

"Don't worry 'bout that. We just need the license," Woodrow replied, still smiling.

"Another thing," Leona continued, "aren't you married already?"

"No, ma'am," Woodrow said. "Never been."

Leona turned her attention to Claire. "What about you?"

"I'm divorced," Claire replied.

"You got proof?" Leona held out her hand. "Documentation is required."

Claire pulled divorce papers from her purse and handed them to Leona, who read every word.

"I'll need to make a copy," she announced.

"Fine," Claire said.

"Twenty cents a page," Leona asserted. "Let's see." She counted the pages. "One dollar sixty cents."

Claire pulled two dollars from her wallet. Leona took the bills and walked away.

"This is surreal," Claire whispered. "It's more a negotiation than a government service."

"I got history with her," Woodrow whispered back.

"Lucky you," Claire said softly.

"So it seems," he concurred.

"I'm also goin' to need driver's licenses and birth certificates or some proof of you two bein' citizens of these United States. Passports will do," Leona said tonelessly when she came back.

Woodrow squeezed Claire's hand.

He was still holding Claire's hand when they left the courthouse seventy dollars lighter and in full possession of their license-to-marry within thirty days. They headed toward Woodrow's truck, passing the towering statue of an angel on the way. Claire let go of Woodrow's hand and walked around the celestial being, reading the monument's inscriptions as she toured the four sides of its pedestal.

"Be ye reminded of the lessons of sacrifice and loyalty written in the service records of those enlisted from Lafayette County, Alabama," she intoned, glancing at Woodrow who didn't say anything.

"In memory of the Soldiers of the Southern Confederacy. Time will never dim their glory."

Again, he stood mute.

"In honor of the Living and in Loving Memory of Our Honored Dead whose Principles of Right as a Sacred Heritage We Bequeath to Our Children throughout All Generations." Claire's voice rose on that quotation. An elderly man in the vicinity stopped and stared at them.

"You tryin' to make a point?" Woodrow asked.

"I'm intrigued," she said as she came to the pedestal's last face.

"Lest we forget. Lest we forget," she read. "Hmmm, I wonder why those words were inscribed twice? Is there any chance the South will ever forget it was forced by defeat to free the slaves on whom its wealth depended?"

"Sweetheart, I'm tired, more tired than if I'd been under equipment all day. Can you give it a rest?"

"Not quite," Claire replied. "As your mama likes to say, I've got my feathers ruffled."

Woodrow smiled. "I see you two gettin' along. That's a real good sign. My mama's a fine judge of character."

"I expect she is," Claire affirmed, "but I'm feeling . . . overwhelmed by what we're about to do."

Woodrow walked to a bench and sat down. Claire joined him.

"Not sure I can live in Alabama," Claire said quietly.

"What's that mean?" asked Woodrow. "You want to tear up this license we just got?"

"No," she said emphatically. "I'm just tryin' to be honest."

"Like you were honest when you came to my bed that night? Did you honestly ask yourself first whether you could live with me?"

"I wanted you. Nothing else seemed to matter at that moment."

"We're not teenagers, Claire."

She didn't reply.

"Way I see it, you either love me or you don't," Woodrow said. "You'll stick or you'll take off, just like Josie, though Josie at least left me Charlie."

"I do love you," Claire said.

Woodrow exhaled. "Well, if you want to call the weddin' off, I'd sure appreciate you tellin' me right now."

"I don't want to call it off. I absolutely want to marry you."

"I live in Alabama, Claire, and I'm not goin' to move."

"Doesn't it bother you that Alabama is the sixth poorest state in the country?"

"Your Northern farmers dump manure and fertilizer in your rivers. And down the mess comes. We got a dead zone in the Gulf, thanks to states like yours."

"Stop! Woodrow, I'm not claiming Alabama is the only state with flaws."

"I don't think you're givin' us a chance."

Claire shook her head but didn't reply.

"We've all got flaws, Claire. To my mind, it's better to fix the things that are wrong where you are, or try at least, instead of runnin' away."

Claire smiled. "My inclination has always been to run."

"I was born in this county," Woodrow said. "There are sacred places for me here. Some of my ancestors were murdered in that grove of old pine 'cause they wouldn't fight in the war between the states. Alabama ground is soaked with their blood. I ain't never had a yen to leave it, 'cept for the corps."

"Woodrow, please understand, I am *not* going to run off. I'm just worried."

"What scares you more—Alabama, or Charlie's baby?"

"Both," she said.

"Think you can hold yourself together 'til *our* baby comes?"

"Yes," she answered him, "I do." And for a moment, looking at Woodrow's face, she felt better. Why, she couldn't say.

Annie had second thoughts about the bus to Birmingham. There was no connection from Birmingham to Lafayette that she could find, and if she called Claire from Birmingham, it would take an hour and a half to pick her up, and right before her wedding, that might make Claire mad.

On the other hand, there was a bus from Minneapolis to Tuscaloosa, which was only a forty-five-minute drive from Lafayette. Tuscaloosa didn't have a bus to Lafayette either, least not that Annie could see on her dad's computer. But the drive by car from Tuscaloosa would be half as long as the drive from Birmingham, and therefore less likely to annoy her sister. Besides, Claire might send Woodrow to pick her up. He would be nicer.

The total cost of the trip worried her. Fifteen dollars from St. Dominic to Minneapolis sounded reasonable, but it was one hundred sixty dollars from Minneapolis to Tuscaloosa. Her savings wouldn't be enough, not unless she raided the money her grandmother had set aside for her, and since that money was in a bank account with both her name and her mother's name, she couldn't take anything out on her own.

The solution, even though it was immoral and probably illegal, was to "borrow" from her father's cash drawer and leave an I.O.U. pledging repayment.

She also needed to fill out an *Unaccompanied Child Form*, which she downloaded from the computer into the printer in her father's office. For *person meeting the child*, she put Claire's name. For *parent/legal guardian*, she put Claire and Woodrow's names. She dug out her birth certificate so she could prove she was older than twelve. For *address*, she wrote down the one on Claire's letter. For home phone, she put Claire's cell. She forged Claire's signature on the bottom. Finally, she deleted from her dad's computer the history of her searches, just in case anyone looked at it to figure out where she'd gone.

Next, she had to pick the right day for her departure. It couldn't be so far before the wedding that they'd have time to send her back. But it couldn't be so close to the wedding that she might miss it if anything went wrong on the journey. She needed to act perfectly normal in the meantime.

Another item on her agenda: find a way to get to the bus station.

The answer was church, of course. She knew her friend Lacey and her mother went to 7:30 a.m. Mass on Sundays. Lacey's mother agreed to pick her up on their way, no problem. When the day arrived, at 6:00 a.m. precisely, she set Patrick on the big bed next to his sleeping grandma, tiptoed downstairs, and left through the living room door before the sun came up.

She reached the county road just in time to recognize Lacey's family's red Taurus approaching.

"Thanks," she said as she hopped into the back seat. No one said anything about the book bag she'd slung over her right shoulder with her wedding clothes inside. If someone asked, she had an answer prepared.

Dawn appeared on the horizon when they left the car and hurried inside St. Philomena. The Mass took a long time due to an endless sermon, but Annie tried not to fidget.

"Could you drop me at the corner by the video store?" she asked Lacey's mother afterward.

"You're not going home?" Lacey's mother inquired.

"I'm on a mission," she explained. "Need to get my brother a present for his birthday."

Lacey's mother seemed to think nothing of it. Lacey gave her a strange look, but Annie was certain she wouldn't say a word. A six-block walk to the bus stop put her and her book bag at the ticket counter.

"Tuscaloosa, Alabama," she said when the agent got to her.

He took her filled-out form and the copy of her birth certificate and looked them over. Then she remembered that the plan called for two separate tickets, one to get her out of St. Dominic as fast as possible, and a second one for Minneapolis to Tuscaloosa.

"Actually, make that a ticket to Minneapolis," she said. "My sister and I are going to Tuscaloosa together."

"Your sister over eighteen?" he asked.

"Definitely," Annie replied. "She's like . . ." She tried to remember. "Thirty-eight." That had to be close.

"OK," the agent said. "Next bus is 10:05." He took her fifteen dollars and gave her a ticket. "Wait curbside," he added. "Boarding's at 9:50."

That meant she had to wait for more than an hour, and all that time her father or her brother Greg could show up. She went into the restroom and hid in a stall. There was one more thing she needed to do.

She'd brought her cell phone along in case of emergency. But she'd seen on a TV show how the police could find someone by tracking the person's phone, so she looked that question up on the internet and found out the police couldn't track a person whose cell phone was turned to airplane mode. So, she played around with her phone until she figured out how to do that. Just before she got on the bus, she switched to airplane mode and felt very 007 doing it.

Finally, a loudspeaker called out her bus. To Annie's surprise, it was already half-full. When it arrived in Minneapolis, Annie had plenty of time to get something to eat before the scheduled departure for Tuscaloosa. At 1:45

p.m. she got on the new bus and took a seat at a window near the front. Half a minute later, a man sat next to her. He looked about twenty years old and had spider tattoos on both sides of his neck.

"Get out of that seat," ordered a woman Annie had never seen before. "Now." The woman made a gesture toward the young man with her arm. Looking sullen, the young man extricated himself and moved on further down the aisle. The woman sat in his spot.

"You mind?" she asked Annie, who nodded agreement.

"Why did you do that?" Annie asked, relieved though she was.

"You didn't belong with that guy. You didn't even know him, did you?"

"No," Annie agreed. "I'd never seen him before."

"Then why'd you let him sit next to you?" the woman asked, standing momentarily to remove her faux fur coat. She sat on it, wrapping its shoulders around her own.

"I don't know," Annie said. "He just did it."

"Honey, people will take advantage any way they can . . . if you let them. What are you doing alone on this bus?"

Annie looked more closely at this person who seemed to assume she had the right to interrogate a total stranger. She resembled an old hippie, maybe old enough to be on Medicare, but at the same time she seemed kind of young in her expression, as if she'd just left a protest march and was on her way home. She wore black jeans and a psychedelic black-and-white sweater that reached down to her thighs. Her hair hung in gray and brown sections that badly needed a trim. The ends were split like crazy. A thick silver band encircled her neck. *Mother Earth*, Annie decided.

"Done looking?" the woman asked sharply.

"I'm s . . . sorry," Annie stammered, looking down. She knew she had a tendency to stare.

"I don't let my grandchildren gawk like that," the woman said, her eyebrows raised.

"I'm Annie Haig," Annie announced, ignoring the lady's criticism since it was fair.

"Donna," the woman said, excluding her last name.

"Pleased to meet you," Annie replied. "I'm going to Tuscaloosa to see my sister." She knew Donna was going to ask anyway.

"Why are you alone?"

"It's my sister's wedding. My parents don't want to go, but I do."

"Let me guess. They don't know where you are."

Annie noticed the absence of a question mark in the woman's voice.

"Not yet," she admitted. "But I'll call them when I get there."

"Do you have any idea what kind of chance you're taking?" Donna sounded angry.

"Sure. But I have to get there."

"Because it's your sister's wedding."

"That's the main reason," Annie said, surprising herself by a realization. "But also, I just had to get out of my house."

"Does your sister know you're coming?"

"Not yet," Annie admitted.

The woman sighed. "Why aren't your parents going to your sister's wedding?"

"My mother's on the outs with both my sisters. With me too, I suppose, now that I've left home without telling anybody. With Claire—she's the oldest, the one who's getting married—I think it's because Claire doesn't take her advice. And she's gone from the family. She left right after high school. We hardly see her."

"And your other sister?" Donna prodded.

"That's worse. My other sister found out her baby was going to be born with Down syndrome. That's when . . ."

"I know what it is," Donna said quietly.

"And she was planning to get an abortion." Annie lowered her voice to a whisper, "So . . ." she trailed off.

"So?"

"My mother and her friends—" Annie paused but then continued, "They wouldn't let her, so the baby was born. But Theresa won't raise him. So now my family's got him."

Donna shook her head. "What do you mean, they wouldn't let her?"

"They took her prisoner," Annie whispered.

Donna closed her eyes. She didn't say anything.

"My sister didn't want to be pregnant with him," Annie explained. "They made her have the baby. My mother and her friends."

Donna exhaled. Annie didn't know what that meant.

"Don't you think that's wrong?" Annie asked, suddenly curious.

"It's not for me to say," Donna replied.

"Oh," Annie said, deflated. "Well, if you ask me, nobody has a right to take somebody prisoner. It's illegal."

"That it is," Donna agreed.

"My mother wants my sister to take her baby back. Otherwise my mother's going to raise him. That's what she says. Both my sisters are in Alabama now. I just want to be where they are. To tell you the truth, I'd stay with them if I could."

"How old are you?" Donna asked.

"Fourteen," Annie said.

"Your parents must be scared out of their minds."

"Maybe," Annie admitted. "But you don't know what it's like. I just had to get out of there."

Donna nodded. Annie decided she was giving out too much information and not getting anything in return.

"Why are you on this bus?" she ventured to ask.

"My youngest is having a baby in Birmingham," said Donna. "I want to be there for her . . . help out however I can."

"That's nice," Annie said.

She wasn't really all that interested in Donna's family affairs, and Donna apparently considered their conversation concluded because she shut her eyes and leaned her head back against the seat.

———•◦•———

It was 11:00 a.m. on Sunday, November 18, four days before Thanksgiving, and Annie was nowhere in sight. Calls to her cell phone went directly to voice mail. There was no response to texts.

Tom sent Greg out searching. The sky was overcast, but he didn't much care if it snowed or not. The harvest was done, equipment stored, the entire crop sold.

Greg came back to the house as Tom fried ham in Maureen's cast-iron pan.

"No one's seen her," Greg said, pulling off his jacket. "I looked everywhere."

"Everywhere *where*?" asked Maureen.

"All over downtown. I saw some girls from her class at that cafe across the street from school. They said nothing was going on. If you ask me, she's hiding here somewhere with a book."

"Too cold in the barn," Tom interjected. "Too cold outside. She's gotta be at somebody's house."

"She's friends with that Lacey Conen," Greg recalled. "I could check with her when we're done."

"Done what?" Tom inquired.

"Eating," said Greg as he washed his hands at the sink. "I'm starving. It's not like anyone makes decent meals anymore."

Tom glowered and seemed about to let loose when Maureen intervened.

"We know with school and the harvest, it's been hard on you," she told Greg. "Especially now with Patrick. But that part will be over soon as he passes his milestones . . ."

"Anyone look in the attic?" Greg suggested after Tom handed him a plate of meat and retrieved a half dozen eggs from the refrigerator. Maureen put sliced bread and butter on the table.

"The attic?" Maureen repeated.

"Yeah, she used to hide up there all the time," Greg said.

"She did?" Maureen recalled Annie's frequent disappearances before Patrick arrived. The attic? She wiped her hands on her apron and was about to head for the stairs when Greg intervened.

"I'll go up, Mom. Right after breakfast."

Tom shook his head. "This is crazy. Patrick's where he don't belong, and Annie can't be found."

"Patrick's right where he belongs," Maureen insisted, smoothing the blanket that covered his sleeping form in the kitchen bassinet.

After eating, Greg checked the attic. No luck. Then he drove to Lacey Conen's house and talked to the girl's mother. Rhonda Conen told Greg about 7:30 Mass and dropping Annie off downtown. Greg raced home and informed his mother, who called Tom from upstairs.

Suzanne O'Brien, who was scheduled to help with Patrick, arrived during the commotion, poured herself a cup of coffee, and sat at the kitchen table as the baby began to stir in his bassinet. Maureen picked him up.

"Since when does Annie go to 7:30 Mass?" Tom wanted to know.

"It makes no sense," Maureen agreed. "I've always had a hard time getting her to the ten o'clock." She soothed Patrick by patting his back as she walked back and forth. That seemed to calm him.

"I could call Rosemary Schmitz and ask her to spread the news on the telephone tree," Suzanne suggested. "If anyone's seen her, they're bound to let us know."

Maureen nodded.

"Over two hundred families are signed up," Suzanne said. "We can reach the ones on duty this weekend, and they'll tell others, and after that information will pour in, just watch."

"Great," Tom said. "Now the whole damn town knows we can't keep track of our kids."

"The telephone tree was set up for parish activities," Suzanne pointed out. "But I guess it's OK to use in emergencies. Did you alert the sheriff?"

"I'll do that now," Tom said and left the kitchen. Greg slipped out too.

"I don't know what's happening," Suzanne complained to Maureen, "but my legs feel so heavy these days."

"Hmmm," Maureen murmured.

"I'm going to have to take it easier," Suzanne said. She held out her arms for Patrick, and Maureen handed him over.

A sheriff's deputy, Antoine Harrison, phoned about 4:30 p.m. and said he was on his way to the farm. He didn't tell her if he'd located Annie.

When he arrived, Maureen had a fresh pot of coffee ready and chocolate chip cookies just out of the oven. She set them on a rack in the middle of the table and plucked cups and saucers from the cupboard.

"Cream?" she asked the deputy.

He nodded as he sat down, placing his hat on the top of a spindle and his sheriff's jacket over the back of the chair.

"I looked at our records before coming out," he told Maureen, "and it seems you had a daughter missing last spring too."

"That was a misunderstanding," Maureen said, staring straight at him.

"From what I recall, there was a baby involved," Harrison continued.

Maureen used a spatula to remove two half-cooled cookies from the rack and placed them on a plate in front of Deputy Harrison.

"The baby's fine. My daughter Theresa is fine. We're talking about Annie, my youngest."

"Your husband said she's fourteen."

"She turned fourteen this past summer."

"And you've been searching among her friends and acquaintances?"

"Yes. Everyone's looking. Her brother was out all morning."

"She's not answering her cell phone?"

"No. We've been leaving messages on her voice mail, but she hasn't called back."

"I'll look into it. Maybe we can track her phone. Is she upset about something?"

"She wasn't upset about anything that we know."

"Does she have a boyfriend?"

"She's too young to have a boyfriend."

"Is her brother around?"

"He's upstairs."

"Could you call him down, ma'am?"

Maureen yelled for Greg. Tom came too, without Patrick.

"I just set him in his crib, and he stayed asleep," Tom said.

They sat around the kitchen table. Greg ate half of Maureen's cookies and drank two cups of coffee. The deputy didn't touch the cookies, nor did Tom, which Maureen took as an ominous sign.

No one in the family knew of a boyfriend, they assured the deputy. Greg mentioned what Lacey's mother had said about dropping Annie off at the video store.

"That's only a few blocks from the bus depot," the deputy pointed out.

"Why would she take a bus?" Maureen asked. "Where would she go?"

"You tell me," the deputy said.

Maureen turned toward Tom, whose expression was blank.

"I'll look into it," said Deputy Harrison, rising from his chair. "If she took a bus, we'll figure out where she went. Meantime, you ask around about a boyfriend. One other thing—" He paused. "Do you want us to open a missing person's file?"

Somehow those words made Annie's disappearance real in a way nothing else had. Tom nodded. "Go ahead and do that," he added.

"I'll get back to you soon as I know more," the deputy said.

After he was gone, Tom told Maureen to call Rebecca Cole, using the line in his office. From the kitchen, he phoned Ben Johnson. Ben was alarmed to hear that Annie was missing.

"You think she mighta gone down South?" Tom asked. "Her sister's getting married on Wednesday. To the baby's grandfather. It's a mess of a situation."

"Anyone from your family attending the wedding?" Ben asked.

"Course not," Tom said. "We got our hands full."

"Maybe I'll go down there," Ben suggested.

"Why the hell would you do that?"

"I've known your oldest daughter all her life, Tom. I'd like to see her get married."

"That so?" Tom let out.

"Call me if you find out more," Ben said. "I'll hold off leaving 'til you get word on Annie's whereabouts."

After the call ended, Tom sat at the kitchen table with nothing to do. Patrick was still sleeping in Maureen's bedroom. Greg was wherever Greg went on a late season Sunday night. Tom didn't have to obsess over the farm at the moment. There was nothing to think about but the fact that he had another daughter missing, and this time he was going to pay attention, damn it.

Maureen came downstairs. "They haven't seen nor heard from her," she said. "But they'll phone us if they do."

Tom nodded. He stared ahead, thinking he should have paid more attention. He should damn well have paid more attention.

If Annie turned up in Alabama, Tom figured he'd best go down there with Ben Johnson. He called Ben back. Ben had no objection.

The family spent a sleepless night, including Patrick. Maureen crashed about three o'clock, and Tom took over holding Patrick in the rocking chair. The next morning, he called Antoine Harrison at daybreak. The guy wasn't in his office yet.

Finally, at seven o'clock, the deputy called back. They weren't able to track her cell phone, he said. He'd let them know as soon as he got any word from the bus company. Their administrative offices didn't open until 8:30, which was why it was taking so long.

Harrison used up Monday morning and most of the afternoon not getting answers. It was like pulling teeth, he told the Haigs. Employees to interview, records to review, lawyers to consult. He was fixed to see a judge, he told Tom on the phone, when the bus company finally informed him that they knew where Annie Haig could be found.

She was on one of their buses traveling its normal route between Nashville and Birmingham. The company had talked to the driver, who was keeping an eye on Annie. The driver would pull over for the state patrol to take her off in Tennessee or Alabama, as the family wished. The bus company manager wanted the family to know that Annie's paperwork had been entirely in order, and that they had followed proper procedure in accordance with regulations at every point in her itinerary.

Tom could breathe again.

But if they had her taken off the bus, he wondered, how would they get her home? Maybe the best idea would be to let her ride the bus the rest of the way, as long as the driver continued to watch her and as long as her sister was waiting to meet her at the other end. He called Ben Johnson. They were leaving immediately, he told him.

"We'll leave at six o'clock tomorrow morning," Ben informed Tom.

———•◦•———

Pal's preferred spot was not his cushion in the back seat of Charlie's Genesis. The little guy much preferred to lie on Theresa's lap. Charlie didn't blame him one bit. When they stopped for a picnic in Tuscaloosa, he planned to nestle his head in similar fashion. Pal would have to settle for the blanket or the grass.

He and Theresa made love every day, more when he got time off. As far as he knew, another baby could be in the offing. He was still in the early stages of this, his first and only passionate embrace of another human being, and he would imperil it for nothing and no one—not even their firstborn child.

Charlie got regular reports from Rebecca, so he knew his son had been discharged from the hospital. But he and Theresa never talked about Patrick's future. The few times he'd tried, he couldn't get a response.

Theresa didn't seem to work at her disinterest, if that's what it was.

Charlie couldn't imagine what she felt, how she should feel, or what she ought to do about it. Whatever she wanted, he'd told her, he would back her 100 percent.

Charlie based his support for Theresa on two lessons from his training. First, that with the use of force comes responsibility. The country had seen in Iraq what happened when you intervened and then withdrew as if the result had nothing to do with you. Officers were fond of quoting the Powell Doctrine: you break it, you own it. That was sound morality and sound diplomacy, and Charlie thought it applied to a whole lot more than military matters.

The women who took Theresa were responsible for everything that happened after. They couldn't walk away as if the tragedy that resulted wasn't their fault. Theresa had the right to make them bear the consequences.

The second thing he understood is that it's impossible to predict fallout. When strategists make assumptions about the outcome of a particular maneuver, they prepare to deal with those results, not other results contrary to expectations. But inevitably, contrary results bedevil the operation. The question becomes not only what did you plan, but what are you prepared to do if the plan goes awry?

Theresa was forcing the women who kidnapped her to cope with a high-needs newborn on their turf, to witness the child's suffering, to ask themselves what sacrifices they'd make to take care of that child.

It had probably never occurred to any of them that Theresa could invoke a law that made the infant whose life they'd saved the ward of their local welfare department. They wouldn't want that. From what he'd heard, pro-life supporters weren't big on the taxes needed to support other people's children after they were born.

So, they'd have to ask themselves how much they really cared about this baby. Were they all hat and no cattle when it came to a child whose existence they'd engineered?

He thought they probably were. These anti-abortion types would tend to walk away once they got what they wanted because it wasn't really the baby they cared about. It was naked power. If there was anything Charlie had seen in action, it was the human yen to take control. Theresa was making those sanctimonious do-gooders look in the mirror and see what they were made of.

Or so Charlie hoped. He hoped and prayed, in as much as he knew how to pray, that once Theresa had made her point, those women would show their true colors. They'd cut and run, leaving the baby up for grabs. In that melee, somehow, his son would come back to his family. He didn't know how it might happen or when, but he knew his father was right when he told him to cling to Theresa.

He had no intention of losing her. That was the crux of it. He supported his wife 100 percent because nothing—no situation or decision Theresa made or didn't make—would ever get him to give her up.

Shortly after noon, they'd stopped to have lunch on a riverbank. It was as beautiful a day as anyone could wish for. Pal scrambled off to explore. He was just smart enough not to let his enthusiasm take him out of sight. Theresa put his kibbles in his bowl with bits of cold salmon. Pal liked salmon, though he preferred chicken or beef.

"You gonna be OK at the weddin'?" Charlie asked as they munched sandwiches and potato salad with the remainder of a bottle of wine from the previous night.

"It's just one afternoon," she replied.

"Think any of your Minnesota kin'll show up?"

"I doubt it," Theresa said.

"Have any regrets about 'em?" Charlie asked, lowering his voice.

She laughed half-heartedly but didn't answer.

———•◦•———

"I'd rather not be a bridesmaid," Theresa admitted when she and Charlie reached his childhood home. His grandmother would have none of it.

"Honey, you can't let your sister down. This is her big day. You're the bee's knees on a day like today or any day after the weddin'. But the day of the weddin' belongs to *her*, darlin'. Now come try on your dress so I can pin it."

Charlie had seen this aspect of his grandmother many times. Most everyone in Lafayette County knew not to mess with Rebecca Cole when she took a tone. Uncharacteristically, Theresa conceded the field. She didn't look at Charlie, but he knew his feelings played a role in her calculations.

Rebecca had cut the bridesmaid's outfit from a 1950s Chanel pattern she'd found in a back room at the dressmaking store across the street from the courthouse.

"It's classic. Won't ever go out of style," she told Theresa.

The fabric was already pinned on a mannequin in the finished part of the Cole attic, a cozy corner that looked more like a fashion boutique than storage for all the old things a family saves up.

"It's matted gold silk," Rebecca said, "low-cut and lined in satin. You've got this flarin' skirt all the way to the ground, off-the-shoulder sleeves, and I made a matchin' cape topped by a hood goes over your head. Just the kind of finery you might wear to a military ball someday."

NCOs don't get invited to military balls, Charlie thought. But he didn't say it. No use dashing the mood. For more than an hour, Theresa stood motionless in front of a full-length mirror. It reflected a vision of loveliness that evoked the Southern ideal. Charlie hadn't ever thought much about fashion, but as he watched his grandmother work on Theresa's gown, he felt mesmerized by his wife. Nothing would ever tear him away from her.

———•◦•———

The bus pulled off the highway numerous times over two days and nights to let travelers disembark or to give continuing passengers a chance to use the restroom and buy a piece of fruit or a plastic-wrapped sandwich. There was too much commotion to concentrate on reading a book. Annie slept as much as she could, the right side of her forehead pressed to cold glass. Sometimes the road got bumpy, or rain on the roof woke her, or the air in the bus turned stale as more people entered, filling it to capacity. Babies cried on their mothers' laps. The driver threatened to eject offenders whenever kids ran up and down the aisle or unruly riders yelled at each other. Someone got sick, but the operator continued on while the nauseated individual used donated wipes to wash his face. Annie mostly dozed in her little space.

The entire journey took a lot longer than she'd thought it would. When they reached Birmingham, Donna gathered her things to get off. It was already dark outside as the bus turned into the station. Annie still had one more leg of the trip, namely the hour's drive to Tuscaloosa. She jolted to attention as Donna stood up.

"You take care, now," Donna warned. "I'm gonna tell the driver to watch out for you. If anybody touches you, you scream, OK?"

Annie nodded.

"And call your sister soon as you get off this bus. You understand?" Those were her parting words.

———•◦•———

There weren't any creepy men on the last leg of Annie's trip. Just college students, mostly female. They paid no attention to her, but she was mesmerized by the glorious prospect of being one of them someday.

Since leaving Minneapolis, Annie had consumed four candy bars, a sandwich, and a can of orange juice. She felt dizzy standing up after the bus abruptly stopped with a hissing sound. Her book bag still lay between her feet and the wall. She picked it up. The college girls exited quickly and almost as quickly disappeared into cars. No one but the driver remained as she got off to face the glaring lights of the depot, which was really just a gas station.

The clock on the front of the building said 6:10 p.m. The driver went into the side door of a flat-roofed garage not far away. Annie walked toward a wooden bench at the edge of the parking lot, turned her cell phone back on, and dialed Claire, who picked up on the first ring.

"Annie," she said in a strange voice.

"Hey, Claire, yeah, this is me," Annie responded, sitting down on the bench.

"Where are you?" Claire practically shouted.

"In Tuscaloosa. In front of the bus depot," Annie said, well aware that Claire's tone did not bode well.

She heard her sister speak to someone. "She says she's outside the bus depot in Tuscaloosa."

"Let me talk to her," said the other person.

"Annie!" Woodrow thundered. "Are you OK?"

She recognized his voice right away. He certainly didn't have to yell.

"I'm fine," Annie informed him. "Hungry, though, and sore from sleeping on the bus."

"Annie, I want you to go inside the station and talk to the agent at the counter. You tell him someone's on his way to pick you up. Then you stay near the counter 'til I get there. OK?"

"How long will it take?" Annie asked.

"Forty-five minutes," Woodrow said. "You stay there, you hear?"

Annie agreed.

The more than forty-five minutes—forty-nine to be exact—that Annie spent in Tuscaloosa seemed like the longest part of her trip. After she'd freshened up in the restroom, she still had a half hour to cool her heels. She walked around, trying to work out the kinks in her neck and legs. She could hardly wait for this part to be over.

The only other people in the vicinity were the gas station attendant and occasional customers, none of whom looked threatening. She tried to tell the attendant that she was expecting someone, but he seemed disinterested. Finally, Woodrow arrived in the same red pickup he'd driven to Minnesota the previous May. At his side was a boy about her age who was doing his best imitation of nonchalant.

"Annie," Woodrow said when he got inside. It wasn't a "Glad to see you" greeting. It was more a "What the hell are you doing here, Annie?"

"Hi, Woodrow," she said, resisting the urge to hug him. Her gaze switched to the boy.

"Who are you?" she asked matter-of-factly.

The boy smiled in the same way she'd seen Woodrow smile.

"Jeremiah Cole," he said as if he were a grown man, which he was not.

"Happy to make your acquaintance," she replied, extending her hand.

"Think I'll wait 'til you're cleaned up," he said, ignoring her outstretched invitation. "Right now, you stink like pig slop."

"What was that you were sayin'?" Woodrow asked, his hand a vice around the back of Jeremiah's neck.

"My apologies, ma'am," Jeremiah got out, wincing. "Your smell is more like a rose garden." He laughed as Woodrow let go.

Despite the aches in every muscle of her body and the noisy ruckus going on in her stomach, Annie couldn't help laughing too. It was nice to see the little snot put in his place, even if her teachers would say what Woodrow did was child abuse.

"I know I smell bad," Annie said sweetly, deciding to meet bad manners with better ones. "I'm looking forward to a hot bath."

"Let's go," Woodrow said.

Annie was glad he didn't want to discuss matters any further until they saw Claire. She had arrived in time for the wedding. She'd rather take her dressing down from the two of them at the same time, and then she could concentrate on getting set for the nuptials.

———•◦•———

Ben Johnson drove an old black Volvo with none of the fancy stuff they add on to cars nowadays. He played public radio's classical music channel until he lost reception. Then he put in an opera CD.

He wouldn't switch driving with Tom until later, he said. He stopped frequently at gas stations and parks— to relieve an old man's bladder. Tom was not used to that kind of self-indulgence, and it was irritating as hell that Ben wouldn't go faster than fifty-five. The average interstate speed was seventy and up, so it was not only irritating but downright dangerous, even if Ben stayed in the far-right lane.

The two men had made their peace after Tom told Ben he wouldn't pay for any more work Ben did for Maureen. That wasn't unusual. Tom had a temper, as even he acknowledged, but his storms passed quickly. Ben was not the type to hold a grudge. "Born wise," people said about him. Ben would show up at the Haig place a day or two after an argument, and both men would act as if it hadn't taken place. Tom never apologized. It wasn't in his nature. But he knew, and the whole family knew he knew—that Ben was the kinder man.

"We shoulda taken my Caddy," Tom observed when they finally crossed the state line. "Much more comfortable, and I'd have us miles ahead of where we are," he added.

"Fifty-five is the safest speed in congested driving," Ben replied without taking his eyes off the road. "Less stress, too."

Tom tried to nap but couldn't. Ben let him take the wheel at the first Iowa rest stop.

"All that caterwaulin' is driving me nuts," Tom complained, referring to the arias blaring out of Ben's console. Ben made no response, but he switched back to the radio.

For lack of anything better to discuss, shortly after they passed Waterloo, Tom let Ben know how he felt regarding Theresa's abandoning her baby, and what that decision was doing to his domestic tranquility.

"Nothing's been the same since," he said.

"We've got to deal with facts in life, not what-ifs or what-might-have-beens," Ben replied. He didn't react to the phrase *domestic tranquility*, which was in the Constitution, Tom recalled, and ought to be guaranteed.

They stopped for lunch at a cafe outside Cedar Rapids. Their waiter was odd, a young man who talked a lot but had a hard time making himself understood. He wrote down their orders with no problem, though.

"What's wrong with him?" Tom asked rhetorically as the waiter walked away, stopping to make high fives with a pair of giggling toddlers in a nearby booth.

"That might be Patrick twenty years from now," Ben suggested. "Grown up and employed and pretty happy. On top of that, he's giving those little boys the extra attention kids crave."

"Jesus!" Tom exclaimed. "You think that's what he'll be like? Ask me, I'd rather not be born."

"You consider that young man's life less valuable than yours?" Ben asked.

Tom shrugged, sick to death of hearing about the upside of Down syndrome. It was all Maureen could talk about.

Their food arrived quickly, a surprise given how packed the place was. Ben took his time eating a ham sandwich with two pickles, an order of onion rings, and a wedge of apple pie topped with a scoop of cinnamon ice cream. Tom wolfed down a cheeseburger and fries and was ready to leave in short order, but it took Ben another twenty minutes to finish his meal, and then he spent an eternity in the men's room.

Tom called Maureen from the parking lot. She was doing all right, she said. Irene Overdale was coming shortly to keep her company. Irene's second cousin twice removed had a child with Down syndrome, so she'd known what to expect. She was great with Patrick.

Maureen seemed surprised that Tom and Ben were only as far as Cedar Rapids.

"Don't get me started," Tom said.

"Now, you call me soon as you find Annie, and you put her on the phone," Maureen reminded him.

"After I've given her what for myself," Tom said.

———•◆•———

Most days, Maureen stood on the overhang of a cliff, holding onto Patrick for dear life. In her mind, that is. When Irene arrived, she hurried her grandson into Irene's arms so she could shower and change.

She cried under the spray as warm water sluiced another day's sweat down the drain. All she did was rock Patrick in the chair by the bedroom window, soothe him when he wailed, take him to the hospital two or three times a week, agonize over Theresa's catastrophic choices, throw whatever they had for food on the table, beg for volunteers from anyone willing to spare an hour or two, change Patrick's diapers, check his breathing whenever she couldn't hear it, feed him four or five bottles of expensive formula per day, and now, obsess over Annie's whereabouts.

"You've taken on a lot," Irene said when Maureen returned in a fresh outfit, her hair still wet from the shower.

"Everyone thinks the better of you for it," Irene added.

The women made their way to the living room, Patrick half asleep in Irene's arms. He smiled at her. Babies liked Irene, Maureen had observed. Perhaps because Irene was so content with them. When Irene's cousin's daughter Rose was born with Down syndrome, the little thing preferred Irene to her mother. Rose had been full-term, her condition a total surprise. She had not developed sleep apnea, and her heart needed only a minor repair—minor by the standards of today when surgery on infants had become routine, or so it seemed.

Rose was ten years old now, and low on energy, Irene said. The child ate too much, preferring high-calorie snacks to fruits and vegetables. That was a problem, as was her weight and her IQ.

Her mother was determined to mainstream Rose in school and hold her teachers accountable. So far, Rose had never had to repeat a grade, but she had trouble keeping up. Her teachers thought she might have hidden abilities they could "tease out" in a more appropriate setting. They meant special education. According to Irene, Rose's mother hated anything with the word *special* in it.

"There's a lot you can take from what my cousin learned the hard way," Irene told Maureen. Maureen didn't want to hear it. She felt tired and frightened, waiting endlessly for Tom to call.

"I don't understand," she lamented. "How could Annie sneak away like that?"

"It's hard for siblings," Irene said. "I know people say it teaches them to be more empathetic, but sometimes too much of the burden gets dumped on them."

Maureen bristled. "Annie's a member of this family, isn't she? I didn't dump anything on her. What do you think this has done to me?"

Irene nodded. "Of course, you're right," she said. "Annie's too young to understand is all."

"She'll understand when her father catches up to her," Maureen retorted. "When I think about how she tricked her friend's mother, and then ran off to the bus station, and us not knowing where she was for almost two days. I always thought Tom spoiled her. Here's the proof."

They ended up dozing, all three of them, Maureen on the sofa, her head on one of the throw pillows, Irene in a chair with Patrick sideways against her chest, his face nestled against the softness of her cashmere sweater. The house was silent.

Miles of farmland wrapped around them, fields separated by Tom's remaining oaks. Their bronze-red canopies sheltered thousands, maybe tens of thousands, of acorns this fall. It was a masting year, and food had fallen to the critters below like manna from heaven. A wind was blowing from the north. It probably meant something was coming in. The birds and squirrels disappeared when a mix of snow and sleet hit the Haigs' steel roof.

"As it is in the beginnin', so shall it be in the end," the preacher intoned. A longtime friend of Woodrow's, Jimmy Solay had come to Lafayette from the winding waters of Bayou Têche.

He stood now on the stump of a pine tree cut down decades ago, its fissured remains barely visible against the living giants behind it. The man was tall and lanky. Stringy brown hair hung to his shoulders. His face and body suggested famine, and a scraggly mustache fell over his mouth. No one knew him well, except Woodrow. He and Jimmy had been Marine buddies and stayed in touch long after the corps.

In Alabama, a couple needed to find a judge or retired judge, an ordained minister, or a church pastor to join them in matrimony. Many judges in the state no longer performed wedding ceremonies, however, due to new regulations regarding gender combinations. It was all or none, the law said. Anyone could marry anyone, as long as both parties were adults. Better none, some judges decided.

Most couples opted for a preacher anyway, and a ceremony in the tradition of the bride's family church.

"You ask me," Jimmy told Woodrow, "those judges are takin' a mean route, and evangelicals—they're just as bad. *Couyon*, we say in the bayou. Sendin' folk away because they ain't matched up to public satisfaction is pure *méchanceté*, and I don't cotton to it. No, sir. Long as both of 'em are old enough to know what they're doin', I'm satisfied."

At home, Jimmy presided over a ten-year-old church he'd established in the parish of Breaux Bridge. That distinction got him approved online in less than five minutes to conduct what he called a "hitchin' ceremony" in the state of Alabama. He'd driven to Lafayette in an old Ford convertible that Woodrow had worked on more than once.

"Woodrow, I'm as ready as a preacher can be!" he'd announced on arrival at the wedding site.

The gathering was small, Jimmy noticed, just the affianced couple, Woodrow's brothers and their wives, a dozen or so of the younger generation, Woodrow's mother, and Woodrow's son and his wife standing as best man and bridesmaid. It was noon with no wind on a blue-sky day. The temperature was fifty-two, up from thirty at dawn. Woodrow's intended wore a low-cut, long-sleeved, white velvet dress with a hooded cape trimmed in rabbit fur.

She looked as serene as any bride Jimmy had ever seen. Since it was her second wedding and Woodrow's first, his friend's betrothed had agreed to let the groom decide the venue. Woodrow picked his family's most hallowed setting, this grove of old-growth pine. The forest was peaceful midday in late November. Jimmy paused a moment before resuming, waiting for whispers and salutations and burps and sneezes to die down. At length, a near stillness settled on the assembled.

Jimmy noticed Annie, the bride's little sister, shivering silently for lack of a coat. She didn't want to ruin her appearance, he'd heard her tell Rebecca, and the two briefly disputed the matter. Jimmy waited them out. He was a man whose hearing had been refined to register the barest swish in placid water and whose patience rose from an innate curiosity regarding the mysterious workings of the world.

"That man can perorate," he'd overheard Rebecca's grandson Jeremiah whisper to Annie. "You know what that means?"

The wisp of a sister shook her head.

"Deliver a grandiloquent oration," Jeremiah told her.

"Grandiloquent?" she whispered back.

"Sort of like pompous," Jeremiah returned. "He speaks English perfectly fine, but he throws in bayou-talk to make an impression."

When silence finally reigned, Jimmy began again.

"Words like *beginnin'* and *end* are favorites among the preacher crowd . . . and by preacher crowd, I mean my competitors who like as not embrace even as sacred an event as a weddin' to rail against Satan's minions. They see 'em 'round every corner. They strain to divide the world between the righteous and the wicked. There's no in-between, they say. In their parlance, the beginning is a heavenly garden no one ever saw, and the end is the evil of here and now, 'til the very moment Death arrives for each of us. Well, folks, that meanin' ain't my meanin' when it comes to these beautiful words, *beginnin'* and *end*. I'm meanin' something true to the flesh and blood we are. I'm meanin' love in all its majesty. This *zanmi* of mine, Woodrow Aurelius Cole, we met in the corps on a mighty hot day, if I rightly recall, and he saw me havin' troubles with a machine whose defects I did not fully comprehend but had been ordered to rectify."

Jimmy drew a deep breath.

"Suffice it to say I found myself in a situation like what folk in the bayous call *gris-gris*. Someone or something had brought me to the edge of insanity, even as sweat poured off my skin like the primeval waters of creation. But Woodrow here . . ." Jimmy waved his arms. "Woodrow stopped what he was about *tout court*, and he made it right for me, and it cost him a dressin' down and a penance."

Jimmy allowed his story to sink in.

"That's the way it is with Woodrow, *mes amis*. He'll help a stranger. It's no small thing to help a stranger. But it's his way, and it will be his way to the end of his days, I can tell you for sure. It will be his way as husband to Claire. They stand together in love and affection today and will do the same fifty years from now. Y'all can plainly see the truth of that."

Jimmy spread his arms wide and then put one hand each on Woodrow and Claire's shoulders. "These two people have found a love in each other that makes 'em a sun unto itself. They generate love like a fire inside 'em that joins one to t'other. It's their character, and character don't change. People may live in desperate times and wear themselves down, flailin' against injustice everywhere they turn, but character . . . character is in 'em from beginnin' to end of their bliss and their travails. Woodrow and Claire . . . their love is true. It's manifest. And therefore I exercise the powers vested in me by the state of Alabama to unite their separate selves in legal matrimony, which is their intent and my priv'lege to impart."

After Jimmy's words, Claire and Woodrow spoke their vows. Jimmy pronounced them *marye koup*—joined together—and the ceremony was over.

———◆•●•◆———

A half hour later the wedding party arrived back at the Cole homestead, where what Jimmy imagined as a hearty *fais do-do* awaited, judging by the piquant scents wafting from inside. Woodrow had hitched two borrowed white horses to a wagon festooned with ribbons to fetch his bride home in style. Legs hanging over the edge, Jimmy sat in the back of the wagon as it approached the imposing house, where he spied two men standing on the front porch, seemingly unbothered by an old German shepherd or by a barking Koda, who hurled himself down the steps as soon as he caught a whiff of his master.

"Koda, slow down, boy," Woodrow ordered, helping Claire alight in her lovely white gown. Jeremiah grabbed Koda's collar before he could reach his target. He pulled him aside as the two men marched off the porch and straight toward them, Tom Haig out front, Ben Johnson right behind him.

"Tom Haig's my wife's father," Charlie told Jimmy, who jumped out of the wagon and made his way toward the house. "Tom's Claire's father too, and Ben's a friend of their family."

"I smell trouble," Jimmy returned.

"You married?" Tom demanded, looking straight at the bride. He added after a moment, in seeming amazement, "My God, you look just like your mother."

"Yes, I'm married," Claire returned, beaming. "And I know I look like Mother in this dress. Rebecca made it. Dad, I'm so happy. Be happy for me, *please.*"

Woodrow extended his right hand toward Tom. "Welcome to our home, Mr. Haig. Your daughter has done me the honor—"

"I'd have stopped it if I could," Tom interrupted. He looked on the verge of tears.

"That's what I figured," Ben said. "Remember what I told you coming down here, Tom. You need to stay calm for once in your life."

Tom swung around. "I thought so," he said. "That's why you took as long as you could driving. I knew for sure when we got here. And you—" He pivoted back to Woodrow.

He stopped speaking for a moment before asking, "How old are you?"

"Remember, Dad, I'm thirty-nine," Claire said. "There's less than ten years between Woodrow and me. As I recall, there's more years between you and Mother."

Tom glared at Woodrow. "You and your goddamn family stole my girls," he charged.

"Now you're going overboard, Tom," Ben intervened. "You and Maureen had three daughters among a pile of sons, and all three bolted on their own. I don't think the Coles made it happen."

"You think I give a damn what you—" Tom protested.

"Stop it, all of you," Rebecca said, appearing with Annie. They'd driven back to the house the long way around. Annie now wore Rebecca's quilt coat.

"Annie, thank God," Tom cried, rushing to embrace her. "What you put us through!"

"I always knew I'd have to pay," Annie said to no one in particular while Tom held her tight.

"Let's head indoors," Rebecca suggested.

"Point is, I succeeded," Annie insisted moments later as she and Rebecca climbed the porch steps. "I made it to Claire's wedding."

Ben Johnson patted the middle of her back as she passed him by. Annie turned her head toward Ben and whispered, "Is there any legal way I could stay here and have Woodrow and Claire be my parents?"

Ben smiled. "Don't think so, kiddo. Best thing for you right now is not to rile your father. He's bound to take you back soon as this is over."

"That's what I figured," she muttered.

Woodrow and Claire followed Annie and Rebecca inside. Theresa turned to climb the steps, holding onto Charlie's arm.

"I need to talk to you," Tom said, standing in her way.

"There's nothing to talk about," she replied, looking him full in the face.

"Your baby's nothing?"

"It's Mother's baby, not mine."

Tom scowled. "Your mother's taken your responsibility on her shoulders, but she's not up to it. You gave birth to that boy, Theresa. By rights, he belongs to you."

"That's not what the law says," Theresa replied. "I was forced. You know that's true, don't you, Dad? You know Mother and her friends turned me over to that maniac, Lucy Meyer. I was knocked out cold. I couldn't defend myself. They kept me from getting an abortion that I had every right to."

Theresa turned to Ben. "Do *you* know?" she asked.

Ben nodded yes. "Your parents have done some real soul-searching on that question, Theresa."

"They can soul search all they want. Facts are facts," Theresa said.

"And abortion is murder," Tom said.

A dull silence ensued. Jimmy Solay watched from a perch he'd assumed at the far end of the porch.

"What about you?" Tom turned toward Charlie. "You OK giving up your own flesh and blood?"

"I support Theresa," Charlie said. "Whatever she decides is right by me. We need to believe her when she tells us what she went through."

Theresa looked at Ben again. "You drove my father here?" she asked.

"Slow as I could," Ben said. "In my car. He came to bring Annie home."

"He came for more than that," Theresa said. "Dad," she added, turning back to her father, "I am finally starting to get through a day without reliving those awful weeks when I was at the mercy of a room full of women who took me out of your house by force. I can't tell you how angry I was with Mother when I finally got free. When I saw her at the hospital, she didn't even apologize, did you know that?"

"You need to claim your baby and bring him to live with you. I know *that*!" Tom said with finality. "Apologizing comes later."

"I told you. He's not my baby," Theresa returned, meeting Tom's glare with one of her own.

"And you don't mind her saying that?" Tom asked Charlie.

"Told you before. I support my wife," Charlie said evenly.

Tom looked back and forth between them. Then he turned and walked out into the yard, his shoulders slumped. He faced a line of pine trees at the top of a hill and stood there like a statue.

Ben cleared his throat. "Mind if I venture a question?" he asked Theresa, who looked for a moment as if she might go after her father. "Would you tell me why you didn't stay in Minnesota long enough to press charges against the women you say took you against your will?"

Theresa seemed surprised.

"I know the truth when I hear it," Ben went on. "So I'm not denying what you say happened, Theresa. And I'm the first to admit kidnapping is against the law. But if what you say is true, you have every right to file criminal charges against those women . . . against your doctor, too. I'm asking, if you were kidnapped, why haven't you done that?"

"And let them become martyrs to their cause, which is probably what they want? No, Ben. I wasn't going to give them any more of my life than they already stole. Especially after I found out how hurt Charlie was. What happened to him in Afghanistan wouldn't have happened if he hadn't been trying to get home to find me."

"The way it stands now, you didn't get justice, either one of you," Ben noted.

"No, we didn't," Theresa agreed. "But sometimes the price of justice is too damn high."

"Has anyone from law enforcement contacted you?" Ben asked. "Anyone from the FBI?"

"They've left messages on my phone," Theresa said.

"To which you don't reply?"

"That's right," she admitted. "I can't do it. They'd want me back in Minnesota. They'd turn the whole thing into a circus. I won't put myself through any more, Ben. I won't put Charlie through it." Her eyes beseeched him. "You understand?" she pressed.

"Yes, I understand," Ben said. "Justice is expensive in more ways than money."

"Thank you," she said simply. She broke away, climbed the porch steps, and went inside. Charlie, his head bowed, followed her. Ben thought he saw tears in Charlie's eyes.

He decided to stay outside a bit longer, surveying the mid-day landscape that now included Tom still standing in the Cole front yard, his back to the house. The sky held a few feathery clouds, and the sun shone a little less brightly behind the trees. Tom remained where he was, not moving an inch. Ben wasn't sure how much he'd overheard.

"Lots goin' on," Jimmy remarked from his corner of the porch.

Ben turned around. "Who are you?" he inquired.

The preacher put out his hand. "Jimmy Solay. Officiant at this here weddin' your friend Tom don't seem so happy about."

Ben smiled and shook Jimmy's hand. "Tom might come 'round yet," he said. "I'm Ben Johnson, bride's family friend."

"Good to meet you, Ben. I don't know anything 'bout the bride's *famille* or what their troubles are, but I'd say there's a whole lot of *misère* goin' on."

"If you mean misery, I'd say you're right," Ben said. "Not sure we'll get it smoothed out anytime soon. Tom is heartsick."

In the quiet that ensued, Jimmy remarked, "My daddy used to say *le père de famille* got no choice 'cept to let his *garçons* wander off once they reach an age, but he don't like it when his *petites filles* grow up and git . . ."

"No, they don't like it," Ben agreed.

Mid-afternoon on the day Maureen imagined her eldest daughter was attempting holy matrimony with a Southern heathen, she phoned Matthew, her eldest son, who lived eighty miles away.

"What are you doing?" she asked when he picked up.

"Getting ready for tomorrow." He sounded out of breath. "Mary's washing the turkey. I'm cleaning the house. It's our first time, you know. Before this, we either went to Mary's parents' place or to you at the farm."

"Would you please put your wife on the line?" Maureen said.

"Uh . . . sure. Mary? My mother wants to talk to you."

"Should I save the neck, heart, and gizzard for an alternate dressing?" Maureen heard her son's wife ask as she took his phone. "Organ meats make it richer . . . Yes, Maureen?"

"Mary, I need my family with me this year," Maureen told her simply. She waited to let the question sink in. It didn't take long.

"We can't, Maureen. Didn't Matt tell you? You could come to our house, though."

"Mary, you know the situation with Annie. Tom's gone to bring her home, and I'm alone with Patrick. I want you both here at the farm. Bring the kids."

"Maureen, we spent the whole morning shopping. I've got a nineteen-pound turkey in the sink and a house full of groceries. My parents will arrive in the next two hours. We can't."

Maureen exhaled loudly.

"Your son is cleaning the house," Mary resumed. "You trained him well, I must say . . . and I'm about to set the table in the dining room. It's a lot of work, Maureen. Gives me an appreciation for all the Thanksgivings you hosted over the years."

"I need my family here," Maureen got out between gasps for air, as if she were trying to prevent a stronger reaction.

"I'll put Matt back on," his wife said. Maureen heard her whisper, "It's out of the question . . . I wish you'd turn your cell off."

Matt's voice came back. "Mom," he said.

"Matthew, I need you and your brothers to come here for Thanksgiving . . . I thought I could handle being alone this year, but I'm at the end of my tether. I want you to call every one of your brothers. *Now*, Matthew. This is an emergency."

"Uh . . . OK," Matt said.

He sent texts to Paul, David, Mark, John, Andrew, Luke, and Greg, suggesting they discuss the situation.

"Mom in meltdown. Wants us home for Thanksgiving. Skype?" he tapped out.

He got a text from Greg in less than a minute. "Too far away. ND."

He called Greg. "What are you doing in North Dakota?

"I'm at my girlfriend's dad's farm."

"I thought for sure you'd be home."

"I've got my own life," Greg said defensively. "School's been a bear, and this is my only chance for a break."

"Greg, I've never heard her this bad."

"Well, I have. You ask me, she's taken on too much."

"Someone has to go there."

"Not me," Greg snapped. "You guys are closer." He hung up.

With Greg out of contention, the discussion continued in a Skype session. All five of the married sons, including Matt, exempted themselves.

"Mom invents emergencies," Mark pointed out. "This isn't the first time. You wanna know what I think . . . I think she's teed off that we've given in to our wives' wanting Thanksgiving in place."

"You mean with our in-laws," Paul said.

"Exactly. Thanksgiving in St. Dominic isn't practical anymore. Mom and Dad need to come to us."

"They have chores on the farm," John observed.

"Not much this time of year," Andy said.

"You know, Andy, you and Luke not being married, you'd be free to go up there," Paul said.

"That's what my Mary says," Matt concurred. "One of the unmarrieds should keep her company."

"Can't," Luke said. "I have other plans."

"I will," Andy offered. "Don't forget, guys, Mom has Theresa's baby, and the kid's a preemie."

"Thank you, Andy," Matt said loudly, and the others chimed in.

"I'll leave in the morning," Andy said. "Driving will be safer then."

"Bring food," David suggested.

"Of course, I'll bring food!" Andy told him.

After they'd finished, grateful texts surfed their way to Andy's phone.

The next day, Andy called his mother before he left. She didn't answer. That worried him. With a turkey and premade fixings in an ice chest, he drove to the farm in record time, barely missing a speed trap on Highway 694.

Once there, he parked near the kitchen door. His mother's car was either in the pole barn or she was gone. He got out of his vehicle and brought the food inside, at which point Zip greeted him, wide-eyed and panting. There wasn't much in the refrigerator, so he crammed everything on the shelves.

When his mother didn't appear by the time he was done unpacking,

Andy yelled upstairs. Zip's food bowl lay empty on the floor, and his water bowl was empty too. Andy filled both and watched Zip gorge himself.

A search of the house revealed no one. All Andy could think was that, whatever happened, it happened to Theresa's baby. His next stop had to be the hospital.

There he found his mother asleep, curled into a ball in one of the armchairs inside the NICU. He could see her through the glass as a nurse instructed him on how to prepare his own entry. He knew what to do. What he didn't know was how bad he would feel that his mother sat alone in a hospital with an obviously sick infant on Thanksgiving Day.

Pneumonia, a nurse told him. Maureen had brought the baby in around five o'clock that morning. They thought it might be a complication from exposure to the flu. When did Andy have his flu shot? He shook his head.

Andy would need a flu shot immediately, the nurse said, and so would everyone who came into contact with the baby. It took two weeks for the shot to be effective. Maureen had one in September, but apparently a friend of hers who'd held the child yesterday did not.

The nurse was incensed. Andy avoided eye contact. He felt really sorry he'd skipped the shot at work. He'd have to stay outside the NICU, he was told. His mother continued to sleep. The baby was out of sight. Not exactly the way Andy expected to spend Thanksgiving. But there it was. He left the building and called his father.

"We're on our way home," Tom said. "Right after dinner. Ben insists we eat first. Said he's not going to leave on an empty stomach . . . and like a fool I let him drive his car."

"He's probably right about eating," Andy observed.

"How's your mother?" Tom asked, changing the subject.

"She's sleeping." Andy didn't tell him where.

"Good," Tom said.

———•◦•———

William watched his grandmother cut the lattice for the top crust on three apple pies lined up on the kitchen table. Most of his friends' mothers made apple pie in a skillet, but Rebecca baked her pies, twelve inches in diameter, using what she called her "historical porcelain bakeware" that were nothing but shallow, fancy-edged bowls that had been wrought from refined clay, hand-painted, and glazed to sell for hard coins (not Confederate notes) after the war.

The dishes showed scenes of life on imaginary plantations and always included white pillars and balconies where young ladies stood in hoop-skirt dresses. Magnolia trees blossomed. Fields of cotton rolled to the horizon. Vague figures bent over in the distance.

"Who gets these dishes when you're, you know, gone?" William asked.

William, the second youngest son of Rebecca's youngest son, Lewis, figured now, age nine, was a good time for him to start understanding practical things, especially if they had to do with money.

"I haven't decided yet," Rebecca said.

"How much you 'spect they'd fetch?"

"You know, William, people hard up in those times made and sold whatever they could to keep their babies' mouths filled. These lyin' pie dishes were part of that destitution, which makes 'em part of history."

"*Lyin'* dishes?"

"Look close," she advised. "Plantations and masters. I see white people like my father's family, the ones who owned slaves. There they are sashaying on their balconies, but where are the people in bondage? Those dots in the distance? These plates don't show their misery. In my opinion, they're nothing but propaganda 'bout the war between the states."

"I know all about the war between the states," William informed her.

"Hmmm," she said, unhappy with a nubbin of lattice dough. She flicked it into a bowl of apple cores.

"Anyway, I want to ask somethin' different," William said.

"Thought so," Rebecca returned, stirring peeled and sliced fruit, sugar, cinnamon, and a dash of vanilla in a cast-iron pan on the stove. The apples came from an orchard north of Birmingham. It took over an hour to drive there. William and several of his cousins had accompanied his grandmother to the orchard numerous times.

"What happens when a girl in high school gets pregnant?" William ventured, staring at the pies and not at his grandmother. As he well knew, rule number one in talking to adults was never look straight at somebody's face when you ask embarrassing questions.

"What brings that on?" Rebecca inquired. She poured pie filling into another of the dishes.

William hated it when adults answered a question with a question. In this case, there was no avoiding it if he wanted an answer.

"A girl at my school is goin' to have a baby," he informed her matter-of-factly.

"How old is she?"

"Fifteen," he said.

"How is it you know she's goin' to have a baby?"

William sighed. "She's my friend Elijah's older sister. It's all Elijah's family can talk about."

Rebecca shook her head.

"What happens?" William persisted.

"Does the family know who's the daddy?" Rebecca asked with a scowl.

"No!" William thundered. "OK, maybe. Elijah didn't say. I jus' wanna know what happens after a girl gets pregnant."

Rebecca went silent. Then she said, slowly, "Way it is now, the girl has all the power."

"What does that mean?"

"It means she gets to decide what to do. She and her parents. Not the boy. Do you know how babies get started?"

William near panicked. "I know all about it!" he said emphatically.

"Are you sure you got the right information? Did your daddy have a talk with you?"

"I know everythin', Gramma. That's *not* my question."

"I see," she said. "Well, imagine for a moment you were fifteen and *you* were the daddy. You would be powerless to decide what happens."

"What does that mean?" he asked again, irritated. "Really, Gramma, why can't you jus' say?"

"It means she can abort the baby. In case you don't know, abort means pull it out so it can't grow anymore. It means killin' it even before you know if it's a girl or a boy. The father gets no say."

"How come he gets no say?"

"It's not his body. It's *her* body. If her parents are willin' to drive her to where they abort babies, and if they give their permission, she can do it, and the boy might not even know. And sometimes the girl doesn't even need her parents' permission."

William clenched his hands into fists.

"But in the South, that's not what usually happens," Rebecca continued.

"What usually happens?"

"Around here, the girl and her parents usually decide to bring the baby into the world. However, once the child is born, the mother can make other decisions without the boy who fathered the child getting a say in them either. For example, she could decide to give the baby to somebody else. It might be that the boy would never get to see his son or daughter. He might never even know about it."

"That's not fair!" William interrupted.

"But if he does know about it . . . like most of 'em . . . the only thing the boy can do is ask a judge to let *him* raise the baby. He'd need to have his parents behind him on that or the judge would likely say no."

William didn't interrupt this time.

"But his parents might be mad," Rebecca went on, "because they'd know a lot of the work of raisin' the baby would fall on them. They might tell him if he wanted to keep it, he had to make sacrifices."

"What kind of sacrifices?"

"He might have to give up sports and come home right after school every day and mind the baby. If his mama didn't want to do it, he might have to wake up in the middle of the night to give the baby a bottle and change its diaper. Things like that."

"What if he doesn't want to raise up the baby but he wants it to be alive and he wants to see it sometimes?"

"He'd have nothin' to say about that. Maybe he'd get to see his baby, maybe not . . . If the girl keeps it, which is what usually happens, she could decide she didn't want the boy to ever see it."

"Can't the judge make her?"

"The judge might tell her to let him see the baby. But maybe she just won't. Then the boy would have to ask the court for help, and to do that, he'd have to spend money to hire a lawyer to get the judge to make the girl let him see his baby. And all that time they're fightin' in court, his baby is growing up without knowing his father."

"How much money does a lawyer cost?" William asked.

"Probably quite a bit. Depends on how stubborn the girl is and whether her family decides to fight the boy about it."

"Why would they do that?"

"Maybe they're mad that he got the girl pregnant," Rebecca said.

William didn't say anything.

"And speaking of money, the boy would owe the girl money for the baby, even if she never lets him see it . . . Now if he were a poor boy who had no money, there's not much the girl could do. But if the boy were like you, with a bank account, well . . ."

"I got a bank account?"

"All you kids have bank accounts. It's not a lot of money. But whatever is there, the judge could make you pay it month by month for the baby. So, it wouldn't be there for you when you need it for college or whatever."

William kicked the table leg.

Rebecca glared at him. "Watch out! I don't want my pies slidin' on the floor."

"It's not fair," William protested.

"You're old enough to know *fair* is not the point," Rebecca said sternly. "Reality is the point. And the reality is you would have no power. The girl would decide. I think that's what gets some folk mad as all get-out when a girl in high school gets pregnant. They don't like it when a girl has power, as she does under the law right now."

"Can't the law be changed?"

"Hope not," said Rebecca. "Woman's got a right to control her body."

"What about the boy? Why doesn't *he* have rights?"

"He does. He's got the right to keep his zipper zipped, if you know what I mean. Nine times out of ten, it's the boy who pushed the girl to get all this started."

"Well, I don't want none of that to happen to me," William said angrily, shoving the pies toward the center of the table.

"Most boys don't," Rebecca acknowledged. She turned off the burner under the last of the filling. It stopped bubbling in seconds.

"Fact is, most of the boys who start these babies don't help much after the child is born. The girl is on her own with only her family to help, *if* her family hasn't chucked her out. Lots of times the boy goes on as if nothin' happened. People don't gossip 'bout *him*. They gossip 'bout the baby's mama. That's not fair either, William . . . And don't forget, the girl and the boy are both at fault. Unless the boy forced her. Then it's a whole 'nother matter. Then he's a criminal."

"I don't wanna start any babies," William announced.

"Then don't," advised Rebecca. "It's on you."

William sat at the table for a while, long enough for Rebecca to lay the lattice on the first pie. Her pies had delicate crusts. She didn't work the dough much, to keep it from getting tough, she always said. Rebecca felt there was nothing more the mark of pie-making failure than a heavy, stiff crust.

"I'm goin' home," William said tonelessly.

He had a six-mile walk if he didn't wait for his daddy to come in from work. But he decided this new information would take some time to reflect upon.

———◦———

Once her youngest daughter was back in Minnesota, Maureen felt Annie had a lot to make up for. All three of her daughters made her wish again that she'd borne only sons.

Since Annie's disappearance, Maureen had stopped attending Mass on Sundays, despite the sin of it. That was partly because of Patrick's ordeal and slow improvement—a calvary God alone understood—but it was also because she could not bear to look her fellow worshippers in the eye after what Annie did. What must they think of a mother whose daughter ran off in secret to a state a thousand miles away? She'd been unchaperoned, and she'd stolen money to pay for the trip.

"Annie's a complete and total failure," she told Tom.

"My Annie a failure? Nuts," Tom said. He went back to reading *Farm Journal.*

"She makes me so mad," Maureen insisted. "Sometimes I think she's not worth the powder to blow her to hell."

Tom didn't react.

"This was the worst Thanksgiving of my life," she added.

"That Annie's doin' or Patrick's gettin' sick again?" Tom queried, looking up.

"Both. But at least it isn't Patrick's fault."

"Then whose fault is it?" Tom asked.

She didn't like his attitude, so she left the room. Maybe, Maureen thought, in the weeks and months ahead she could find it in her heart to forgive Annie. But not yet. For one thing, several women from church had called to interrogate her. There was no other word for it. They fished for information she couldn't or wouldn't provide. Helen Swanson made so bold as to ask outright if Annie was pregnant. The nerve of the woman. After ending the call, Maureen crossed Helen off the list of those she would allow to help with Patrick. She had always held such a high opinion of Helen because of her dedication to St. Philomena's choir—but no longer. Mean was mean, and not to be forgotten.

In the weeks that followed, Annie tended to Patrick and did whatever else she was told. She was allowed no phone calls or visits with friends. She fell asleep with Patrick in her arms at night and sometimes took him to her bedroom after supper, giving Maureen a badly needed respite. Maureen hadn't slept well since Patrick came home after Thanksgiving. Her schedule was hectic, especially on days when the physical therapist came to help Patrick exercise.

They worked on what the therapist called "gross motor skills," most of them still beyond Patrick's capability. Maureen watched her sit him up from a reclining position over and over. Eventually he would learn to crawl, stand, and walk by himself—all things other babies learned in a shorter time. But the important thing was not how long it took Patrick. The important thing was that he be able to get there at all. The therapist tried to stretch the sessions a little more every time, so the movements would become ingrained in Patrick's memory and ultimately become part of what he took for granted, like any other child. Maureen felt energized after Patrick's therapy, and worked with him herself, mimicking what she had observed. She loved him more every day, even when he fussed or screamed bloody murder, but especially when he managed a smile.

Out of the blue, Charlie got a call from Aaron Short, who introduced himself as guardian ad litem for Charlie's biological son. Mr. Short didn't have to tell Charlie who he was.

"I keep in touch through my father," Charlie told him. "He talks to his friend Ben Johnson all the time. So, he pretty much knows what's going on in the Haig household."

"Then your father has probably also made you aware that your son was hospitalized for pneumonia over Thanksgiving," Aaron Short said.

"Yes, sir, I am aware," Charlie said. "I was relieved to hear my son's been discharged since then, and that he seems to be doing OK."

"He's doing OK for the moment. They think the pneumonia was probably viral. He'd been vaccinated for bacterial pneumonia before he left the NICU the first time. I'm glad, by the way, to hear you call him *my son*."

"He is my son, sir."

"Well, that's the way the court is going to see it when I make my report about custody. Maureen Haig talks about him as if he were a permanent part of her family. I can't seem to get her to understand otherwise."

"My father is looking for permanent custody too, whenever the question comes before the court," Charlie said.

He sat on a bench outside the military treatment center on base. He'd just been examined to see how his back was holding up. His superiors wanted him looked at every two weeks to make sure he could handle the heat and stress of the program before they sent him off to Fort Jackson for DI training.

"Does that mean you yourself are not looking for permanent custody?" Aaron asked.

"I don't think I could make it work, sir. It would threaten both my marriage and my career in the army."

"I see," Aaron said.

Charlie let a silence fall between them.

Aaron Short broke it. "Can I ask you something else?"

"What would that be, sir?"

"I'd like to meet in person with you and your wife. I could fly out there, if you'd be amenable. I'd like to talk to you both about the court hearing that will eventually determine where your son will grow up, where his permanent home will be."

"I'm not sure my wife will want to be involved in that, sir," Charlie said.

"I'm not talking about tomorrow. The hearing might be several months from now. But I need to prepare a report outlining the possibilities before us and giving the judge my assessment of which situation would be optimal for your son. And to do that, I need to get to know you and your wife. This is not a typical custody case."

"A few months probably won't make much difference, sir. My wife wants to put the whole thing behind her."

"Legally, she can do that. But it's not going to be so easy for you, Charlie. If you two face things together, sooner or later the court will want to know where you stand because you, sir, are the logical parents. You're young enough to give your son his best chance in life."

"My wife doesn't see him as her son. I do. It's hard for us to face things together, sir, given that difference in our attitudes."

"Do you think she'd be willing to come before the court and explain what happened from her point of view?"

"I doubt it," Charlie said. "She can't hardly bring herself to talk about it with me."

"If I came out there and spoke to you both, in private, at a time and place that's comfortable for you, would that be feasible?"

"I can ask her, but I can't tell you now whether she'd agree."

"Would you ask her, please? To tell you the truth, Charlie, I want to explore every option for the best life your child can have, and to do that, I've just got to talk to you two together."

"I'll ask her, sir."

"OK. We'll leave it at that. I'll call you back."

"Let me call you."

"OK, Charlie. You call me."

———•◦•———

Claire received a passel of texts from Annie in January.

patrick too much I need help

It was late afternoon. Annie was probably just home from school and already assuming responsibility for Patrick.

I'm the school pariah even Lacey won't talk to me.

Claire knew she should respond, but what could she say? She also knew if Woodrow saw Annie's texts, they'd upset him no end. He might get into his precious truck, drive to Minnesota, grab Charlie's baby, and bring him back to Lafayette just in time to get himself arrested. Claire knew that fear was irrational. Woodrow wouldn't do something so reckless. Still, the thought unnerved her.

Their own baby had started to kick. Every night in a ritual, Woodrow kissed her stomach, murmuring proposed names, supposedly to get the baby's opinion. Gad . . . Barnabas . . . Ephraim . . . Hepseba . . . Ishmael. The preponderance of boys' names suggested he wanted a son.

"We're going to have a little girl," she teased him.

"Hope she looks like you," he came back. Always that grin and the melting look on his face.

"I never thought you'd come round to me," he said once.

"You gave me no encouragement," she pointed out.

"That woulda sent you flyin' for sure."

She had no answer, especially since she hadn't imagined life with anyone could be this sweet. She worried, though, that Woodrow would make Charlie's son the new focus of his life, if he got hold of him.

In February, when Claire was about to enter the sixth month of her pregnancy, Woodrow announced he was prepared to stop having sex completely so as not to alarm the baby. Claire's obstetrician said not to worry, and to just refrain from wild and wooly stuff. Woodrow relished that phrase.

One day, Claire brought up Annie's situation with Rebecca, who was kneading bread at the time.

"Not right, what they're doin' to your sister," Rebecca agreed.

"I don't know how to help," Claire said.

"Not much you can do 'til the child gets down here."

"That's the thing. I'm not eager for him to get down here."

Rebecca sighed. "You're leery of lovin' somebody who's an abstraction, and it's no wonder. All you hear is what Annie tells you, and she's overwhelmed. I don't understand that there aren't other people Maureen can call on. I thought Minnesota was supposed to have programs for everything."

"I don't understand either," Claire admitted. "As for empathizing with Theresa and Charlie's baby, I'm feeling short."

Rebecca smiled. "We don't feel the same for everybody, and not everybody has the same capacity. Take Woodrow. He always brought the injured bird home. He'd patch it up, feed it, wait 'til it could fly again. It's his nature. Fixin' things, I mean."

"It's not my nature," Claire said.

Rebecca took her hands out of the old ceramic bowl her great-great grandmother had brought over from England. She covered the bowl's exterior with a clean cloth and washed her hands at the sink.

"Person don't know her nature 'til it's tested, Claire. Wait on this. See what happens. You're roilin' yourself into a stew 'fore you even know what's what. Patrick might charm the socks off ya."

Claire stood up. "I'm not good at waiting," she said.

Rebecca shook her head. "That's 'cause you got too much imagination and hardly any faith. Now *hold* on," she said, noticing the way Claire's face darkened. "I mean faith in Woodrow. Faith in your marriage. Faith in this family. You know, we Coles stick together. Even my other daughters-in-law, they don't like me much. They think I've got altogether too much say because I run the business . . . And they don't approve when a body's not a Baptist. I was surprised they even came to your weddin', to be honest. But they know, every one of 'em, that I'd be there, the whole family'd be there if anything happened to them. I don't get the impression your people up North come runnin' when there's trouble. They're spread out, your mama tells me. And they're scared stiff of her . . . I do admire some things about Maureen. But she's not the star at the center of her solar system."

Yes, Claire thought. A mother's the sun at the center. She and Theresa and Annie were planets that flew into space when the center would not hold. "I don't know," Claire said, mainly to end the conversation.

"Talk it over with Woodrow. Important thing in a marriage is to talk everything out. Consider each other's feelings. You might be worryin' 'bout something's not gonna happen."

"You mean, if Patrick doesn't come here?" Claire suggested.

"Or if he comes here, and it's not like you expect."

———•◦•———

Yankees are quick to think the worst of the South. That's one of the first things a Southern boy learns as he comes to recognize that the war between the states never did end. The howitzers fell silent more than a century ago and now sit idle as statues, but the assumptions by outsiders regarding the culture and morality of the Southern way of life endures to this day. Woodrow saw it in Aaron Short's appraisal of the quality of care available to a child with Down syndrome in Lafayette County.

He called Aaron twice a week to check on his thinking. Woodrow knew that Annie was miserable, and the Haig household was stressed to the limit. Aaron Short knew it too, and so did Ben Johnson. That level of stress couldn't be good for Charlie's son, Woodrow pointed out. But Aaron wouldn't budge about his requirements, and, between the lines, he gave Woodrow the impression that he thought folks in Lafayette County weren't organized enough to do the best that could be done.

"You think we're yahoos," Woodrow submitted.

"Not at all," Aaron said without missing a beat. You couldn't insult the man.

"I think we deserve a chance before it's too late," Woodrow asserted.

He was well aware, and sure that Aaron was too, that time militated against moving a child. The longer it took, the more likely it was that Charlie's son would end up stuck in Minnesota. Woodrow suspected Aaron wanted Theresa to change her mind. He didn't think that was likely to happen.

It didn't help Aaron's conscience to know that Tom thought of his grandson as a liability and a hindrance, while Maureen looked on him as a test of her moral rectitude. In Woodrow's opinion, they were both irrational people, and they were both too old to raise Charlie's son. But he didn't say that to Aaron.

Rebecca didn't help the Coles' case when she told Aaron—in a conversation to which Woodrow was not privy at the time—that she didn't believe in interventions. "He'll be somebody's burden all his life, Aaron. Way I see it, we'll help Patrick's medical problems however much we can, but mostly we'd just let him be. He'll get more pleasure blowin' dandelion seeds than he would with a world of interventions."

"He needs to learn the basics," Aaron said.

"Even if learning's torture?" Rebecca asked. "Maureen told me about his exercises."

"Everything will be harder for him. The exercises come backed by experience. That's why he needs help from specialists," Aaron insisted.

Woodrow damn near hit the roof when he heard about that back and forth.

"Don't you lecture me," his mother warned. "You think I'm gonna spend day after day drivin' back and forth to Tuscaloosa just so Patrick can sit with some kid fresh out of disability school and learn to say 'Ooooo'? We're practical people, Woodrow. We know when academics take over, they can muck things up more'n anyone."

"That's true," Woodrow admitted, "but this guy holds all the cards. He's guardian ad litem. That means we can't get Charlie's son to come live with us unless Aaron agrees."

Claire came back from her daily walk in the middle of their argument. She closed the kitchen door quickly to keep the chill outside. She was in a good mood. She moved differently these days. She carried a sketchbook and drew pictures in charcoal and couldn't stop smiling as signs of spring appeared.

"What's going on?" Claire asked, noting Rebecca's expression.

"Patrick," Rebecca said, "and who gets him."

"Ah," Claire said, rolling her eyes as she looked at Woodrow.

Aging is the process of a body losing itself bit by bit, like limbs falling from a dying tree. Maureen would soon turn fifty-seven, Tom seventy-one. But Tom looked and acted more like sixty, while Maureen ached in every appendage.

She knew she was far too young for the way she felt. The past six months had put a decade on her body. But aches and pains didn't matter. Maureen was determined to match the standard her mother had set when her older brother Peter contracted polio. Peter spent a year in an iron lung and more years getting his strength back as he learned to walk again with the help of crutches and braces. Like her mother, Maureen was determined to labor indefatigably in the Lord's vineyard and never, ever give up.

After Peter was released from the awful breathing contraption that kept him alive, her sainted mother had dedicated herself to her son's every waking moment. It was as if her younger children ceased to exist. In the first years of her life, Maureen hardly had a mother.

Now, she'd become a woman of legend herself, chosen by the Lord to perform the impossible. She would teach Patrick to walk and run and jump, to flex his muscles and his mind, to become even better than *normal*, whatever normal was, and she would accomplish those feats as her mother had accomplished hers, with the *Grace that brought us safe thus far*, with amazing grace that must and would be sufficient.

It didn't even matter that the only church friend who regularly helped with Patrick was Irene Overdale. The others had mostly fallen away. But Maureen didn't complain. She carried on.

One Wednesday afternoon in March, halfway through the penitential season of Lent, Irene held a giggling Patrick in her arms while Maureen baked. It was such a joy to fill the kitchen with delicious smells again.

"I have news," Irene said, making funny faces at the baby.

"What?" Maureen asked, not expecting much.

A long silence ensued before Irene filled it. "This is hard to say, Maureen. It never seemed the right time. But I have to tell you. Jerry and I are planning to move."

"Where?" Maureen asked, flummoxed.

"We're not sure yet. Jerry says he's waited all these years to retire, and now he wants to live it up while we still have our health. He's partial to Hilton Head. For the golf. Or maybe Florida or Mobile. I keep telling him we should stay away from the coast with all this climate change, but he's bound and determined to live on the water. Or at least within walking distance of a sandy beach."

"Is this a second home for the winter?" Maureen wondered aloud.

"No," Irene admitted. "It's going to be year-round. Jerry thinks winters are too long here and our taxes are way too high. He says we can't afford the cost of two houses. I tried to tell him I don't want to give up our roots, especially our friends at St. Philomena."

"What did he say to that?"

"He says we'll make new friends and find a new church. He's never been sentimental, you know. He joined St. Philomena for the business contacts, and now he doesn't need them anymore."

"Irene," Maureen got out before she became too choked up to continue. She had to sit down.

Her friend looked mortified. "I'm sorry, Maureen. I really am. This is a lot to spring on you. But it looks like it's happening soon, and I didn't want you finding out from somebody else."

Maureen took a deep breath and tried to control herself. "When?" she asked quietly.

"We're going to look at places from now until June. If we find something we like, Jerry wants to remodel top to bottom. He'll hire a contractor and when they're done, we'll move in sometime around September. That's his plan."

"How do *you* feel?" Maureen asked. "Doesn't your opinion count?"

"To tell you the truth, I'm up for a little adventure," Irene admitted.

"I'll miss you like crazy," Maureen pointed out.

"I'll miss you too," Irene said, "but other people will step in. You'll see."

Maureen tried to hold onto her smile. "Lately, I've only had a couple of volunteers. You've been the most reliable."

Irene didn't respond. Maureen couldn't help but wonder how much of the assistance she'd received in the beginning had diminished because of the scandal brought on by Annie running off to Alabama. That, or her friends found it harder than they'd anticipated to find time for somebody else's special needs baby.

Maureen couldn't stand the thought of losing Irene. It shouldn't matter, she reminded herself. Somehow, the Lord would provide. The Lord had a plan, surely. She just didn't know it yet.

After Irene departed, Maureen got down on the living room rug with Patrick and watched him wave his arms and legs, using his tummy as an anchor. Zip came near and sniffed. Patrick flailed in Zip's direction. The tips of his fingers landed on Zip's nose.

"No!" yelled Maureen. "No nose touching." She grabbed an antiseptic tissue and wiped Patrick's fingers. He protested and cried, but then forgot.

"My mother will never give up," Theresa told Charlie.

As far as Maureen was concerned, the moment of conception produced a being that belonged eternally to Theresa, and was as precious as Theresa, even if that being were smaller than a grain of salt. Theresa reported to it, like a worker to her boss. Maureen Haig could see things no other way.

Therefore, in her mother's view, the baby she called Patrick could not be shuffled off to someone else just because it would take extra work to raise him, or because there would be no end to raising him, or because he interfered with Theresa's vision of her life with her husband, or because Theresa simply did not want a son she had been forced to bear.

"She thinks I'm on the hook and can't get off. That's why I won't ever go back to Minnesota."

"If you like, I could check the mail from now on and throw your mother's letters away so you wouldn't have to see them," Charlie offered.

"Yes, do that," Theresa agreed.

"Or you could read her letters, look at the photos, maybe answer her. You know how I feel about my son," Charlie said, opening the refrigerator to retrieve a beer.

"You can feel about him however you want. I know you talk about him all the time when your father calls. I know Woodrow wants to bring him to Lafayette. I know you want me to meet with Aaron Short to talk about taking him ourselves. I just don't want to be sucked into any of it."

"No one's tellin' us we have to raise him," Charlie said, uncapping his Red Horse and pouring the amber contents into one of the glasses Theresa kept in the freezer.

"Oh, yes. Oh my, yes! He's a weapon, Charlie. If I were still in St. Dominic, my mother would get the whole town to hound me. But she can't because I'm here. So, she writes letters that are really aimed at you. She'll come between us if you let her."

"I won't let her," Charlie made clear. "But I think you should answer one of her letters, even if it's only to tell her what you're tellin' me."

"That would feed her obsession," Theresa maintained.

"This—whatever we're doin' now—feeds resentment. That's no good either," Charlie returned. "You can't change the past."

Theresa sat in a rocking chair Charlie had moved into the kitchen, next to a window looking out at their garden.

"I'm not trying to change the past," she said, moving rhythmically back and forth. "But we've got our own baby to worry about. I'm so scared something will go wrong again."

Charlie set his glass on the table and moved toward the window, kneeling in front of his wife. He put his hands on her pregnant belly.

"We won't let that happen," he assured her. "You've had all the tests."

"I don't trust them," she said.

The lone obstetrician at the base hospital said everything looked fine. Theresa had even flown to Atlanta to have the tests repeated, and she got the same results. The DNA screening checked out normal. The ultrasound looked normal. But she had lost her optimism. Everything and everyone aroused suspicion.

"I'd appreciate it if you'd pick up the mail from now on," she told Charlie. "When you see my mother's handwriting, toss the envelope. Toss anything from Claire too."

"Christ, the women in your family are hard on each other!" Charlie exclaimed as he got up. "Why don't you like Claire?"

"She deserted the family when I needed her," Theresa shot back. "Your mother deserted you. You know what that feels like."

"Haven't you and Claire deserted Annie?" Charlie asked. "My dad says she's having a tough time." Theresa didn't answer.

Charlie considered desertion a puzzle beyond his ability to comprehend, as Theresa well knew. But he was always careful not to accuse Theresa of abandoning his son, not when so much had been forced on her.

"You know," he suggested, "being sisters and pregnant at the same time, you and Claire could share the excitement."

"I'm not excited," Theresa returned. "I'm too scared."

Charlie put his hand at the back of her neck, leaned down and kissed her head.

"We'll be OK," he promised.

———•◦•———

Patrick's tricycle arrived via FedEx, its cardboard container deposited on the front porch by a muscular young man who scurried into his truck when he saw Zip rushing toward him. His vehicle left a cloud of dust as he drove away. Nothing for the recipient to sign, Maureen concluded.

She decided to let the box sit outside until Tom came back in. Patrick wouldn't be able to mount his new tricycle anytime soon, but she liked the idea that it would be ready when he was. Designed to help him develop the essential motor skills he would need to catch up to others his age, the bike was a symbol of progress in Patrick's recovery. Maureen needed it to be there, if only to look at.

According to materials she'd received in the mail, her grandson could likely start using the bike at age two and a half to three. It would improve his balance and coordination, and give him a sense of freedom. His self-esteem would soar. Maureen planned to have Tom install concrete or blacktop over the entire gravel driveway all the way to the mailbox. That smooth-pedaling distance would expand Patrick's sense of the world. Like every kid, he needed a big horizon.

Patrick was now eight months out of the hospital, and therefore eight months was his real "adjusted" age, according to the specialists. They felt he was progressing remarkably, given his rocky start. Every time a doctor talked like that, Maureen beamed.

She had already purchased a nest swing, a sort of hammock shaped in a circle that Tom would attach to trees in the yard as soon as he could find the time. In it, Patrick could study the sky, the birds, and the hanging branches as he watched summer take its course.

He had an unfortunate tendency to look down a lot of the time. But in his nest swing, he would naturally look up. She would read to him after settling him into the swing, or he could take naps in it. Maureen had all kinds of plans.

This warm June day, though, she spent alone in the kitchen. St. Philomena's Spring Festival was over, and though a success compared to previous years, it had not brought in enough money to pay for the second quarter installment on the church's roof repairs. To make up the difference, the fundraising committee decided to hold a baking contest.

Maureen planned to recreate a cake her mother had made, one she could still taste if she thought hard enough. There was liqueur in the filling, possibly Vandermint. The recipe included melted dark chocolate as well as butter and cream. There was coffee in it too.

Ben Johnson stopped by in time to test the results of her first experiment.

"Cake with coffee and liqueur is nothing to sniff at," he said. "Especially if a cup of your fine brew comes with it. Therefore, I offer myself as a taster."

When Ben had consumed the last crumbs, he asked how Patrick was doing.

"Annie has him upstairs," Maureen replied. "School is out, so she's here the whole day."

"Mind if I go up?" Ben always requested, never assumed. Maureen appreciated his manners.

"Go," she said, waving her arm toward the stairs.

When he appeared in the doorway, Ben found Annie in her bedroom with Patrick, holding him in place with her left arm while trying to turn the pages of a book with her right hand. Ben peered sideways to see what it was. Jane Austen, *Sense and Sensibility*. He approved.

Annie looked up. "Just the man I was hoping to see," she said. Ben smiled back. "Did you know my sister Claire's having a baby any day?" Annie asked him.

"Maureen didn't mention it," he replied, settling into a chair. "But I've heard all about it from Woodrow."

"I wish I were there," Annie said ruefully. Ben said nothing. "That's why I want to hire you," Annie added.

"Hire me for what?" Ben asked.

"As my attorney," she replied, reaching into her pocket. "Here's a dollar." She handed him a crumpled bill. He took it.

"That means you're my attorney from this moment on," Annie said.

"Well, that depends," Ben told her. "What kind of legal advice are you seeking?"

"I don't want advice. I've already made up my mind. I want action," she said.

"As in . . ."

"As in I want to divorce my parents and move to Alabama."

"Annie—"

"You know the school year is over—"

"Meaning you've got three years left."

"What do you think my grade point average was for the whole of freshman year?"

Ben stared at her.

"B-minus," she informed him.

"Is that so bad, given all that's happened?" Ben asked.

"It's a fake B-minus. At best, maybe a C." Ben continued to sit, mute. "I'm not a C student, Mr. Johnson."

"You've never called me Mr. Johnson before," Ben pointed out.

"Nobody's ever called me a B student before," she said, growing vehement. "I'm an A student. But you'd never know it. I didn't even get to do all the reading in my courses. My math is worse. I got a fake C. It should have been a D or an F."

Patrick began to stir, twisting his head from one side to the other. His little fists poked the air.

"Why would your school give you fake grades?" Ben asked.

"Because they don't want anyone to know I'm not getting a good education. It might make the school look bad. They don't care about reality. Just the way things look."

Patrick began to cry. Annie pulled his head against her chest. That soothed him enough to stop crying for the moment. "Tell me, does a kid deserve a good education?" Annie demanded, "Or is that only if her family is not a mess?"

Ben looked her in the eye. "You deserve a good education, Annie. You're entitled to one."

"So will you take my case?" Annie pleaded, lowering her voice to calm Patrick. "I want to file a lawsuit right away so I can be with Claire and Woodrow before the end of summer."

Ben shook his head. "Before we talk about a lawsuit, Annie, perhaps we should try another tactic."

"What?" Annie asked as Patrick began to squirm again. "Look, he wants out of my arms." She set him on the floor.

"Negotiation," Ben said. "I've always found that bringing two sides together to talk things out, as long as both parties are willing, is preferable in the long run to filing a lawsuit. Lawsuits bring out the worst in people."

"I figure a lawsuit is what I need to get their attention," Annie argued.

"But isn't that why you just hired me? Let me work on this before we take any drastic steps."

Annie nodded. "But there's got to be a limit," she insisted. "I can't wait 'til fall."

Ben nodded. "I understand," he said. "Time is of the essence."

"Yes!" Annie agreed.

Patrick raised his arms, wanting Annie to pick him up again. Ben watched them, noting Patrick's insistence and Annie's quick response. Annie was Patrick's lodestar, he thought. But she was also a child herself.

9

Claire was no expert on childbirth. At four in the morning, she wasn't sure if she were dreaming the ripples that shot from her ribs to her knees, or if they were cousins of the pointless, random pains that had plagued her on and off for weeks.

By five o'clock, she was sure. No longer able to lie beside Woodrow, his arm around her middle, she extricated herself from the bed and sat in a rocking chair, watching him sleep. She was in labor. She was sure of it now. Claire swayed front to back, letting her feet alternately lift from the floor and return again. Her spine hurt. Her stomach rumbled like an underwater volcano.

She turned the clock on the shelf. 5:06 a.m. Another wave arrived.

It was still dark. Birds were starting to rustle outside the open window, softly at first, the beginning of their morning rituals. She tried to make them out by their calls to each other, to remember their species names, to concentrate on something other than the pain, but she couldn't recall a single avian variety by its designation or song. Their flutterings mirrored the flutterings inside her belly, and as their sounds grew louder, so did the agitation inside her, slowly building to a crescendo . . .

A major tremor hit at 5:21. Fifteen minutes apart and getting stronger. A few feet away, Woodrow slept entirely unaware.

Their baby was a girl, she knew. She wanted a girl, though a girl frightened her. Where was her template for raising a girl? Woodrow didn't care, he said, boy or girl. She didn't believe him.

Whatever the gender, an infant would be born to them this very day.

Their child would arrive in spring, nature's favored season for new life. A spasm ran through her. She gasped.

The internet had informed Claire that Alabama was no place to have a baby. The state of Alabama had the highest rate of infant mortality in the country. She wondered if she was insane to have married a Southerner, to trust his birthplace to protect her life and the life of her soon-to-be-born infant daughter.

She liked her doctor, though, a woman in her fifties who had "caught babies," as she put it, for more than twenty-five years. She more than liked her. She had confidence in her, and she knew the hospital had emergency obstetric services on an upper floor in case something went awry.

She also knew that she was perfectly healthy. She didn't smoke, drank alcohol sparingly before she got pregnant, didn't drink at all during her pregnancy, gained the right amount of weight, walked several miles every day, slept well, had normal blood pressure. Her ultrasounds looked good. Her amnio checked out.

On top of that, she realized that worry was normal. All the books implied it with their lists of things to do and things to avoid.

Yet, though no one ever wrote it out explicitly, having a first child at her advanced age—she was an *elderly primigravida*—presented a serious complication, perhaps reason enough to panic. To have her daughter here in a world far from the people and places she'd known for most of her life turned panic into terror. She couldn't help it. Another spasm hit.

Claire floated between contractions. It was hard to concentrate on how far apart they were. She wondered if she should rouse Woodrow. But she didn't want to worry him prematurely.

Then he stirred. His hand searched the sheet beside him. Finding nothing, he pulled himself up in their bed and saw her.

"Is it time? Why didn't you wake me?"

Claire smiled, or grimaced—she wasn't sure.

"Yes," she told him.

He rushed toward her.

She felt another contraction, this one of a higher order and awfully close to the last. All hell was breaking loose.

"You want to get dressed?" Woodrow asked.

She shook her head no, bent over in the chair, and felt herself picked up. Woodrow carried her down the stairs. Her nightgown was wet. Rebecca appeared from the kitchen. Woodrow talked. Claire couldn't talk.

"Missus Cole, would you like some ice chips?"

Where was she? Were they in the hospital already? Woodrow stood next to the gurney and held her hand. Claire opened her mouth, and a nurse whose face reminded her of someone whose name she couldn't remember smiled down warmly at her.

Oh, yes, they were in the obstetrics ward. She remembered the ER's automatic doors. Before that, the bumpy ride on that stretch of road that seemed to magnify everything. Woodrow had been driving.

The doctor fastened a white mask on her face as she entered.

"Shall we see how you're doin', sweetie?" she asked before lifting the drapes over Claire's legs and disappearing headfirst.

"You're more than halfway, but I'm not quite sure about the size of the baby's head. I'd like to get some pictures."

Claire heard Woodrow say something.

"We're goin' to do an ultrasound. OK, Claire?"

She nodded. The bed moved, rolling of its own volition. Woodrow held her right hand. A nurse on the other side put fingers on her wrist.

Scoot over, they said. She tried to scoot over. People took hold of her in numerous places, and she found herself on another surface, hard and unforgiving.

"The head's in the right place, but it's big for the pelvis. Cervix is fully dilated. We might have to consider a cesarean if she doesn't progress."

"Then do it!" That must be Woodrow yelling at the doctor. So much for catching babies.

What came next? She couldn't remember. This was too hard. She couldn't think of anything except when it would end.

They were rolling again, down another corridor, lights flickering. It was a different room entirely, sterile, an operating room, metallic. It smelled of disinfectant.

"The baby's pulse is good. We'll give it another ten minutes."

Her beautiful daughter would have to be pried, yanked, maybe bribed to come out. Otherwise cut out. Woodrow looked awful. His face contorted, as if she were looking at him through wavy glass. She lifted her head and caught a smile she didn't believe she'd ever seen on him before. She almost laughed. If that smile had been meant to reassure her, it failed miserably.

Then she fell back on the table. Ten minutes was way, way too long.

"I'm dying," she got out.

"No one's dyin' on my watch," her doctor said, as Claire stared at the ceiling.

Time stretched. She didn't think she could go on. Then she felt something wet.

"A girl. You have a little girl, Miss Claire."

A girl. It was over. Their baby was born, and it was a girl. She'd always known it was a girl.

They wiped her daughter dry, sucked the mucus from her mouth, and set her on Claire's abdomen, while beneath the drapery, things were happening that Claire could not feel. She was alive from the baby up, the mother of this absolutely adorable creature whose skin had turned to velvet. The baby's gaze moved back and forth. Her tiny face scrunched up. There were indentations in her forehead. Her eyes engulfed her face.

"We're cuttin' the cord now, Claire," her doctor said. She heard the scissors snap.

"What'll you name her, Miss Claire?" asked one of the nurses.

Claire looked at Woodrow, who came into sharp focus for the first time since they'd left their bedroom. He looked back at her, apparently speechless.

She remembered. He would name a boy. She would name a girl.

"Ariane," Claire said. "Ariane Cole."

"That's a name pretty as she is," Woodrow said, grinning.

The doctor lifted her head from beneath the drapes. "We're going to have to stitch you up a bit," she announced, "but you came through just fine, Claire."

"Mmmmm," Claire said, kissing Ariane's forehead.

———·•·———

"The Olsons donated forty-six pounds on Tuesday. That brings the total to over six hundred pounds," Maureen announced as she set a platter of scrambled eggs on the table.

"Pounds? You mean British money?" Tom asked, shoveling half the eggs on his plate.

"You know better than that," Maureen snapped.

"She means pounds of food for the food shelf," Annie informed her father.

"Guess I know what comes next," Tom observed. "I'm supposed to buy cases of this and that and deliver it to the church where they'll weigh it, so everybody knows what number of pounds the Haigs donated. You ladies are not stupid, I'll give you that."

"Generosity needs a nudge, and the best nudge is competition," Maureen concurred.

"So, how many pounds you want me to get?" he asked, reaching for the bacon. Maureen put two slices of toasted sourdough bread next to his plate.

"Sixty, at least," she replied, "Here's a list."

Tom read it out. "Old-fashioned oatmeal in cylinder boxes, largest size. Cans of coffee. Canned condensed milk. Cloth bags of beans, barley, and rice. Soups, all kinds you can store on a shelf. Powdered milk. Canned tuna and salmon. Breadcrumbs. Tartar sauce. Also bars of soap, toilet paper, paper towels, and packages of diapers."

Maureen poured more coffee.

"Soap and paper are not food," Tom pointed out.

"People need them," she said.

"And diapers can't weigh much. You'll spend a lot and not get equal credit in pounds," he added.

"Don't be such a miser. People need them."

"If they can't afford diapers, they shouldn't have kids."

"You sound like a Republican. Do you want them getting abortions because they can't afford a baby?"

"I *am* a Republican," thundered Tom. "So are you!"

"You think too much about money," Maureen retorted.

"You may have noticed, my darling bride, that now is not a good time for farmers. We were lucky to break even last year."

"There've been plenty of good years in the past, and there'll be plenty more to come," Maureen said.

"I don't see why we should buy anyone disposable diapers. Cloth diapers were good enough when I was born. Good enough for our own kids, as I recall."

"Then you're not a true Christian," Maureen concluded. "Nobody uses cloth diapers anymore."

Tom stopped arguing. For a brief moment, the kitchen was quiet, until Patrick squealed with pleasure as he threw a handful of scrambled egg on the floor, part of a game with Zip, who scarfed it up the moment it hit and licked the residue.

Patrick squealed again, unhappily this time. Annie wiped his nose.

"He might be coming down with a cold," she informed her mother, feeding Patrick the tiniest bits of buttered bread with the crusts cut off.

The phone on the wall rang. Annie rushed to answer it. "Annie, honey, that you?" said the voice.

"Woodrow!" Annie gushed.

"Got news, sweetheart . . . Claire had our baby last night."

"Whew!" Annie whooped. "Wow. Ohhhh, Woodrow, is it a boy or girl?"

"A beautiful little girl. Looks like her mama, for sure."

"What's her name?"

"Ariane. Seven pounds, two ounces."

"Are you home already?"

"No, we're at the hospital. Your parents there?"

Annie looked at the table. She put the phone to her chest so what she said wouldn't be audible.

311

"Claire and Woodrow's baby was born," she whispered. "Seven pounds, two ounces. A girl."

Her parents stared at her. Neither got up. Even Patrick seemed to have caught the drama of the moment. He stopped throwing bits of toast at Zip.

"Aren't you going to say something?" Annie asked. When they didn't respond, she got back to Woodrow.

"Ah, they were here just a moment ago."

"You tell 'em, OK?" Woodrow interrupted.

"Sure, I'll do that," Annie said. "How's Claire?"

"Mighty tuckered. It took all day. She's asleep now, and the baby's under lights for jaundice. I'm goin' back and forth between 'em in a state of awe and amazement. Never thought I'd be a daddy again."

Annie smiled, and Patrick seemed to take the smile as a gift for him. He giggled in response and raised his hands, a signal he wanted out of the high chair and into his favorite person's arms.

"I'll call back," Woodrow said, "when Claire's awake and eaten something."

"OK," Annie whispered. She put the receiver into its cradle and moved toward Patrick, untied the towels that kept him attached to the high chair, and pulled him up as he smashed tiny fingers against her cheeks and nose.

"Did you get that?" Annie asked her dad.

Tom nodded. "Seems I'm a grandfather again."

Maureen's face fell into her hands. She emitted a cry, rose, and ran out of the kitchen. Annie turned toward her mother's rushing form.

"Leave her be," Tom said.

Patrick began to whimper. The phone rang again, and Annie answered. Finally, it was Ben Johnson. He'd be over to the farm this evening, if that was OK with her parents.

"Yes, it's OK," Annie assured him without asking anyone. She hung up and faced her father.

"Who was that?" he asked.

"Ben Johnson," she said.

"What's he want?"

"He wants to talk to you and Mother tonight."

Annie left the kitchen to hold Patrick on her bed upstairs for a nap. He slept in fits and never made it through the night. She needed to lie down with him, or he would scream them both to exhaustion.

Patrick woke from his nap an hour later, most of which Annie had spent reading *Madame Bovary*. Tragic story of a brainless woman, in Annie's opinion, but she liked the way the author put things.

A clang of metal on metal had awakened Patrick. Annie carried him downstairs where she encountered several tin buckets, a pile of old towels and washcloths, sponges, two kinds of detergent—clear and blue—a gallon of white vinegar, and a mop. Her mother was cleaning the kitchen, which she tended to do when overwrought.

"Why are you upset?" Annie asked.

"Wouldn't you be upset if your daughter had a baby off the grandfather of the baby's cousin who is right there in your arms at this very moment?"

"It's a *new baby*! Can't you be happy for them?"

"Not one word of this to anyone, you understand? You will *not* tell your friends that your sister had a baby down South with those Southern people and their incest and their heathen ways. The neighbors don't need to find out."

"Incest?" Annie repeated incredulously. "There's no blood relation between Claire and Woodrow. Besides, I don't have friends anymore."

Maureen didn't answer. Annie kissed Patrick's cheek.

"If you could fight so hard for Patrick's life, why can't you welcome this new baby?" Annie asked.

"Because I'm embarrassed," her mother admitted. "If you tell people, I'll be publicly embarrassed. So don't you say one word about Mary's baby to anybody. Do you hear me?"

Annie kissed Patrick's forehead. He had stopped fussing and was now intent on reaching for a sunbeam on the counter. She decided to take him back upstairs.

"Ben Johnson's coming over tonight," she told her mother on her way out of the kitchen. "He wants to talk to you and Dad."

Ben Johnson, Tom, and Maureen sat at the kitchen table as always, but there was no idle chatter this warm Friday evening. Commodity prices, weather predictions, land sales, tariffs, and whatever else served as topics of interest in farm country didn't enter the conversation. Tom and Maureen didn't even tell Ben about the new baby, though Ben had already heard from Woodrow, who'd called near dawn.

"Remember, I'm not paying you to work for Maureen anymore," Tom reminded Ben.

"I'm well aware," Ben said.

"He's advising me out of the goodness of his heart," Maureen observed.

"You can thank him with the goodness of that," Tom replied, pointing to dessert.

In the middle of the table sat a thirteen-inch apple pie still warm from the oven, slits in its crust venting cinnamon mist. It happened to be Ben's favorite, especially if topped by slow-churned vanilla ice cream. But Ben had decided not to accept any pie tonight. He reckoned it would be unwise to let himself feel beholden in any way. He didn't even say yes to coffee. He wore a suit and his Allen Edmonds shoes.

Tom sat freshly showered and in clean clothes, his reading glasses sliding down his nose. He leaned across the table as Maureen got up, fussed at the counter, filled Tom's coffee cup, poured one for herself, and finally returned to her chair. After several attempts, she gave up on serving anyone pie. Only Zip indicated interest, making a small circle before settling himself in a pile next to Tom's feet. The kibbles in his bowl lay untouched.

"I had a talk with Aaron Short yesterday," Ben said. "Aaron hopes to head out soon to meet with Theresa and Charlie at Fort Benning . . . before he makes his recommendation to the court on Patrick's custody arrangement."

"He's on his way to Alabama?" Maureen gasped. "Ben, does that mean they've changed their minds about claiming Patrick? They want him now?"

"Georgia," Ben told her. "Fort Benning's on the border with Alabama, but it's in the state of Georgia. Thing is, Charlie will be transferred in a few weeks to Fort Jackson in South Carolina. He's going to be trained as a drill instructor there, seeing that his wounds make it medically unfeasible for him to continue serving as a regular troop in the field. He has a strong desire to stay in the army, and the army is bending over backwards to see if maybe he can do that despite the odds—by that I mean given how serious his wounds are."

"I don't understand," said Maureen. "What do his wounds have to do with Patrick?"

Ben scowled. "Maureen, his injuries occurred when he was trying to get home to look for Theresa. If it weren't for Theresa's disappearance while she was pregnant with Patrick, he wouldn't have been wounded in the first place."

Maureen flushed. "I don't see what any of that has to do with Patrick's situation now."

"Just listen to the man, Maureen," Tom said quietly.

Suddenly, Tom reached toward the center of the table, picked up a knife, and cut himself a generous slice of the apple pie. Zip rose from his curled position on the floor and nudged Tom's knee with his nose as Tom set the wedge of pie on his plate.

"Aaron wants to talk to them together, face-to-face, before Charlie leaves for South Carolina," Ben explained. "Charlie will be gone for nine weeks. Theresa will stay at their home in Columbus until Charlie gets back. So, this is Aaron's best chance to find out their current thinking before he makes his recommendation to the court."

"Change your mind about pie, Ben?" Tom asked.

Ben shook his head no.

"You're missing out," Tom said.

Maureen saw both sides of the issue as if an imaginary piece of silver flew in the air, turning and turning, about to land, heads or tails, depending on the Lord's will. Heads, she would keep Patrick and raise him in a good Catholic home in all the wonderful ways she'd planned. Tails, Theresa would come to her senses and claim the son she should never have abandoned in the first place. Maureen honestly didn't know which side of the coin she wanted to land face up. She was just going to have to trust in Divine Providence. Thy will be done, she said in silent prayer. Thy hallowed will be done. Not my will but Thine, Oh Lord, now and forever, Amen.

Suddenly, another thought occurred to her. "Maybe Theresa should come back here while Charlie is gone to this Fort–wherever," she suggested. "She could make amends to everyone."

"That won't happen," Ben interrupted. "Theresa will stay where she is. She has a job on post at Fort Benning, and she has friends among the other wives. Besides, she's pregnant again, and she wants to have her baby there. The other army wives will help her."

"I don't see why–" Maureen continued.

"It won't happen, Maureen," Ben said again, somewhat harshly. Then he sighed. "I'm sorry. This is a difficult conversation."

"These things should be plain common sense," Maureen said. She looked at Tom. "Don't you have anything to add? Wouldn't you like Theresa to come back home while her husband is off getting trained in South Carolina?"

"This isn't Theresa's home anymore," Tom said.

"That brings me to the second part of what I'm here to tell you," Ben announced.

Tom finished the last bite of his pie and put his plate on the floor for Zip to lick. He did it much to Maureen's annoyance, but she didn't say anything. She wanted to hear what else Ben had to tell them, hoping against hope it was something positive.

"It has to do with Annie," Ben said.

"What about Annie?" Maureen asked, surprised.

"She's carrying too much of the load in this house," Ben said. "She's taken on too much of Patrick's care, in particular. I've noticed it whenever I stop by. So has Aaron, and so has the social worker from the county welfare office."

Maureen's expression hardened. "Annie's not allowed to help with

Patrick? Since when is that legal? I didn't think the Constitution allowed courts to interfere with families."

"Annie's doing more than help," Ben said. He waited for his words to register. "You and she are pretty much it, as far as Patrick's care is concerned," he added, looking at Maureen.

"What are you suggesting?" Tom asked.

"Annie's still a child herself, and her number-one job is to get a good education," Ben pointed out. "That's not happening. I've heard about her report cards. Her progress is below her capabilities."

"Who's showing you her report cards?" Tom demanded.

"Are you suggesting we bring in someone from outside to help with Patrick?" Maureen inquired. She thought that might solve a lot of their problems, and she was sure, no matter what Tom said, that they could afford it.

"What I'm suggesting is that you let your daughter sleep and study the way she needs to in order to excel in school. She's at her wit's end trying to keep up, and her preferred solution, I'm sorry to say, is to go live in Alabama with her sister."

"Oh, not Alabama again," Maureen said disgustedly. "I'm so sick of hearing about Alabama."

"This situation has a lot of people concerned," Ben said. "When you two got temporary foster custody, it was with the understanding that you would take care of Patrick with help from your church friends. You wrote it all up in your care plan. I don't see your church friends here anymore."

"Annie doesn't mind taking care of Patrick," Maureen insisted. "It's good experience. One day she'll have a baby of her own. That said, I do agree we could use an extra hand. Sorry to say, my friends at St. Philomena don't seem to have as much time for Patrick as I'd hoped."

"Outside help is one point we could agree on, then," Ben said. "That is, if you two want to petition the court to adopt Patrick."

"I don't agree," Tom said. "We're not getting outside help."

"Well, that's a problem," Ben said. "Because if Theresa doesn't change her mind, and if Charlie's allowed to relinquish physical custody, the court has to decide between you and the Cole grandparents for permanent custody leading to adoption; that is, if we're going to keep the family connection intact."

"We want the family connection, don't we, Tom?" Maureen implored.

Tom didn't answer.

"If something doesn't change soon, Aaron Short will probably recommend that Patrick go to the Cole grandparents," Ben said. "And I'll tell you who'll back him up—Bev Hagen. Patrick is the most expensive baby Stears County has had in years. Bev wants someone to adopt Patrick as soon as possible. And I'll tell you something else. She'd love to have the US Army pay for Patrick's NICU care."

"Most expensive can't be true," Maureen objected, ignoring the rest. "There have been other Down's babies in this county. They must have been expensive too."

"Maureen," Ben searched for the right words. "I'd recommend you not use the phrase, *Down's baby*. Say *baby with Down syndrome*. Some people might take offense at *Down's baby*."

"For heaven's sake!" Maureen exclaimed. "What does it matter? The Coles are heathens. We're Catholics. That's why we've got him, and it's why we should keep him. As for being expensive, how dare you put a price on his life!"

"He's not only a baby with Down syndrome, Maureen. He was a micro preemie."

"He's not a micro preemie anymore! Those expenses are in the past," Maureen pointed out, raising her voice.

"They may be in the past as far as you and I are concerned, but Bev has a budget to worry about, as well as future expenses for Patrick. What she spent on him already, she can't spend elsewhere. That's why she's looking to the army."

"What are we talking about?" Tom interrupted. "The way I see it, Theresa can take him back or the Coles can adopt him. Either way is fine with me. Maureen and I are too old for this. He doesn't belong with us. He's not our baby. End of story."

Maureen stood up to face them both, looking down into their obstinate faces.

"Theresa has us all on tenterhooks while she decides if she wants her child or not. Then Mary has a baby of her own in some far-off, godless family," she got out, her voice strengthening as she went on, "and now the Coles want to take my Patrick into that same family. And Tom, you don't even care what happens as long as it's not us. And Ben, you're not on our side anymore. This is too much!"

Ben didn't reply. He dismissed the thought of saying something blunt, like *why did you force Theresa to have a baby she didn't want and wouldn't keep?* That was his personal opinion based on a low regard for the combination of religiosity and kidnapping. But it wouldn't be helpful to say it. So, he just looked at Maureen and said nothing.

"I guess you told us all you're gonna," Tom summed up, seemingly unperturbed by Maureen's outburst.

"Guess I have," Ben said.

Maureen pulled a handkerchief from her pocket, blew her nose, and left the room.

"See yourself out," Tom advised Ben before heading outside himself.

———•◆•———

On Tuesday, June 18, 2019, Aaron Short flew American Airlines via Charlotte, North Carolina, on his way to Columbus, Georgia, the military town north of Fort Benning where Charlie and Theresa Cole had settled. They lived in a neighborhood called Rosehill. He found it on a city map. The house that Woodrow's son and his wife leased was a little over eight miles from the fort. Aaron planned to take an Uber from the airport rather than rent a car. His visit wouldn't last long. He would succeed, or he would not.

The layover in Charlotte was about an hour and a half. During the final leg of his flight, Aaron rehearsed, working from notes he had overprepared for his meeting with Theresa, much the way he routinely overprepared for court. Judges had told Aaron that nobody appeared before them as ready to do battle as he, and that was true enough. Aaron hated having to go into court. Establishing a reputation as someone other lawyers dreaded to meet in front of the bar—that highly symbolic line separating authorized participants from clients and spectators—helped him stay out of the arena much of the time. If he had to go in, he'd show up overprepared, and he'd use every weapon at his disposal, especially if the future of a child was at stake.

His plane hit the tarmac with a gentle thud and taxied toward the gate. "Welcome to Columbus," the pilot announced over the intercom, citing time and temperature. It was eighty-eight degrees, on its way to ninety-four. The sky was clear. It would be partly cloudy later, but there was no chance of rain today.

Aaron had never been to Columbus before. It was the site of the last battle in the Civil War, but the military town had settled into a relatively peaceful rhythm in the present day. Its crime rate was higher than a city its size could brag about, but some neighborhoods were safer than others—Rosehill among them.

Columbus boasted a few museums that sounded interesting. Aaron read descriptions of them in a travel brochure stuffed into his seat pocket. But that was only to pass the time; he had no inclination to see museums that day, nor would he stroll the promenade along the Chattahoochee River, pretty as it looked in pictures.

As passengers began to deplane, Aaron took a deep breath. Theresa didn't want to see him. Charlie had begged her. She'd relented when Charlie said, "I'm asking you to do this for me the same way I accepted your decision to give up custody of our son when he was born."

318

Tit for tat. It worked when people were fair-minded. Aaron hoped that Theresa would be fair-minded enough to undertake the task he was about to set before her. He knew he needed to convince her face-to-face.

Charlie told him the meeting was a 'go' in an early morning phone call that Aaron had feared wouldn't come. "Make it soon," Charlie said, "while our talking it over is fresh in her mind. She's pregnant," he reminded Aaron. "She has mood swings."

Aaron's partner drove him to the airport an hour later, and Aaron bought a full-price first-class ticket on the next flight out.

"Good luck," Roger whispered, and kissed him sweetly on the cheek.

"I needed that," Aaron quipped. Roger's goodbye kisses were his lucky charm. Still, he'd felt a sense of dread, hoping the day would find Theresa in a braver disposition than she'd shown in the past.

If Theresa said no, he wasn't sure what he'd do next. Maureen's age aside, he'd had more than a few doubts about her from the beginning. Now, he was convinced she and her husband should not get permanent custody of the child Theresa Cole had borne prematurely eleven months before.

Mitchell Gunderson and Ramona Eggers had laid it all out for him—how and why they believed an abduction had taken place prior to the child's birth. Aaron knew how unusual it was for the FBI to disclose information on an open case. Since the rules are relatively relaxed in family court, he thought he could get their evidence admitted in his report, backed by Theresa's testimony. Without Theresa, the plan wouldn't work.

The FBI was on a tear, Ramona Eggers especially, to locate and prosecute a woman named Lucy Meyer. Theresa's appearance in family court was part of their strategy. They had not been able to get through to Mrs. Cole despite multiple efforts. They hoped that if Aaron could convince Theresa to testify in the custody battle, her testimony would help them build a case against Lucy Meyer later on—a woman who had probably coerced others before Theresa, and would surely do it again. They wanted Theresa to eventually agree to testify before a federal grand jury.

Charlie had arranged with his CO to be home when Aaron arrived. Charlie had to be there, Aaron had emphasized. The ask they were about to make went against everything Theresa had said she was willing to consider.

She had turned her back on this baby. Aaron hoped she hadn't turned her heart off too. He wanted the weight of her testimony to fall on the side of Woodrow Cole and his family.

He would have to show the court that in this particular instance, Alabama—while maybe not ideal—was a better place for the child than the Haig home in Minnesota. To that end, he needed to convince the judge that the only family-linked alternative for the child—Maureen Haig and her husband—failed to qualify for custody by dint of Maureen's participation in a crime. To prove a crime had occurred, he needed Theresa.

———•◦•———

No one told Maureen it would look so ordinary. A decision affecting Patrick's future was likely to be made in this unimpressive low-ceilinged room with no paneling or Latin inscriptions or murals on the walls. The judge's bench was scarcely more imposing than the rest of the court. Maureen wasn't sure what she expected, but surely something more like on TV.

She and Tom were the first to arrive. Twin tables had been placed on opposite sides of the room, each with chairs facing the judge. They sat down on the right-hand side.

Their lawyer, Randy Lamers, felt they had a good case, stemming from the fact that they were what he called "custodians of record." Courts favor keeping children where they are rather than disrupting their sense of security by moving them, he said. It was known as the *stability factor.* Absent violence or abuse, the stability factor prevailed in most cases.

There was certainly no violence or abuse in the Haig household. Maureen admired Randy's intellect and was sure he knew what he was talking about regarding the stability factor. As far as Tom was concerned, Randy's primary qualification was his willingness to take their case pro bono.

"Not one cent for lawyers," Tom had warned Maureen when they found out the other side had hired a woman who specialized in custody battles. She had a law degree from a prestigious school in St. Paul. A lot of important people, including a US Supreme Court justice, were alumni of the same school. That's how prestigious it was.

The clock moved glacially until the other side's attorney entered at 8:50 a.m., along with Woodrow and Rebecca. Maureen had spoken with Rebecca Cole many times on the phone, but she had met her only once, at Theresa's wedding. She didn't make eye contact now. If someone of Rebecca Cole's common sense thought Patrick should be ripped away from the only home he'd ever known—well, there was nothing to talk about.

Randy arrived five minutes before the judge, who was not the person Ben had told them would preside. Instead, a white-haired woman in black robes walked in at exactly nine o'clock and introduced herself as Judge Judith Van Handel. Maureen was sure she and Tom had voted for her in the last election. So, this was Judge Van Handel's courtroom, her court reporter, and her bailiff, as Randy had explained last night. The judge they'd previously expected had recused himself for reasons Maureen couldn't begin to understand.

An unopened manila envelope lay on Maureen's lap. It was a copy of Aaron Short's report to the court. It had been delivered to them by Aaron personally, and to Randy by mail. Maureen couldn't bring herself to break the seal and read it. She wasn't sure that Randy had read it either. She knew he had a busy schedule and was fitting their case in pro bono because of their church connection. Randy was a prominent parishioner at St. Philomena.

Outside in the corridor, Annie sat on a bench holding Patrick. At the last minute, she'd begged to come along, and Maureen had allowed it.

Maureen looked around nervously. The judge's bench and other furniture in the courtroom were fabricated out of bullet-resistant fiberglass, a guard had informed them on their way into the building. The same guard made them walk through a metal detector and put personal items in a bin for someone to x-ray. The atmosphere seemed designed to intimidate, and it succeeded. She had never felt so frightened in her life, not even last fall when Annie disappeared. Deep down, she had known during that tribulation that Annie would be fine. But the thought of losing Patrick at his tender age brought a whole different level of fear. Patrick had no way to defend himself and maybe never would. Not only his life and his chance to be normal, but his very soul was in danger. Before they left the house for the courtroom, she had engaged everyone on the telephone tree to pray for him.

Judge Van Handel spoke in a voice that surprised Maureen. At first, she'd seemed like an unimpressive person up there on the slightly raised bench, not very tall as she surveyed the room. Her defining features were shiny white hair and a wide face, and she looked like the kind of woman who probably held acceptable opinions about goings-on in the community. She wore no makeup and hardly smiled. All in all, she appeared respectable. Maureen hoped she was a good Christian.

Her voice had an edge, however. Maureen considered herself capable of sizing people up as soon as she met them, women in particular, and this lady amounted to more than a first glance revealed. When she talked, the room fell silent. It was not the volume or the tone in which she spoke. It was the authority of years, Maureen decided. Conviction. Something a person couldn't fake.

"I've read the guardian's report on this minor child whose future custody arrangement comes before the court today," Judge Van Handel said, "and it concerns me like few circumstances I've seen in my thirty years on the bench. There are numerous claims that are troubling. This court intends to take the time and devote the attention necessary to make sure that we get the permanent custody decision right for this child, and to that end, I'd like to hear from all sides before we explore the more disturbing aspects of this case as outlined in the guardian's report."

The judge looked at Randy, and Maureen wondered whether Judge Van Handel knew him. If so, she considered what she might think of him—whether the judge held Randy in high regard. She also wondered what the so-called *disturbing aspects* were that Aaron Short had apparently put in his report. She very much regretted not reading it.

"Randy Lamers representing the Haig family, Maureen and Thomas Haig, Your Honor," Randy said, standing up. He sounded ill at ease. Maureen got the distinct impression that he hadn't read the report, or maybe he'd read it quickly right before the hearing began. In either case, she suspected he didn't understand either what the judge was talking about when she mentioned disturbing aspects.

Next to Maureen, Tom sighed audibly. She wasn't sure what his sigh was supposed to convey, but Tom had promised on his mother's memory that he would make every effort to support her, short of lying about what he thought should happen. She knew he wanted Patrick to end up in Alabama. She knew he wanted her to say as little as possible in the courtroom. She'd begged him not to voice his own opinions and to let the judge sort things out in an intelligent way. By intelligent way, she'd meant submissive in spirit to the infinite knowledge and wisdom of the Lord in His Divine Providence, but she hadn't enunciated those specific words to Tom, lest he roll his eyes.

The judge looked toward the table on the other side of the room, where a woman stood up in high heels that any sane person would fear breaking an ankle in. She wore an elegant pantsuit with a V-neck and no blouse underneath, tiny gold earrings, a fancy watch, and no other jewelry—meaning she probably wasn't married. She had what Maureen guessed was a hundred-dollar haircut. How could a woman like that possibly know what it meant to raise an abandoned child, much less a child with Patrick's many challenges?

"Rose Kinkaid representing the family of the baby's father, Your Honor. They would be Staff Sergeant Charles Cole, United States Army, the child's natural father; Woodrow Cole, the child's grandfather; and Rebecca Cole, the child's great-grandmother."

"Is anyone representing the child's natural mother?" the judge asked.

"The child's natural mother will represent herself," Rose Kinkaid said.

"Is she present?"

"She and the child's natural father are present and willing to testify," Rose Kinkaid said.

Maureen looked around frantically. Neither Theresa nor her husband were inside the courtroom. What did the other side's lawyer mean when she said they were present, she wondered. Present where?

"Then let's proceed," the judge said. "As I understand the current circumstances of the child, he is not yet one year old, having been born prematurely on July 27, 2018."

She looked in turn at Randy Lamers and Rose Kinkaid. "Yes, Your Honor," they said simultaneously.

"He is currently in good health, but he's experienced numerous medical emergencies during his short life," the judge went on. "He seems to have come through those medical emergencies well and shows good stamina and high energy levels, according to recent evaluations." No one disagreed with that assessment.

Judge Van Handel then allowed affidavits to be entered into the record from Beverly Hagen, director of Stears County Child Protective Services, about the county's oversight of the premature infant's care in the NICU at St. Dominic Hospital, along with a separate report about state and county supervision of ongoing temporary foster care in the home of the child's maternal grandparents. She allowed further affidavits from the child's doctors and nursing staff at St. Dominic Hospital. Those described medical interventions and the progress the child had made as well as a report on his current health conditions. Randy Lamers submitted an affidavit containing details of the Haig family's ongoing temporary foster care of the child and the participation of numerous church volunteers in his care. The Stears County social worker assigned to supervise the child's care entered her report. A letter to the court from Maureen's circle of friends at St. Philomena lauded her as the child's tireless champion and protector. Rose Kinkaid entered an affidavit from the Cole family attesting to the paternal side of the family's ongoing concern and desire to participate further in the child's care and upbringing.

When all these affidavits had been read and entered into the record, Judge Van Handel scanned the courtroom. "Now I'd like to hear directly from the principals in this custody dispute," she announced. "Since the Haig family has enjoyed the benefit of temporary foster custody, I'll hear from them first."

She looked at Randy, who looked at Maureen and called out her name. Maureen stood up, nervous beyond her ability to conceal.

"Would the witness please approach the stand?" the judge requested.

Maureen walked over to what was really just a chair. She raised her hand and swore to tell the truth, solemnly, sincerely, the whole truth, before Almighty God, repeating the words after the court officer. She tried to repeat exactly what she heard. Then she sat down. She couldn't stop shaking.

"Would you like a glass of water?" the judge asked.

"Yes, please." She took a few sips from the half-filled glass proffered by Randy, then handed it back to him, careful not to drop it.

"Proceed," the judge said to Randy.

Randy asked her questions. She told him everything about Patrick, all the details, answering as best she could remember about his premature birth, his months in the NICU, her devotion, all the precautions and preparations she'd made to bring him home, how she'd hoped and prayed that his mother would return and reclaim him, how determined she was that Patrick have a normal life no matter what and that he make progress in all his exercises, how happy he seemed to be now, and most of all, how much he was loved.

When she finished answering Randy's questions, Maureen felt she'd done well. She thought the questioning was over and that she could go now. But it wasn't over. The judge had questions too.

"Mrs. Haig, I have to caution you at this point. You are under oath. That means that any untruth spoken by you could be held against you in a court of law. A lie under oath invites a charge of perjury. Knowing that, you need to decide whether you will answer the questions I'm about to put to you. Do you understand that you do not have to answer any or all of my questions if you feel that your testimony could put you in legal jeopardy before this or any other court?"

Maureen didn't know what to say. She looked at Randy. "What does she mean?" she asked. Randy approached her.

"Just tell the truth," he said quietly. "Everything you tell Judge Van Handel has to be the absolute truth."

Maureen nodded vigorously. "Of course," she said.

"In that case," Judge Van Handel said, "I must tell you that there is in the report submitted to this court by Aaron Short, as guardian ad litem for the minor child in question, a contention that the child's mother was kidnapped from your home early in her pregnancy, and that you were present during this kidnapping and that you were a party to it. Will you tell this court whether that contention is based on a true event?"

"A kidnapping?" Maureen repeated.

"Yes, that is the contention," the judge affirmed.

Maureen could sing the second, third, and fourth verses of hymns she loved without glancing at the words in the hymnal. She could remember what food someone served at a wedding years after the fact. She possessed her full mental faculties. There was no kidnapping. She wondered what in the world gave Aaron Short the idea that a kidnapping had taken place.

"Theresa was upset when she found out that Patrick would be a special needs child," Maureen explained to the judge. "It was a surprise. No one expected it. She needed time to prepare herself for everything that would mean. I invited some friends over to help her come to terms with it. Afterwards, she wanted to be alone. That caused all the trouble. She went away to think."

"Are you saying she was not taken by force and removed to some place that she could not subsequently leave?" asked the judge.

"I don't know where she went," Maureen said. "I really don't. People kept asking me, and I had to tell them that she went away to think. I didn't know when she'd come back until the day she did. That was when Patrick was born. She'd been in some kind of accident. But I don't know how that happened either."

"Mrs. Haig, are you acquainted with a person named Lucy Meyer?" the judge asked.

"Yes," Maureen said. "I've met her."

"Was she in your home on the day you described?"

"Yes, she was there."

"Did she participate in forcing your daughter to leave with her?"

"No," Maureen said. "She stayed behind. Theresa left before she did."

Judge Van Handel had no more questions for Maureen. She asked Randy Lamers if Thomas Haig had anything to add, but Tom shook his head and Randy declined to call him to the stand. Randy told the judge that he had no further witnesses, at which point Judge Van Handel allowed Rose Kinkaid to begin calling witnesses of her own.

Rose Kinkaid began by calling Theresa Haig Cole. Every head turned as the door at the back of the courtroom opened, and Theresa walked in, alone. Maureen's heart leapt. For the first time, she noticed that Annie must have come into the courtroom at some point and was sitting on a chair near the back, next to Ben Johnson, with Patrick in his cloth carrier nestled against her chest. Theresa walked by them.

Visibly pregnant, Theresa wore a pale, demure dress, empire waisted, with a classic boat neckline, short, fitted sleeves, and four tiny buttons at the bodice. The dress fell below the knee. Rebecca had helped Theresa find it in an Atlanta boutique.

"You need to feel safe in what you wear," Rebecca told her as they'd shopped. "Then you'll be fine on the stand."

"I just want it to be over," Theresa had said, more than once.

They'd spent two days in Atlanta, prepping psychologically. Charlie and Woodrow were worried sick, and Theresa was still unsure what she'd tell the court. Rebecca was there to calm everyone. Their flight to Minneapolis was delayed for mechanical trouble, but they'd made it, finally, the night before the hearing.

It's too bad, Maureen thought now, that Patrick's face was half hidden in Annie's blouse. His little eyes were probably closed. He didn't see his beautiful mother enter the courtroom. *Wouldn't it be wonderful,* she fantasized, *if Theresa turned around at that very moment and went back to where Annie was sitting and Annie handed Patrick to Theresa, and all of this was over?*

But Theresa walked straight toward the front of the courtroom. She didn't look at Maureen or her father. Her face was set in a way Maureen had seen many times on Tom. It was a look Tom took when his mind was made up. It usually didn't bode well.

The court officer swore Theresa in, much the way he'd sworn Maureen in, and Maureen's hand went to her throat. She had no idea what her daughter would say, but she desperately wanted her to say that she had changed her mind about everything, that she wanted Patrick back to her bosom, that her leaving had all been one long horrible mistake, and that she bitterly regretted running off and even thinking for one second about the possibility of having an abortion, which the Lord had not allowed to happen, blessedly, through His Divine Favor, His Endless Mercy, and His Providential Grace.

"Mrs. Cole, you are the natural mother of the child in question during this custody hearing?" Judge Van Handel asked.

"I gave birth to the child in question on July 27, 2018," Theresa replied, her voice quivering slightly. "I had no choice. His birth was forced on me."

"In what way was the birth of the child forced on you, Mrs. Cole?"

"I was kidnapped on May ninth, 2018. It was toward the end of my first trimester, and I had just found out that something was wrong with the baby. My doctor, Dr. Michael Ryan, wouldn't tell me *what* was wrong. He wouldn't give me the test results. He allowed two women who were unknown to me to come into the exam room at the clinic where I had sought prenatal care. I found out when I returned to my parents' home that the child would likely be born with Down syndrome. My parents' living room that day was filled with women my mother had invited to prevent me from leaving the house. They all knew or suspected that I planned to have an abortion, which was my legal and constitutional right. They helped orchestrate a kidnapping to prevent that possibility. I was rendered unconscious by some kind of injection during the kidnapping, and after that, I was held against my will until the day I escaped in late July. That's why I say that the birth of the child was forced on me."

"You were held in captivity between May ninth and the date of the birth of your child?" Judge Van Handel asked her.

"Yes. I escaped on July twenty-sixth, but I was hurt during the escape and that caused the premature birth."

The judge didn't ask another question immediately, as if absorbing what Theresa had said. Theresa took that moment to look out at the people in the room, among them Aaron Short in the first row of chairs. His eyes were warm, encouraging. She was glad he was there.

It was a small courtroom. She was glad of that too. Glad that family law courtrooms are typically private, not filled with gawkers and curiosity seekers. In her mind, testifying had always seemed like something she'd have to do in a large arena, with cameras flashing and protestors wearing T-shirts emblazoned with slogans, and signs waving about, and the judge pounding a gavel to silence the din.

It wasn't like that. She felt profoundly grateful because the relief she suddenly experienced came over her undiluted, unopposed by the arrogance of people who felt they owned not only her body, but her character and her future.

"After the child's birth, you surrendered him to the state of Minnesota under the Minnesota safe place for newborns law, is that correct?" the judge asked Theresa.

"Yes. I looked it up in the hospital on the morning after. I thought it said safe haven law when I read it. In any case, I informed the hospital staff, and they arranged to take custody of the baby."

Theresa noticed that the Cole family attorney, Rose Kinkaid, was letting the judge ask the questions. She didn't know why. Maybe the judge decided who got to ask questions. Maybe it was better that way, she thought. Maybe it didn't matter who asked the questions, so long as the facts got into the record. Her testimony about the kidnapping was what Charlie wanted so that Woodrow could get permanent custody. She was doing this for Charlie, she reminded herself. She wished they had allowed Charlie into the courtroom, but they'd been told he couldn't enter until he testified, and their lawyer, Ms. Kinkaid, wasn't even sure that Charlie would be called to testify that same day.

"Surrendering the child was a decision you made in the immediate aftermath of giving birth then?" the judge asked Theresa.

"Yes," Theresa told her. "It was a decision I made a few hours after the birth."

"Did you have occasion to regret that decision in the days and weeks afterward?"

"No, I did not," Theresa said firmly.

"If the same circumstances were before you now, would you make the same decision?"

"Yes, I would."

"You have no desire to reclaim custody of your son? I'm sorry to repeat what must seem like the same question, Mrs. Cole, but the court wishes to be absolutely sure that you have no hesitation about permanently surrendering legal custody of this child."

"I understand," Theresa said. "No, I have no desire to reclaim custody."

"Do you understand that, while you are legally entitled under the law in the state of Minnesota to relinquish custody, the child's father is not? The exception that the law makes for the mother is in furtherance of the child's safety, since an alternative for a distraught mother might otherwise be to abandon a child in circumstances that might lead to the child's death. For the child's legal father, there is no such exception. He is still bound by the law for the child's protection. Even if a father surrenders physical custody, he cannot easily surrender custody obligations, since these include Social Security benefits, child support, and inheritance rights."

Theresa waited a long moment before replying. "That may be the case," she said evenly, "but I want the court to understand that I have no intention of raising a child I was forced to bear. If my husband chooses to raise this child, he will do so without me."

Another silence occurred. Judge Van Handel looked out into the courtroom. Her eyes seemed to focus on Annie, who had remained seated toward the back, one hand splayed against the baby's head to hold him steady. The child twisted his body momentarily and made a sound. It wasn't a cry, more of a wheezing in his throat. Annie responded by rising from her chair. She left the courtroom, holding tight to the baby. Ben Johnson rose and followed her.

Maureen turned when she heard the sound of Annie leaving. She rose too and would have followed Annie out of the courtroom, but Tom's hand gripped her arm.

"Stay put," he said. "This is almost over, I hope."

Reluctantly, Maureen sat down again.

Rose Kinkaid stood up. "Your Honor, I wonder if we could recess briefly before calling my next witness. We have a lot to consider, and I'd like to confer with my clients."

"Yes, I'll grant a recess," Judge Van Handel said. "There is a great deal of information to absorb here, including the question of whether the child should remain where he is even on the basis of temporary foster custody. I'd like to meet with the attorneys for the two sides seeking permanent custody and with the guardian ad litem in my chambers to discuss that matter, but first I need to review the evidence at hand. If court can reconvene tomorrow morning at nine o'clock?"

She looked at Randy Lamers, Rose Kinkaid, and Aaron Short in turn. No one answered immediately. Randy appeared uneasy.

"Please approach the bench," Judge Van Handel said.

That's when it hit Maureen. Nothing would be decided today. She realized that this judge might actually believe Theresa's absurd testimony, her lie about a kidnapping, a lie born out of her sinful refusal to take responsibility for her own child.

Maureen tried to picture again exactly what had happened the day Theresa disappeared. So much had been said. She'd replayed it a thousand times in her mind, remembering different things on various occasions. She did recall feeling that it hadn't been handled well.

There was no help for it, she decided finally, but as always to trust in the Lord. She had to hold onto her faith that it would turn out well, if only the Coles would go away. Then the facts would sort themselves out. They had to. She put her right hand into her pocket, intending to pray her rosary. It wasn't there.

— • • —

Woodrow caught up with Tom and Maureen in the courthouse lobby. He and Tom stopped to talk, but Maureen disengaged her arm and continued walking, paying no attention to the voices behind her. When she reached Tom's Cadillac in the middle of the municipal parking lot, she felt faint and put her hand on the car to steady herself. She took it off immediately. The car was too hot to touch. Behind her, she heard footsteps and turned, hoping for a split second that Theresa had followed her out. But it wasn't Theresa.

"Guess we're invited to your place," Rebecca Cole said, looking at ease in the blazing sun. Maureen wondered how she could seem so calm after what just happened in the courtroom, after Theresa had told that monstrous lie about why she had given up Patrick.

In the distance, Tom and Woodrow walked toward them at a leisurely pace.

"Where's Theresa?" Maureen asked Rebecca. She wouldn't mind so much having the Coles in her home if Theresa came with them.

"She and Charlie went back to the hotel," Rebecca said without explaining why.

The last thing Maureen wanted was to sit down with these two remaining Coles and chat with them about Patrick as if he were something to be cut in two, like the poor baby in the Old Testament. Before she could make that fact clear to Rebecca, Annie arrived.

Annie's face looked red, as if she'd been crying. Rebecca kissed Annie's cheek and smiled at Patrick, who yawned in response. Maureen paid no attention to what they were saying. All she could think was that Patrick's fate would soon be decided by a judge who might not understand the morality of the situation, a judge who likely lacked the wisdom of King Solomon and wouldn't choose the right mother. Maureen had just arrived at this grim conclusion, and it terrified her.

"We'll follow you in our car," Rebecca said, as if it were the most natural thing in the world, as if she were a cousin or a friend.

Maureen got into Tom's Cadillac. "Nothing makes sense," she said to Tom. He didn't reply.

Hot air rushed out of the vents when Tom turned the engine over. Maureen lowered her window, though there was no cool air to be had that way either. Annie settled into the back next to Patrick after she'd strapped him into his car seat.

"I don't think Randy's up to the job," Maureen admitted as the Cadillac crossed St. Dominic city limits. The air conditioning finally began to put out cold air, so Maureen closed her window.

"Especially now that Aaron Short has turned against us," Maureen went on. "I never expected Theresa to say the things she said. She convinced Aaron she was kidnapped, and I think even the judge believed her!"

Tom still didn't say anything. He didn't speak at all for more than a mile after that, then suddenly he pulled over to the road's unpaved edge and stopped the car.

"I don't know why I let you go on and on with this," he told her, once they were fully at a standstill and the dust had settled. "Those lawyers warned us in Minneapolis. What you said on the stand today could get us in a lot of trouble. Really bad serious trouble! You lied under oath! For Christ's sake, Maureen, you've got to use your head a little bit."

"We need someone new to represent us," Maureen told him, ignoring all the rest of what he'd said, except for Tom's remorseless habit of taking the Lord's name in vain.

"No, we don't need somebody new to represent us," Tom said.

"Yes, we do. And you need to stop violating the second commandment. I'm not sure if it's a mortal sin, but even if it's only a venial sin, you've got enough punishment stacked up to last a hundred years in purgatory. Think about that!"

"Maureen, we can't afford a new lawyer. And we're too old to raise a kid. I've been patient about this way too long. But I'm telling you now, once and for all. What you want is not going to happen. Especially after what Theresa said in that courtroom."

Maureen decided not to argue with him in the car. Annie said nothing. Patrick began to fuss. The Coles' vehicle was right behind them, stopped dead in the road.

<hr/>

The South is blessed with storytellers. Woodrow had been raised on the literary wealth of his region, and he knew the best tales can take a mind on weird journeys, into macabre situations, with dire outcomes unforeseen until the very last moment. Spinners back home had nothing on Maureen, though. Woodrow could see the punctuation marks in her eyes as she pretended all the more, extending the yarn she'd spun on the witness stand into her pretty parlor.

"It never happened," Maureen insisted over rum cake and coffee served on her rosebud patterned china.

No one immediately contradicted Maureen's contention that a kidnapping did not occur, though Woodrow was tempted to say it out loud.

"Theresa was not taken out of this house by force," Maureen insisted a second time. "She chose to leave of her own free will so she could clear her mind of all the fears she had. Her fears overtook her because she'd lost her faith. That's why she lied in court today. I see it clearly now."

"That's not our understanding," Rebecca said.

"Faith is our wall against fear," Maureen continued as if Rebecca had not spoken. "We must build that wall high. Theresa was too weak to build it at all, and I blame myself. I thought to have raised her with faith enough to endure whatever the good Lord sent, but I was wrong. Her faith was frail."

"Every time a babe is born, that's a mark of faith in the future," Woodrow said laconically. "By the way, this rum cake's the best darn thing I've tasted in a long while, 'cepting Mama's peach pie, of course."

Maureen smiled briefly. "My rum cake is a recipe handed down over three generations," she told Woodrow. "I made it at four o'clock this morning. Shows you what an upset this is. No way to sleep before going into court. All I did was toss and turn last night, so I figured I might as well get up and do something useful."

"Well, it's mighty fine," Rebecca said.

To Woodrow, his mother seemed about as tense as a woman in the woods with a single break shotgun facing a ten-foot bear. Yet there they were, he thought, eating cake in the living room of a Minnesota family unbeknownst to them two years ago, while enjoying the breeze that flowed across the room thanks to a pair of open windows on each end. They sat there listening to malarkey the like of which he'd never heard before.

Tom remained pensive in an old, deeply cracked leather chair dyed a color that matched the skin on his hands. Rebecca and Woodrow perched on the sofa in front of the coffee table, and Maureen occupied the outer edge of a wing chair.

"Where's Annie?" Woodrow asked suddenly.

"Upstairs with Patrick," Maureen replied. "Where'd you think she'd be?"

"Just wonderin'," Woodrow said, setting his empty plate on the coffee table. "You know, Maureen," he continued, "our families are tied together like caught fish on the end of a pole. We're never gonna swim free of each other. Best we accommodate ourselves to that reality, I 'spect."

"I have no idea what you're talking about," Maureen told him flatly.

"Fish on the end of a pole are dead," Tom finally put in a few words.

"Well, first they flop around a bit," Woodrow said, widening his smile. "Their gills collapsin' and such."

"Meanin' what?" Tom persisted.

"Meanin' we got ourselves a situation . . . Now I decamped from Lafayette not lookin' forward to this court procedure and not likin' one bit that I had to leave behind your daughter and your granddaughter, precious to me both. I had no choice but to temporarily abandon them in Lafayette while this bickerin' goes on up here, the reason bein' that we truly want what's best for this child y'all call Patrick. We don't think it's fittin' that he grows up so far away from his own mama and papa."

"My impression," Tom interjected, "is that neither his mama nor his papa got much goddamn interest in him."

Maureen glared at Tom.

"That's not true," Woodrow said. "I can tell you his papa is sick about what's going on. As for Theresa, she's so full of—" he paused. "Might as well say it. She's full of rage and hellfire 'bout the way she was taken prisoner once she decided to have an abortion."

"Will you quit spouting that lie!" Maureen yelled at him.

"No, ma'am, I won't stop sayin' it 'cause it's not a lie," Woodrow insisted as Rebecca reached for his hand and squeezed. "*Force majeure* is what it was," he added.

"Force what?" Tom said.

"Force majeure," Woodrow replied. "Irresistible compulsion. Like when one country invades another, and there's no way to prevent it. They call that force majeure. You and your church lady outfit used overwhelming force against Theresa. She was not at fault. You were. Everything that came from your using force majeure against her is on you. All of it, including this squabble we're having over who's gonna raise Charlie's son." Woodrow stopped talking.

"We think you need help with Patrick is all," Rebecca interposed, looking straight at Maureen. "Claire and Woodrow have been exchanging messages with Annie, and they think Annie needs to stop takin' so much responsibility for the child."

"What right do you have exchanging messages with Annie?" Maureen demanded. "That nonsense has to end."

"I don't think it's nonsense for all of us, every person in this room, to care about Patrick's future. We just disagree on the particulars," Rebecca said.

"Patrick was born in Minnesota," Maureen retorted. "He lives in Minnesota. He'll grow up in Minnesota with a lot more services and better doctors and a firm faith foundation, none of which you can give him. Let's be honest about that."

"I 'spect the judge'll have something to say on the matter," Woodrow put in, "given what all she heard today."

"Enough," Maureen said, standing up. "I think we've discussed everything we can. Unless you're willing to back off and let us raise Patrick here where he belongs, we don't have anything more to say to you."

"I'm sorry to hear that," Rebecca said, not standing up. "For the baby's sake, I'd hoped we could work something out."

"You can leave this house right now," Maureen emphasized. She led the way to the front entry. Rebecca and Woodrow rose and followed her with obvious reluctance. Maureen didn't look at either one as they departed. She kept both hands at her sides.

Outside, Zip sat on the porch, watching mournfully as the door opened and closed with nothing deposited for him.

———◦•◦———

It was the darkest mystery Annie had ever encountered in her near-fifteen years on earth, darker than the mayhem in any suspense novel she'd read, or creepy happenings in a horror film, or anything revealed about spies and charlatans in articles about real-life bad behavior.

There were only two possible explanations for what had occurred in the courtroom that morning, an occurrence to which Annie herself had been a witness: either her mother had deliberately lied to the judge after she'd sworn to tell the whole truth and nothing but the truth; or her mother was just plain crazy. If her mother turned out to be crazy, Annie didn't think she could deal with it.

She wondered if there were different kinds of crazy. Her mind automatically went to Jane Eyre and the dreadful woman in the attic who turned out to be the secret wife of the man Jane loved. She was quite sure her mother wasn't crazy like that. Her mother wasn't about to set their house on fire.

But Theresa's kidnapping had really happened. Theresa wasn't lying. So, if her mother wasn't crazy, she had to be the one lying. Still, her mother didn't act like a person who was lying. She didn't have a guilty look on her face. Annie wondered if maybe her mother was lying to herself, and if she believed herself totally because she wanted so badly to think that Theresa had gone off on her own. Maybe her mother imagined that Theresa had stayed out of sight on purpose all the while she and Claire and Woodrow and the sheriff's deputy and lots of other people had been looking everywhere for her.

Annie decided to search the internet to see if there were any plausible explanations—perhaps a medical condition—that could make her mother behave this way. Her father's computer had a big screen that made information easier to read and digest. Her cell phone didn't seem adequate to the task. So she took Patrick into her dad's office at the end of the hallway upstairs and set him on the floor on his back, glancing down occasionally to see that he was still OK.

She typed her question into Google: can people lie to themselves totally? It turned out the answer was yes, people can and do lie to themselves, and they do it quite a lot. Wow. That was a surprise.

Annie wondered if she ever lied to herself. Maybe she did. But not often and never for very long. She'd found the truth has a habit of reminding a person it's there.

According to an article she found, the phenomenon was called *cognitive dissonance*. Annie had never heard of cognitive dissonance, but it sounded like a scientific diagnosis of something that must be fairly common if there were articles about it on the internet. However, the examples in the articles seemed to be of lies that people deep down really knew were lies. In other words, they were more like rationalizations.

Her mother's lying in the courtroom was bigger than a rationalization. It was such an immense, important lie that Annie could hardly believe her mother could hold onto it without recognizing, after Theresa testified, that her own version was, in fact, a lie.

She looked down at Patrick. He smiled back up at her. He was a happy baby and had no idea about all the fuss people were making over his future. He needed a diaper change, she suspected. Annie closed the tabs she'd opened on her father's computer, picked up Patrick, and took him down the hall to the changing table in her parents' bedroom.

President Lincoln loved to tell tall tales, she recalled as she removed Patrick's diaper. She didn't think telling tall tales had made President Lincoln a liar. Telling tall tales was entirely different from what her mother had done in the courtroom, however, because lying about a crime isn't a tall tale. Lying under oath is much more serious than telling an ordinary lie, which in turn is more serious than telling a tall tale that most people know is just a joke.

Lying without knowing you're lying is a sickness, Annie decided, which seemed to her like a gentle way of saying *crazy*. That took Annie back to square one. She didn't think she could accept being a girl with a crazy mother.

⎯⎯•⬦•⎯⎯

It happened in the middle of the night. Something woke Maureen. Her face felt strange. She tried to rouse Tom, who snored on his back beside her, but nothing came out of her mouth.

⎯⎯•⬦•⎯⎯

Ben Johnson arrived, finally, at a quarter past four. He was the first person Tom called. Tom hadn't even told the boys. What was the use of rousing his kids in the middle of the night when they were nowhere near and couldn't do a damn thing? Ben at least could be there.

The hospital corridor was cold. They wouldn't let Tom advance any further, and Tom wouldn't be anywhere else, so he resigned himself to standing in refrigerated air. The sight of Ben hurrying down the space between them warmed him like an oven door flung open.

"What happened?" Ben asked, searching Tom's face.

"Might be a stroke," Tom said.

"When?" Ben asked.

"Don't know exactly. A little after three. I called 911. They let me inside the ambulance. It took forever to get here, and they kept asking me questions along the way."

"Should I inquire at the desk?"

"I've been inquirin' 'til they're sick of the sight of me."

"Don't crack up, Tom." Ben put his arm on Tom's shoulder. "We need to go somewhere, sit down, and have a cup of coffee."

"Not me," Tom said.

"For me, then. I'm an old man, partner, and I was sound asleep when you called. I'm not entirely awake now."

Tom looked at him but said nothing. A woman walked past with a cart. They had to move to the edge of the corridor to let her through.

"Maureen is such a vibrant woman," Ben said. "She's what, fifty-six? Fifty-seven?"

Tom didn't answer.

"'Course things can happen anytime. No one has a right to tomorrow." Tom gave him a dirty look. "Sorry. I shouldn't have said that. Don't have my wits about me this early."

Tom said nothing.

"Let's get out of here," Ben insisted. "We're not doing Maureen any good like this. Maybe the cafeteria is open."

"I'm not hungry," Tom snapped.

"Of course, you're not hungry. But we're just clogging the hallway in case they need to move somebody in or out."

"This is my fault," Tom said. "I hit her with lying under oath while she's drowning in her fight for the kid. She probably thinks they'll arrest her. How could I have been so stupid?"

Ben put his hand on Tom's biceps. Tom let himself be led, stopping at the desk to say where they were headed. The attendant said the cafeteria began serving at five o'clock.

The place was empty except for workers setting up for breakfast. Tom and Ben sat down and stared at a bank of floor-to-ceiling windows on the hospital's ground level.

"We're facing east," Ben said. "The garden is almost invisible now, but it'll light up when the sun rises. Less than an hour, I'd say."

"What the hell you talkin' about?" Tom asked.

"I haven't seen a lot of dawns in my life. I'm just observing that in farm country, it's a glory to behold. The sight of the land coming back."

"Are you fucking crazy?" Tom suggested.

"No. I'm just trying to stay optimistic. The doctors might be able to reverse what happened to Maureen. Everything might come back like it was before, or close to it. That's what we're hoping, isn't it, as we wait for the sun to rise?"

"If she comes back like she was before, I'd do whatever it takes to keep her safe."

"What does that mean?" Ben asked.

"Just what I said," Tom replied. "She's more to me than the goddamn farm."

"Where's Patrick?" Ben asked suddenly.

"He sleeps with Annie," Tom said. "She's got him most nights now."

"We should call her."

"And tell her what?" Tom spit out, his voice rising. The cafeteria workers turned in their direction.

Ben lowered his to a whisper. "She's probably scared stiff. At least I can tell her where we are . . ."

"Yeah, do that," Tom said, "but not here. I don't have the juice right now."

When Ben came back, they drank more coffee. "Annie already let Woodrow know," Ben said. "He and Rebecca are on their way over to your place."

"What the hell!" Tom objected.

"Somebody's got to be there with her," Ben insisted. "I called Aaron Short too. He's going to inform the county. They'll probably want to send a social worker to check on things. If I know Aaron, he'll stop by to make sure the baby's all right."

Tom shrugged. His mind was not on Annie and the baby. His mind was on Maureen.

Ben checked several times again with the stroke unit upstairs. No information yet. Just as the hospital garden appeared, Ben decided to have breakfast. Tom waved his hand in disgust.

"As if I could eat!" he told Ben.

Ben said he couldn't help it. He had an appetite, so he ordered two eggs over easy, bacon, sourdough toast, jam, and a pancake on the side, plus a large orange juice and a pot of coffee. He spread it out on the table and put plates and cutlery down for both of them. Eventually Tom decided to eat, and eventually Ben ordered a second breakfast.

Twenty minutes later, Ben decided to try again upstairs. He came back saying Maureen's doctor could meet with Tom shortly.

Ben and Tom took the elevator to the fourth floor and were ushered into a room with a TV, some straight-back chairs, and two of the older-style armchairs, as well as a table with a lamp and a pile of magazines. They'd been sitting there close to an hour when a woman in a white coat came in, Dr. Carolyn Allen.

Tom muttered to Ben, "Too young."

She sat on a chair across from them. Tom allowed that Ben could stay in the room as a friend of the family.

"Your wife is resting," Dr. Allen told Tom. "We did a number of tests, including a CT scan followed by an MRI. She's had what's called a thrombotic stroke on the right side of her brain. A thrombus is a blood clot. We didn't see any sign of a hemorrhage, by which I mean the CT scan didn't show bleeding in or around the brain. That's critical because the damage caused by hemorrhage can be irreversible. In addition, the MRI confirmed that the injury was recent," she said. "I'm wondering now if you can tell me exactly when you became aware something was wrong."

"In the middle of the night she made a noise I never heard before," Tom told her. "I called 911 and they came, but it took forever."

"The paramedics said they arrived at your house between five and six minutes from the time of the call," Dr. Allen remarked after consulting her notes.

"Seemed like a half hour," Tom said.

"You called 911 immediately?"

"Yeah," Tom said.

"Time is often distorted in a crisis," Dr. Allen said.

"Maybe," Tom said. "I wasn't paying attention to the clock."

"According to the EMS report, their trip, from the moment they set out to when your wife reached our stroke unit here, was just over eighteen minutes. Mr. Haig, time is critical in this kind of disruption to normal blood flow. Less than a half hour means the clotting occurred shortly before we got to her. Based on that assumption, we used medication to dissolve it once we found its location."

"Will she recover?" Tom asked urgently.

"It's hard to predict. She could make a significant recovery, but she may have to relearn some things. Since she's relatively young and healthy—she doesn't have diabetes, doesn't smoke, has never suffered a coronary event—those are all factors in her favor."

"I want a definite answer," Tom said.

"There are no definite answers. When the brain is injured, it needs time to heal, but every case is unique. However, even when nerve cells have died, the brain can rewire itself. New neurons can migrate to the point of injury. And the brain has a great deal of redundancy. Other parts of the brain can take over and—"

"When can she come home?" Tom broke in.

"We'll keep her here for observation at least the next five days. We don't want a recurrence, so it's important not to rush things. After that, she'll probably need to spend some time in a rehab center."

Tom didn't react.

"We're lucky to have you available to help Maureen so quickly," Ben broke in, leaning toward Dr. Allen. "I know the whole family's going to be grateful, once everybody knows how much you've done."

Dr. Allen smiled and stood up. "That's why we're here," she said, before shaking Ben's hand. Tom's head was down, his hands clutching the edge of the sofa.

"You can see her for a few minutes, but I'd advise you not to try to talk to her," Dr. Allen added to Tom. "She's sedated, and we don't want her agitated. But it might help if you squeeze her hand to let her know you're there."

"That word *recurrence* hit me like a fist to the gut," Tom told Ben later, adding, "I've got nothing against women doctors, but I wonder if she's the best we can do."

"We'll talk to some of the nurses," Ben suggested. "They always seem to know what's what. She certainly seemed competent to me."

———•◦•———

Annie left a voice mail in the wee hours of the morning. Claire didn't hear it until after she'd fed Ariane, who woke about six.

"Mother had a stroke last night. Ben Johnson's at the hospital with Dad. Woodrow and Rebecca are on their way over. I don't know any more. Will you call Theresa?"

Annie was not known for parsimony in word or opinion, Claire informed Ariane after listening to the voice mail, twice. That she left such a short, shocking message indicated not only a dearth of information but an inability to talk without breaking down.

When Ariane seemed sated, white bubbles popping out of her mouth, Claire put her on her shoulder for a series of burps, then laid her gently in her bassinet. Immediately, Ariane fussed. She wanted to be held at all times. Claire picked her up again, took her down to the kitchen, and walked around Rebecca's scarred table.

Once she herself had been as tiny as Ariane, even tinier at six pounds, four ounces. Her grandma probably retrieved her when she cried. Even now, Claire could remember her grandma's face, the deep wrinkles around her eyes, the blood vessels showing through her thin skin. At Grandma Miriam's funeral, she couldn't contain herself. All she did was cry through the Mass, at the graveside, in the house as she packed to return to the Cities. So why wasn't she crying now? She was certainly sorry. She felt something.

Woodrow called about nine o'clock. The news was positive, he said. They thought her mother would recover, but it would take time. He and Rebecca planned to stay with Annie and help take care of Patrick as long as Tom allowed. They'd informed their attorney. Aaron Short had talked to the judge. Tom was still at the hospital. Ben went home to sleep. Her mother was in intensive care, but her vital signs were good.

He waited for Claire to react, but she had no reaction. Woodrow said he'd call back in a while.

Afterwards, Claire rocked Ariane to sleep. She returned her to her bassinet and called Theresa, who thanked her and ended the conversation as if they were strangers on a bus.

———•◦•———

Technically, Tom's eight sons were farmers. They all held stock in the family business. None of them, not even Greg, lived on Haig land anymore or did a lick of work. On occasion, Tom reminded his boys that they were officers of the corporation, every one of them. They needed to take responsibility for the future of their birthright.

In the end, he'd beseeched them to at least take an interest in corporate decisions currently under consideration. He'd always kept them apprised of loans he planned to take out to purchase land or equipment. He'd phoned them in the evenings to talk about good news and bad. When they'd chafed under the frequency of his calls, he set up an email system to send group messages to which he seldom got replies.

The Haig Corporation sat on a mountain of debt. Yes, he'd made mistakes. He hadn't wanted last year's soybeans to wait out tariffs in storage and maybe be worth even less in the spring, so he'd sold them at harvest for what he could get. He was lucky to come out even.

He'd gambled on new equipment, figuring he'd have his son Greg's help in the future and could maybe buy more land, even as the price of land went up and up.

Then he got thrown for a loop when, at eighteen, Greg met a girl at school and got engaged. The girl's dad plowed more than twice Tom's acreage, and now Greg and this girl, whom he and Maureen had never met, were working on her family's farm in North Dakota. Tom had resorted to hiring help to get his crops planted last spring.

Sitting here now in this county building, waiting for further word from the hospital on Maureen's condition, he felt his farming days were coming to an end.

"What do you think, Tom?"

Tom blinked. He occupied a metal folding chair at a conference table in an office whose air conditioning had a rattle no one had bothered to fix. Around the table were Aaron Short, Ben Johnson, Woodrow, Rebecca, Annie with the baby strapped to her front, and Beverly Hagen, the child services woman who had interrupted his thoughts. The Coles' lawyer was not in the room. Neither was the lawyer Maureen had brought in from church—Randy or Andy Something.

"What do I think about what?" Tom asked.

"Tom," Ben Johnson said, "we've been talking about the court's options here. It's likely Maureen can't continue taking care of Patrick. Given what she's gone though, we think she needs to concentrate on getting well."

"I don't appreciate being talked to as if I'm an imbecile," Tom told Ben. "You're damn right she needs to concentrate on getting well," he went on. "How the hell is she going to take care of Patrick when she can't get out of bed on her own?"

Patrick stirred. He usually slept when Annie put him in his cloth carrier with the front of his body pressed to her chest. She kissed the side of his forehead and rubbed his back until he fell asleep again.

"Tom, would you be amenable to Aaron Short and the Office of Stears

County Child Protective Services joining forces to petition the court—I'm referring to Judge Van Handel—to allow Patrick to be transferred to the home the Coles could provide for him as temporary foster parents in Alabama?" Bev Hagen asked, adding, "Later on, they could begin the process leading to formal adoption there."

Tom looked around the table. Both the Coles kept their mouths shut. Aaron Short stared him full in the face. The whole damn situation was waiting for his decision, he realized, and that was fine, since he had decided long ago.

"Let him go to Alabama," he announced. "Sooner the better. I don't want Maureen coming home to see him carted off in front of her."

Annie's gaze flew to Woodrow, who looked like he was trying to suppress a smile.

"I need to stay with Patrick," Annie told everyone. "He can't be in Alabama without someone he knows to hold him. That would be too much of a shock."

Tom shook his head. "Maureen's going to need you," he said. "I can't have you running off to Timbuktu."

"Annie is the person Patrick's most attached to," Woodrow offered. "It won't help Maureen's recovery if she's upset that Patrick has no one he knows to comfort him. He'd feel abandoned, and Maureen might worry to no end, and that might send her blood pressure in the wrong direction."

Tom considered that possibility, and the more he considered it, the more he didn't want the situation Woodrow described.

"I've got to go along with Patrick," Annie emphasized.

"Maybe it wouldn't be a bad idea," Ben chimed in. "Just to the end of the summer, Tom."

"Who would take care of Maureen?" Tom threw out. "If Annie's going, then Mary has to come home."

"We'll need to work that out," Ben said, raising his hand, palm side open in Woodrow's direction as if to say, "Hold back!"

"We need to work a lot of things out!" Tom said loudly.

"What's Maureen's prognosis?" Aaron Short asked gently. "Since only family can see her, I—"

"She can't talk!" Tom shouted. "It takes two people to get her in and out of a wheelchair!"

Patrick stirred again and began to whimper. Annie kissed his head and stroked his back.

"I reckon that's too much to expect of Annie," Woodrow suggested.

"Don't you tell me what's too much to expect of Annie," Tom snapped.

"I am truly sorry, sir. Didn't mean to step into what's none of my business. But Annie's not a nurse. She's not trained to take care of her mama, and she's not strong enough to carry Maureen's weight on her shoulders. As for Claire, she's got a new baby all her own. She can't take care of her mama at the same time. That's all I'm sayin'."

Tom nodded. It was true enough. There was only one person qualified to take care of Maureen, and that was he himself, Tom Haig, her husband. His wife was *his* top priority.

"If we're going to do this, we need to consider the transition in practical terms," Bev Hagen interjected. "If you talk to your insurance provider, I'll see what our program can do to bridge the gap between when Patrick leaves Minnesota and when he becomes a resident of Alabama," she told Rebecca. "And, of course Social Security disability should kick in for Patrick. You'll have to explore all the possibilities."

"Would you apply for Medicaid in Alabama?" she added.

"Don't think we'd qualify," Rebecca said.

"Do you have private insurance that would help cover Patrick's care?"

"We've got the corporation's insurance, which covers Woodrow, so it should cover Patrick once he's legally adopted him," Rebecca said. "Until then, we might need a separate policy."

"You'll need to check limits," Bev suggested. "I should warn you, your company's premiums are likely to go up substantially once you've adopted. You'll have to discuss that with your other workers. You may also find your insurance doesn't cover everything, or that it covers less as the years go by."

"We'll just have to make do," Rebecca said.

"I can help with savings," Woodrow said.

"Helping is expensive," Tom threw in. "That's why those women who *saved* Patrick are nowhere to be seen now when the bills come due."

Tom tuned out the rest of the meeting. It amounted to details about family court, and therefore was not of much interest to him. Bev Hagen said something about informing their respective attorneys. Aaron Short said he'd take care of that. Tom got up and walked into the hallway when the whole thing seemed over. He needed to get back to the hospital as soon as possible.

He wouldn't tell Maureen anything. Damn the day, he thought, that Theresa came to live with them because her husband got sent overseas. Damn the day Patrick was born. Damn the day Maureen decided to raise him. The whole sorry mess grew out of events he couldn't stop from happening because, for the most part, he didn't know they were happening until it was too late.

He knew now. He needed to concentrate totally on Maureen and nobody else.

Annie knew Patrick's progress wouldn't have happened without her, though she didn't want or expect credit. She had no problem minding him some of the time, she'd told Rebecca. As long as it wasn't all of the time. As long as she got to read—she'd just started *I Know Why The Caged Bird Sings*—and as long as she could sleep enough so she could concentrate. If those things happened, there wasn't much to complain about. Like Patrick's world, hers had been transformed. She was free.

But freedom came with an asterisk. All along the drive from Minnesota, her mother's face had flashed on signposts and the fronts of grocery stores. Her mother in a hospital bed, her eyes closed. Her mother in a wheelchair, pushed by some unknown nurse. Her mother's head on her chest because the stroke interfered with holding it up.

How much of that awful situation was her fault? Annie knew her guilt was great. For months she'd made her plight known to all and sundry, and in so doing, she'd wrecked her mother's health.

The worst of it was that she didn't want to go back to Minnesota. Claire took her to inspect Lafayette High School where classes wouldn't start for more than a month. It was hard to judge its strong points without meeting her future teachers and fellow students. She wasn't worried, though.

As for the guilt part, it was her punishment. She had to endure it.

On the plus side, Jeremiah went to Lafayette High.

Tom wiped Maureen's nose and mouth. It terrified him to see her like this. He debated asking his daughters to come home. Theresa probably wouldn't, given the grudge she nursed against her mother. Mary and Annie didn't want to. He could tell by their voices on the phone. The boys found time on weekends and left looking more depressed than when they arrived. They didn't haul the grandkids along. They had that much sense.

He and Maureen might be alone, but they had each other. She smiled at him when he walked into her room at the rehab place. For some ridiculous reason, he thought he could entice her back to health with flowers—whatever looked fresh in the garden shop downtown. Got to keep her spirits high, everybody said. He told her what kind of flowers he brought every day so she could try to say the word.

The morning arrived when he entered her room to see her out of bed and sitting in a chair with no restraints. She could use her bad arm now to hoist herself, the nurse told him. He knew he was too close to analyze improvements as they occurred and that half the improvements he saw might be wishful thinking, but today he was certain.

"Maureen," she said almost distinctly. "Maureen." A twofer. Sitting on her own. Speaking her name.

The staff was impressed. Dr. Allen was impressed. Maureen had improved "beyond expectations," and since she continued to experience additional improvements in the days after, the nursing home released her in mid-September, just when Tom could no longer afford time away from the farm.

Moving Day was a Monday morning thick with the promise of rain. Tom's fields needed moisture. It looked to him like this year might be his last before he leased the land to tenants. He wanted a good harvest, of course, but Maureen came first. The farm came a distant second.

The staff helped Maureen into the passenger seat of his Cadillac and belted her in. A nursing assistant would follow and make sure she got settled properly and that a home exercise schedule was set up. Aides were assigned to check on her.

Tom had installed a hospital bed in the living room after moving the sofa against the back window. His sons helped. He put a cot for himself nearby in case she needed anything in the night.

Not a week passed before too many people knew Maureen was home. The landline rang off the wall. He told callers the same thing, yes, she was back and getting better, yes, he was taking care of her with help from the rehab center, yes, it was slow going, no, his daughters weren't with her, and *no*, the callers shouldn't come by.

Tom needed to search for workers to help with the harvest, and workers were hard to find. Greg said he'd be there soon as the harvest was done in North Dakota, but Tom wasn't sure he could count on his youngest anymore. He called around and advertised his willingness to pay cash at the end of the day for whatever help he could get. He knew everyone would want to bring in crops at the same time, precisely when the right time came. It was still too early.

———◦•◦———

Five days after Woodrow brought Patrick to the university hospital in Tuscaloosa, his doctors still weren't ready to discharge him. They'd cleared up the infection he came in with but felt they needed to do more to boost his immune system before letting him go. Woodrow assured them that everyone in his family was real careful about hygiene. That wasn't enough, he was told. Patrick had missed out on the antibodies expectant mothers pass on to their babies during the final three months of pregnancy. He'd also missed out on the continued flow of immune-building proteins in breast milk—an early advantage in life that he just didn't get. Patrick's immune system was fragile.

Woodrow would have preferred an immunologist with a few more years' experience. But the head of the department said the newly minted young man assigned to Patrick's case was highly qualified and Woodrow should trust him. On a hallway bench outside Patrick's room, he mulled his choices—be patient and leave Patrick where he was, take him to the hospital in Birmingham, or pull out all the stops and get him to a top medical center like Emory in Atlanta or Johns Hopkins in Baltimore.

"Mr. Cole, may I talk with you awhile?"

Woodrow looked up and saw a middle-aged woman wearing scrubs, with a name tag that read *Hannah*. Within seconds, he was on his feet.

"Something happen to Patrick?"

"No, Mr. Cole. I'm here to chat with you on another matter if you don't mind. My name is Hannah Bedford."

"Sit down," Woodrow said, relieved and wondering if it had something to do with forms he might have filled out wrong.

"I work in another department," she said, "but I've heard about you and your son."

"He's my grandson," Woodrow told her.

"Yes, well, I also saw the ad you put in the hospital bulletin. The one about someone to help take care of your . . . grandson."

"Yeah?" She now had Woodrow's full attention.

"You see, I have a brother who needs a job, and he's real good with children. I trusted him with my gran' babies these past five years. He wouldn't hurt them in any way. I know that. They love him dearly."

"Why hasn't he been able to find a job?" Woodrow asked pointedly.

"Because, sir, and I hope you'll hear me out on this subject . . . Because Henry is an ex-convict. He's applied for a hundred jobs. But people don't look deep. They see he has a record and think no further on it."

Woodrow scrutinized her. She seemed to be gathering her thoughts before going on, so he put his question up front. "What was your brother in for?"

"A fight twenty-two years ago."

"Somebody died," Woodrow surmised.

"A boy he'd known all his life. They were both eighteen."

"He was tried and convicted?"

"He admitted his guilt and took the punishment. It killed our mother. He was her youngest. She never saw him again."

"Well, ma'am, I'm sorry to hear that. But I don't see how—"

"Just meet him, please. Wouldn't cost you a cent. Just let him come by and spend time with your grandson. He deserves for someone to take at least a little interest."

Woodrow hunted for words to let her down.

"He was a model prisoner," Hannah Bedford continued. "That's what the warden said in his papers when they let him go. Can't a model prisoner at least get a conversation? You know, Mr. Cole, none of us is everythin' we could be. All of us got somethin' wrong, one way or another."

Woodrow nodded. "OK," he said softly, "write down your number. I'll think on it and maybe call you. Maybe, you understand?"

Hannah Bedford gave him a card with her name and phone number. She nodded and walked away. Woodrow didn't plan to call her. Then, as the day wore on, he thought maybe he would.

———◆———

Hoping it would please her, Tom took Maureen to church one Sunday in October, the day after neighbors arrived unannounced and harvested three hundred fifty acres in a single day. He was grateful and embarrassed, especially when a crusty old fart named Toby Hitchens hugged him like a long-lost brother.

He'd always found that relations stretch in farm country. They were as tough outstate as city bonds are brittle, at least in Tom's opinion. He was in a good mood as he wheeled Maureen down the aisle at St. Philomena for her treasured time of week, ten o'clock High Mass with the full choir, including a soloist.

They settled in a pew near the back. Tom was aiming to stay the duration until an usher approached about twenty minutes in and apologetically asked them to leave. Maureen was making noises, he said, and it was bothering other worshipers, so maybe it would be better if they tried a different service in the future. The 7:30 a.m. was sparsely attended. Tom didn't argue with the man, but a part of him felt he should be sainted for holding his tongue.

He wheeled his wife back down the aisle and drove her to a bakery where they sat in his Cadillac with a box of cookies and coffee on the armrest between them. Tom had the front passenger seat set back, making it easier for Maureen to slide in with his help. He possessed the strength to lift her weight, quite a feat for a man of his age, he thought.

Maureen didn't seem upset about leaving church. She knew her jabbering annoyed people, but Tom reminded her that "jabbering" was necessary.

She needed to relearn how to say things, and Dr. Allen thought she was making progress, and that was enough for Tom.

Her appetite had improved steadily. Snug in the idling car on this chilly Sunday morning, she devoured four chocolate chip cookies and two cups of black coffee. She drank too much coffee, Tom knew, but Maureen loved the stuff. Let her enjoy every minute of every day.

What he thought of as their "jabbering life" continued into November, a series of days that started in the morning at seven when Tom helped Maureen out of bed, guided her to the bathroom where he had installed safety bars in the shower, held her toothbrush with his hand over hers so it wouldn't fall to the floor, put her on the toilet when she wanted, washed her face, brushed her hair, and squeezed eye drops into both eyes.

Whenever one of his sons came by, he took the opportunity to go shopping. Ben also shopped for him. The basement bins were bulging. The fruit cellar was stocked to the top shelves. The freezer was almost full. The generator had enough propane. Tom figured they could manage a two-week weather emergency if it came to that. Hell, they could probably last two months.

Maureen laughed a lot, he told Dr. Allen. The immediate and the tactile made the most impact—a landscape, the fur on Zip's back, the crackling sound of old records on the turntable he'd dug out of the basement. She seemed happier than she'd been in years, strange as that might seem, given what she'd been through. He held her up when they danced to the music of their youth. Dancing was good, Dr. Allen said, as long as he was careful she didn't fall. She mustn't fall.

———•◦•———

Since the harvest was done, Ben proposed Thanksgiving in Alabama as a chance for Maureen to reconnect with her daughters, whose companionship might be more empathetic than the boys'.

"Women are just plain better at soothing the spirit," he said.

Thanksgiving would be a perfect time since Tom had no more work on the farm. Everything was sold, even the hens and the pigs Tom had left. The corn went at a loss since the price had plunged due to oversupply and the exemptions for ethanol refiners. Tom was lucky to get two-thirds of what he paid for new equipment he'd scarcely used. At the end, he had nothing but old equipment, the land itself, and soybeans that had to be put in storage because the market was dead again this year. Maybe 2020 would be better.

Never mind next year, Ben insisted. They had more immediate things to think about. Truth be told, if anything happened to Tom—some medical emergency of his own—Maureen would need her daughters. That was the argument that won the day. Ben took the initiative to call Rebecca, who said they would be welcome as could be for Thanksgiving.

Tom worried that it might be too soon for Maureen to travel and that maybe she wouldn't want to be seen by the Coles until she was back to normal.

"Time is not our friend," Ben reminded him. "The longer we wait to help her reconnect with your girls, the harder it will be."

Tom had no answer for that.

"Maureen is just now at the point where I can understand her pretty well," Ben observed, "and you understand everything she says."

Tom nodded.

"Do you want to take a drive to see your daughters?" Ben asked her.

She said "Yes," clearly and distinctly. Tom and Ben eyed each other.

"If we take this trip," Ben told Tom, "I can drive or you can drive, up to you, or we can trade off driving. In whatever car you want. Or we could fly."

"I'll drive," Tom said. "In *my* car."

"Agreed."

"Who'll take care of Zip?"

"Expect we'll find a neighbor," Ben said. "I'll look into it."

"If we go, we stop whenever Maureen wants," Tom decreed.

"For sure."

"And we turn back if Maureen changes her mind."

"Absolutely," Ben said.

Maureen looked intently at Tom.

"When I think about it," Tom said quietly, "I have to ask myself—what if something did happen to me? Who'd be there for Maureen? The girls need to mend fences with her."

Ben nodded.

"OK, then," Tom said.

"We'll drive slow and easy, two, maybe three nights at motels so Maureen can get her rest," Ben advised.

"Yup," Tom agreed.

Ben put his arm around Tom's shoulder. "I've got high hopes," he said.

"Just what we need." Tom remarked, cracking half a smile.

Maureen reached up and touched the small of Tom's back with her bad arm. "Conickid," she said.

"What's that?" Ben asked.

"Connected," Tom said. "She says we're connected. Guess we are."

———•◦•———

Rebecca called Theresa early on the Saturday morning before Thanksgiving. Theresa answered after the second ring.

Rebecca frequently called Theresa early in the day. She knew Theresa would recognize her voice, so there was no need for preliminaries. The baby was close by. She could hear him sucking air, probably in Theresa's arms.

"How's he doing?" Rebecca started.

"Just woke from a nap," Theresa replied, a smile in her voice. "I'll nurse him in a few minutes."

"Can't hardly believe I'm a great-gramma again."

"You should see how he's changing. Every day he looks different. He cries a lot, of course. I think at this age their brains are growing so fast, it frightens them."

"You sound pleased."

"We are. Now we know how it's supposed to be. Charlie is happier than I've ever seen him."

"Do you miss your work on the base?"

"There'll be plenty of jobs later on," Theresa replied. "This is Wyatt's time."

Rebecca paused, letting a long moment of blank intervene before she broached the topic.

"Theresa, I'm calling about Thanksgiving," she said.

"Charlie still isn't certain he can get enough leave. We hope he can."

"It has to do with your mama."

Theresa didn't respond. Rebecca could hear Wyatt's breathing and a little complaint he made as some kind of movement took place, perhaps Theresa sitting down.

"Your daddy and Ben Johnson are bringin' her with 'em for Thanksgiving. They asked to visit. I think they want us all to sit down and talk things out. You know, your mama's gone through a lot, Theresa."

"We're not coming then."

"Honey—"

"Rebecca, there's nothing to talk about."

"Are you sure?"

"I'm absolutely sure."

"She's still your mama. She'll always be your mama."

"No. That bond is severed."

"You can't mean that, Theresa."

Theresa didn't answer.

"Sweetheart," Rebecca exhaled and then took another breath, "I was in the garden with Patrick the other day. We had one of those last bursts of summer. It was so pretty. I took him into a patch that gets a lot of sunlight.

It's out of the way. I call it my secret garden, and there was this rose bush against a fence. It was done bloomin' months ago, but part of it started bloomin' again that afternoon. I almost thought it was spring. Patrick was in my arms, and we went up close, and the look on his face—I wish you could have seen it. He was enraptured. You know, Theresa, we think so much about whether he's ever going to be coordinated enough or smart enough, but I swear to you, he's got feelings enough, normal human feelings. There was pure amazement on his face."

Theresa sighed audibly. Rebecca could hear that she'd put Wyatt to her breast, Wyatt who was so much younger than his brother, not yet able to distinguish a rose from a turtle.

"Rebecca," Theresa came back, speaking slowly and distinctly, as if to a puppy needing to learn a rudimentary lesson, "you have to remember that Patrick is not my child. I don't know how many times I have to say it. Please do not expect me to feel guilty or sing kumbaya or dance around his successes. It's not going to happen. Neither is any connection with Maureen. Please understand that."

"You won't even spend time with her at Thanksgiving?"

"No, I won't. Charlie can come to Lafayette if he wants. He can forgive her. He can embrace Patrick. Whatever he chooses. But I won't do it."

"I had to ask."

"Now you've asked. Now you *know*, Rebecca."

Rebecca had no idea what else to say.

"Keep in mind, though," Theresa went on, "there is a chance Charlie and Wyatt and I can come for Christmas."

"You're always welcome, all of you. Of course, you'll see Patrick if you come."

Theresa laughed. "This little guy just bit me."

"Oh! Guess he wants your full attention."

"Rebecca, I'll ask Charlie to call you later tonight if you'd like."

"You do that, darlin', and I'll tell him what we said. You know, we don't ever give up in this family. It's the Civil War in us, I guess."

"The Civil War's in me, too, Rebecca." Theresa paused. "Bye," she said and hung up. Rebecca hung up too.

"Well, that didn't sound too good," Woodrow remarked, bouncing Patrick on his knee as the boy giggled.

"Everything worthwhile takes time," Rebecca replied. "I haven't given up."

"So, they're definitely not coming for Thanksgiving?" Annie inquired.

"Not this Thanksgiving, she says."

"I'm gonna talk to Claire about it," Annie said. "Maybe she can think of some way."

"Ariane had a tough night," Rebecca replied. "Let it wait 'til later."

"It's just not right," Annie said. "I'll never understand my family."

"If it's any comfort to you," Rebecca said, "I never understood mine . . . Now, let's start gettin' ready. How about we bake some pies?"

<hr />

Much to her supervisor's disappointment, Theresa planned to stretch maternity leave well beyond three months. There was no assurance, she was told, that her job would be there when she was ready to come back. In all likelihood, someone would replace her—probably not someone as popular with new families on base as Theresa had become, but that someone might have seniority if and when Theresa returned.

Theresa understood. It didn't matter, she said. She would stay home with Wyatt as long as she felt her son had need of her. She would nurse him longer than most babies were nursed. That way her immunities would continue to transfer to her son during the critical months before he started immunizations. With his mother home, Wyatt would get used to a schedule that rarely varied. He could breastfeed whenever he showed an interest, and that instant gratification, she felt, would give him a deep sense of security that might follow him throughout his life.

She, Wyatt, and Pal kept each other company whenever Charlie wasn't around. Charlie had missed Wyatt's birth due to his DI training, and now he was missing a lot of Wyatt's firsts, but frequently absent fathers went with the territory as far as the army was concerned. It was something Theresa had to live with.

The days were long, but she didn't mind. Not when she had the wonder of Wyatt in her arms. Charlie came home every night long enough to kiss Wyatt in his crib and spend some time next to her before he had to be back on base by 5:00 a.m. In between platoons, he would get at least two weeks off, he promised, maybe more. Theresa looked forward to that.

Charlie had proposed they drive home to Lafayette for Christmas. He still called Lafayette *home*. Theresa suspected he wanted Wyatt to meet his older brother. She had no objections. She'd resigned herself to Charlie's emotional bond to the child she'd been forced to bear, the son who would never be hers. Despite their rocky start, she and Charlie had stuck it out, each making whatever adjustments the other needed. She was proud of that.

When the doorbell rang on Friday, December 13, she hurried to answer it so whoever was on the other side wouldn't ring again. Wyatt was sound asleep in the bedroom. Pal padded along with her, growling faintly. She looked through the door viewer. A woman in a dark pantsuit stood alone on the porch. Theresa opened the door.

"Theresa Cole?" the woman asked.

"Yes?"

The woman opened a double-sided ID badge with her photo on one side and FBI in large letters on the other.

"My name is Ramona Eggers," she said. "FBI. I've been trying to reach you. Could we talk awhile?"

Theresa bristled. "What do you want?" she asked.

"A half hour of your time. I've flown in from Minnesota hoping to see you. It's important."

Theresa hesitated. This woman was from that FBI field office in Brooklyn Center, she was sure of it. Ramona Eggers had been leaving phone messages for months. Theresa had never responded, but if she didn't talk to her now, the irritating intrusions would just continue. She opened the door.

"Please keep your voice down," she said. "My baby's sleeping."

"Of course." Ramona Eggers stepped inside.

Theresa offered her coffee or tea. Agent Eggers chose tea. Theresa put a kettle on the stove and sat across from the woman, who'd opened a flat, padded black briefcase and pulled out a laptop she set beside her on the sofa.

"I'll be as concise as I can be." Agent Eggers smiled slightly.

"Please." Theresa wanted the woman to be as concise and brief as she could possibly be. Reminders of what had happened in Minnesota that awful summer of 2018 were about as welcome as cockroaches crawling out from underneath her stove.

"The FBI has a watchlist," Agent Eggers said, "as you may be aware."

"It's not something I think about," Theresa responded.

"It's a list the bureau constantly updates," Agent Eggers continued. "We look for threats. That's our job. One of the people I've tried hard to locate, since even before your case came to our attention, is a woman named Lucy Meyer. I believe you came into contact with Lucy Meyer the summer before last."

Theresa nodded. Just the mention of Lucy Meyer's name caused her throat to constrict. She pulled Pal up onto her lap, from where the little fellow scrutinized Ramona Eggers curiously. He had ceased growling, though.

"What she did to you—I should say, what I believe she did to you—is part of a pattern in her behavior that we've established through indirect evidence," Ramona said. "Lucy Meyer's not an easy person to track. She has a network of accomplices, many of them deeply involved, others incidental, some of them people who help her without knowing what they're getting themselves into. I believe your mother was one of those people. I don't think she had any idea who Lucy Meyer was when she met her."

Theresa didn't respond. She felt as if she'd been transported a year and a half into the past. A flood of bitter memories rose from wherever they'd buried themselves.

The kettle on the stove began to whistle. Theresa set Pal down and rushed to stifle the burner before the noise woke Wyatt. In the kitchen, she filled a teapot with chai and poured milk into a small pitcher, put both on a tray with mugs, and brought the ensemble into the living room. She set the tray on an ottoman.

"Have you found her? Is she under arrest?" Theresa asked, her voice shaking.

"She's being watched. It's not constant surveillance but we know roughly where she is. We're not ready to arrest her, but we are trying to build a case. For that, we need the kind of testimony we can present to a federal grand jury. Witness testimony."

"You've convened a grand jury?" Theresa asked, alarmed. She knew what was coming.

"No, we don't have a grand jury convened at present. The climate isn't right at the moment. I think you probably realize that the investigation at a local level didn't go very far when you disappeared in May of 2018. The will was not there. Your neck of the woods is pretty—"

"Yes, I know. It's pro-life. But that's no excuse for allowing a kidnapping to happen without law enforcement seriously searching for me."

"You were ill-served," Agent Eggers agreed. "We talked to everyone we could in St. Dominic at the time, and they just clammed up. The BCA got the same response. When you left the state, our investigation stalled, but it didn't stop. Nothing stops an investigation in a case we haven't cleared."

"So, what are you doing now?" Theresa asked. "You haven't made any arrests; you don't have a grand jury."

"We're looking forward," Agent Eggers interrupted. "Under the fifth amendment to the Constitution, a federal grand jury has to be called by a federal district attorney. The FBI can't just set one up. The Minnesota federal district attorney right now is an appointee of our current president, and, as you know, our current president is squarely in the pro-life camp. The FBI is not likely to see a federal grand jury impaneled to investigate a kidnapping orchestrated to prevent an abortion. Not at this moment. We could file paperwork, and they'd just slow-walk it. But—"

Theresa looked closely at Agent Eggers. She was middle-aged, maybe forty, short-statured, possibly Hispanic. Her face was full, and her eyes were intense. They were dark, almost black. She had curly brown hair that fell in ringlets from a part on the left side of her head. Everything about her was neat and clean, from the impeccable white shirt she wore to her dark suit. There wasn't a speck of lint or dirt anywhere on it despite a trip halfway across the country.

"But what?" Theresa prodded her.

"But 2020 is an election year. Our current president may not be our president after the inauguration that follows November 2020. That means Minnesota may get a new federal district attorney, chosen by a new president."

"All that sounds a long time away," Theresa pointed out. "It's eleven months just to the election."

"I play a long game," Agent Eggers confirmed.

"You want me to testify."

"I want you to tell me now everything you remember. I want as much detail as you can give me. I want you to repeat what you tell me to a federal grand jury when we get one. Who knows what 2020 will bring? It could be a whole different world."

Theresa nodded.

"Will you do that?"

"I wanted to put it all behind me."

"If you put it all behind you, Lucy Meyer is free to do to someone else what she did to you. We're in the middle of a kind of civil war here, Theresa. It's only going to get worse. If we don't fight for each other, then who will be there for the next victim when Lucy Meyer decides she has the right to take another woman prisoner?"

Theresa nodded. From the bedroom she heard a cry. Wyatt.

"Would you like to meet my son?" she asked Agent Eggers. "I'll nurse him while you take my statement."

Agent Eggers nodded, smiling. "Yes," she said. "I'll set up."

Theresa left the room. Wyatt looked up at her from his crib, expecting immediate attention.

"Sweetie." Theresa leaned over.

After she'd put him into a new diaper, Theresa carried Wyatt into the living room, where Agent Eggers was pouring herself a cup of chai. Pal sat on the floor, staring intently.

Theresa settled into the rocking chair that Charlie had only recently returned to the living room from the kitchen. She watched Wyatt find her breast.

"I dream about it sometimes," she said. "I see Lucy Meyer's face. That's what I'd like to stop."

"Then testify," Ramona Eggers replied. "Testifying is how you take your power back."

Theresa nodded.

"I never thought about abortion until that day, May ninth," she began. "The need for one seemed to come out of nowhere . . ."

Acknowledgements

Warmest thanks to everyone who helped bring this novel to fruition, including Sonja Bonner and Sam Chapin for taking the time to read first drafts and make helpful comments; Joan Hackel for valued legal advice; editors Kerry Aberman and Alicia Ester for critiques, suggestions, and inspiration; Tina Brackins for cover and layout design ideas; and Lily Coyle, for having confidence in me and for staying firm at the helm of Pond Reads Press.

Most of all I'd like to thank my husband Paul, whose contributions are manifest in every aspect of our life together.